Lily Quinn

• VOLUME 3 •

NATALIE & ERIC SEVERINE

LOOSE LEAF
STORIES

Cover art by Gwynn Tavares
Edited by J. Cameron McClain
and Amber Presley

———

This is a work of erotic fiction.
It is not intended for minors.
All characters, organizations, places and events portrayed in this book
are either the product of the authors' imagination or are used fictitiously.

———

Find more of our books at LLStories.com

LILY QUINN BOOK #10

A MADE
Man

Chapter ONE

We faced each other across the empty rooftop. We may as well have been on an island out in the bay – the street below was a river of silver fog in the light of the rising moon. The evening air thumped with music, blasting from five different live bands performing all along the Quay. The festival was far away, though, and only the deepest bass notes carried across the distance, throbbing like the night's own heartbeat.

So this was my guy – if "guy" was even the correct word... He looked male, but sure as hell wasn't human. At least, not entirely human. What I could see of my target's skin was a patchwork of red and white, and a single sharp horn curved up from his right temple. The eye on that side glowed with scarlet hellfire.

I advanced on him slowly, swinging my hips. Okay, so maybe black fatigue pants and tank top weren't the sexiest clothes I could have selected from my closet, but I figured I could still pull off the femme fatale look. I wasn't even certain if this thing had the equipment for fucking, but I certainly looked forward to finding out.

"Hey, big guy," I said. "The College wants a word with you. And I have to admit that I wouldn't mind a piece of–"

That was as far as I got. The monster reared up to his full nine-foot height and let out a decidedly not-seduced roar of pure fury. The wind off the bay whipped long black hair out behind him like a war banner. It only grew along the right side of his head, though, like some kind of crazy midnight mohawk. The hair on the other side was shorter and much lighter, as though it had come from somebody else entirely.

Because it had.

He closed the space between us in two long, loping strides and swiped at me with his sinister hand. And I mean that in every sense of the word – that left hand was bigger than a grizzly bear paw, with bright red skin and black claws like oversized fishhooks or under-sized meat hooks.

I dropped to one knee and yanked a silvered knife from the top of my boot. Claws whistled through the air just over my head and I slashed at the tendons of my bounty's leg, really hoping he even *had* tendons on that side. He whirled, bent and grabbed for me with his right hand. This one was smaller, with skin only a shade darker than mine and no claws. A human hand.

I sliced across his side and was rewarded with a deep grunt of pain. But his huge left hand came down as I stabbed for his ribs again and seized my blade in long scarlet fingers. I yanked, but even with all my sex-powered strength, I couldn't twist it free. If the knife was cutting into the beast's palm, he didn't appear to notice. His burning red eye flared and smoke rose from between his tightening fingers. My knife blade glowed orange, then softened and ran like melting wax. Molten steel and silver dripped from the monster's fist and sizzled where it fell to the cool rooftop.

"Shit!" I gasped, releasing my knife and jumping back. "Okay, haven't seen that one before."

There was a gun thrust into a holster at the small of my back, but I suddenly wasn't so sure I wanted to whip that out. Melting bullets that close to me seemed like a bad idea.

I blocked a punch from the big guy's smaller, less knife-melting hand, but even that sent a brutal shock through me. It was like being kicked by a horse. I felt bones breaking and flesh bruising, and then the hot golden surge of my sex-powered body rushing to heal the damage. This thing wasn't only bigger than me – it was stronger, too. Considering that I'm a half-succubus who can punch through brick walls, that was saying something. Fortunately for me, I'm more than just strong.

When he slashed at me with that blazing red left hand again, I hammered him back with some of the good old Evaine-fu she had been teaching me since high school. I laid into him with a couple of jabs and uppercuts, a spinning back-kick and then a wicked elbow-strike. The monster curled in on himself, throwing up those long arms as a shield. I stepped in closer to inspect my work and maybe offer the big bastard another chance to come along quietly.

Wrong move. He lashed out with both arms, flinging me back through the air. I slammed down into the edge of the roof with a gut full of broken ribs and my bounty let out another roar like the world's most pissed-off lion. A single sharp fang shone like a dagger in his mouth.

More blazing sexual energy went to work rebuilding my shattered bones. Fuck, I was burning through my reserves at a record pace tonight. But I guess that's what happens when you go toe-to-toe with half a rage demon, even when he's stitched up with pieces of a human man. There's a damn good reason Merlin sealed all of the demons away in the Nether.

The patchwork horror charged, moving so fast that even I could barely track his movements. My hand tightened on the edge of the roof, crushing the concrete into powder. When the monster leapt at me, I hurled the broken concrete up into his mismatched eyes. Ha, the ol' dirt-in-their-eyes trick!

While my mark was still swiping at his face, I jumped up and flipped acrobatically over his head. Too bad he didn't see that bit of badassery. I wrapped my arms around his thick neck and held on. Yeah, I know that it would have been sexier to do it with my thighs, but let's be honest: sex was off the table and it's a hell of a lot easier to choke someone out with your arms.

He grunted and whirled, but if I thought he couldn't reach behind himself to grab me off his back, I was wrong.

Dead wrong.

That long, muscled red arm snapped up and closed on my shoulder. Sharp black claws bit into my skin and hot blood soaked my shirt. The monster lifted me up, my feet kicking in empty air, and threw me off the roof. I fell six stories through the night and slammed down into the street hard enough to pound a Lily Quinn-shaped crater into the asphalt.

Groaning, I tried once, twice, and then a third time to stand. My whole body was a knot of agony that wasn't fading nearly as fast as I would have liked. I managed to look up just as the monster leapt from the rooftop and slammed down into the street. He stalked through the swirling silver fog toward me.

Shit. This wasn't going well.

I needed to get to my car. A ton of fiberglass and steel would slow this big demonic motherfucker down, right? It had worked for the werewolf, Dominic. Sure, that encounter had landed the i10 in Max's garage for months, but I was ready to make that trade all over again if it would give me an edge now.

I turned on my heels and bolted through streets as dark and empty as my worst nightmares. There was that to be grateful for, at least – no witnesses. There were thousands of people out on the waterfront, dancing and shouting and listening to bands that filled the night with music. But I was alone and even those sounds were fading, replaced by the racing of my pulse and the pounding of my feet against the pavement. Was I heading away from the festival? Or was I so low on power that even my senses were failing?

I ran, but not fast enough. I didn't have the energy to move at anywhere near my top speed. How fast is that? Well, let's just say that when I really cut loose, I have to replace my shoes afterward. But not now.

I heard a single low growl just before the huge, malformed silhouette materialized from the fog. He slashed obsidian claws across the back of my thigh and blood streamed down my leg. I sprawled into the gutter.

"Fuck!" I gasped.

The only thing within arm's reach was a dented garbage can emblazoned with a crusty city seal. I grabbed and flung it up at the monster with the last of my strength. He took trash and pitted aluminum full in the face, and I heaved myself to my feet again.

I ran blindly through the misty city. Where the hell was I? Gray fog obscured any street signs or familiar landmarks. I jammed my hand into my pocket, searching for my cell phone. GPS didn't give a shit about the weather and I just needed a little help to orient myself, but I felt the screen cracked under my fingertips.

Silhouettes in the fog. I dropped my phone back into my pocket and lurched the other direction, but they were too many and too small to be my mark. Just a few drunken, staggering festivalgoers. None of them noticed one more stumbling woman on the road and soon they were gone again. I could have shouted out to them, I supposed, but what good would that do? How could they help? My job was to keep people like that safely away from monsters like–

"Shit!" I cried.

Like the one charging at me from the side. How the hell had he gotten around me like that?

I grabbed the gun from my belt. It was loaded with silver and had survived the six-story drop better than my phone. Now I would just have to hope it would slow the big bastard down before he got close enough to use that red-hot hand.

I pulled the trigger again and again, slamming five silver slugs right into the massive red and white shape running toward me. He reeled, but didn't stop. I swore again and jumped back, but my bleeding leg was too slow. A fist the color of blood and the size of my head smashed into my chest. My world exploded into snapping, shattering pain.

Lights swam across my vision and I blinked them away, dimly aware that I was no longer standing. I lay on my back, surrounded by broken glass and looming white figures. With a startled cry, I tried to bring up my gun and put a bullet through the nearest one, but the weapon was gone. Had I dropped it or had it been melted like my knife...?

The pale shapes didn't move, but continued to stare down at me with blank, unblinking eyes. Mannequins. I lay half on top of a toppled clothing rack and shards of the store display window sliced deep into my skin. I tried to stand. My legs shook and my feet slipped in the spreading puddle of blood. My blood. I couldn't hold in a moan of pain and even that hurt. Something sharp jabbed into my lung when I breathed.

And none of it was healing. I was out of energy.

I rolled over onto my stomach, whimpering as glass cut into my belly, and groped blindly for my gun. A shadow fell across me, deep and dark even by the wan light of the streetlamps outside.

I looked up. The red and white monster ducked through the shattered window. He stalked through the broken glass on huge, bare feet and loomed over me, tensing muscles that seemed to have been carved from stone... or forged from steel in the raging inferno of hell. His right eye burned. I couldn't see the one on the human half of his face at all. My vision was going gray and dim.

The demon half of his face grinned and he reached down with that massive red hand, ebony claws extended. I tried to throw my arms up defensively, but they were heavy and unresponsive. I could barely move. I was going to die on the ground, too weak and beaten to even fight back.

The monster froze and jerked upright. The tip of his long crimson horn gouged an inch-deep furrow into the ceiling.

"Master," he growled in a voice that sounded like two gravestones fucking.

But then he pressed his hands against the side of his head and let out an ear-splitting cry of absolute agony and terror.

"No!" he screamed in another voice entirely. "Let me go!"

His huge body trembled and he lurched, almost overbalancing to join me down on the ground. But he wheeled away and then bolted back out the ruined window, smashing a chunk of concrete from the frame without even appearing to notice. He vanished into the dark fog.

I was too weak to wonder what the fuck had just happened. My body was so cold and heavy. I was a statue carved out of pain. I would have screamed with the effort of crawling if I only had the breath. I tasted blood in my mouth.

I tried to crawl out of the store, hopefully toward my car or at least a nice quiet alleyway, but my stupid numb legs wouldn't respond at all. I finally spotted my gun under a nearby rack of shirts, but didn't have the strength to retrieve it. It was all I could do to fumble my cell phone out of my pocket. The screen was a spiderweb of cracks and I dropped it twice before managing to turn it on. That couldn't have been good for my chances of actually getting it to work. The display lit up and shone red with my blood. I couldn't read anything on it. I held down the button.

"Call..." I gasped.

Call who? I couldn't think, couldn't move. Everything hurt, but even that was fading too quickly. I was dying and alone and scared. God, so scared.

"Call... Max..."

The speaker hissed and popped, but it rang and then I heard Max's distorted voice. "Hey, Lil. What's going on?"

"...Help..." I whispered.

"Lil? Lil! What's wrong? Where are you?"

Something cold was dragging me down into the darkness. It was so heavy and I was so tired... The phone slid from my grasp and consciousness followed close behind.

Chapter
TWO

I was somewhere soft and everything hurt. Even my eyes ached as I cracked them open. A pale blur resolved itself into the familiar pattern of my bedroom ceiling. Smaller blurs became the windows that usually looked out across the shiny steel and glass jungle of downtown. That view had cost me a little over four million dollars, but now the curtains were closed and I was glad. I felt vulnerable and naked.

Because I *was* naked, I realized. My sheets were smooth against my bare skin and rustled quietly as I tried – and failed – to sit up. There was gentle pressure on my shoulder, pushing me back down into the bed. I didn't fight. I couldn't.

"Don't try to move, Lil. You're in bad shape."

I blinked and pulled the rest of my bedroom into focus. A metal mixing bowl sat on my nightstand, full of broken, bloody glass. Tweezers lay beside the bowl, also stained red.

Max sat on the edge of the bed, wearing a neat white dress shirt and dark crimson tie. His sleeves were rolled up to the elbows and he was wiping his hands on a towel already spotted in blood. More red smudged his nice shirt.

Max...

My lips moved, but his name didn't make it past them. I managed a weak moan and one of my hands twitched toward him.

"You're still bleeding," Max said. His voice was soft. "Not that you have much blood left. I'm no doctor, but I'm pretty sure your ribs are broken, too."

I was no doctor, either, but I had to agree. My body was cold and unresponsive. Numb, too, but not numb enough to blot out the dull throb of pain from my back and legs. My side was full of fire and every shallow breath made something sharp stab into my lungs. That seemed... bad.

"Lil, you have to heal. And I can't take you to a hospital. Not without a lot of questions that I know you don't want to answer."

Max stood and draped the bloodstained towel over the bowl. He tugged the knot of his tie down until it came loose and dropped the length of red silk to my bedroom floor. Max unbuttoned his white dress shirt and the glow of my bedside lamp threw the chiseled lines of his chest and stomach into stark relief. It felt like a lifetime since I had seen him like that. Ever since he started dating Taya.

Max slid into the bed beside me. He was so warm and solid against the deathly chill closing in around me. Faintly, I heard myself whimper.

"It's going to be okay, Lil," Max said.

Gently, he kissed my forehead and bright, hot energy surged through me like someone had poured molten gold down my spine. I gasped.

"I'm here," he told me.

Max kissed the tip of my nose. Another blinding jolt of power. His lips left a tingling afterglow in their wake as he moved down. So delicately, Max kissed my lips. Just a light brush of his mouth over mine at first, but then again, giving me the deeper kiss that I craved. That I needed.

I broke the kiss unwillingly.

"Taya..." I whispered.

"It's okay. She knows I'm here. She knows what we're doing," Max said softly. He kissed me again.

Max's hand slid across the sheets to my knee. I almost didn't feel it through the icy numbness, but then his fingers were sliding up my thigh, trailing warm lust that kindled life back into my frozen nerves. I suddenly felt every laceration red-hot on my skin and I gasped against Max's lips at the pain. He deepened our kiss, tasting and caressing, and the sharp edge of pain faded as my cuts began to heal. Max's touch moved up between my legs. I inhaled his breath and desire.

I managed to raise one hand to Max's shoulder and pulled him against me as tightly as I could, but I was so weak. There wasn't enough blood left in me to tempt a starving vampire. But I clung to Max as he pressed a single finger carefully into me.

Max wrapped his other arm around me and held me with all of the strength that I didn't have. He worked a second finger in beside the first and then twisted them inside me, tracing a spiraling pattern against the tightness of my pussy. I moaned quietly and bit Max's shoulder. His lips brushed my ear.

"I've got you, Lil. You're going to be okay. We're going to fix this."

"Yes," I sighed.

I closed my eyes and gave myself over to Max. His fingers moved with swift, sure strokes inside me and I floated in the sweet golden heat of his desire. He withdrew, but before I could whimper my disappointment, Max's touch was sliding up to the raised bud of my clitoris. He coaxed me so gently to climax that I didn't even realize that I was cumming until I was already moaning Max's name. His gentle fingers danced over me, inside me and guided me up into the dizzying heights of pleasure.

I reached for Max again, my hand crawling agonizingly slowly down his body to the waist of his black slacks. Whimpering, I tried to push my fingers inside, but succeeded only in prodding weakly at the hard plane of his stomach. God, I was pathetic.

Max took my wrist in one hand. He gathered up my other wrist, too, and firmly pressed them into the pillows above my head. I'm not the kind of girl who lies there in bed, but for the first time since I was eighteen, I was too weak to move Max. Every ounce of sexual power he was giving me went to healing my broken body and I needed more.

"Easy, Lil," Max said. "You're still hurt."

Max kissed me again and then trailed his lips down to my chest, over my mending ribs. The sharp pain retreated from his touch and when he closed his mouth over my nipple, I gasped the first real deep breath in... however long since Max came to my rescue. My spine arched and I let out a moan.

"Now that sounds a little better," Max said with a small smile.

"I want..." I whimpered. "I need..."

"I know."

Max withdrew his hand from between my legs and unbuckled his belt. My fingers curled and I ached to shove his pants down, but Max was still holding me pinned against the bed.

So I just bit my lip and watched him kick off his slacks and then a pair of silk boxers the same color as the tie he had been wearing. This wasn't how he dressed at the garage... I tried to remember what Max said when I called him. Had he told me where he was? I didn't recall any background noise, but then, I could barely hear my own desperate plea as I lay bleeding in the glass.

I forgot my questions entirely as Max finished pulling off his clothes. His cock was long and hard, straining toward me with all of the urgency that I was too wounded to act on. I moaned, though, and felt Max's answering surge of lust.

He slid up through the sheets to make sure I had a good view and then closed his hand around the full, flushed length of his dick. Max's fingers were still shiny wet from being inside me and moved smoothly along his cock. His fist pumped slowly – Max wasn't trying to pleasure himself or just cover me in his bright white cum.

This was for me. Max was making a show of touching himself in a way that the men in porn just never did. If their performances were a cheap circus, then Max's sensual stroking was an opera.

It was beautiful and it was powerful. I burned with Max's desire for me. There was no pain in my body now, only need. I wrenched my hands from Max's grip and flipped him easily down into the sheets. His dark blue eyes flew wide as he hit the mattress beside me. I grabbed his cock triumphantly.

"Lil, be careful!" Max protested. "You're hurt!"

I descended on his cock like a starving woman. I stuffed the big, blunt crown between my lips and swallowed his entire length in one ravenous gulp. Max groaned and my head spun. I didn't care if I could breathe or not. Saliva ran from my overstuffed, overeager little mouth and drooled along Max's dick. I still didn't care.

"Slow down, Lil!" Max panted.

I shook my head, not taking my lips off him. Instead, I reached between Max's legs and cupped one hand around his balls. They were heavy and blazing hot. I felt his lust boiling there, a bottomless font of sexual energy for me. I drank it all up desperately, but wasn't even close to done. I wanted Max's cum, too.

He placed one hand against the base of my spine and traced a long, delicate line up my back to my neck, then laced his fingers through the red tangles of my hair. His precum ran across my tongue, salty and musky. The taste was so uniquely *Max* that it sent a shiver through my body, coiling between my legs just shy of orgasm.

Then Max's hips rose from the sheets. His head fell back into the pillows and his groan sounded like it echoed up from the very bottom of his soul. He came hard and set me off, too. Thick, creamy heat gushed between my lips and down my throat. I was more than ready for it. I needed it. I drank every drop eagerly. Warmth filled my belly and pushed back the terrible, icy cold. The pleasure rose higher and higher with each pulse of cum that Max pumped into my mouth.

I sucked the last drops of semen from him and held them there, swirling my tongue through the sticky mess, and rose to my hands and knees on the bed. I looked up at Max and let out a wordless sound of need. He understood and positioned himself behind me, grabbing my hips. His cock still stood out utterly and unflaggingly hard from his body. I threw my head back, his spunk running down from the corner of my mouth, and refused to swallow. Not yet, not until Max was inside me. I wanted to be full of him, front and back. When Max speared his cock into me, I finally swallowed with a loud moan.

"Please fuck me," I gasped. "Give me your cock, Max. It's been so long."

"Yes," he agreed in a voice that had gone rough at the edges.

Max's hands tightened around my waist, holding me there and pounded his dick into me with single-minded intensity. Max wasn't being gentle anymore. He knew better, knew that I could take it now. Every impact of his hips made my breasts bounce beneath me, tipped with pink nipples that were so hard that they ached. I braced myself against the headboard and pressed back into Max with even more force than he hammered into my streaming pussy. He fucked me harder. Max held nothing back, giving me every ounce of lust and every inch of cock that he could.

I reached around to place my hand on Max's hip and pushed. He responded instantly and withdrew, but only long enough for me to roll onto my back. I spread my legs and Max was between them again before I could even voice my request. He buried his cock in my pussy and his face against my chest, kissing and sucking my nipples as he drove himself into me. Sensation poured through me like a flood, a primal force of nature that couldn't be stopped.

"Max!" I screamed.

I clung to Max and held him close, fingers tangled into his sweaty blond hair as he devoured me. When I could take no more, I pulled Max's face up to mine and kissed him, moaning my climax into his mouth.

His body tensed against me and trembled, then Max's voice rose along with mine. I heard the coming peak in his groan, tasted it on his tongue, and wound my legs around his waist to hold him close. Max poured his pleasure into me – bright, hot cum and the even brighter, hotter blaze of his desire. I locked my lips against Max's and rode the waves of ecstasy. Even healed and charged up, I wasn't strong enough to fight it. But who would want to? Max gave me everything he had and I willingly opened myself to it all.

After what felt like an eternity, I finally collapsed back to the bed, panting. Max fell into the sheets beside me, too, and then gathered me into his arms. My body was no longer bleeding or broken, but I was suddenly weary right down to my core and I yawned.

"Go on, Lil. Get some sleep," Max said. "You need it."

My eyes were already drifting shut, but when darkness swallowed me this time, I wasn't frightened.

Chapter
THREE

When I woke up again, the curtains were still drawn, but a few slender golden rays of morning sunlight knifed across the room from between them.

Max lay in bed beside me, with my cheek was pressed into the hollow of his shoulder and my leg draped over his. His chest rose and fell slowly, peacefully. Max was awake, though – his fingers combed slowly through my hair, stroking and smoothing it.

I jerked upright in my bed. No, I didn't clutch the sheets up under my arms. That bullshit is for television and movies. Max has seen me naked and I wasn't about to get shy about it now. But I was more than a little weirded out. I can count the number of times I've let a guy stay the night on one hand with five fingers left over.

"How're you feeling?" Max asked.

"What? Uh..." I shook my head. "Strange. And I probably look like shit."

While I've never been one for a lot of makeup, I was still pretty sure my hair looked like it had played host to an orgy of squirrels.

Max smiled. "You're gorgeous, Lil. As always."

I turned to get a better view of Max. He still smelled like sex and faintly of cologne. His dark blond hair looked as though it had been neatly styled before I got my hands on it. Speaking of which, how had I even done that?

"How the hell did you find me last night?" I asked. "I passed out before I could tell you where I was."

Max leaned over the side of the bed, riffled through the heap of his clothes for a moment, and then pulled out his cell phone. He unlocked it and pointed to an icon on the home screen.

"I pinged your phone for a location," Max admitted. "This app is just supposed to be for finding your kids if they go missing, but the whole thing is... uh... kind of shady, legally. You could probably report me for stalking or something, if you wanted to."

I laughed. "No way. You saved my ass last night. Plus, I think it's more legal than my sex-powered monster-hunting."

"Probably."

"Have you ever used it before? That stalker app?"

Max shook his head. "No. But I installed it about a year ago, just in case..."

"In case of shit like this?"

"Yeah." Max's smile faded. "I got down to the Quay and managed to get you to my truck before the cops showed up."

"Did you see my gun?" I asked.

Max nodded at me. "Yeah. It's in the living room. I didn't think it would be a good idea for the police to find it."

"Good calls," I said. "Thanks."

"Lil, what happened last night? How did you get so beat up? What the hell could have done that to you?"

"The College calls it a golem," I said.

"Golem? Like those clay men that other bounty hunter makes? Sabra?"

"Yeah, sort of. As I best understand it, a golem is any artificially constructed creature. What Sabra makes are homunculi, which I guess would technically be a type of golem. But that thing last night wasn't made of clay."

Max's brows drew down and he twisted a corner of the bed sheet between his fingers. "What was it made of, then?"

"He was more like... like Frankenstein's monster. Someone built this guy, but not from scratch. They stitched him together from two different men."

"That's... horrible," Max said.

"Not men," I corrected with a shudder. "Only half of that golem was human. The other half was a demon, Max. A real demon."

"Like your mother?" Max asked quietly.

I shook my head. "Succubi are demons of lust. This one was a demon of rage. You should have heard him– On second thought, no. I hope you never have to hear a roar like that."

"Fuck, Lil." Max pulled his knees up against his chest and gave me a worried look. "Aren't demons supposed to be banned from Earth? That's the entire point of the Seal of Avalon, right?"

"That's what the College says. So either someone summoned a demon just to chop it up, or maybe the Seal isn't everything that the wizards claim."

"Or something else is happening," Max suggested. "Remember last year? That fairy stole a book called *The Gates of Avalon*. That was all about Merlin's Seal, wasn't it?"

Max was right. And last I heard, the College was discussing that particular issue with Finn and Muir, a pair of wizards currently in a whole magic cauldron of trouble for summoning a succubus. There was definitely something going on with demons and the Seal of Avalon. But damned if I knew what it was.

"Were you powered up last night?" Max asked.

I smirked at that. "Yeah. The College bounty said this golem washed ashore a mile or so down the bay from the Quay and triggered some kind of magical sensor. Since we're in the middle of the Quay Festival, I stopped by on my way. Two birds, one stone and all that. It took me all of five minutes to find three festival guys up for sharing a hot redhead."

"But it wasn't enough?"

"No. This guy is powerful, Max. He's a real demon. Or at least half of one. That's probably why the College wants him caught yesterday. The bounty is ridiculous."

The reward that the College was offering for the golem's live capture was just about enough gold to start my own federal reserve. I climbed out of bed and stood, stretching. I wasn't sore, but I was absolutely starving.

Max remained in bed, thick arms wound around his knees. He watched me closely.

"This thing is dangerous," I said. "And it's still out there. I have to find him again."

"Lil, he kicked your ass. Can't you work with some of the other hunters on this one? Or maybe use your wish?"

My favor from Madu Tau, the air djinn who subtly ruled most of Cairo and who I had fucked so impressively that he granted me a single wish. I had forgotten all about that. It would have been pretty damned useful last night.

I opened my mouth to say so, but then my stomach growled like a hunting werewolf. Max blinked.

"Wow," he said. "Okay, I tried to clean up as much as I could, but I'm pretty sure you're still going to want that shower. By the time you're done, I'll have some breakfast ready."

"Thanks, Max."

He slid out of bed and I walked into the bathroom. There were smudges on the mirror above the sink that tickled memories of last night – Max carrying me to the bathroom and starting the shower, me running my hands down his back, then fucking on the countertop so long that the shower went cold and not caring at all about the stupid water as Max shot another sticky white load all over me. I smiled into the mirror.

Apparently we hadn't exactly slept through the night. Somehow, that made Max staying over feel a little less weird.

As I turned on the shower and stepped under the hot spray, I sifted through everything else that happened last night. The golem kicking my ass and then... leaving? I remembered two voices: one crying out in fear and the other so low, angry and violent that it made even an experienced hand at bloodshed like me shudder.

So why had that golem left me alive? I doubted it was any particular mercy on his part. No, something interrupted the monster before he could finish the job. That second voice had been pained, frightened. Was that why he ran? I shuddered to think what in the worlds could scare a creature like that.

It took some effort and a little swearing to untangle my hair, but I eventually managed to shampoo it all out. Then I briskly scrubbed the rest of my body clean of blood, sweat and cum. Max had done a pretty good job cleaning me up last night, but he was right – he had missed a few spots.

By the time I stepped out of the shower and grabbed a towel, the scents of breakfast were wafting out from the kitchen. I dried my hair and grabbed my robe from a hook on the back of the bathroom door. I had burned through every ounce of sexual energy from the guys at the Quay Festival and then all Max gave me after that, plus probably about ten thousand calories. I was ready to eat a dozen eggs, an entire pig's worth of bacon, and a loaf of toast. And it smelled like Max was already serving it up.

When I padded out into the living room, Max stood in my kitchen, wearing just his red silk boxers and my fuzzy white bunny slippers. A huge plate sat on the counter, piled up with a massive omelet, bacon and sausage. Another plate contained pancakes with syrup, and toast smeared with butter and jam. Max held a steaming cup of coffee in one hand and a heaping tablespoon of sugar in the other, but he wasn't moving. He stared out across my condo with his mouth hanging open.

I followed his gaze, assessing my closest weapons. The sword under the couch? The gun beneath my nightstand? The block full of knives in the kitchen? If that big patchwork fucker tracked me back here, I was going to... But the golem wasn't who stood in my living room.

It was Evaine.

"Holy shit," I gasped.

Evaine stood in front of a window Max must have opened. Sunlight gleamed off her armor. Real armor and I don't mean Kevlar. Evaine wore a burnished silver breastplate buckled over glittering chainmail and her platinum blonde hair was pinned up into a knot against the nape of her neck. I had never seen my teacher wearing anything other than normal clothes. Always pale and elegant, but not like... this.

Somehow, I didn't think Evaine was here for a threesome with Max and me. Her expression was deadly serious.

"Evaine?" I asked. "What's going on?"

"Lily, do not hunt the golem," she said.

I blinked. I'm not sure what I was expecting, but certainly not *that*. Evaine's never offered unsolicited advice on my job before and even when I asked for her help, I didn't count on a call back. I adored Evaine, but she was always rather remote and mysterious. Her picture would have been the dictionary entry for *enigmatic* if only she weren't too reclusive to show up for the photo.

"I... uh..." I said helpfully. "What the fuck, Evaine?"

"This hunt is too dangerous. Stay away from the golem."

"What about the other hunters?" I protested. "The size of this bounty is going to have them visiting from the Castle to cash in. I only edged out Doyle and Griffith last night because they don't like teleporting inside city limits and both of them drive like little old ladies."

"Wizards appreciate the value of restraint, care, and caution," Evaine said, putting her hands on her hips. "Stand down from this hunt, Lily. I will kill the golem."

"You?" I asked. "*You're* going to hunt that thing down?"

Now my mouth hung open, too. Evaine had taught me every trick I knew, but she wasn't a bounty hunter. Evaine was a... Well, I had to admit that I didn't really know *what* she was. Evaine sort of lived on Avalon and sometimes called herself the island's keeper, but I had no idea what that involved.

I crossed my arms. "I can handle this. I've fought that golem before."

"And got your ass kicked," Max said from the kitchen.

"Hey, whose side are you on anyway?" I asked, scowling over my shoulder at him.

"Yours, Lil," Max said. "Always."

I turned back to Evaine. "Are you warning off all of the other hunters? Are you visiting Stefano next?"

"No," she answered. "The magi must not learn what I am doing. I need to move quickly if I am to reach the golem first, before the College can catch him."

"Wait, what? Evaine, you've always worked with the wizards before! Even the High Magus does pretty much whatever you tell him to. Now you're going behind their backs to hunt down the golem? What the hell is going on?"

"That's dangerous for you to know."

"Hey, I'm not a kid anymore. I deserve to know why you want me off the job!"

Evaine frowned at me. I longed to kiss those pouting pink lips, but I was way too angry. My teacher closed her eyes for a moment and then sighed.

"This golem... will make the College ask questions," she said. "Questions that I do not want them to answer."

"I... what?" I asked. I really wanted answers, too, but those answers were already confusing the fuck out of me. "Isn't that sort of their job?"

"Those questions are dangerous to you, Lily."

"To *me*? Why?"

Evaine's expression hardened and she didn't respond. I stalked across the living room toward her.

"Fine," I said. "If this guy is so damned deadly, then let's hunt him down together."

"No!"

The force of Evaine's answer brought me up short. In nine years, she's *never* raised her voice like that. Not to me or anyone else, as far as I know.

"Evaine..." I said.

"No, Lily. This golem presents the greatest threat you have ever known. I will deal with it. I must discover how it was able to leave the island. Avalon let it go for a reason—"

"Wait, time out!" I shouted, holding up my hands. "Avalon? The golem came from Avalon? Like me? What the *fuck* is going on here? Tell me!"

Evaine gave me a look that was half proud, half pained. But she shook her head. "Lily, I must have your word that you will not pursue the golem. You're already in enough danger."

"Evaine, this is bullshit and you know it! If you love me at all, then talk to me!"

"Because I do love you, I cannot. My need is not yet that dire. Though it may be before this ends."

Despite Evaine's beautiful voice and flowing accent, her words hung in the air like storm clouds. I held her eye as long as I could. The sunlight off her armor was almost blinding.

"Come on, Evaine," I said. "Don't start keeping secrets from me now! Please!"

"I have always kept secrets from you," she said in a hard voice. "Since the day you were born, Lilith."

She was right. Evaine knew who my father was, but she never told me. How much more had she kept from me? I had to admit to myself that I had no idea. How much did I know about Evaine at all, really?

I dropped my gaze to the floor and swallowed a painful lump in my throat.

"Fine," I said at last. "I'll sit this one out."

She actually seemed surprised. "You will give up this bounty?"

"Yeah."

Evaine studied me for a moment and finally nodded. Without another word, she turned away and stalked out through the front door. I wondered briefly what the doorman would make of Evaine in all her shining silver armor. But then I doubted that he would even see her.

When Evaine was gone, Max let out a long breath.

"I don't think I've ever seen you give up on anything in your life, Lil," he said. "Are you really going to back off now?"

I looked up at my best friend. "Oh hell no. If Evaine won't tell me what's going on, then I'll find that golem and make *him* do it."

Chapter
FOUR

I shoveled Max's breakfast into my mouth without taking the proper time to enjoy it, but I had to hurry. Evaine wanted to get to the golem before the other bounty hunters and I had to get to him before she did.

"Something's going on, Max," I said between bites. "Something big. But Evaine won't tell me what. I don't know where she learned to fight, but Evaine's one of the world's true badasses. What the hell is she doing hunting down a bounty? That's my job!"

Max nodded and slid another stack of pancakes onto my plate. I drowned them in maple syrup and dug in ravenously.

"So what's the plan?" Max asked.

"Phone call," I answered through a mouthful of pancake.

"Your phone is a wreck, Lil. I'm surprised you even managed to call me last night."

"Spares in my desk."

Max went to my desk in the living room and fished around in the top drawer until he found two extra phones. He held them up. I pointed to the one in his left hand with my fork. It was the newer model, already pre-loaded with all the apps and contacts I needed for work.

Max carried the phone over to the counter and set it in front of me.

"You should just start buying these things in bulk," he said.

"Yeah," I agreed. I swallowed and turned on the new phone, then began scrolling through my contacts list. "Okay, if I'm going to be dumb and go hunting the scary golem that Evaine has expressly warned me to stay the hell away from, let's see if I can at least be smart about it."

Max laughed and gave me a dimple-cheeked smile. I selected Dorian's number and hit the green *call* button.

"Good morning, Lilith," Dorian's slightly creaky voice answered after a single ring.

"Hey," I said. "Dorian, I'm working the golem job. The original bounty posting had a location yesterday, down at the south end of the Quay. Do you know if that information is still good?"

"I don't believe so. Stefano and Doyle both called earlier this morning, inquiring about the same thing."

So my golem had moved on. Where was he now? I would bet a stack of gold bigger than my breakfast that all of the other hunters had the scry network booked solid to find him. Good idea, but I wasn't a wizard and couldn't use the College's magical surveillance system.

"Dorian, why is there such a huge bounty on this guy?" I asked.

"The golem is half demon, Lilith. That can't be permitted and should not be possible. We need to stop that creature quickly, and learn how he came into existence."

Max shifted his weight back and forth, making the ears on his borrowed bunny slippers twitch curiously, but he didn't say anything. He knew better than to talk while I was on the phone with the College. That was a one-way ticket to nine years of magically erased memories.

"That's all?" I asked. "I mean, you don't know what this has to do with Avalon?"

There was a pause on the other end of the line. When Dorian spoke again, I could practically hear the old wizard's bushy brows scrunching up.

"Avalon? Lilith, have you learned something about this golem? Perhaps you should come speak to the High Magus."

Now it was my turn to hesitate. What little I knew – which was more questions than answers – came from Evaine. It was one thing to try to beat her to the golem, but it was another to rat her out to the College. I sighed.

"No, Dorian," I said. "It's nothing. Thanks for the update."

"I'm sorry that I don't have more, Lilith. Good hunting."

"Yeah, I hope so. Talk to you later."

I hung up the phone and spun it contemplatively across the countertop. No help from the College on finding the golem, and they didn't know anything about his connection to Avalon or the Seal there. What the *hell* was going on?

"What's next?" Max asked.

"Last night, I had a rough location from the College and found him with my police scanner. Some driver almost hit my golem down in Southport, but he hit the car first. So that's where I focused my search. Wizards have a mild allergy to modern technology and I swear it's the only reason I can even compete with their magic."

I tapped the Fuzz Radio app icon on my cell phone and soft police chatter filled the kitchen. But when I scrolled through the transcript feed, I frowned.

"What's wrong, Lil?" Max asked.

"I don't see any new police reports that look like my guy. Plenty of drunk and disorderlies down by the bay, but nothing that could be the golem."

"Maybe one of the other hunters caught him."

"Already? Then why would Evaine show up here with her predictions of gloom and doom? And Dorian would have told me if the hunt were off. It's more like…"

"Like the golem's laying low?" Max suggested. "Hiding, maybe?"

"Yeah, that's what I'm thinking. Where, though? I don't know enough about him. That thing could have killed me last night, but then he just... left. Why? I still don't know. He sure as hell wasn't scared of me or my gun."

Max's jaw tightened. I guess even my best friend hadn't realized just how close I came to death.

"There are a lot of places to hide in Southport and along the Quay," he said.

That was true. How long would it take me to check every single one? Too long. I wasn't certain how Evaine planned on finding the golem, but I was pretty sure it was better than driving around and looking under bridges.

Fuzz Radio droned out a continuous stream of mostly minor crimes, nearly all of them reported in or around the Quay Festival. Indecent exposures, lewd conduct, thefts and a couple of assaults with artisan beer bottles and stuffed animals. I smirked in spite of myself. The annual festival was a week-long party that shut down ten square blocks along the Quay and filled them with food, over-priced merchandise, and lots of drunk people in crazy costumes.

"No fair," I said. "There are about fifteen thousand people at the festival, all having a lot more fun than me right now."

"That's a lot of people."

Max raised one eyebrow and I grinned at him. It *was* a lot of people. At least ten times the usual crowd of the Quay, even during the height of tourist season. I didn't have access to the wizards' scry network, but I had other networks. Maybe I could get all those thousands of eyes and cell phones to work for me.

I left Fuzz Radio playing in the background and opened up another app, something that not even the most adventurous sorcerous bounty hunter would dare to tangle with: social media. I hit the *Near Me* button and the screen was instantly filled with photographs from the Quay.

There were hundreds of them. Thousands. The Quay Festival isn't Halloween or even held in October, but it's a bit like a slice of Mardi Gras mixed with a dose of Burning Man. The festival attracts some strange people and even tempts the normals to get their weird on. There were photographs of all sorts of costumes and cosplay. I could swipe through pictures all day and miss the one I needed.

I chewed my lip for a moment and then searched the tags for *golem*. Zero results.

"Fuck," I muttered.

Max looked over my shoulder. "*Golem* is what the College calls that guy, yeah? The technical term?"

I nodded.

"Try *Frankenstein*," Max said.

"But that's the name of the creator, not the monster," I objected.

"Yeah, but most people don't know that. Or don't care."

The search results proved Max correct. I found my golem on the first page. Not in the background or under some overpass, but right in the middle of the festival. There had to be a hundred pictures of him and it was easy to see why.

The human half of his face was strong and square-jawed, with a single high cheekbone and brown eye so deep and dark that it was nearly black. The demonic half of his face was the blood-red color that I remembered so well, with long, thick ebony hair like spilled ink. The horn that arced up from his right temple was a slightly darker scarlet than his skin and ended in a sharp point. I had the sudden desire to run my hand along the curve of it. The features on his demonic side were heavier, cruder and his red eye burned with a savage intensity even in photographs.

His clothes looked like thrift store fare: worn jeans and a t-shirt that must have been huge but were nonetheless stretched tight over the golem's massively muscular body. There appeared to be several holes in the shirt, too.

Bullet holes.

So my shots had found their mark, apparently. I squinted at the pictures, but the shirt was black and I couldn't tell if there were any bloodstains. A few bullets certainly hadn't slowed the big fucker down much...

He wasn't posing for the photographs. The golem was stooped over or drawing back in every shot, sometimes with his mismatched hands raised to cover his face. He hardly even seemed like the same monster who had nearly killed me last night. I touched my fingertips to my ribs and winced at the memory. If he hadn't run, I'd be dead. But there was no mistaking the brute, even if his posture was all wrong.

Max whistled. "That's the guy who got you last night?"

"He's even bigger in person," I said.

I searched through comments on the pictures, hoping that someone at the festival would mention where they had seen him. But most of the comments were about how awesome and fucked up the costume was, wondering what exactly he was supposed to be dressed up as and how the hell he had pulled it off. No help there, and the background was different in every photo. My golem was on the move.

"The cops are pretty thick out around the Quay during the festival," I said. "Someone might eventually notice him holed up under an overpass, I guess, and then things would get messy."

"But no one gets arrested just for dressing up at the festival," Max finished. "As long as they have all their naughty bits covered. He's hiding in plain view, isn't he? A tree in the forest."

"More like a sequoia in a community park, but yeah."

Max frowned. "Why, though? Lil, if this golem is as dangerous as Evaine says, why is he hiding? You said he's half rage demon."

"Yeah."

"Then why isn't he in the middle of a murder rampage right through the middle of the Quay Festival?" Max asked. "Is he hiding from you?"

"Not a chance. I barely scratched that guy. No, he's scared of something else."

Max caught my eye. "Maybe that's why Evaine wants you off this hunt, Lil."

"I don't know. But I'm going to find out. And catch his big red ass before he can decide that ripping people apart sounds like more fun than hiding."

I leaned against the kitchen counter and Max stepped in close. He smelled like sex and good, homemade food. I wanted to lick him all over. His deep blue eyes were serious, though.

"Lil, that guy almost killed you last night," Max said in a low voice. "And we've never known Evaine to jerk you around. Are you *sure* you want to do this?"

"If that golem is trying to stay under the radar, maybe I can use that to my advantage somehow. If not... well, I'll figure it out. He knows things, Max, and Evaine wants to kill him before the College can ask questions. I *have* to find out why."

Max nodded. "Alright then, Lil. But you're not going anywhere near that golem without topping off."

"What?" I asked.

He grabbed the red sash of my robe and tugged it loose. The silk slid open to bare a long stripe of pale skin from my throat all the way down my body.

"Wait," I said.

My pussy had other ideas and mostly just drooled, but I did my best to ignore it.

Max stopped with one hand halfway beneath my robe. "What is it?"

"Last night, I was half dead. Maybe more than half. You saved my life."

Max smiled hugely at that. Damn, those dimples were adorable. I really missed sitting on them.

Focus, Lily!

"What about Taya?" I asked. "You said she knows..."

Max nodded. "She does."

"Taya knows that you fucked me last night? And that you're offering to do it again now? She's a great girl, Max, and I don't want to mess things up between you two."

"I know, Lil. But it's alright. I can do whatever you need me to."

Relief flooded through me... Another feeling, too, that was hot and somehow heavy. I suddenly couldn't breathe. My nipples rose into hard points of sensation against the soft cloth barely covering them. Max pushed the robe off my shoulders and it slithered down my body. Goosebumps prickled my skin, but I wasn't cold.

Max pulled me into his arms and kissed me. One hand slid up my spine to cup the back of my head while Max's lips pressed against mine. His mouth still tasted like coffee and cream. I seized the waist of his boxers and tugged, but the band caught on the end of his hard cock and the silk tore in my hand. I bit Max's lower lip in frustration and yanked the ripped boxers off his body. His mouth blazed a white-hot trail along my jaw and down my throat.

"I've missed you, Lil," Max said softly.

His hands raced down my back again, leaving contrails of heat across my skin. He grabbed my ass, traced the curve of it with his fingertips, and then lifted me up off my feet. Max shoved the dishes aside with one elbow and set me down on the counter. Faintly, I heard something crash on the floor, but I didn't care, not when Max was lowering himself to his knees.

"Yes," I said, moaning. "I need you, Max."

He buried his face between my thighs and kissed me there with just as much passion as he had my lips. Max's tongue caressed my clit and inside me, teasing me closer and closer to the peak of orgasm, then over. My back arched and my cries echoed through the kitchen.

I wound my legs around Max's neck and grabbed a handful of his hair. His strong fingers ran up my thighs and held my hips, pulling me even closer. Max licked me until his jaw had to be sore, but that man was tireless. I squirmed on the cold granite countertop until my wetness streamed down his chin.

I yanked Max to his feet and kissed him, tasting the tang of my juices on his tongue. With my lips still pressed urgently to his, I groped blindly until I found the maple syrup. Thankfully, that wasn't what had fallen off the counter. With one thumb, I spun the cap off the top and it went flying fuck knew where. I tore my lips from Max's and leaned back. His eyes widened and I winked as I poured the maple syrup into amber streams across my breasts. The sticky cold oozing across my skin made me gasp.

Max devoured me. He sucked my achingly hard nipples into his mouth and licked maple syrup from the sensitive pink nubs. Like the good boy that he very much was, Max traced his tongue along every last winding golden line down my chest and belly, lapping and cleaning up sweet syrup from my skin.

But when he moved toward the gleaming drops dotting my thighs, I pulled Max upright again. He panted rapidly as I held him there, then stared when I thrust two fingers into my pussy. They made soft wet sounds as I slid them in and out. Max's jaw tightened, but I didn't release him. When my fingers were dripping, I withdrew them with a sigh. Max struggled a little in my grip, but went still as I painted curving lines up along my spread thighs, swirling my juices and dark gold syrup together into shining lines all across my skin.

I finished with a glistening spiral over my hip and then held up my hand. Max grabbed my wrist and wrapped his lips around my fingers with a low sound of pleasure. His eyes fell shut as he drank down the mixture of my wetness and maple syrup. His tongue was hot on my skin and I let out a moan.

Max tore his mouth off my fingers and pushed me down against the counter. My legs came up and he was between them in a heartbeat, tongue racing over the shining lines I had traced on my thighs.

His desire blazed and I gasped at the feel of it flowing into me. My pussy ran so wet that I felt a puddle forming beneath me on the granite.

"Lil…" Max groaned. His breath was warm on my wet skin.

Max would have stood there licking me all day, but I had kept him waiting long enough. I planted one heel in the center of Max's chest and pushed him away so I could slide down from the counter. I turned around and bent over the edge, pressing my breasts against the cold stone. I reached under myself and plunged my fingers into my pussy until they were hot and wet again. Max's breath caught as I slid them up and rubbed slippery circles over the tight hole of my anus.

"Fuck my ass, Max," I said.

I leaned against the counter and grabbed my buttocks in both hands, spreading myself for Max. I lay my face on the granite and my breath fogged the polished surface as he stepped in behind me. Max's cock nudged insistently into me, harder and harder until the clenched tightness had no choice but to yield with a soft, sweet pop. I gasped. There was always pain along with the pleasure, but would you think less of me if I said that's part of the fun?

Now wasn't the time to take it slow and not just because I wanted all of the sexual energy that I could get before hunting that golem down again. It seemed like ages since I had taken Max up my ass and was surprised how much I missed it. I guess he had, too – Max wasn't taking it easy, either. He pressed me into the counter, shoving himself deep into my butt. I felt Max's breath warm on the back of my neck.

"Yes… Lil…" he said.

"More, Max. Fuck my ass hard!"

He already had me pinned against the counter, with no room to move or writhe, the ring of my anus stretched and forced open by Max's dick buried there. He drew back and then hammered his cock home again, his hips impacting loudly against my ass.

The sounds of Max driving himself into me became wet slaps as I gushed. I moaned into the counter with every thrust, with every blazing hot stroke of penetration. And then I screamed as the pleasure rose like a tidal wave, crashing over me. Max held my hips and slammed his dick into me, stoking the wild storm of ecstasy inside of me.

I clutched at the counter, reaching desperately for something to hold onto. My questing hand closed on a coffee cup and crushed it into powder. I dug my fingers into the granite countertop until the stone cracked beneath them, and held on as Max fucked my ass as hard as I had told him to.

His hands moved along my back, fingertips trailing lightly over my sweat-slicked skin as he pounded himself into my ass. Orgasm surged up from my core, meeting the gentler waves of pleasure from my back. Max traced the line of my spine and sweet sensation followed his every touch. When his fingers slid into my hair, I could barely see through the haze of searing lust.

"More," I gasped.

"Yes, more," Max said.

His fingers curled into my hair and he pulled. My back arched and I clawed at the broken countertop as he yanked me up against him. Max's chest and stomach were as hard as the granite, but hot where the stone had been cold. Muscles flexed against me as Max drove his cock deep into my ass.

He pulled my head to one side and bit at the soft flesh of my throat. Max's other hand came up to squeeze my breast, catching my nipple between thumb and forefinger. He pinched and then twisted, and the pain-pleasure of it lanced through my body. I didn't know how much more I could take.

"Yes," I whimpered. "Fuck me, Max!"

He kissed my neck with bruising force and tugged back on my hair again. I gasped and stared up at the ceiling. The entire counter wobbled under my clenching hands.

Was that me or an earthquake...? My whole world was spinning off its axis, spinning on the long shaft buried deep within me.

"Cum inside me, Max!" I cried. "Shoot it right up my ass!"

"Yes, Lil!"

Max shoved his hand down between my legs. His cock impaled my ass in a last balls-deep thrust and his fingers slid into my pussy. I was so full of Max, of the pleasure and the bright lust that he gave me. And then his cum poured into me; so much hot, sticky spunk that it ran down my ass and thighs in ivory streaks.

It was so deep, so hot... I screamed out wordlessly and, to my surprise, squirted wetness all over his fingers. I've certainly gushed before, but never actually squirted – that was always more Evaine's thing than mine. But now there was too much sensation, too much ecstasy and it spurted from my overwhelmed body to leave droplets glittering across the kitchen floor.

Max released my hair and I fell forward, sagging against the countertop. I groaned as he slowly withdrew his spent cock from my ass and his hot white cum ran in a creamy river between my legs. Max wrapped his arms around me, all gentleness again.

"You okay, Lil?" he asked.

"Mmm," I said.

I slumped to the floor and Max went down with me, holding me against his chest amid the remains of breakfast and my broken kitchen counter. His legs stretched out to either side of us and Max was still wearing my wide-eyed bunny slippers. Oh, the things those slippers have seen. I giggled and Max's arms tightened around me.

"I missed you, Lil," he whispered into my hair.

"You, too," I groaned. "Damn, if you had been the one to fuck me last night, maybe I wouldn't have gotten my ass kicked."

Max laughed.

It took a few minutes before my bones would agree to support me again and then a couple more until my legs worked enough to stagger over to my bedroom. Every wobbly step made Max's load drip from my ass and I grinned as I climbed back into the shower. Messy sex is absolutely worth it. Every time.

When I had cleaned up all of the syrup and spunk, then dried off – again – I went to my closet to pick out a costume for the Quay Festival. Most of my costumes aren't exactly what you would call *family friendly*, but I figured I could put something together that wouldn't get me thrown right back out of the festival before I found my golem.

I selected an admittedly tiny pleated plaid skirt, white blouse, vest and striped tie: my favorite wizarding student uniform. Red and gold, of course. I may be underhanded and sneaky at times – when the job demands it or I just feel like it – but let's just say my house name doesn't rhyme with *shivering*.

I returned to the bathroom to tie my hair up into a long copper ponytail and grabbed a pair of costume glasses, then checked my reflection. It wasn't exactly the most creative cosplay, but I looked good and would blend in with the rest of the festivalgoers. With any luck, my half-demon quarry wouldn't even recognize me until I was right in his big patchwork face. I spun a quick circle and wondered if "Professor Maxwell" would try to give me detention. I was, after all, a very naughty girl…

Out in the kitchen, Max was crouched down with a broom and dustpan in hand, sweeping up the shattered plate that we had first shoved off the counter. The syrup and semen were already mopped away, too, and Max had cleaned up the broken granite. His bare back and ass flexed as he worked.

A sexy naked man cleaning my kitchen? I nearly threw myself at Max all over again.

With an effort, I restrained myself. I remembered what Evaine had told me – or, more precisely, what she had *not* told me – and the answers I wanted to find. The thought sobered me.

Max rose and turned to look at me. His eyes widened and his cock stirred. "Wow, Lil. Are… uh… we going to play?"

Reluctantly, I shook my head. "Later. Right now, I need to find that golem before Evaine does. I'm not sure why he's hiding at the Quay Festival, but I'm damned well going to find out."

I collected my gun up off the coffee table, where Max must have set it down last night. There were still a couple dried red fingerprints on the grip. I ejected and checked the clip. About half full. I grabbed a fresh magazine of silver bullets from my desk, reloaded and racked the slide. After setting the safety, I tucked it under my blouse and vest.

Max watched me. He was still obviously aroused, but his expression had become serious again. "This is dangerous, Lil."

"I know."

"Is there anything that I can do?"

"To help me or to talk me out of this craziness?" I asked.

Max's eyes were earnest and very, very blue. "Either."

"No," I told him.

Max took a deep breath and nodded. "Alright, Lil. I'll finish up here and then head back to the garage. You call me there if you need *anything*."

It was already getting to be late morning, but I supposed that was one of the perks of Max owning his own business: he got to set his own hours. No more getting fired for taking time off to fuck me. I kissed Max goodbye, grateful to be able to put it on his lips where the kiss belonged, and left.

Chapter
FIVE

 I took a cab down to the Quay. Unless it had been towed, my i10 was still where I parked it last night, the windshield doubtlessly bristling with tickets. There was parking at the Quay Festival itself, of course, but it was expensive and absolutely did not guarantee that I wouldn't come back to a car covered in streamers and Silly String... or something worse.

No thanks. I could deal with the i10 later.

The cab driver dropped me off about a block away from the festival. Any closer and he would have been stuck there in traffic for the next hour. Even from a distance, I felt the bass beat of music vibrating through my bones and heard the buzz of overlapping voices. The air as I walked into the Quay was full of the smells of food, from hot dogs to artisan pastries. The doors of every shop and restaurant were thrown wide open, their windows displaying colorful banners and their flashiest merchandise.

And the people... Even if the Quay weren't closed to cars for the festival, there wouldn't have been room for a single vehicle on the road. Every street was packed with people, the entire population of a small city jammed into ten blocks. There were locals and tourists dressed up like me or dressed down for comfort. Every sidewalk was filled with vendors under tents and pavilions, or just set up on folding tables or blankets laid out on the sun-warmed concrete. Thousands of people talked, shouted, laughed, and sang to each other across the festival. The sound drowned out even the crashing of the ocean against the Quay.

I almost regretted that I was there on College business. The Quay Festival is one of the brightest, most beautiful gatherings in a city already known for its chaotic, overpriced wonder.

Not that *everything* was so beautiful and impressive. Ten steps into the festival, a guy clutching two plastic cups of beer in each hand offered to show me his 'wand' and spilled one of his drinks trying to thrust his hips suggestively.

Oh, I am *so* seduced.

I moved on. There were other offers, catcalls and whistles to mark my passage. Generally, I ignored those, too. One teenage boy in green and black robes actually jumped out into my path and pointed his wand at my skirt. He winked artlessly at me and opened his mouth to chant the levitation charm, but I grabbed the wand and yanked it out of his hand.

"Fuckus offius," I said, tossing it off onto the sidewalk a few feet away.

The boy shot me a venomous look – I wasn't sure if it was for taking his wand or for getting the spell wrong – and then scrambled off through the crowd. I wouldn't have felt the least bit guilty if the little creep got his hand stepped on trying to retrieve his wand.

Served him right. If I want to be treated like a piece of meat, I'll tell you. Literally. Just ask Max. But otherwise, I don't want to hear the shitty pickup lines. No one does.

So if I wasn't interested in guys and girls floundering to get under my skirt, you might be wondering why the hell I had bothered with the costume at all. For one, it was fun to get dressed up. There's nothing like kicking ass in a costume to make me feel like a damned superhero.

But I had another reason for getting my wizarding pride on. If Evaine was trying to get to the golem before the College hunters, then so was I. Not much I do pisses off the real wizards more than dressing up like a fake one. Seriously, last Halloween was a fiasco. I doubted even Sabra – who was so reclusive that I had never actually seen her face – would pass up a chance to lecture me about the factual inaccuracies in everyone's favorite fantasy series. If any of the College hunters were here at the Quay Festival, I would know it.

I moved through the crowd, searching for the red and white golem. Almost half of the huge throng wore costumes of one kind or another, from five-dollar face painting to full-body mascot suits. I watched for anything red, but that didn't narrow the field very much. I must have seen hundreds of foxes, ladybugs, Little Red Riding Hoods, Teletubbies, Power Rangers, Angry Birds, and even one grinning man dressed up as a lobster.

I stopped to stare at a woman dancing in front of a stage in what appeared to be a ball gown made entirely of rose petals. A pair of graceful butterfly wings arced out from her shoulders and shone in the sunlight like stained glass. I would have bet half the golem's massive golden bounty that those wings were real. The Quay Festival attracted even the fae out to mingle, safe in humanity's shared certainty that fairytales were made up. The fairy caught my eye and winked.

I winked back and kept searching.

The costumes that gave me a start every time were the devils. Every man or woman in red and horns made my heart skip a beat. I may have been stubborn and curious enough to go looking for the golem again, but I hadn't forgotten how close he came to killing me last night. Max gave me a hell of a lot more sexual energy than the festivalgoers yesterday, but even if that was sufficient power to take on half a rage demon, there were a lot of civilians around. I might be able to stand up after being suplexed on a fire hydrant, but what about the thousands of other people at the Quay?

By noon, though, I still hadn't spotted my golem. Was I just missing him? The festival was huge and full of people. What if he had moved on and found somewhere else to hide? Had one of the other hunters worked faster than me? If the wizards had a bit of the golem's claw or horn, any one of them could divine where to find him right about now...

What if Evaine got him first? This whole thing with her was weird. It felt like I was saying that more and more over the last year. What the fuck was going on?

I had never thought of Evaine as a warrior before, even though she was the one who taught me how to fight. It just didn't seem very... *her*. What did I really know about Evaine, though? She had taught me all about myself, but rarely said much about her own history. Hell, most of the College sorcerers didn't even call her *Evaine*. They called her *Lady*. Not *Lady Evaine* or anything like that. *Lady*, like it was her name.

I remembered seeing a picture of her in *The Gates of Avalon*. And Evaine told me once about another cambion student, long ago. Merlin. *The* Merlin.

Evaine wasn't human. She had said so herself. But even though the College respected her, she wasn't a wizard, either. She was certainly magical, and I don't just mean the mysterious disappearing act. Evaine knew songs that healed Max back when I was a teenager and couldn't control my powers. To this day, I've never heard anything quite like that.

I glanced over my shoulder in the general direction of the fairy woman, though I doubted she was still hanging around that particular stage anymore. Could Evaine be a fairy? I didn't think I'd ever seen her flinch from iron, but I wasn't sure I had even noticed her touching it at all.

Maybe Evaine was more like Ptah, someone who used magic to change from human into... something else? Or was she a djinn?

The only other creature I had even known to disappear and reappear as silently as Evaine was Madu Tau, the air djinn.

None of these questions were getting me any closer to my golem. I shook my head and pushed through a knot in the crowd. They had gathered around a juggler in a red and black harlequin costume who briefly attracted my attention when he lit his clubs on fire. Cool, but not a golem.

I wasn't getting anywhere. There was too much to see. In this throng, the golem could have slunk right past me, as long as he kept his huge head low, just like in most of the photos I saw that morning.

The smell of something sweet and deep-fried wafted by. Breakfast with Max had been sort of cut short. The same amazing sex that had my senses sharpened to a razor edge also meant that my stomach growled at the scent.

The scent. My golem might have been able to look like a part of the festival crowd, but he wasn't one of the humans. He wouldn't smell like them. What would he smell like...?

I stopped on a corner of the sidewalk, closed my eyes and inhaled deeply. The bounty posting at the College said the golem had come ashore south of here. Evaine said she didn't know why Avalon had let him leave. Avalon was an island, so the golem must have crossed the water to get here. I smelled seawater, but we were right on the Quay. No help there.

Okay, what else? Steel. The golem had melted my knife in his hand. That would leave a scent... But I smelled a lot of hot metal. The Quay Festival always brought out the Renaissance faire crowd, too, and there were at least three blacksmith's booths set up. I needed to narrow it down more.

Silver and gunpowder, maybe? I had shot silver slugs into the golem, too. My guns always left a scent, a cordite smell I was forever washing out of my clothes and hair. I turned a slow circle and sniffed the air, hunger forgotten.

There! I detected the faintest cordite whiff of gunpowder and silver, steel and seawater. And blood... my blood and his. A lot more of mine, though.

The day was warm and not too windy, but there was always a soft breeze coming off the ocean. It led me back and forth as I followed the trail, sometimes in frustrating loops. But that also meant the scent was fairly fresh, not yet blown away. I was paying such close attention to the smells swirling through the air that I nearly ran into a group of excited tourists trying to get my picture on their phones. I posed for exactly five seconds and then hurried on while two of them were still asking for my number.

I caught a glimpse of red out of the corner of one eye. Not in the road, but half-hidden behind a weather-beaten kayak rental shop. I touched the gun tucked under my vest. If I could creep up close and put a whole magazine of silver right between the golem's eyes, that might at least slow him down for a few seconds. But I had no desire to flash my gun – much less fire it – in a street full of witnesses.

Besides, I wanted answers from the golem. It wasn't until I was slipping quietly between the kayak shop and a neighboring bistro that I realized I had no idea how to get them.

I stepped around the corner, behind the shop. Brightly colored plastic kayaks sat in tiered racks, each one chained and padlocked into place. My golem hunkered down at the end of the little aisle, his back against a weather-beaten gray fence and his long, mismatched arms wrapped around his knees. His head was bowed and I could clearly make out several bullet holes in the shirt stretched nearly to tearing across his huge chest, each one ringed with dark dried blood.

Out of view of the general public, I slid the gun from the waist of my skirt and pointed it at the golem's head, right where the single sharp red horn arced up from his temple.

"Hey," I said, not sure how else to start this conversation.

"No more pictures," he said. "Please..."

The golem raised his right hand palm-out toward me. It was big, but it was human. So was his voice. It was deep and slightly rough – smoky, almost, in a way that reminded me of good whiskey. Was that the same voice I heard last night?

When I didn't immediately retreat, the golem looked up at me with one glowing red eye. The other was a rich, earthy brown. But both pupils dilated when he saw me and his left hand came up, the scarlet one with two-inch-long black claws like monstrous ebony thorns.

"You!" the golem growled.

There was something of the deeper, harder voice I heard before in that word.

My finger tightened on the trigger of my gun.

"Easy," I said. "I just want to talk."

"Then why are you pointing a gun at me?" snarled the half-man, half-demon golem.

He climbed up to one knee and I quickly gestured with my gun for him to stop, not sure if he would obey. But the golem stilled. Fuck, even down on his knees, this thing was almost as tall as I was.

"Because you tried like hell to kill me the other night," I said. "Or have you forgotten that already?"

The golem actually went pale at that. At least, the human side of his face did. Here in person, in the daylight and while he wasn't trying to tear my guts out through my bellybutton, I could finally make out some details. The two halves of his face were sewn together with silvery thread in fine, intricate stitches. The work that I had assumed crude and ugly was, in truth, quite meticulous. But then the golem bowed his head again, hiding behind the long fall of black hair that cascaded from the right side of his scalp.

"That... wasn't me," he said in a low voice.

"Are you saying there's another giant Frankenstein guy running around the city?" I asked, scowling.

"Frankenstein was the creator, not the monster."

I couldn't help it. I cracked a smile at that. Luckily, the golem still wasn't looking at me. I schooled my expression into something more appropriate for a badass monster hunter.

"I mean... it wasn't me," he said, reaching across his wide body to touch his human hand against the human half of his face. "It was me."

Now he touched his fingertips to the red side of his face, then pulled them away as though burned. For all I knew, that was exactly what had just happened. I remembered my melted knife all too well. But I struggled to untangle and make sense of what the golem seemed to be telling me.

"So that was the demon part of you?" I asked. "Not... you? The human you?"

The golem nodded. Okay, this was getting *beyond* weird. I knew he was made up of two men, but were each of them still distinct entities inside him? I had even more questions than before. I decided to start with a simple one.

"Do you have a name?"

He looked up at me, ignoring the gun now. Maybe the golem had nothing to fear from it... I backed away a step and fought to keep my hands steady. I didn't want to start a fight with the patchwork monster here. For fuck's sake, I could hear a man just on the other side of the kayak shop, arguing with his kids about whether or not it was time for ice cream.

The golem laughed, but it was a bitter, unhappy sound.

"Yes, I have a name. More names than I can stand," he said in that smooth whiskey voice. "Reid. Orbias. Reid and Orbias."

When he said the second name, it came out in a deep, inhuman growl. *That* was the voice I recognized and it sent a chill down my spine. My skin crawled so hard I half worried it might run away without the rest of me.

The golem squeezed his eyes shut and pressed huge hands against his temples with such force that I was pretty sure he would have cracked my skull like an egg. He let out a low groan, but it was in the human voice this time.

"Reid," he panted. "My name is Reid!"

"Okay... Reid," I said slowly. "Why are you hiding out here?"

"My... master," he said in a whisper soft enough that I stepped cautiously closer to hear. "The beautiful demon. He calls to me and Orbias wishes to return. But my master can't reveal himself. Not yet. I don't think he would follow me to a place with so many people. I... I hope he won't."

Another demon. Shit. That wasn't good news.

I glanced nervously up and down the aisle of kayaks, but the only demon here was the big red half of Reid that was Orbias. And my own half-succubus self, I supposed. The golem looked nervous, too. At least, as much as a nine-foot-tall mountain of muscles and claws *could* look nervous.

"You said something about your master last night, right before you ran off," I prompted.

"My master summoned me and I longed to obey. Orbias could not stay, not even to tear you apart. To rend your body and watch blood spill..."

Reid's voice was dropping in pitch. He stopped with a gasp and squeezed his eyes shut.

"I am... trying to control Orbias," Reid said. There was pain in his voice, both sharp and heavy. "He wants to return to my master. But I can't go back."

"Why? Who is this beautiful demon?"

Reid shook his head. Hard. "No. You don't want to know him. You would desire him, but he would be your death. Please, don't ask me about him!"

The golem sounded an awful lot like Kalen when I asked about whoever hired him to steal *The Gates of Avalon*, an employer who frightened even an infamous Unseelie thief so badly that he was more willing to sit in prison than give the College a name.

And a beautiful demon that I would desire even to my death...? That sounded like Ben talking about the succubus who attacked him last year. But Reid said *him*. An incubus, maybe?

I remembered the shadow that came after Kalen in the Hotel Marquis penthouse. I had never forgotten those brilliant, burning golden eyes. And what did Evaine say when the High Magus asked about Avalon at Finn and Muir's trial? Only shadows and dreams moved on the island, or something like that. Shadows like the one that tried to take the book from Kalen.

"Where did you come from, Reid?" I asked.

"The island," he said.

Avalon. That matched up with what Evaine said that morning, but it still hit me like a bucket of cold water. I was about one more icy shiver away from never being warm again.

All of the weird shit that had happened over the last year was beginning to come together, but I still didn't know what it meant. Maybe Reid did, if I could get him to tell me. Carefully. Evaine said that this was dangerous. I might have been a disobedient little student, but I tried not to be a stupid one. If Max hadn't come to my rescue last night, I wouldn't even be alive to wonder about all of this shit.

"Okay, Reid," I said. I switched the safety on my gun and then tucked it back under my shirt and vest. "We need to talk more, but not here. There are a lot of innocent people around. Neither of us wants to hurt them, I think."

"Orbias does."

Reid's huge left hand flexed, showing off his massive, hooked black claws. The golem put his right hand over it and pulled both arms against his chest.

"You're fighting his control. And that's... impressive," I said, then suddenly realized that I meant it. "But let's go somewhere comfortable. Somewhere without witnesses."

Reid narrowed his eyes at me. "You tried to kill me."

"I'm sorry about that, but it was kind of mutual. You were trying to kill me too, remember?"

I smiled at Reid. His crimson eye flared like gasoline thrown onto a fire and I regretted putting my gun away.

"Orbias wants to kill you," Reid said. His voice dropped several octaves. I felt it in my bones. "He rages. I want your blood. I want to tear you apart…"

The golem's hands were still clutched against his massive chest and Orbias' claws tore jagged lines into Reid's already tortured t-shirt. Blood soaked the cloth and I winced.

"I'm scared," he said. "I frighten myself."

"Yeah. You freak me out, too," I admitted. "Come on. Let's get you out of here."

Reid regarded me suspiciously for a long time, but then he rose slowly to his feet. His shredded and ragged clothes almost concealed where my bullets had hit last night, but my sight was still too good to avoid seeing all seven holes across his chest from shoulder to shoulder. I would have been proud of myself for hitting him at all in the state I was in, but to be fair, Reid was the proverbial broad side of a barn.

And, I realized, I felt kind of guilty for hurting the towering golem. Whatever else was going on, I doubted that Reid had asked to be cut into pieces and sewn to a demon. He was scared and in pain and I got the feeling that it had been a while since anyone was nice to him. Reid was fighting off Orbias' control alone, to say nothing of this incubus who called out to the golem's demonic half.

"Let me help you," I said.

I held out my hand to Reid like I would to a wild animal and for a moment, I almost expected him to sniff it. But he simply nodded heavily and stepped in closer, until he was close enough to touch. Gingerly, I put my hand on his elbow, then slid my arm through his. Reid looked down at me.

"Come on," I told him.

I led Reid out from behind the kayak rental shop and back into the street. The golem kept his head down, but especially with me on his arm, there was no way to avoid being stared at. I was pretty sure I even saw the butterfly-winged fairy watching us, a shocked expression on her ethereal face. You would think she had never seen a cambion escorting a half-demon golem from a party before...

I didn't recognize anyone else on the way out. There were a lot of men and women eyeing me discreetly – and drunk ones ogling not so discreetly – but no wizards charging through the crowd with wands drawn. And no sign of Evaine.

Good. I wasn't ready to confront my teacher again just yet.

When we reached the cordoned-off perimeter of the Quay Festival, I shoved my way to the edge of the sidewalk. Even if I felt like hiking eleven blocks out to where I had parked the i10 last night, there was no way Reid would fit into my sleek little silver sports car.

I flagged down a taxivan in record time. Short skirts are helpful that way. I slid open the door and gestured Reid inside. The golem gave me an uncertain frown, but then crammed himself into one of the bench seats. I glanced at the seat belts and shook my head. Not a chance.

"Hey, great costume," said the driver, peering back over his seat at Reid. "How does it work? Is it one of those rigs that takes two guys to wear?"

Reid shot the driver a look that was half rage, half horror, and you can guess which half was which. I climbed into the passenger seat.

"Twelfth Street and Mason," I said. "And I'll give you an extra hundred bucks to keep quiet."

The cab driver didn't answer. But then, I was paying him not to.

Chapter
SIX

*E*ven my usually unflappable doorman did a double take when he saw Reid duck out of the van. He didn't whistle, but just opened the door and called down the elevator. I tipped him an extra hundred dollars, too.

"Where are we going?" Reid asked when the elevator doors had closed behind us.

"My condo," I said. "No one should bother us there."

I stood pressed against the wall. Reid took up most of the elevator. I had almost rented us a nice big hotel suite somewhere, but then reconsidered. I wanted a place that was safe, familiar and contained a lot more weapons in case I needed them. As far as Evaine knew, I had given up the hunt for Reid. She had no reason to return to my condo... I hoped. And while the College hunters were out searching for Reid, none of them would be turning the scry network on me.

The elevator lurched into motion and Reid tensed. Then he looked down at me with an embarrassed expression on half of his stitched face.

"Sorry," he said. "I wasn't always like this. When I was only me. Before I was me and me."

Reid frowned deeply and growled low in his throat. His expression became one of pained frustration. As shitty as yesterday had been for me, I was pretty sure Reid's day was worse.

"It's okay," I told him. "Maybe we can find a way to fix this."

I regretted the words as soon as they left my lips. What the hell could I do? Cut the demon parts off Reid, find the rest of his body and then stitch them back together? Even if I were a real wizard – not just dressed up like a slutty version of one – I doubted that would work.

To his credit, though, Reid didn't look very hopeful. He smiled sadly, silently thanking me for trying, however pathetically. I still wanted my answers, but was also developing a strong desire to dick-punch whoever had made the golem.

The elevator chimed and stopped. When it slid open, Reid followed me down the white-finished hallway to my door. I unlocked it and then waved him inside. Reid stepped through.

"This is where you live?" he asked.

Reid's look of surprise was all too human. For some reason, no one ever expects the four-million-dollar condo. It's not even close to the most expensive place in the city, but it's nice and it's mine. I guess I just didn't seem like the professional sort that filled the rest of the building.

"Home sweet home," I said. I went inside after Reid, then shut and locked the front door behind us. "Let's get you cleaned up."

Speaking of cleaning up, Max had finished taking care of the kitchen. It was spotless. Well, except for the broken countertop, but he had taped over the cracks to keep any more pieces from coming loose. I supposed that I would have to call someone in to fix it later.

Reid let me take him through the living room and into the bathroom. He caught his reflection in the mirror and looked down at the floor. I touched his arm carefully.

"Want a shower?" I asked him. "Assuming you remember how to use one."

I wasn't sure how much Reid recalled of his human life, but the golem nodded and began stripping off his ruined clothes. I got the water going and then reluctantly left him alone in the bathroom. Reid's control of Orbias appeared pretty good for the moment, but how long would that last? If his demonic half took over and started busting up my shower, though, I supposed that the noise would give me enough warning to grab a bigger weapon than my little nine-millimeter. An elephant gun loaded with a pound of silver *might* do the job...

In the meantime, though, Reid needed some new clothes. I went to my desk and flipped open my laptop. I had no idea what sort of clothes Reid liked, but figured that anything would be an improvement over his tattered t-shirt and pants bursting at the seams. Jeans and some shirts in the golem's size required hitting up a couple of specialty websites, but at least I could spring for over-night shipping.

The hiss of running water was still coming from the bathroom. Next on my list: feeding him. When had the golem last eaten? Did he even need to eat?

I went to the kitchen and eyed the contents of my refrigerator suspiciously. No leftovers from breakfast and I had no idea how to cook. Max was the one who took home economics twice in high school. I usually just ordered out, but inviting a delivery boy or girl to the front door when I had a half-demon golem over didn't seem too smart.

The Lily Quinn special, then: a bowl of cereal and a package of chocolate chip cookies. And a gallon of rocky road ice cream if Reid was still hungry after that. With an early dinner sorted, I deposited my gun on my desk – no reason to provoke Orbias more than I had to when there were other weapons stashed all around my condo – and returned to check on Reid.

The bathroom was full of steam and I could barely make out the golem's massive silhouette still in the shower. He appeared to be simply standing under the spray, letting the heat cascade down his back. There was red in the water around his feet that wasn't just a reflection of his crimson skin.

I went to the medicine cabinet and scowled even harder than I had at the refrigerator. The sum total of my first aid supplies was some gauze, tape and tweezers – and even those were new. I recognized the tweezers as the ones Max had used to pull the broken glass out of me last night. In nine years of bounty hunting, I had so rarely come up against a monster who could beat through my sex-fueled healing that I never bothered to buy any medical supplies. Max must have brought these himself.

I removed the bandages and tweezers from the cabinet. What about disinfectant? I never worried about it, since my sexed-up immune system could take on the bacterial equivalent of a tank... But I returned to the kitchen to dig around under the sink and came up with a half-full bottle of rubbing alcohol. I had used it a few times to clean my guns until Max pointed out that alcohol was hard on the finish and told me where to buy the right kind of solvents. That was years ago and the label on the plastic bottle was turning yellow, but I was pretty sure that rubbing alcohol didn't expire.

Thinking of Max and his attentions the night before got me a little warm between the legs, but it also reminded me to get a bowl down from the cupboard. By the time I went back to the bathroom, the water had stopped. My shower was large and I had shared it often enough without any issues, but Reid made it look positively cramped. He climbed out, forced to both step over the lip and duck under the stainless steel door frame at the same time.

I pulled up a towel from the rack and held it out for Reid. He took it with a small nod, but the golem was so damned massive that I grabbed a second towel to help him dry off.

Honestly, I wasn't *trying* to sneak a look... but I just couldn't help myself. Reid's mysterious creator had made him from equal parts man and demon, all neatly stitched together with shining silver thread. I had thought of him as a patchwork, but Reid was far more finely crafted than that. Whoever Reid had been before being disassembled and sewn to Orbias, he was huge and in excellent shape – as close a match as any human could be to a rage demon.

And nothing at all had been neglected in constructing Reid. I couldn't help noticing his firm, muscular ass, one flank taken from Reid and one from Orbias. Or the alternately red and white expanse of abdominal and back muscles all painstakingly joined with precise silver stitching. And his cock... Oh god, his cock. Even soft, Reid's dick was as big around as my wrist and long enough to gag me. It was the color of live coals and made my mouth water.

I felt eyes on me and glanced up at Reid. He was watching me, too. I smiled and finished drying him off. When we were done, I took both towels and tossed them into the laundry basket.

"Okay, now sit down and let me take a look," I said.

I collected the bandages, bowl, tweezers and rubbing alcohol, then led Reid back to my bedroom. Max had replaced the sheets and made my bed neatly before leaving that morning. I had the best friend in the world. No, *all* the worlds.

I sat Reid down on the corner of the bed, put my supplies on the nightstand and got to work examining the golem's vast chest. The damage was both better and worse than I expected. One of my bullets had torn a raw red wound into his right shoulder, then two more across his chest, but his left pectoral was hard red demon flesh. I clearly remembered bullet holes all across the front of Reid's shirt and where I had cut him once with my knife before he melted it like a birthday candle. But now there were no injuries or even scars on his smooth scarlet skin.

"That silver didn't do very much, did it?" I asked, rolling up the sleeves of my tailored white shirt. "I guess it's not only lust demons who heal fast. Well, at least that's half the work done."

I took off my costume glasses and set them aside, then gripped Reid's arm just below the wound and gently poked my tweezers into the ragged red hole. The golem jerked away and growled like a distant thunderstorm. His demonic right eye flared with ember light and the temperature in my bedroom shot up a few degrees.

"Hey, I'm trying to help," I said.

Reid's burning red eye dimmed a bit and his growl became a deep sigh.

"Sorry."

"It's okay. Your life has been pretty fucked up lately. But I want to help you, if I can, and I'm hoping that you can help me."

Reid nodded slowly, though his jaw tightened when I grabbed the first bullet with the tweezers and began prying it free.

"What... what's your name?" he asked, grunting as I pulled out the flattened piece of silver and dropped it into the bowl sitting on my nightstand.

"Lily Quinn." I brandished the bloody tweezers and gave a little bow. "At your service."

I practically had to sit in Reid's lap to go after the remaining two bullets. They were good shots, if I do say so myself, and buried deep in the impressive muscle of Reid's chest. He snarled and clenched his fists, but didn't lash out at me. I bit the tip of my tongue in my teeth as I dug the remaining two silver slugs from his chest. They clattered heavily into the bowl.

"Why are you still alive?" Reid asked. "Orbias thought he killed you last night."

"Well, your worse half wasn't entirely wrong," I said. I cut a few squares of gauze and then picked up the rubbing alcohol. "Brace yourself. This is probably going to sting like a motherfucker."

I poured alcohol over the bullet holes, sopping up the excess with more gauze. Reid growled and Orbias' claws sliced a yard-long section of my sheets into ribbons.

"Sorry," I said, blotting the wounds dry with another piece of gauze. "Anyway, I *would* have been dead, but my best friend came to my rescue."

I measured out some white medical tape and secured the last three squares of gauze over Reid's injuries. It wasn't perfect work, but at least the bullets were out.

"But you're not even hurt," Reid said, looking up and down my body. My costume exposed quite a bit of it.

"That's because I'm a cambion."

Reid jumped up to his feet, dumping me unceremoniously onto the bedroom floor. There was nothing distant about the thunderous growl he let out this time. The storm was right on top of me. I threw myself to one side and thrust my hand under the nightstand, to the automatic pistol hidden down there and closed my fingers around the grip.

"So... you've heard the word before, then," I said, fighting to keep my voice steady.

"You're the daughter of an incubus," Reid snarled down at me. "Like *him*, like my master!"

Incubus. Called it.

I didn't feel very victorious, though.

"Actually, it was my mother," I told Reid. "She was a succubus. She fell in love with the wizard who summoned her. And starved to death because he didn't love her in return."

The golem let out another bone-rattling growl and my hand tightened on the gun under my nightstand. The bullets were lead, not silver... But it wasn't like the silver had made much difference against Orbias. He was sewn together with the stuff.

Reid, however, seemed just as susceptible to bullets as any full-bodied human.

"Reid, stop." I kept my voice as firm and calm as I could. "You're only giving Orbias what he wants. He's a rage demon. Get angry and he'll take control again."

The golem flexed his left hand, brandishing his wicked black claws. Reid squeezed his eyes shut and took several deep, shuddering breaths. I kept my hand on the gun and didn't move.

"You're... right," Reid said at last, opening his eyes. The demonic one still glowed, but less furiously now. "Thank you, Lily."

"For what, exactly?"

"For not shooting me."

"I left my gun on the desk," I said.

"You have another one down there. I can smell the steel and powder."

Reid's half-demon senses were just as good as mine, apparently. Slowly, I released the pistol and stood. The golem and I stared at each other for a long moment. Finally, I touched my fingertips to one of the bandaged squares on Reid's chest. A spot of blood shone red against the white gauze.

"Does it still hurt?" I asked.

"Less than before," said Reid.

Gently, I traced the line of silver thread stitching the two halves of his chest together. "Do *these* hurt?"

"Yes," Reid admitted and then tapped a long, taloned finger against his forehead. "But not as much as it hurts here. I'm made of two men... Well, one man and one demon. Orbias is always fighting me for control. He longs to return to his... our... master with blood on his claws."

The pain in Reid's voice was deep and simple. He wasn't asking for a solution or even sympathy. The golem gazed up at me and his expression turned into one of wonder.

"You're like me," he said. "But... not like me. You're beautiful."

I actually blushed a little at the unexpected compliment and smiled.

"You're pretty damned sexy, too," I said.

"No," Reid answered quickly, with some of that familiar but still frightening snarl. "I'm a monster!"

"Hey! First of all, I've fucked more than a few monsters and a lot of them were very fine pieces of supernatural ass. Second, you *are* beautiful."

The golem gave me a quizzical look. I touched my hand to the center of Reid's chest, where red flesh met white, where I felt his powerful heart beating under my touch.

"Right in here," I said. "Horrible things have been done to you, but you've restrained Orbias from kicking my ass at least three times since lunch. You're holding back a demon, Reid. A demon of fucking wrath! I don't know who you were before, but the man you are now is nothing short of amazing."

Carefully, I ran my hand along the hard red curve of Reid's horn, following the arc of it down, and laced my fingers through his long, thick black hair.

I tilted Reid's head back and kissed him. His whole huge body tensed, but the golem didn't shove me away and I felt a hot spark of lust. It was small, almost shy, but burned with such intensity that heat rushed through me.

I withdrew just a bit. Reid's eyes were closed and his heartbeat raced to match mine.

"Did you like that?" I asked.

He nodded.

"Can I do it again?" I asked.

Reid nodded a second time, still not looking at me.

I pressed my lips to his. He sat frozen on the edge of my bed for a moment before opening his mouth to me. I traced the tip of my tongue delicately along his lower lip. Reid gasped, but then sighed as I deepened the kiss. I don't know which tongue his creator had given the golem, but it was warm and agile. He tasted somehow spicy and his desire was so hot that it burned.

I felt something sharp against my tongue and drew back. That single fang hung like a dagger on the right side of his mouth. It was a bit like a vampire's, but much longer and thicker – meant to rend and tear rather than simply puncture.

Reid had finally opened his eyes and the human half of his face was blushing nearly as red as the demonic half. I felt a tug at my skirt and looked down, expecting to see Reid's hand there. Both of them were at his sides, grabbing the edge of my bed, but the golem's crimson cock had swelled into something truly massive and was still rising. The tip had caught the hem of my pleated skirt and lifted upward as it grew. Reid followed my gaze and then back up to me. Shame and desire warred across his face.

I reached out and wrapped both hands around his huge length. The golem's dick was almost painfully hot in my grasp, like he burned with some unimaginable fever. I stroked down to the base – so thick now that I couldn't even come close to touching my fingers around it – then back up to the tip. Reid's grip on the edge of the bed tightened and I heard sheets tearing.

"Did you like that?" I whispered.

Reid nodded.

"Can I do it again?"

He nodded quickly, staring at me and holding his breath. His heartbeat hammered like a great drum and the tempo rose as I caressed his immense cock, exploring its length and weight.

"Lily, I want..." Reid said, half stammering and half growling and with absolutely no idea how to finish the sentence.

I put one finger to his lips and reached beneath my skirt to hook a thumb through the waist of my underwear. I tugged them down over my knee socks and Reid bit his lower lip hard enough to make his fang dimple the skin above his chin. My panties were just plain white cotton, but completed the student image perfectly. When I dress up, I don't skimp.

The white cloth was dripping wet. I stepped out of my panties and held them up to show Reid. His mismatched eyes were wide. I told him that he was beautiful – would he believe me now?

I slid forward, straddling Reid's thighs. The golem's impossibly long cock twitched in his lap and the spark of lust I felt inside him burst into a furious golden inferno. Taking a dick of his size was going to be difficult, but I had no intention of letting that stop me.

Max had already powered me up considerably and Reid was only giving me more.

Reaching down with both hands, I grabbed the golem's cock and held it tightly. Reid was so big that I had to spread my legs wide to sit in his lap and balance on the tips of my toes to position myself. One brush of my wet, eager pussy over the crown of Reid's dick made us both gasp.

He was amazingly hot. And I don't mean sexy, though he was, in an imposing, rough-hewn sort of way. No, I mean... literally. Reid's demonic cock had grown even more feverishly hot, blazing against me like something on fire. I remembered my melted knife from the night before and took a deep, steadying breath. This wasn't safe or smart, but I didn't care.

Slowly, I sank onto Reid. I watched his huge dick disappear up beneath my skirt. The sight was delicious, but even better was the sensation of thick, red-hot hardness penetrating me. I fell down and down onto him, accepting inch after inch, invasion and invitation all at once. I let out a breathless moan as I took Reid to the hilt. All of him.

It wasn't easy with the golem's monstrous cock shoved deep inside me, but I began rocking my hips. He let out a low, groaning growl and shredded another handful of sheets with his demonic black claws. But Reid's right hand rose to my thigh, tracing the line of it up under my skirt to cup my ass.

The heat of him was incredible. I felt it burning through me, the blaze of Reid's cock and of his desire. Could I catch fire? I didn't know, but I sure as fuck didn't want to stop. I rode Reid faster, impaling myself on his dick, grinding my hips and clit against the hard planes of his patchwork body. Hotter and hotter, higher and higher... I was stretched so tight on Reid's demonic cock. There was pain, but that pain was only the leading edge of sensation. Beyond was pleasure. Hot, brilliant golden pleasure and lust.

"Reid!" I moaned out.

I clutched his broad shoulders as I came, bucking in Reid's lap, and my pussy dripped wetness all along the thick length of his cock. His eyes were wide as he took in the sight of me cumming on the end of his long prick. I kissed Reid and felt Orbias' dagger fang against my lower lip, drawing a bead of blood there. I wasn't safe with the golem, but how could I be? He wasn't even safe with himself.

I drew myself up as best I could to the big head of Reid's dick, but my knees were weak and even my long legs weren't quite long enough to make the movement an easy one. I fell down onto Reid once more with a loud whimper.

"Like... like this?" he asked in a deep, tight voice.

Reid grabbed me around the waist with both hands, long fingers touching at my spine and naval. He picked me up easily, lifting me to the tip of his cock. Before I could gulp down a single breath, Reid was yanking me onto his dick again.

"Yes!" I cried out in a breathless, raw voice. "Give me your huge fucking cock!"

He did. Have you ever heard the term *slam piece*? I don't use it often and never really appreciated that it might be applicable until now. Reid's hands tightened around me and the golem growled as he hammered me down onto his dick. Maybe he realized that he didn't need to be gentle with me, that I could take it rough. Or perhaps Reid simply couldn't help himself anymore. He had been containing and restraining Orbias for the last day and now he was free to loose some of that pain and aggression, to feel something good and sweet in return.

Reid lifted me until my toes actually came up off the bedroom floor and then lowered me just a little, fucking me with only the thick head of his cock. He held me prisoner there until I was squirming and begging in the golem's unbreakable grip before finally pulling me down and spearing me fully on his monstrous red length.

He pounded pleasure into up me and I threw back my head, screaming out my orgasm like a war cry. My hair was a wild copper mess, my tie tugged loose and my shirt yanked free from my skirt. And god, the *heat*... I would have torn off my clothes if I could move in Reid's grasp any more than to thrash in helpless ecstasy. I was soaked all over, streaming wetness from my overfilled pussy and sweat from the rest of my body.

The sensation of Reid's great demonic cock hammering up into me kindled fires all along my nerves, lighting them like fuses. His heat flared and the golem's already massive shaft was swelling even bigger inside me. My ecstatic scream was breathless as Reid surged to his feet. He slammed me down onto his dick twice more and I felt his huge body trembling against mine.

With a groan like a shifting tectonic plate, Reid heaved me off his cock and threw me to the bedroom floor. I barely managed to get my knees beneath me and grabbed the golem's jutting crimson dick. It was slick and red-hot under my hands, probably hot enough to burn a human. But I wasn't human and I wasn't letting go.

A single long stroke was all it took. Reid roared and white arced out from his cock. The golem's cum was phosphorescently bright and almost glowed in the air. It splashed against my cheeks, making me gasp. The droplets were thick and hot, like candle wax oozing across my skin. Reid's load shot out over my lips and the bridge of my nose. It ran in vivid lines down to soak my shirt and dripped from my chin onto my rumpled skirt.

When it was over, I looked up at Reid and smiled. The golem was panting and staring down at the huge mess he had made. I didn't want him thinking that all of this was unwanted, that *he* was unwanted.

So I licked my lips slowly, deliberately. Reid's spunk was still hot and tasted spicy. I showed him his cum on my tongue, then swallowed it all and winked. He blinked and another brilliant white pearl of cum trickled from his cock to splatter down onto my skirt.

When I stood, I wobbled a little on my feet. Reid caught my arm and helped me stand.

"Are you alright?" he asked. "That..."

"Was amazing?" I finished.

Another shy smile spread across Reid's face. "That would have hurt a human woman. Badly."

"You may be a monster, Reid," I told him. "But so am I."

Chapter
SEVEN

My wizard costume was far beyond salvaging. Even my best dry-cleaner wouldn't be able to do much against what seemed like half a gallon of white-hot demon spunk. So I stripped out of my ruined skirt and blouse, balled up the whole outfit and chucked it in the trash.

Since Reid's new clothes wouldn't arrive until tomorrow morning, I grabbed a sarong out of my closet. Orbias' huge clawed hand wasn't very good for managing knots, so I helped Reid tie it around his waist. I pulled on my robe and found my bunny slippers replaced neatly at the foot of the bed. I slid them on and led Reid to the kitchen.

He gave the meal I had set out a skeptical look, but that didn't stop him from devouring the cereal and cookies. I wondered if I should call Max – Reid could probably use some warm homemade food. In the meantime, I started emptying everything edible from the cupboards out onto the counter. Reid had finished a huge bowl of cereal and was tipping the last cookie crumbs into his mouth with no signs of being full. The golem ate like I did after a job.

The living room curtains were still open and the sun had set outside. It was the middle of summer and even at this late hour, scarlet light glowed along the horizon, coloring the western sky as though bloodstained. The city was already steeped in shadows and the road below my condo flowed with white headlights and red taillights. Thousands of windows were lighting up one by one, squares of radiance that marked out places where humans lived and worked even as night fell.

It was about the time I usually would have kicked a guy out the door, but I couldn't do that to Reid. He was a hunted man and might kill someone if Orbias gained the upper hand in their internal battle. The other hunters were still out there, searching for him. And so was Evaine.

"Reid, who made you?" I asked.

The golem froze with a second bowl of cereal halfway to his mouth. His expression became pained.

"I'm sorry," I told him. "Really. But I need to know. Who is your master?"

Reid lowered the bowl again and let out a long sigh. He looked tired. No, exhausted. But he nodded slowly.

"I don't think my master was the one who made me," Reid said in a heavy, thoughtful voice. "There was a man there, too, on the island. A wizard. I smelled my blood on him."

I leaned against the counter. "Tell me everything you remember. Please, Reid. It's important."

"I don't remember my real life anymore. My human life... But I don't recall Orbias' life, either, so maybe that's a fair trade. The first thing I remember is the island. There were mountains and a forest, I think, but it was so dark. It was a strange place. It didn't feel real. Or too real. I'm not sure which."

"That must have been Avalon," I said.

"I don't know... but *I* do." Reid growled and scratched four new lines across my already tortured granite countertop. "I mean that Orbias knows the island, Avalon. Reid doesn't. I'm sorry... This is difficult."

"Yeah," I agreed. "I'm sorry, too. But I need to hear about this. What happened on the island?"

"My master was there. The beautiful demon, the incubus with the burning golden eyes... The wizard brought me there, I think. He was the one who made this body and presented it to my master."

Reid had paused to rubbed his temple, just below where Orbias' red horn curved up from his wild thatch of thick black hair. It hadn't exactly been neat before, but after our bout in the bedroom, Reid's hair was really a mess. I should probably offer the poor guy a comb.

Later. Right now, I needed answers. I had put them off for long enough.

"What did the wizard look like?" I asked.

Reid thought. "About your age, I think. He had dark hair and no beard. But I wasn't watching him."

That wasn't much of a description and didn't immediately ring any bells, but I didn't know very many wizards. There were hundreds of them across North America and hundreds more serving the Castle in Europe... Which was assuming that whoever Reid had seen was a Merlinic wizard at all. There were as many traditions of magic in the world as there were cultures.

"We were both kneeling before my master and we were all inside a circle of stones. Old standing stones, like Stonehenge," Reid said, then cocked his head at his own choice of words. "I guess I do remember a few things."

"What happened there?" I asked.

"My master commanded me to stand, then took me to the center of the circle. There was another rock there, smaller than the others and sticking up out of the ground. It didn't look like anything important, but the beautiful demon told me to put my hands on it."

I frowned. Why? Was this some kind of demonic version of the test the College gave me nine years ago? Was the incubus making sure that Reid was demonic enough? Or human enough?

"I wanted so badly to make my master happy," Reid told me in his smooth whiskey voice. "Both of us, Reid and Orbias. We would have done anything he asked, anything to please our master. But when I touched the stone, it... cracked."

That didn't seem like much, but neither had filling a cup with water. A cup that Vincent Myrdon called the Grail and which tested the purity of my heart, he said. So what was Reid being tested for? To judge by the unhappy expression on both halves of the golem's face, his test hadn't ended as well as mine.

"It wasn't a very big crack," said Reid. "Not enough to harm the stone much, but the beautiful demon was furious."

"What was supposed to happen when you touched that stone?" I asked. "What was it? Did they ever tell you?"

"I... think I knew once. At least, Orbias did. But that was before the wizard cut us apart. Not everything was stitched back together. Whatever was supposed to happen, that crack wasn't it. My master hit me and I flew out of the circle."

"That's when you ran?"

"Yes."

Reid closed his eyes. Suddenly, he didn't seem hungry anymore. His head sagged and his single long horn hit the overhead light, setting it swinging. He opened his eyes again and scowled magnificently at the wavering lamp. Orbias' fury-red eye flared and his left hand darted out, grabbing the fixture and crushing it easily. Broken glass rained down over the counter.

I remained silent until Reid regained control of his body. The golem looked down at the shattered glass in his cereal. For a moment, I wondered if he intended to eat it anyway, but Reid pushed the bowl away.

"I'm sorry, Lily," he said.

"It's okay," I told Reid, smiling a little. I pointed to the taped-over cracks in the kitchen counter. "That's what happens when *my* demon half gets her way. I'll get it all repaired later. How did you escape from the incubus?"

"My master was speaking to the wizard, telling him that I wasn't good enough. They weren't watching, so I ran. I came to the sea and heard my master calling to me, to Orbias. He wanted to go back, but I was so frightened. I jumped into the water and I swam... I don't know for how long."

"Avalon let you go," I said. That was what Evaine told me that morning. She also said that if the mystic island let Reid leave, it was for a reason. "What happened then?"

"I thought I would drown, but I swam until I washed up under that big red bridge. I tried to hide, until you found me. I was so tired and Orbias was so angry with us for running away. You know the story after that."

"The incubus was still calling for you," I said, nodding. "Orbias wanted to go to him. But you hid instead."

"Until you discovered me again. Why were you looking for me?"

"You're part demon, Reid, and when you entered the city, you tripped some kind of magical alarm. The College of wizards has put a bounty on you."

"Why?"

"They're afraid of you," I answered. "They think you're dangerous."

"They're right."

I sighed, not quite sure what to say to that. I didn't know that I agreed... or disagreed, exactly.

I crossed my arms over my chest and looked down at my bunny slippers. After a long moment, I raised my eyes to Reid again and drew a deep breath.

"Okay," I said. "I still don't know what any of this has to do with me or why Evaine didn't want me on the job, but that doesn't really matter anymore. We're dealing with wizards and demons and that means you need to talk to the College."

Reid's mismatched eyes narrowed and his claws gouged another quintet of lines into the granite. I reached across the counter and put my hand on top of his.

"Hey," I told Reid. "It's going to be okay. The High Magus is... well, he's kind of a dick, to be honest. But he's also the most powerful wizard this side of the Atlantic. He knows his shit."

"He'll kill me."

"No. I won't let that happen," I said firmly.

I squeezed Reid's hand and then went to my desk, where the cell phone I had been using to find him that morning sat beside my gun. I picked up the phone and scrolled through my contacts to Vincent Myrdon's number. I hit the *call* button and gave the golem what I hoped was a reassuring smile.

The line rang once and then the phone shattered in my hand. I yelped and dropped the broken pieces to the floor. Reid jumped to his feet with a leonine snarl and whirled. Evaine stood in my living room, just like she had that morning, still wearing her gleaming silver armor.

And she looked pissed.

Chapter
EIGHT

y mouth fell open. I don't get caught with my pants down very often. Okay, I actually get caught with my pants down fairly frequently, but only literally.

What the hell was Evaine doing here again? Her expression was hard and cold. I had never seen my teacher look like that, not even when I slacked off during our most important lessons. Evaine was truly furious.

Reid's head snapped up and his red eye burned with hellfire. He flexed his demonic hand, something dripping from his black talons that smelled poisonous and left smoking scars on my kitchen floor. The golem started toward Evaine, but I flung myself in between them.

"Reid, no!" I cried.

The golem lurched to a stop with another deep, dangerous snarl and I spun back to face Evaine.

"What the fuck?" I shouted. "Why did you break my phone? That's the second one I've lost on this job!"

"You can't tell the College what is happening here." Evaine's tone was icy. "I said that *I* would deal with the golem, Lilith. And so I shall."

I remained standing between her and Reid, my hands thrown out to either side. Evaine took a step toward me, armor clinking like silver chimes. I gulped.

"Lily, who is this woman?" Reid asked in a low voice. "Is she one of the hunters?"

"I didn't use to think so," I muttered. "But now I'm not so sure."

"You should have been more careful," Evaine said. Even her usually lyrical accent had become hard. "The golem's hiding place was far from perfect and you were seen leaving the Quay."

The fairy in the rose-petal dress at the festival. The College had a good relationship with the Seelie court and the fae were probably happy for a chance to make up for Kalen Silverwind stealing *The Gates of Avalon*.

"Shit!" I said. "How long until the College hunters get here?"

"Not long," Evaine told me. "They will come for the creature and they will ask him questions that must not be answered."

She was only a few inches away now, staring down at me with ice-blue eyes. But I didn't get out of her way.

"He's not a creature." My voice shook. "And none of this is his fault! There's a demon, an incubus–"

"I know," said Evaine.

I felt like someone had just slapped me. I gaped at Evaine.

"You... know?" I asked. "Then why are you hunting Reid? He's innocent!"

Evaine stood close enough to kiss. "Is a gun innocent of murder? His guilt or innocence no longer matters. The golem is dangerous, Lilith, to the world and to you. Get out of my way. He must die."

"Why?" I leaned closer until I felt the metallic chill of Evaine's armor through my robe. "I don't understand! Yes, he's dangerous and unpredictable and demons are a big heaping pile of trouble. But... but you're talking about murdering an innocent man. I know you, Evaine. You wouldn't do this!"

"I would do it," she said, "to save you."

"But *why*? That doesn't make any sense!" My hands clenched into fists at my side and I shouted right in my teacher's face. "What are you talking about? What the fuck does any of this have to do with me?"

Evaine's silver-blonde brows drew down and her eyes suddenly looked so old, so sad. I sensed Reid's massive presence drawing closer behind me, listening.

"Think about what the golem is," Evaine told me. "Half human, half demon."

"I know! So what?"

"His master was trying to create a cambion. Like *you*, Lilith."

Now I did stagger back from Evaine, suddenly unable to pull air down into my lungs. My heart pounded and the echoes shuddered through my whole body. Like me? Why?

I felt Reid's human hand on my shoulder, holding me up, but Evaine was still speaking. She advanced on us like a wrathful goddess with each word.

"Thus far, I have been able to conceal your existence from the demons," she said. "Even the College doesn't recognize your significance... and they never can. I have tried since you were born to keep you safe, Lilith. To protect you. But you have defied me. You have hunted the one creature I forbade to you! You have taken him into your bed and now stand in my way when I *must* destroy him!"

My eyes burned with tears and my pulse thundered in my ears. My mother died when I was born. I had never known her. Somehow, that didn't hurt as much when Evaine was there with me. She taught me everything I knew. She taught me strength when I was weak, bravery when I was scared. For nine years, Evaine had been better than a mother to me.

In all that time, she had never been this angry. This morning, it had seemed so plucky and cute to ignore Evaine's command, to go hunt down the golem anyway. But I shook off Reid's hand and stood up straight. I met Evaine's stare, though tears made my vision swim.

"You *can't* just kill Reid, Evaine," I said through clenched teeth. "Find another way!"

"If the College learns why this golem was created, they will kill both of you. Even your father would not hesitate. And if Asmodai finds you, it will be even worse."

"Wait, what? My father?" I asked.

Evaine's expression softened just slightly. "There may not be another chance to tell you. Yes, your father, Lily. High Magus Vincent Myrdon."

My heart stopped. A hundred strange comments and indecipherable looks came together into a single truth. My mother was a succubus, but my father was a wizard. I had known that since I was eighteen years old. But now I knew which one: the High Magus, who stood in judgment over me. Vincent Myrdon had summoned a succubus and she fell in love with him. But he didn't love her and she died because of it. And he didn't love me.

There was something running down my cheeks. Not tears this time, but Evaine's fingers. Her anger wasn't gone, but there was pain in her eyes. Something harder to name, too, that made me want to throw my arms around her.

"I'm sorry, Lily," Evaine said. "You should have found out more gently than this, but I fear there is little time left. Let me protect you. Let me kill the golem."

"He doesn't deserve this." My voice was ragged.

"Perhaps not," Evaine agreed slowly, quietly. "But he is beyond my protection. You are not. Not yet. Stand aside, Lily. Please."

"No."

The rage flashed in Evaine's aquamarine eyes, but I swore I saw tears there, too. She kissed me softly and drew back.

"And to think that the College ever doubted the purity of your heart," Evaine said. She smiled and my heart ached. "Lily–"

Fire erupted in the middle of my living room. Smoke alarms screeched and then sprinkler heads popped down from the ceiling.

Water sprayed across my condo, but the flames only sizzled and rose higher. They burned so brightly that I could barely look at them. But when the man stepped out of the fire, I couldn't *stop* staring.

He was gorgeous. I've fucked some pretty damned hot men and women, but the newcomer was so beautiful that I could only catch my breath in swift, desperate gasps. The figure standing in front of the flames was tall. Not quite as big as Reid, but not shorter by much. His waist-length hair was the deep, perfect black of a starless night and his skin wasn't just tanned or bronzed. It was gold, burnished like something unutterably precious, and I longed to taste it. A pair of slender, graceful ebony horns arced up from his forehead, almost invisible against his black hair until he turned his head to look around the room. And his eyes... They shone like golden rings, burning with a brilliant inner light. I *knew* those eyes. I had seen them before, when his shadow came to claim *The Gates of Avalon*.

I was dimly aware of Reid falling to his knees behind me, prostrating himself before his master. The incubus' glorious golden eyes lit on Evaine and a painfully perfect smile spread across his face.

"Evaine," he said. "Still so lovely, even after all these centuries."

His voice was as sweet and rich as the best honey and wetness ran unbidden between my thighs. I would have done anything to make the incubus speak to me with that voice.

"Asmodai," said Evaine.

She turned to face him, standing between me and the demon. The smoke alarms continued to scream and water rained down all around us.

"Still fighting for the humans, Evaine?" Asmodai asked.

"You know they're worth fighting for," she answered evenly. "After all, you loved one of them once."

"We've all made our... youthful mistakes. And now I shall rectify mine," Asmodai said. He looked past Evaine to Reid. "You've found my golem. An imperfect attempt to create a cambion, I admit."

Evaine's hands clenched into mailed fists and her silver armor gleamed in the firelight. But Asmodai was wearing armor, too, all gold and lacquered black that outlined his body without detracting one bit from his perfect male form. He raised a gilded, gauntleted hand and pointed at me.

"But her... She's the real thing, isn't she?" Asmodai asked. "I didn't believe it possible, yet here she is. Such a lovely child..."

"She is not for you," said Evaine. She reached across her waist and placed one hand on her hip. "You will not have her, Asmodai."

The demon laughed a deep, rich laugh. "I will. Even you cannot stand against me, Evaine. I am a prince of the Nether. I am the Lord of Lust."

Evaine lifted her empty fist as though drawing a weapon, but then something the color of moonlight shone in her hand: a sword. It was a simple blade, with a battle-scarred steel crosspiece and un-adorned pommel. But Reid seemed to recognize the sword and let out a long, low growl. Even his master's golden eyes widened.

"Excalibur..." Asmodai breathed. The incubus' handsome, confident smile faltered. "That blade is not yours to wield, Evaine."

"Arthur still sleeps. I gave him this sword once, and will return it to him before he wakes."

Excalibur shone with a cold silver radiance as she raised the scarred blade. Asmodai held out one hand and an elegant golden sword appeared in his grasp, its gilded length wreathed in flames. The demon lord took a sweeping, graceful step closer and Evaine brought Excalibur down into a low guard position.

"Lily, you must go," she said. "You are not ready for this battle. Not yet."

"You want me to leave you? No fucking way!" I cried.

I was a monster hunter, not a cheerleader. No way was I going to just stand around while Evaine fought off an incubus. I sprinted toward my desk and the gun sitting there, but Asmodai was already closing in on Evaine.

Metal rang on metal and sparks sprayed across my living room as Evaine parried a lightning-quick slash of Asmodai's burning golden sword. The demon whirled, long black hair fanning out around him, and swung again before my heart could finish a single beat. Evaine leapt back just as quickly and Asmodai's blade sliced through my desk. It collapsed into a heap of wood and glass, the edges red-hot and smoking.

My gun spun out across the wet floor. I dove for it, arm outstretched, and my fingers closed on cold steel. Just over my head, Evaine and Asmodai came together once more in a storm of steel. Their swords clanged off one another like the peels of some great heavenly – or perhaps hellish – bell.

I rolled over onto my back, took aim and fired at Asmodai. My bullet didn't even mark his shiny black and gold armor. The incubus darted a look down at me, smiling, and that single glance made my whole body go weak. My pussy pulsed with wet heat and I gasped in unwilling desire.

Evaine parried Asmodai's blade and slammed her shoulder into his stomach. The demon slid gracefully away, then thrust his sword at Evaine. She barely turned it aside in time and the flames left a scorched mark across the pauldron of her silver armor.

"Golem... Reid!" Evaine cried. "Take Lily and go!"

"On the contrary," said Asmodai. His voice made my knees weak. "She will succeed where you have failed, Orbias. Bring the girl to me."

Reid trembled in the kitchen, still kneeling with both huge arms wrapped around himself. He dug his nails into his shoulders, each limb fighting to hold the other back. Blood ran from where Reid's left hand clawed into his skin and the golem let out a terrible strangled sound somewhere between a scream and a sob.

"Leave him alone!" I shouted.

Evaine had forced Asmodai back with a pair of slashes, but now the demon was regaining his lost ground. My teacher's face was hard and platinum ringlets lay plastered against her neck by sweat and water. Asmodai, though, was still smiling. Still perfectly beautiful and handsome.

I finally managed to scramble to my feet and ran to the couch. A flaming cut through the armrest had sliced deep into two of the white cushions and leather sizzled as the sprinklers tried in vain to put out the fire. Water slicked my red hair and robe against my body. My bunny slippers were soaked right through.

I kicked over the couch and it splashed down into a growing puddle. The sword strapped underneath was nearly as long as I was tall... and it was dusty. I hadn't touched one since Evaine's lessons when I was in high school. But now I wrenched the blade free and aimed my gun at the incubus.

"Evaine!" I called out as I ran to her side.

Asmodai stepped into my charge, his hand extended toward me. I fired, but another bullet just rang off his bright armor. I cocked my sword over one shoulder, trying to remember everything Evaine had ever taught me about using the thing.

"Come to me, child," Asmodai said.

Even through the blare of fire alarm and hiss of falling water, I could still hear Asmodai's every word. They slid over me, into me. I moaned at his command and faltered.

The water was nearly ankle-deep in the living room, but Evaine ran right across the rippling surface and threw herself at Asmodai, staggering him away from me. The demon spun to face her again and a ring of golden flame detonated like a bomb around them both. The impact slammed me back into the kitchen and my sword went clanging and clattering across the floor. Reid crashed through the counter, sending shattered wood and granite flying in every direction.

"Orbias, bring me the cambion!" Asmodai ordered.

Reid pulled himself onto his knees, shaking his head. His left hand closed on a piece of what used to be my kitchen counter and the polished stone shattered in his fingers. I jumped to my feet and Reid looked up at me. Cascading water matted the golem's black hair to his face. He snarled. The sound was bestial, furious.

"Lily, run!" Evaine called out in a ringing voice.

"What makes you think I'm going to start listening to reason now?" I cried. "I'm not leaving Reid and I'm not leaving you!"

I pointed my gun at Asmodai, but then there was a flicker of red from behind me. Reid pounced, grabbing me in his huge arms as though I were no more substantial than a blow-up doll. I swore and tried to bring my gun around to get a line on the golem. But he was holding me too tightly and even my sex-powered strength was no match for his.

Reid's terrible black claws pricked through my robe and into my skin... but they didn't tighten. He clutched me tight to his wide chest and ran for the front door.

"No!" I screamed. "Let go of me!"

I saw Evaine for just a moment over Reid's shoulder. Excalibur was locked against Asmodai's flaming sword. Water hissed off gold and silver armor. The incubus' burning eyes flashed with deadly rage, but Evaine only smiled serenely as Reid smashed through my front door and carried me away.

Chapter NINE

*R*eid didn't bother with the elevator – he bolted down stairs blurred by his speed and my tears. I screamed and pounded my fists against the golem's bare patchwork back. Reid grunted in pain, but didn't release me.

He burst out through the front door of my building, but the doorman was nowhere to be seen – probably off calling the cops or fire department or the fucking National Guard. Was that why the street outside was so empty? The barren sidewalk tickled my memory. This reminded me of something, but I was too angry to care.

"Put me down!" I cried.

Once we had crossed the road, Reid finally released me, but kept his hands tight on my shoulders. I still had my gun. I could still help...!

I tried to run back across the street, but Reid yanked me to a stop and I stared helplessly up at my condo. Blinding golden light flared through my windows and then the glass erupted outward into silvery shards. They rained down into the road below and I heard the steely ring of sword against sword. Flame billowed from my shattered windows while water sheeted down the side of the building.

"What the fuck?" I shouted. "Demons can't come to Earth! That's the whole point of the Seal of Avalon! What is that Asmodai fucker doing here?"

"There was a human on the island, too," Reid said. His words sawed back and forth between his human and demon voices. His claws tightened on my shoulder, drawing blood that mixed with the water soaking my robe and ran down my arm. "The wizard. Merlin's spawn can summon demons and that one serves Asmodai. Our... master..."

My voice shook too, but with sobs. "Why did Asmodai want a cambion? Why is he doing this?"

"I don't–"

Something exploded above and a great fireball spewed from my condo like a gout of dragon's breath. More glass fell in a rain of glittering shrapnel across the pavement and I felt the heat of the flames even ten stories below. What was that? A gas line? More demonic fire?

"Lilith!"

The shout wasn't from Reid, but I knew that voice.

There were finally people hurrying up the road. Six of them.

I recognized Stefano in the front. His dark eyes fixed on me and his hands hovered over his belt full of alchemical reagents. Tall, tattooed Griffith loomed over short Clio beside him. Doyle clutched a polished wand in his white-knuckled fingers and kept staring up at the ruins of my condo. He ran alongside Redmond, who held his bow drawn and low, with a runed arrow nocked against the string. And the huge, lumbering shape of one of Sabra's homunculi came last, its rough clay body poorly concealed under a flapping trench coat.

That's why the street was empty. The wizards had cleared it – there were fewer witnesses that way.

"Who are they?" Reid asked.

"The College hunters," I said. "All of them."

I opened my mouth to call out to Stefano. Evaine was up there, fighting for her life. Surely every single bounty hunter in the city could help her defeat Asmodai. And the wizards... This was the battle they were born for, right?

But I was interrupted by Orbias' bone-shaking growl. The golem snarled something in a language I had never heard before and hoped never to hear again. It was deep, hard and ugly. He turned away from me and lurched a huge step toward the closing hunters. At a command from Stefano, they spread out, leveling weapons and spells at Reid.

"No." I gasped at the golem. "They can help you! They're wizards. Maybe they can... can fix what happened to you. Don't fight and they'll take you alive!"

Reid stopped and looked down at me. The fire in his demonic eye flickered. "But... Evaine said they can't know why I was made. That it will put you in danger, Lily. That your father will kill you if he finds out."

"That doesn't matter right now!"

"Lilith!" Stefano and the rest of the wizards were still far enough away that he had to shout, but drawing in step by cautious step. "What's going on? The scry network is blasted half to hell! What are you doing with the golem? Get back!"

Reid grabbed my wrist, the one just below where I gripped my gun. He fell to one knee and yanked me close, pressing the barrel to his forehead.

"Kill me," Reid said.

"What?" I cried. "No!"

I tried to pull away, but Reid snapped his huge demonic hand up over his human one. He snarled and the obsidian claws sliced deep wounds into his own skin as Orbias fought Reid for control.

"Asmodai still calls to me, Lily," he said in a low, pained groan. "My master summons Orbias to war, to tear apart these... traitors... To deliver you into his hands."

Reid's teeth ground and I heard one crack with the effort as the golem shifted my gun. He pulled it over against the pale, sweat-beaded human half of his face. Stefano shouted my name, telling me again to stand back and demanding answers.

"It has to be here," Reid said. "Where Orbias can't heal. This is the only way to keep you safe."

"No!" My protests came out in a strangled sob. "We didn't get this far just to kill you now!"

Reid's human eye closed. The demonic one burned and his left arm clawed at his right as the golem trembled with the strain of keeping his body still.

"Hurry. I... don't know how much longer I can hold Orbias back," he said. "Please, Lily. It hurts. Being me hurts."

I could smell saltpeter and wolfsbane, hear the heavy tread of booted feet. The wizards were close now. Sabra would send her homunculus in first, to engage Reid and buy time for the others to cast their spells.

"Wait for a clear line of fire!" Stefano shouted. "Lilith! Get out of the way!"

I didn't. I stared down at Reid, kneeling before me with my gun to his head. Tears ran from his closed eye and then turned to steam when they fell against the red flesh of his chest.

"I'm sorry I couldn't help you," I whispered.

"You are helping me, Lily."

Reid held his hand over mine and helped me pull the trigger. The shot was such a tiny noise compared to the sound of his body falling to the ground. Stefano ran in and skidded to a stop beside me, staring down at the dead golem. The demonic half of Reid's face was twisted with rage, but the human side was finally calm. Peaceful.

I wiped my eyes and turned to Stefano. My voice cracked when I spoke. "Come on. There's another demon and Evaine is up there fighting him!"

Stefano snapped his gaze up to me, nodded, and then looked at the other hunters.

"Doyle, conceal the body," he instructed. "Sabra, keep your homunculus down on the street. Everyone else, let's move!"

I didn't want to move. I wanted to sit in the middle of the road and cry like a child. But Evaine...

I ran with Stefano across the empty street, but the only sound was the pounding of our footsteps. No more clash of steel or scream of fire alarms. Maybe Evaine had finally disarmed Asmodai and the two were going at it hand-to-hand now? Or better yet, would we find Evaine sitting on my ruined couch, Excalibur across her lap and the demon's handsome head on my coffee table?

By the time the other hunters followed me into the tenth-story hallway, doors were open and my neighbors were calling out, wondering what was happening. What was all the noise? Was there a fire? What was I doing in a dripping wet robe and did I want to come inside to take it off?

I ignored all of the questions and shoved my way toward my condo through the growing crowd. Stefano barked a short order to Griffith, who began pushing the curious onlookers back, but not dispersing them. No, there were memories to be altered and I supposed that work would be easier if the wizards could keep all the witnesses together in one place.

That was their job.

Mine was to find Evaine.

I burst through the remains of my front door and into a wasteland of smoke, burnt furniture and murky black puddles of water. Asmodai was gone.

"Evaine!" I shouted.

I ran through the condo, calling her name. The floor was alternately searing hot and icy cold under my slippered feet. My couch was in two pieces that flaked away to ash in my hands as I grabbed the smoldering frame and tossed it aside. Redmond yanked Clio out of the way just in time to avoid being hit.

Evaine lay beneath. Her silver armor was dented and scorched. Her braid had come undone and now wet white-blonde curls lay in tangles around her shoulders. The water around her was stained red and I couldn't see Excalibur anywhere. Evaine's eyes fluttered open.

"Lily." Her voice was so quiet that I had to lean close to make out the words. "The demons know about you now. Asmodai will come for you."

"Fuck that guy," I said. "I'm not worried about him. Not with you here to protect my dumb, defiant ass."

Evaine smiled and raised her hand up a few inches. I took it and pressed her fingers to my cheek. She was so cold. I kissed Evaine's palm, trying in vain to warm her.

"Come on," I said. I hated the awful, broken sound of my own voice. "Just sing that song you used to heal Max when we were kids. This can't be any worse than dealing with a stupid teenage cambion, right? And... and then we can go kick Asmodai's ass together. Girl's night out."

"I am slipping beyond Avalon's reach," Evaine whispered. "Soon I will enter a realm that even that isle does not touch."

"What the hell does that mean?" I cried. "Evaine! No, don't go!"

"You are loved, Lily. Always. Remember that."

And then she melted away. Armor and all, Evaine turned to water in my arms and was gone. I clutched uselessly at the puddle where she had lain until someone touched my shoulder.

"The Lady of the Lake is dead," Stefano said. "There are preparations to make and magic to be done here. It's time for you to go, Lilith."

Stefano helped me to my feet and led me away from my shattered life.

LILY QUINN BOOK #11

Chapter
ONE

The old truck rumbled along a winding highway that led out of town. I leaned my head against the window and watched the city fall away below as the road curved up into the coastal mountains. Six lanes of highway dwindled to four, and then barely two. The truck was well-maintained, of course, but the engine still wheezed a bit as the air grew thinner with the high altitude. The glass of the window against my cheek was warm, but the air blowing in from outside smelled of bitter-sweet pine sap and cold, stony earth.

I kicked my hiking boots up onto the dashboard and switched the air intake over to *recycle*. Max downshifted again and glanced over at me.

"I don't want to ask if you're okay because I know you're sick of everyone asking," he said. "But... Lil, are you okay?"

"No."

Max nodded and drove in silence for a bit, guiding his truck through the increasingly sharp turns of the mountain road. For a moment, I had a breathtaking view of the bay and red spires of the bridge spanning it, but then they were eclipsed once more by the green of pine trees and the black-flecked gray of granite boulders.

A few minutes later, we passed the first weathered wooden sign marking out the edges of the national forest. Max pointed to the yellow *closed* notice taped over it.

"Will we even be able to get into the park?" he asked.

"Yeah," I answered.

"Is it closed because of the uh... what is it?"

"Yeti."

Max nodded. "Yeti. As in a sasquatch, right? Bigfoot? What are they like?"

"Big, savage and smelly," I said. "Dangerous."

"So not exactly a monster you can take to bed before you take it down. Well, maybe..." Max smirked, dimples marking his cheeks. "You're a kinky girl, Lil."

I shook my head. "I'm not fucking a yeti."

"Well, that's what I'm here for. To keep you powered up."

"Yeah," I said. "This might take a few days and it's not like I can rely on a steady stream of hot forest rangers."

"And I own actual camping supplies," Max pointed out. "I don't think you even had a sleeping bag."

"Back when I owned anything."

Max fell silent again. Each breath fogged my window in wispy white plumes for a moment before they faded. Outside, the road shoulder had all but vanished and only a dented aluminum guardrail separated us from a long, rocky drop.

"Lil, why did you take this job?" Max asked quietly. "It doesn't seem like you want to be out here and it's not like you need to work. You have enough money stashed away to live in luxury for the next hundred years."

"I had to get out of the city for a while. Besides, what the hell else am I supposed to do with myself?"

I've been hunting down monsters since I graduated high school. There was no other profession I knew. This was what Evaine had trained me for... I squeezed my eyes shut. I wasn't sure if I had any tears left to shed, but didn't feel like risking it. I felt Max's hand on my knee. He didn't keep it there long.

"I don't really know what's going on or what happened to your condo," Max said slowly. "And that's okay. You don't need to talk about it if you don't want to, Lil. But you've been living in that hotel room for the last month…"

"It's fine. Like you said, I've got the money."

"But you don't have to do that, Lil. You could always crash with me until you get back on your feet."

I kept leaning against the truck window and cast a sidelong look at Max.

"It's fine," I repeated. The words came out a little harder than I meant them to. "Besides, what about Taya? Even if she's okay with you and me suddenly being fuck buddies again, I really doubt she would be thrilled with me living at the garage."

Max glanced at me. There was something in his expression that I couldn't quite figure out before he returned his attention to the road. We drove without speaking for another ten minutes, each one ticking by in glowing blue lines on the dashboard clock.

"So," Max said at last. "What's the plan? Is there a particular technique for hunting yeti? Uh, is *yeti* singular or plural?"

"I think it's both."

"How many are we dealing with?" Max asked.

"Just one. And trust me, that's enough. It's already killed two campers and put a park ranger in the hospital. He's still in critical condition."

Max frowned. "I read that story in the news. They said it was a mountain lion."

"And the ranger probably even believes that. The College wizards rewrote his memory and then went to a lot of work to get the whole forest shut down. Only hunters are allowed up here until someone kills that yeti."

"How do you plan to do that, Lil?"

"Pretty much by wandering around and smelling delicious," I admitted. "That's how Stefano catches werewolves, by being both the bait and the trap. Yeti are man-eaters and I don't mean metaphorically like me. It should be nice and hungry by now."

Max went a little pale and his hands tightened on the steering wheel, but they remained steady enough. I gestured through the windshield to a gravel parking lot up ahead, closed off with a battered yellow gate. A chain wrapped around the gatepost, but wasn't locked into place.

"This is it," I said.

Max nodded and pulled to a stop. I got out of the truck and pushed the gate open, then closed it again when he drove through. I followed at a trot as Max parked and then climbed down from the driver's side.

"I thought the forest was shut down until the hunt is over," he said, pointing.

A neat black Mercedes sat on the other end of the lot. The coat of dust it had picked up on the drive into the park seemed conspicuously out of place on the shiny obsidian paint job. I didn't recognize the car.

"That doesn't look like a forest service vehicle," Max noted. "No government plates. Maybe it belongs to some tourist who ignored the *closed* signs?"

I shrugged. "Maybe."

Max waited for me to say more. When I didn't, he lowered the tailgate of his old truck and began unloading our gear. There were two huge backpacks, each bulging with supplies. One of them even had a hunting rifle strapped to the side.

"Borrowed it from my dad. Just in case," Max said, catching my look. He nodded to a small, weather-beaten building at the end of the parking lot. "That's our last real bathroom. Need to use it?"

I didn't really, but I took advantage of an actual toilet seat under my ass while I could. And a chance to cry for a few minutes without anyone asking me what was wrong. The sound of my sobs echoed in the shitty bathroom stall.

When I was done, I blew my nose into a handful of scratchy one-ply toilet paper, flushed and washed up with some half-frozen water from the sink. I checked the mirror. My eyes were rimmed in red and I looked tired. After the destruction of my condo, I had paid top dollar for a luxury hotel suite, but I still missed my own bed. I was pretty sure I would miss it even more after a few nights sleeping on the ground.

In theory, I could track down and bag the yeti in a single day, but doubted that I would get that lucky. I rarely was these days, it seemed. But Max said that he could take as much time away from the garage as we needed, so the length of our camping trip depended entirely upon our food supply and how good a hungry yeti's nose was.

After splashing some more cold water on my face, I exited the bathroom and returned to the truck. Max had finished unloading our gear and was crouched down, inspecting the tires. The truck had been an old junker back when Max rebuilt it in high school and the beast was going on ancient now, but it was practically the only thing that had been his alone since his little brothers were born. Max had lost his virginity in that truck and it had a hell of a lot of sentimental value.

Not only to him. My first time had been in the bed of that truck, too. With Max.

He picked a rock out of the tire's tread and glanced up at my approach. If Max noticed that I had been crying, he didn't say anything about it. He just stood, patted the truck and held out one of the backpacks to me – the one without the gun.

"You ready to get moving, Lil?" he asked.

I nodded and strapped my pack into place. When everything was situated, we consulted a sun-bleached map posted at the base of the trail and started hiking.

Max set a brisk pace up into the mountains. I had not been camping since freshman year of high school, but Max clearly hadn't been as lax as me. He was in excellent physical condition and made me work to keep up. I wondered briefly if Max ever forgot that I'm not always super-powered. Sex fueled the succubus half of my heritage, but without it, I was only an ordinary mortal woman.

But I remembered all of the frowns, the worried looks that Max gave me every time I blundered into battle against the worst monsters of the supernatural world. I remembered how close I came to death just a few weeks ago. Max was the one to pull the glass out of my lacerated body, to give me the sex that I needed to come back from the brink. He hadn't forgotten how fragile I really was.

Max climbed up over a slab of granite and then paused under a towering sugar pine to look down at me. There were only a few clouds in the sky and the early autumn sun shone bright between interlacing tree branches. Sweat poured along my spine.

"You okay, Lil?" Max asked over one shoulder.

"You make this look so easy," I panted. "Is there anything you're not good at?"

"Um, hunting down dangerous monsters? That's what I keep you around for."

Max flashed me a dimpled smile. I wanted to smile back, but I just couldn't do it. How could Max smile at me after I had utterly failed to save Reid? When all I could do to give the golem some shred of peace was to kill him?

How could anyone still smile when Evaine was gone?

I swiped my sleeve across my eyes and followed Max up the mountain.

Chapter TWO

Cell reception was absolute shit out here in the middle of the wilderness, but my phone still worked just fine as a clock. It was a little after three in the afternoon when Max and I stopped to set up camp in a half-circle clearing beside the trail. There was a narrow gap in the trees that gave us a view out across the mountains and distant silver-gray ocean that probably would have been breathtaking if I gave a crap.

We could have hiked a little longer, but the clouds were beginning to close in. It wasn't cold yet, but we were losing the light and there wasn't much use in tripping and breaking an arm in the premature twilight. Besides, we were basically setting out a meal and hoping that the yeti would accept the invitation. I needed to be ready in case dinnertime came early. So far, all of the yeti attacks had occurred higher in the mountains, but I had no idea how hungry it might have gotten in the two days since the College shut down the park.

I sat on a more or less flat slab of granite jutting out from the forest floor while Max stripped off his shirt and got to work setting up our campsite. I could tell a tent from a canteen, but that was about the limit of my camping expertise.

Max dug a fire pit and raised the tent in record time, finally starting to sweat. His pale skin and golden hair gleamed in the fading sun. For a moment, Max looked almost otherworldly, like something that had stepped out of the fairy market. He paused in hammering the tent pegs into the ground and wiped the back of his hand across his forehead.

"If you're undressing me with your eyes, Lil, I could just take off my pants and finish the job," Max offered.

That wasn't a bad idea. The whole point of Max being here with me was to fuck me every day, to keep me topped off with enough sexual energy to beat the crap out of a yeti whenever we found it. But I hesitated.

"Does Taya really know that you're here with me?" I asked. "I mean, do you tell her every time we're... together? Shouldn't I text her before jumping your bones?"

At the very least, if Taya was willing to share her boyfriend, I figured I should buy her a car or something to thank her. Did she like Corvettes?

Max sighed. He gave the tent peg one final blow, hard enough to flatten the metal head. Then he stood, dropped the mallet into his backpack again and came to sit next to me on the granite. It was still warm from the day's sun.

"Lil, Taya's... not in the picture anymore," Max said.

My stomach lurched. "What? What happened? You said Taya was okay with this!"

"I said she knew," Max corrected softly. "That night you called me, half dead, Taya and I were out. It was our three-month anniversary. I took her to a nice restaurant. Spending money I didn't have, really. But when you called, I... left."

I stared at Max. Suddenly I remembered the white dress shirt and red silk tie Max had been wearing the night Reid nearly killed me. Dressed for an anniversary dinner out with his girlfriend.

"What?" I asked.

Max ran one hand through his hair. "Taya knew I was going to you. I had to tell her that much. She asked if it was a hook-up... and I said yes. But I couldn't tell Taya any more than that. Not without saying things that would have made her think we were crazy and might have put her in danger."

"And... and Taya left you?" I felt something like steel bands tightening around my ribs. "Because of me, Max? Because you were with me?"

"It wasn't like that. Taya said that she could see which woman I was loyal to. She didn't sound angry about it. Just... sad. I think she already kind of knew. But I didn't have time to discuss it with her. I had to get to you, Lil. I left. *I* left Taya."

I jumped to my feet and my hands clenched at my sides. "No, Max! This is stupid! When we get back, I'll talk to Taya. I'll explain everything. I'll tell her what I am, what I do."

"She won't believe you."

"I'll twist a tire iron into a knot or something and *make* her believe it. I'll fix this!"

"Lil, don't," Max said.

"Why the fuck not?"

"Besides the fact that you're not supposed to? Besides the fact that Taya is a good woman and I don't want the College to carve out her memories because of me? I signed up for all of this when I was eighteen, Lil. But Taya didn't."

"Yeah, besides that," I mumbled.

Max reached out and grabbed my wrists, tugging me closer. My feet were heavy and unresponsive, but right then, Max was stronger than me. With him still sitting on the rocks, we were just about the same height.

"Because Taya was right," Max said. "I'll always choose you, Lil. I would have left Taya at the altar to come to you."

"Don't be an idiot!"

"I promised you, Lil. And that promise means more to me than anything else in the world. I'll always be there for you."

Max's expression wasn't as sad as it should have been. In fact, he was smiling. I didn't understand why.

"It was a special night. Taya's an amazing girl," I told him. "You should have stayed with her!"

Max pulled me another step in, until we were face to face. "You would have died, dummy."

"I... I could have crawled to your neighbor's house and fucked him," I said in a shaking voice.

Max stroked my hair back from my forehead. "You were halfway across the city from my garage. And my neighbor is eighty-seven. *He* would have died."

"I should have called Stefano..."

"He might have been halfway across the country hunting down some werewolf. Or off in another world, like the Tower or wherever the fairies live. Does Stefano get cell reception on other planes of existence?"

"No..."

"You needed me, Lil," Max said. "So I was there. I always will be. End of story."

I didn't know what to say to that. Max had given up Taya... for me. What *could* I say? Max was the best friend a half-succubus girl could ever ask for, far better than I deserved. It hurt that he had to lose something he wanted just for me, but Max was smiling. One of his hands was still on mine, the other cupping my cheek. He didn't seem to regret his decision at all.

Sometimes I tried to show Max how much he meant to me with presents. What the fuck else was I supposed to do with all of my money? But Max always put his foot down if my gifts became too extravagant, always stopped me long before I ever got anywhere close to what he deserved.

Words were even harder. I barely passed high school English. And then I only managed it with Max's help.

I'm half lust demon. There's just one language in which I can really express myself properly. I leaned in close and pressed my lips to Max's. His eyes fell shut and I tasted the breath he had been holding. My heart lurched painfully, pleasurably in my chest.

Max still held one of my hands, but I ran the other along the firm planes of his chest and stomach, down to the front of his jeans. He gasped and hardness rose against my palm. I squeezed and his gasp became a deep, hungry groan.

"Time to get you charged up?" Max asked in a thick voice. "In case the yeti shows?"

"Yeah," I whispered. It was almost the truth.

Max's desire burned. The sinking sun had vanished behind clouds, but I wasn't cold at all. I raked my nails over Max's bare chest, leaving red lines across his skin, and grabbed his shoulder. Our mingled lust wasn't enough to take on a yeti just yet, but it made me strong enough to push Max easily against the black-flecked white of the granite beneath him. The rough stone must have scratched his bare back, but Max didn't complain. Of course not. He never did.

I flicked open Max's belt, then tugged his jeans and boxers off down his legs. His cock fell free, lying long and hard against his stomach. I inhaled the scents of pine, sea and Max's sweat. My breath caught somewhere between a gasp and a sob, and my heart hurt even as it raced. I took Max's hand in my own shaking one and placed it over his dick.

"You just... hold on to that for a second," I told him.

Max's expression became serious, but he nodded and closed long, strong fingers around his flushed shaft. I stood and stripped my shirt off over my head, then draped it across a nearby rock. My bra came next and now I did gasp as the cooling air brushed my nipples and raised them to tiny pink peaks.

I unbuttoned my shorts and pushed them down my legs, then had to stop and awkwardly unlace my hiking boots. Max laughed at my hopping dance as I tried to kick them off. I felt myself blushing, actually embarrassed.

"Shut up, country boy," I said as sternly as I could. "You just jerk that cock."

Max stopped laughing at once. "Yes, Lil."

He watched me raptly and ran one hand along the length of his dick. His touch was light, but Max's entire body tensed with each stroke. A bead of white precum dripped from the flushed head of his cock onto his stomach and gleamed there like a liquid pearl. Max reached down with his other hand to caress his balls, rolling them gently until the color of the delicate skin there deepened to a dark rose. His eyes closed again and his hips strained upward.

"Max," I said.

His eyes opened. The deep blue of them was a slender ring around the dilated black of his pupils. I threw one leg across Max and straddled his thighs. He stared up at me, hands still going on his cock. I grabbed his wrists and pushed his arms over his head, pinning them against the stone, just like Max had with me the night he left Taya to come save my life.

I wished he hadn't done it, but Max was right – I wouldn't have survived without him. I was furious with Max, sad for what he had lost and grateful for what he had given.

Reaching beneath my body, I ran two fingers up the underside of Max's dick, which lay flat against his stomach once again. At my touch, Max let out a long, loud groan. I steadied myself with one hand on his chest, then slid up along his body. I came to rest with Max's steely cock pressed between my legs, hot and smooth all the way from my clit to my ass.

I leaned into Max and began rocking my hips. Not tilting them or angling myself to thrust his cock into me, just sliding the softness of my pussy along the length of Max's dick. Every movement left wetness dripping across his flushed skin. I moved up and down until Max's cock gleamed. Pulling back to inspect my work required me to release Max's wrists and his hands rose in an instant to cup my breasts, caressing my cold nipples with the urgent heat of his touch. His strong fingers kneaded my tits, nails biting slightly into the soft skin.

My back arched with pleasure. I moaned and I rubbed myself faster over Max. The firmest pressure against my clit was at the broad base of his cock, but at the top, the crown was so hot that it sent shivers racing up my spine. And the swift, wet contact along every inch sent Max's glorious golden sexual energy coursing all through me.

Max wasn't making as much of a mess as I was, but it was close. Pale precum oozed from the head of his dick, leaving white streaks across his abdominal muscles and mingling with the little puddle of my own wetness. I swiped a finger through the slickness and then stuck it in my mouth. The taste of Max and of me mixed together made my hips rock involuntarily. Pleasure took over, consuming my senses. A single finger did little to stifle my screams of climax as my smooth rocking became wild thrashing and grinding against Max.

I bit almost savagely at my fingertip, lashing the skin with my tongue for *all* of Max's salty, musky taste. When there was none left, I reached behind and beneath my writhing body to grab Max's balls. They were tight and heavy in my hand.

Max groaned and his hips rose under me. One light squeeze and his cock throbbed between my legs. It went so hot against my pussy that I gasped, and then a long line of white shot straight up along Max's body. Dripping ribbons of cum splattered his chest and stomach, even leaving a few ivory drops across his jaw.

"God, Lil," Max panted.

He leaned up on one elbow and hooked a strong arm around my neck. There were pine needles tangled in his tousled blond hair.

Max pulled me into a deep kiss. His tongue traced over mine and left us both breathless. Max's cock remained as hard between our bodies as the stone beneath us.

I pulled back, panting and gasping. The granite was hard and gritty against my knees, so different than being in a bed. Wind made the trees sway and a few more fragrant green needles fell around us. The forest moaned softly along with me as I wrapped trembling fingers around Max's dick again. I squeezed and a thick pearl of semen welled up from the tip, splashing down onto his flat stomach.

Max's fingers curled into my breasts and sweat sparkled in his hair. The smear of white spunk along his tightened jawline was every inch as sexy as any grease smudge. Maybe even better... I kissed the angle of Max's jaw and then worked my lips down until I tasted warm cum. I licked it up hungrily.

My fingers still encircled Max's dick, not quite able to touch all the way around. I held him there, lifted and then finally impaled myself on his cock with a long moan. Max slid his hands from my breasts, down my sides to my hips and helped pull me onto him.

By the time I had taken Max's entire length, my body shook and my pussy ran as wet as any mountain stream. My nerves burned with overstimulated ecstasy. When I looked down at Max, smiling up at me and spattered utterly unselfconsciously from neck to navel in his own bright white cum, the pleasure crashed over into the hot, electric thrill of climax.

I descended on Max. I rode his cock in hard, desperate movements and pressed myself tightly against him. Between breathless cries, I kissed my way along Max's neck and followed the oozing ivory trails of semen with my tongue. I traced every line and licked them clean, down and across the muscular expanse of his chest. I didn't know what kind of food Max had packed and I didn't care. Right then, I felt like I could live on nothing but Max's cum for days.

I swallowed sticky mouthfuls and it slid down my throat to join the searing heat of his dick inside me.

Max held my hips in his large hands, guiding me on top of him. His cock filled the deepest places in my body and then pierced even deeper. My cries rose, sounding out the same long, relentless orgasm that hadn't stopped since I mounted him.

I licked up every drop of hot white spunk that I could reach. When I could drink no more without climbing off of Max, I whimpered in disappointment. He smiled at me and released my hips. He put one arm behind his head and ran the other over the hard ripples of his stomach. When Max raised his hand again, it was covered in his cum and mine. My lips parted and Max fed slick fingers into my mouth. I sucked them with a muffled moan. His eyes fell half-shut as my tongue caressed his skin and my pussy milked his cock in tight, smooth contractions. His desire flared and his dick swelled inside me. Pleasure burned through me like wildfire and my muffled screams were growing frayed, breathless.

"Lil," Max said. "Lil, I'm..."

That was as much warning as he could give me. Max's voice became a deep groan that echoed up from his very core. He pulled his fingers from my mouth and wrapped both hands around my waist. One, two more thrusts and then molten heat filled my pussy, flowing from Max and into me. It pushed me up, higher and higher. For a moment, I forgot everything that we had lost.

Panting, I collapsed onto Max and he cradled me against his chest. His skin smelled and tasted of sweat, stone and sex. I closed my eyes and breathed in the scents of him. Max stroked my back in long, wandering lines.

"Thanks, Max," I sighed.

Chapter THREE

We cleaned up with some towels and wet-wipes Max had packed. He sealed the wipes into a plastic bag, but we left the towels draped over a low tree branch. I *wanted* the yeti to smell me, after all, and come searching.

In the meantime, though, I got dressed again and helped Max finish making camp. We had used up most of the remaining daylight fucking, so we had to work quickly in the last violet glow of twilight. Max directed me through building the fire while he did pretty much everything else. I even managed not to burn the whole forest down.

While I gathered a little last-minute firewood, Max folded potatoes and vegetables into foil. He pushed them under the logs at the edge of the campfire to cook, then unpacked a bag of sourdough rolls and some kind of sausages wrapped in white butcher paper.

"Just because we're camping doesn't mean that we have to eat s'mores all night," Max said.

I dropped my armload of branches a few yards away from the fire and Max grinned up at me, but the expression faded when I didn't return his smile. He opened the small cooler beside him and pointed to a bag of marshmallows inside. A sizable stack of chocolate bars were stuffed in beside them, too.

"Well, not *only* s'mores," Max amended.

The moon was rising, but the thickening clouds obscured it into a silver smear low on the jagged horizon. There wasn't much wind, but the night grew swiftly cold. I sat down across the fire from Max and wrapped my arms around myself.

"Max, why didn't you tell me you and Taya broke up?" I asked.

Max watched me through the red and orange flames as he skewered a few sausages on extending metal forks.

"You were bleeding out at the time," he said. "If I told you, Lil, you would have stopped me from... helping. And then what? A hospital? How well would a bunch of medical records have gone over with the College?"

"Not well," I admitted. Reluctantly. "But that was a month ago. Why are you only telling me now?"

Max wasn't smiling anymore, either. He sighed. "Honestly, Lil, I didn't even want to say anything today. You've been so devastated since whatever happened with the golem job... Since Evaine died. I didn't want to hurt you more."

"Then why tell me at all?"

"I can't stand lying to you, Lil."

"Well, it wasn't really a lie," I said. "You just didn't tell me."

Max poked at the roasting vegetables and turned our sausages in the fire. A look of such pain flashed across his face that my stomach twisted into a knot. Was Max mourning Evaine? She had been his friend, too.

"I'm sorry," I said.

Max looked up again, but now his expression was just confused. "For what?"

"Never mind."

All of the sexual power Max had given me still coursed through my body with hot golden light. I could have picked up that boulder we were fucking on and chucked it halfway out to the bay. But I didn't have the energy to explain everything I was feeling right now. The wounds were too fresh and too deep... as a dozen or more empty tissue boxes and overflowing trash cans back in my hotel room could attest.

I wrapped my arms around my knees and sat in silence, listening to the night. The fire popped and hissed. Wind whispered through the tree branches. Stone cooled and settled after the day's warmth, groaning out notes so long and deep that I doubted Max could even hear them. He saw my expression, though, and sat up straight.

"Is it out there, Lil?" Max asked.

"Huh? What?"

"The yeti. Do you hear it?"

I shook my head. "Oh, no. If it were, you would hear it, too. Like I said, yeti are big and dumb. They aren't particularly stealthy hunters."

"Are they uh... native to this area?"

"I don't think so. They come from up north, in Canada and Greenland."

"Let me guess. Global warming has been driving them out of their forests, right?"

"Kind of the opposite, actually," I said. "The lumber industry has sent a lot more humans into their territories. Yeti don't exactly have many natural predators, so the rise in food led to a sort of population boom. They've even spread out into some parts of Europe and Russia."

Max whistled softly and began fishing our dinner out of the fire. The sausages were nearly done, but after a brief inspection of the vegetables, Max folded the foil back up and pushed them deeper into the campfire.

"What about werewolves?" he asked. "They're wilderness hunters too, right?"

I nodded slowly. "Yeah, mostly. Yeti and werewolves run into each other sometimes, but not often enough to keep the yeti's numbers down."

"So who usually wins? Between a yeti and a werewolf, I mean?"

"The werewolf," I said. "A pack of yeti *might* be able to take on a fully transformed werewolf, if they worked in groups. But yeti only barely tolerate each other long enough to mate."

Max smiled. "Then we're good. I know you can take on a werewolf and come out on top."

"In more ways than one."

The joke slipped out before I could think. Max's smile widened until the firelight cast dancing shadows in his dimples.

"Well, werewolves are pretty much the most dangerous things in our world, right?" he asked.

"Short of an elder vampire or pissed-off djinn. Or a demon."

My voice broke. I remembered Reid kneeling at my feet in the road, telling me to kill him because the constant war with his demonic half just hurt too much. I remembered pulling the trigger and watching a good, tormented man die. I remembered running away before the golem's body was even cold because Evaine was still up there in my burnt-out condo, fighting for her life against the incubus who had created Reid. Fighting for *my* life.

Max didn't try to make me talk any more. He finished cooking dinner and we ate quietly, then made hot chocolate in a saucepan over the fire. When the flames burned low, Max and I moved into the tent and left the flap open so we could keep a watchful eye on the glowing embers.

Our sleeping bags were laid out next to each other across the tent floor. We stripped down to our underwear and crawled inside them. There were no stars and even the moonlight had vanished entirely behind clouds, but the fading coals provided more than enough light for my sex-honed senses. Max lay silently beside me, arms crossed beneath his head and staring up at the tent ceiling.

It felt strange to be spending the night with someone. The only time I'd ever slept anything but alone in my bed was by accident, the night that Reid tried to kill me and Max came to my rescue. This was different, but my brain was too damned tired to freak out about it. It gave me a big middle finger and told me to fuck the hell off, so I closed my eyes.

But I couldn't sleep. The evening was cold and I could not get comfortable. It wasn't just the hard ground... I did the same thing every night in my stupidly soft hotel bed back in the city. Scenes of Evaine and Reid's deaths played over and over in my head. My eyes stung and I squeezed them tighter shut.

"Lil?" Max asked.

"What?"

"Come here."

I felt his hand close on my shoulder and then our sleeping bags sliding over one another as he pulled me up into his arms. Max's fingers laced through my hair and he pressed my cheek down against his chest.

"You can cry, Lil," Max whispered. "It's okay. I won't ask you any questions or if you're alright. I know you're not."

His arms were so warm around me. I curled my fingers into Max's sleeping bag, clutching at the cloth hard enough that it tore under my nails.

"Max, do you miss Evaine?" I asked.

"Yeah, Lil. I do." His arms tightened around me and his voice cracked. "I miss her a lot."

Max kissed my head and I felt the warmth of his tears trickling into my long hair. I buried my face against his chest and sobbed. Max and I clung to each other and cried like we were children all over again until I soaked his sleeping bag in tears. It hurt... but it felt good, too.

By the time I finally cried myself out, my eyes felt even more sore than they were that morning. I drew a few deep, shuddering breaths and nuzzled against Max's shoulder. He was still quiet, but his fingers caressed one of my wet, tear-streaked cheeks. Outside the tent, the remains of our campfire crackled. A blackened piece of wood snapped and threw a short fireworks display of sparks up into the darkness.

The huge tear-soaked patch at the top of Max's sleeping bag was growing cold enough to raise goosebumps along his skin. I folded the edge down and rubbed my hand over Max's bare chest, trying to return some of the heat he had lost. But the goosebumps didn't go away as his skin warmed.

"Lil..." Max breathed.

An answering heat rose and coiled inside me that made my heart clench all over again, but not in grief this time. I slid my hand down Max's chest and followed the narrow trail of hair leading from his navel to the waist of his boxers.

"You... don't have to, Lil," Max said. "I'm not trying to..."

"I know."

"Anti-yeti session?"

"In case of yeti, yank cock," I murmured with a tiny smile.

Max reached between us, down into my sleeping bag and splayed his fingers across the soft skin of my belly. I wondered if he could feel the flutters inside me there.

The muscles of his stomach tensed as my hand slid into his boxers and gripped his thick cock. Max groaned into my hair. His hand mirrored mine, circling around my navel and then moving to trace the waist of my underwear. His fingers pressed between my legs, stroking my pussy through my panties. The thin fabric soaked swiftly and my fist tightened around him.

Max's already hard dick grew hotter in my hand and I felt his breath warm along the side of my neck. I tilted my hips and parted my legs as best I could in the confines of the sleeping bag to give Max better access to my aching pussy. Through my wet panties, he rubbed a close spiral over my dripping sex and throbbing clit.

I bit Max's chest to stifle a soft whimper. His hips rose insistently against my hand and then his heartbeat sped as I ran my curled fingers up along his length. I traced my thumb over the rounded head of Max's cock and he gasped.

"Yes, Lil," he whispered. "Oh god...!"

It felt good to be wanted. To be needed. I moved my hand in long, slow strokes along Max's dick. He groaned and pulled my panties to one side, baring my dripping pussy to his touch. Max's fingers weren't rough – he moisturized regularly and I had noticed a little bottle of his favorite lotion in his backpack earlier – but after a decade of working in garages and kitchens, his hands were calloused and tough. Max trailed them so lightly over me that it felt like butterfly wings.

I gasped at the sensation and bit Max's chest again. A tight, hot knot was swelling deep in the pit of my stomach. I jerked Max's cock with growing speed and urgency as he used two fingers to gently spread me open. He paused there, leaving the most sensitive part of me exposed and vulnerable. I whimpered and wetness ran down the cleft of my ass.

"Max..." I said.

He nodded and finally slid one finger into my pussy. The bright glow of ecstasy cinched tighter inside me and Max's cock pulsed hot in my grasp. I moaned into his chest and my hips rocked desperately against his hand. My sleeping bag was just a tangle around my thighs by now. Max's finger moved inside my pussy and touched all of the secret, sensual places within me one at a time, building my pleasure with care and precision until my whole body shook with it.

I was falling over the edge and desperately needed to bring Max with me. I squeezed my eyes shut and forced my hand to slide smoothly along his cock in quickening strokes. Max's breath came in ragged, uneven gasps and I felt his heart pounding to match the drumbeat in my own chest.

He wasn't done with me. Max pulled me closer against him, twisting his finger inside me so he could change the angle of his hand between my legs. He buried his face in the red tangles of my hair and ran his thumb up to my clitoris. Max touched it lightly, but even that gentle brush made lightning jolt along my spine. I screamed out the orgasm I had only barely been keeping at bay.

When the finger still in me curled, pressing against the sensitive little nub of my clit from within, I screamed louder. Bright lines of sensation seared through my body, tugging and pulling at every part of me. I grabbed Max's wrist in my free hand and ground myself helplessly against him. I kept the other moving along the length of his dick by sheer force of will.

"Oh fuck, Lil. Yes!" Max panted.

My angle wasn't ideal, but I wasn't about to let that stop me. I pumped Max faster, trying to keep up with the wet, hot quivering of my overstimulated pussy. My senses were drawn so taut that I couldn't *not* feel every exquisite inch of Max's cock – the silkiness of his skin, the delicate tracery of blood vessels and the blazing hard heat beneath that was subtly ridged like folded steel.

Max's fingers trembled against me and inside me, but he was just as determined as I was. Even when he let out a deep groan and his dick throbbed in my grip, Max refused to stop touching me. Hot semen cascaded over my hand and wetness gushed along his fingers. We came together, tangled with one another and our sleeping bags shoved awkwardly halfway down our writhing bodies. Our hands moved frantically, fumbling in the throes of climax until we both collapsed soaked and spent to the tent floor. Max and I held each other tightly for a long time, kissing and tasting one another's panting breath.

Finally, Max reached out and grabbed the package of wet-wipes.

"Better clean all of this off before it gets cold," he said.

I nodded and we set to work. The heat we had created inside the tent dispersed quickly, though, even after we closed the flap.

Max and I were both shivering by the time we finished filling up the plastic bag with used wipes, especially once his boxers and my panties went into another sack for laundry.

When I was done cleaning up, I practically dove back into my sleeping bag. Max laughed, but I heard his teeth chattering, too. He climbed into his own sleeping bag again and pulled it tight around his neck.

"Want to zip our bags together?" I asked. "We would be warmer that way, right?"

"Yes," Max answered slowly. His eyebrows were raised so high they were just about crawling up into his tousled blond hair. But he smiled. "If you want to, Lil."

"Yeah."

We slipped out of our sleeping bags and braved the cold just long enough to zip them together, then scrambled back inside. Max put his arms around me and within a few minutes, we both stopped shivering.

Care to guess how long before we were fucking again? Whatever you guessed, it was too long.

Chapter
FOUR

*M*orning came early when there were no walls to block out the sun. The tent made a valiant attempt, but was no substitute for the hotel blackout curtains I had kept closed for the past month. I sat up and scrubbed at my eyes until I could see again, then checked my phone. Six fucking thirty.

I looked over at Max. One of his arms was draped across his face, the other hooked loosely around my waist. I had spent the night with a guy. In the same sleeping bag. On purpose. And the world didn't end.

Gently, I shook Max awake. His eyes cracked open, then widened when he saw me beside him. I guess he was shocked by the intactness of the world, too. Max sat up and stretched, smiling a hell of a lot more than I was. Pink scratches from my nails ran all across his chest like arcane designs.

Once I took care of Max's morning hard-on and topping off my powers, we ate breakfast and broke down camp. I found a few ripped bits of paper that looked like they had come from the sausage wrapper the night before. The teeth marks were far too small – and not torn out of our flesh – to belong to the yeti.

"Looks like a raccoon got into it," Max said, glancing over my shoulder. "Or maybe a fox."

"I guess the yeti hasn't been hungry enough to come down this far," I said. "We'll need to get higher up."

Max nodded and went to work burying the latrine pit. Not my favorite part of our little camping trip so far, by the way. Max covered it under just a foot or two of dirt so we weren't leaving any unpleasant surprises for the next campers, but if we somehow missed the yeti on our way up into the mountains, I wanted it to be able to find my scent.

The sun had risen sufficiently high to stab me right in the eyes, but by the time Max and I were buckling our backpacks into place, the blue sky was already dotted with a fresh batch of clouds. They were fluffy and white, but thick enough to cast chilly shadows when they passed over the sun.

Full on sexual energy now, it was much easier to keep up with Max's long-legged stride. In fact, I could have raced for the peak and left him in the dust without even breaking a sweat. But that kind of pace might have made it hard for the yeti to keep up, too, and I hadn't forgotten that I was bait.

The forest thinned a bit as we hiked further into the mountains. Ferns gave way to low, bristly grass and patches of bright yellow flowers that swayed like dancers when the wind picked up. Our view to the west was hazy with the morning's coastal fog and the city was concealed under a soft blanket of gray, but I caught a few bright pewter flashes of the ocean spreading out beyond.

We stopped a little bit after noon and ate some sandwiches. I might have snuck a couple of chocolate bars, too, while Max pretended not to be looking. When we were done eating, he bent me over against a pine tree, shorts shoved down around my ankles, and fucked me from behind. I gripped the poor tree so hard that I tore out chunks of bark and wood. My cries echoed across the rocky mountain slope and hopefully sounded just like a dinner bell to a hungry yeti.

Max's breath heaved and he poured hot, gooey cum inside me. When we were done, I cleaned up as much as I could – busily filling yet another plastic bag with wet-wipes – but spent the next hour feeling sticky sperm soaking into my panties as we hiked. I was seriously considering asking for a matching load up my ass when I smelled something.

Max stopped beside me on the trail. He scanned the trees and rocks with narrowed eyes.

"What is it, Lil?" he asked.

I sniffed the air again. "There's someone else up here."

"Yeti?"

"No, it smells human. Male, I think. And recent."

"Maybe whoever came in that Mercedes we saw below?" Max suggested. "Is he in danger from the yeti?"

"Anyone in this forest is in danger from the yeti," I said.

Max frowned. "Then I really hope we find it first."

"Yeah."

We kept moving. I picked up the pace and before long, even Max was panting. The clouds were growing thicker and closing over the sun again, but he was still sweating. Max gulped down the last of his water and then pointed through the trees to a small stream winding between the rocks.

We detoured to refill our canteens. There were several large sealed bottles of water in my backpack, but Max wanted to save them for emergencies. There hadn't been enough spare time when he was a kid for Max to join the Boy Scouts, but he sure acted like one. He crouched at the edge of the stream and fished something out of his pack.

"The water's flowing pretty fast and we haven't seen anything bigger than a bird living up here, so it's probably safe. But just in case, use one of these," Max said.

He ripped open a foil packet and handed me a tiny red-brown tablet. I sniffed and made a face. Max laughed at my expression as he dropped a matching one into his own water. He screwed the cap shut and shook his canteen briskly.

"Iodine?" I asked.

"And some other stuff that will help kill off any pathogens that might be in the water."

I groaned. "You mean from animal poop."

"And urine," Max reminded me with a dimpled smirk. "Yeah. The iodine will taste a little strange, but–"

A pine tree with a trunk as big around as my thigh exploded into splinters. The huge furry shape that had just smashed through it reared up, snarling and slavering. It was the size of a grizzly bear, with elongated limbs covered in ropey muscle and matted gray fur. The face was something between a gorilla and a bulldog, all twisted together into a mask of savage rage and hunger.

"Yeti?" Max gasped.

"Yeah," I said. "I'm definitely not fucking that!"

If you were expecting a big goofy ape thing, you were wrong. This monster was all claws, hair and death.

The yeti threw back its malformed head and let out a guttural howl. Foam flecked the tusks thrusting up from the beast's heavy jaw. The yeti lowered its lumpish head, brandishing a pair of thick, curling horns like those of a ram, and charged.

It was coming right for us. Plan successful. Yay! And also, shit!

I leapt into motion, meeting the yeti's charge with a shoulder to its sinewy midsection. Up close, the reek of rotting meat churned my stomach. The yeti growled and lashed out at me with claws like dirty bone knives. I ducked the first swipe and answered with an uppercut to the yeti's ugly face, but those rangy arms and legs had a lot more reach than I thought. The yeti kicked me back and then raked its talons across my midsection. They ripped through my shirt, deep into the flesh of my stomach. I hit the ground hard and blood stained the dirt red.

"Lil!" Max shouted.

"I'm okay," I panted, hoping he could hear me.

The yeti's oversized foot came down at me. I barely rolled aside in time to avoid those hairy toes and their hooked yellow claws. The gashes in my belly were no longer bleeding and were now swiftly healing shut. I sprang to my feet and jumped back before the yeti could try disemboweling me again. I would need to watch my range more carefully.

A gunshot cracked deafeningly. A patch of the yeti's filthy fur flicked and a tiny spatter of brackish blood joined mine on the rocky earth. Max stood ten yards away, hunting rifle pressed against his shoulder. He worked the gun's bolt and sighted down the barrel again.

The yeti spotted Max and roared. Stinking saliva sprayed from its mouth and then the yeti was loping toward him. Max's eyes went wide, but he didn't move. He pulled the rifle's trigger and slammed a second shot into the yeti's ribs. The huge monster dropped to all fours and lowered its head for the charge. Instead of running like a sane human being, Max let out a long, steady breath and chambered a new round.

Max had bought me precious seconds to finish healing and now the yeti was turned away from me. I sprinted down the slope toward it, my legs pumping so fast that they became a blur. As the yeti coiled for the final pounce, I leapt and landed on its back. I wasn't heavy enough to bear it to the ground, but I hooked one elbow under the monster's arm in a half nelson. I wrapped my other arm across the yeti's tree-trunk neck, groping for the leverage to snap its spine. But the yeti was nearly as strong as a werewolf and thrashed like a sack full of pissed-off anacondas in my grasp.

"Hold still, you smelly fucker," I grunted. "Shit!"

The yeti twisted and raised its free arm to slash at me. Max brought up his hunting rifle, narrowed his eyes and fired. But I was right on top of the monster and Max aimed low to avoid me, just grazing the yeti's swinging arm. His bullet didn't even draw blood through the yeti's thick, fetid hide, but Max had its attention again.

I planted my knees against the monster's spine and yanked, but it wasn't enough. Max had underestimated the yeti's reach, too. Its unpinned arm lashed out and Max flew back in a spray of blood. He slammed into the ground on the far side of the hiking trail and tumbled down the steep slope toward a cliff that dropped away into the valley far below.

"Max!" I screamed.

I released the yeti's throat and jammed the point of my elbow into its shoulder. The yeti sagged to its shaggy knees, howling in pain. I jumped off and as soon as my toes touched stone, I was already sprinting down the mountain.

Max had rolled onto his back and his legs kicked for purchase as he slid out of control. His heels dug deep furrows into the stony earth, but it was too late – he was falling over the edge. Max twisted and just managed to grab onto a jutting tree root. My heightened hearing picked out the loud pop of Max's shoulder as his fall jerked to an abrupt halt. He dangled there over a hundred-foot drop.

I half leapt, half fell the final yards to the cliff's edge, slipping and skidding just as Max had. I dug my fingers so hard into the rocks that I distantly felt my fingernails splitting, but I lurched to a stop above where Max clung to the mountainside. Blood sheeted down the front of his torn shirt and Max's face was terribly pale. His arm trembled with the effort of clinging to the tree root.

"Just hold on, Max," I said. "I've got you..."

I grabbed the thick strap of his backpack with one hand. For a heart-stopping moment, the tough nylon slid through my blood-and sweat-slicked fingers, but I tightened my grip. Not daring to move too quickly, lest the strap snap and drop Max, I heaved him up and back onto solid ground. He collapsed beside me, panting and gasping. I wrapped one arm around Max and held him close against me as I peered up the slope.

The yeti was gone.

Chapter
FIVE

By the time Max's shaking legs could hold him again, all of my wounds were gone. I grabbed a clean sweatshirt from my pack and kept it pressed tightly to Max's lacerated chest as we limped back up the slope. As soon as we clambered over the wooden railing of the hiking trail, I tried to get Max to sit.

"We have to stop that bleeding," I said.

Max shook his head. His face was still horribly pale and sweat darkened his blond hair. He staggered and sagged against me.

"Not here," Max gasped. "Too much blood already. The scent might bring the yeti sniffing around again."

I wanted to argue, but he was right. So I took Max's backpack and slung it over mine. It was heavy and awkward, but I was more than strong enough to handle it. Once that was done, I wrapped one arm under Max's shoulders and the other behind his knees. He weighed well over two hundred pounds, but I scooped Max up easily and carried him back down the trail.

"We're going the wrong way," he protested.

I just growled in answer and stopped at the first level place I found, a small clearing that I remembered seeing earlier that day.

There wasn't much room and it wasn't marked as an official campsite, but I was in no mood to be picky.

Hastily, I unrolled one of our sleeping bags and laid Max out on top of it. First, I had to take care of his chest. There was an awful lot of blood and Max's skin felt cold and clammy.

I ripped off the remains of his shirt and balled it up with the bloody sweatshirt I had been holding against the wound. I chucked them both as hard as I could out across the trail. My super-powered throw would have made the most juiced-up quarterback envious. Max was right about the blood scent and I had no desire to get the yeti's attention again.

The clouds had turned gray and heavy, transforming the afternoon into premature evening. I searched quickly through my backpack until I found a little LED lamp and switched it on. I set it on a fallen tree nearby and inspected Max's injuries with my heart in my mouth. Four deep slashes ran from his right shoulder, across his chest and ended just on the left side of his sternum. I prodded them gently, eliciting a low groan from Max. The worst of them had probably nicked a couple of his ribs, but the bones weren't broken and had successfully protected the vital organs beneath.

"So... so am I going to turn into a yeti?" Max asked in a ragged voice.

"No, dummy," I said. "That's werewolves."

"Are you sure? I could use that kind of toughness right now. The yeti didn't even seem to feel my bullets."

I couldn't tell if Max was really scared or just trying to lift my spirits with a stupid joke. Either way, he offered me a wan smile. I didn't return it.

"There's a reason I didn't bring any weapons," I told Max. "Anything short of an elephant gun loaded with napalm is like a bee sting to a yeti."

"That's why you went in close for the neck break."

"Yeah."

"What kinds of problems are we looking at here?" Max asked in a slightly steadier voice, dipping his chin down toward his wounded chest and shoulder.

"Blood loss and infection," I said.

"Neat. There's a first aid kit packed in the front pocket of my backpack. No stitches, but there are some butterfly bandages and rubbing alcohol."

"That's going to hurt like hell," I warned as I retrieved the kit from his pack and laid the plastic box open across the log.

Max laughed weakly. "Because getting these scratches didn't hurt at all. I don't know if I can handle a little disinfectant."

"If you don't shut up and lie still, you don't get a lollipop when we're done," I growled.

"Oh?" Max asked. "Are we playing doctor, Lil?"

I found the small bottle of rubbing alcohol and poured it carefully over Max's chest, wincing as his pale face contorted in pain. His jaw clenched, stifling a cry. I wiped away the blood and cleaned around the wound as gently as I could. With Max's help, I closed each of the deep cuts with the first aid kit's entire stock of butterfly bandages, gauze and then a thick layer of white medical tape.

"Shit, that's going to scar," I said.

"It's okay, Lil. Now what?"

"Let's take a look at that arm."

Max sat up slowly, leaning back against the fallen tree that held our lamp and dwindling first aid supplies. The skin around Max's left shoulder was bruised a terrible purple-black from taking the full force of his fall over the cliff. I touched a protruding knob of bone that wasn't supposed to be there and Max bit back another sound of pain.

"Dislocated," I said. "Alright, this is going to hurt like hell, too."

Max nodded. "Do it, Lil."

I placed the palm of one hand flat over the bulge and grabbed Max's left wrist in my other hand. He squeezed his eyes shut and I took a deep breath. I wanted to pull the shoulder into place, not rip his arm off. I yanked sharply and pressed down, guiding the bone back into its socket with another loud pop.

Max couldn't stop himself from screaming this time, but it was short and then he sagged against the log. He lay there panting and sweating for a moment, then finally opened his eyes and smiled at me again.

"So do I get my lollipop now?" Max asked, panting.

"I'm all out."

"Got anything else to suck on?"

"You nearly died!" I said. "Shit, I wish sex would heal you up like it does me."

"I'll be fine, Lil."

I shook my head and stood. "No, Max. You might get an infection. You might tear open those cuts. You might snap your shoulder right out of the socket again."

"I'll be careful," Max said, looking up at me with a frown. "You still need to catch that yeti."

"Not a chance. I'm taking you down out of these damned mountains and to a hospital."

I slammed the first aid kit shut, threw it into one of the backpacks and leaned over Max to scoop him into my arms again. He raised his right hand to stop me, wincing.

"Lil, we can't leave yet," he said. "The yeti–"

"I don't care about the fucking bounty, Max!"

"No. But you care about the people that thing will kill if you don't stop it. We know there's someone else up here. What if the yeti finds him?"

Max held my gaze with steady blue eyes until I sank down beside him. I slumped against the log, staring into the low, darkening gray sky.

"Stop being so... wonderful," I told him.

"I apologize for nothing."

The lightness in Max's voice was somewhat undercut by the hiss of pain as he scooted closer to me on the sleeping bag. Carefully, he reached out and laced his fingers through mine. I let out a shuddering sigh.

"Why did you volunteer to come with me on this job?" I asked. "And why the hell did I let you?"

"You needed help, Lil."

"From your cock, not your gun. What the hell were you thinking? That yeti could have killed you!"

I turned to look at Max, but he didn't even flinch as my voice rose. I wanted to slap or kiss that calm, serious expression off his face. Didn't Max know how close he had come to death today?

"Lil–" he began.

"I can't lose you, too!"

Max's eyes went wide and his hand tightened around mine. I felt wetness on my cheeks, but I wasn't crying. It had started to rain.

"Evaine's dead and... and I don't even understand why," I said. I couldn't breathe. "She was protecting me, Max. Trying to help, just like... like you. And she died."

"You're worth fighting for, Lil," Max said softly. "And worth fighting with, when you make us."

"Evaine warned me not to hunt Reid. She was trying to protect me from the demons, from the College. From Asmodai, from my father..."

"Your father?"

"Vincent Myrdon."

"The High Magus of the College?" Max asked incredulously. "*He's* your father?"

"Yeah. Evaine told me."

Max listened while I talked. The words came slowly at first, about how I tracked Reid down at the Quay Festival and brought him home to answer my questions. About how innocent and broken the golem had been, about the one night we had together and how little I could do to ease his pain. I repeated everything Reid could tell me about his creator, the beautiful incubus, Asmodai, and the mortal wizard who served him.

By the time I reached the part where Evaine appeared in my condo to confront me about hunting Reid again, the rain was falling hard enough to mask my tears. Max didn't interrupt even as cold water soaked his hair and ran down his bandaged chest.

"Evaine said that Asmodai was trying to... to create a cambion," I said.

"Like you."

I nodded. "Yeah."

"Why?"

"I don't know."

I told Max about how Evaine had revealed my father's identity and warned that if the College ever learned why Reid had been created, Vincent Myrdon would order my death. His own daughter. I still didn't know why and there had been so little chance to ask questions, to understand anything that had happened.

Max didn't press me for answers that I didn't have. He pulled me as close as he could into his injured arms while I tried to tell him through hiccuping sobs about Asmodai's fiery arrival, how Evaine fought the incubus and begged me to run. To escape.

I told Max how I had defied Evaine again and refused to leave, how Reid had carried me away. How I shot him down in the street outside like some kind of rabid animal before the College hunters could find out why Asmodai wanted a cambion. And how it was all fucked anyway because Evaine was dead and the incubus was gone by the time we ran up to my ruined condo.

"Stefano called her the Lady of the Lake," I told Max. Rain drenched my clothes and they clung to my skin. "Like the stories about King Arthur we read in school. Evaine gave him Excalibur and taught Merlin how to use his powers."

"Just like she did with you."

"I guess that's why the wizards always listened to her. I should have listened, too. Then maybe–"

"You did the right thing, Lil," Max interrupted in a hard voice. "Maybe not the smart thing, but you helped Reid. And you tried to help Evaine. Never regret that."

"I still don't understand what Asmodai wants from a cambion. What if... what if I'm dangerous, Max?"

"Don't even say that, Lil. You protect people. That's your job. You're good at it and you love it. You're not dangerous."

"My own father thought I was," I said, wiping rain and tears out of my eyes. "That's the point of that whole test thing when I was eighteen."

"Have you told the College about any of this?" Max asked.

"Some. Stefano debriefed me afterward. I told him about Asmodai appearing in my house and his wizard accomplice, but that's it. Evaine and Reid gave up too much to keep... *something* secret from the High Magus for me to go running my mouth."

"The High Magus... your dad. Shit, Lil. Does he even know you're his daughter?" Max asked.

"Yeah, he knows," I hissed. "How did I not see it before? It seems so fucking obvious now... But he never said anything. No, High Magus Myrdon was more worried about what would happen if anyone ever found out that he had a half-succubus daughter. Shit, no wonder he was so hard on Finn and Muir. Vincent's seen *exactly* how wrong things can go when you screw with a lust demon."

"Your mother loved him," said Max. "A *demon* fell in love. How unbelievable is that? And things didn't go wrong – they had you. That's... amazing. Anything that resulted in you being born wasn't a mistake, Lil. It was a miracle."

Max said it with such conviction that it made my heart ache. I leaned in and crushed my lips against his, kissing him fiercely and tasting rain. Max wrapped his good arm around me and pulled me in close.

"Lil?" he asked quietly.

"What?"

"You said the golem... Reid... had a huge bounty on him. Right?"

"Yeah. Massive."

"You didn't take the gold, did you?" Max murmured against my lips.

"No."

Rain slicked my shirt to my skin and turned it into no barrier at all against the feeling of his body pressed to mine. Max's fingers traced my spine and my shiver had nothing to do with the drops of cold water rolling down my skin.

"Even though hunting Reid cost you pretty much your whole life?" he asked.

"I just couldn't take money for killing an innocent man."

"That's my girl."

Max rewarded me with another long, deep kiss. He slid both hands down my back to my waist and held me tight, then hissed out a pained breath at the pressure.

"Careful," I admonished him. "If you hurt yourself, I'm hauling your ass to the nearest hospital. Fuck the yeti."

Max laughed, though the sound was still a little strained. "I thought you said we weren't doing that."

"I'm not losing you, Max."

"No," he agreed. "You're not."

I kissed Max again. And again and again, until his gasps were no longer ones of pain. At first, I thought he was shivering from the rain, but swiftly realized that it was something else entirely – he was shaking with the effort of restraining himself. Max knew I meant every word I said, that if he made his wounds any worse, I really would abandon my hunt for the yeti.

"That's my boy," I told him.

Max clutched at the small of my back, his nails scraping lightly over my rain-slicked skin. I walked my fingers down his chest and felt his heart pounding even through the bandages. Cold silver rain pattered in the trees and wind tugged them into a swaying dance around us.

"Lil, please," Max gasped. "I want you so much..."

My fingers reached the waist of his jeans. The cloth was wet and heavy, but not even close to a match for my strength. Max groaned and his head fell back against the log as I pulled his cock free from his pants. With a couple of swift, eager strokes, I coaxed Max's already rising length into full, feverish hardness. The muscles of his arms and chest tightened. I kissed the tip of his nose and gave it a little nip as a reminder to be still.

"You promised me something to suck on," Max reminded me. "Since we're out of lollipops."

I raised one eyebrow.

"I promised nothing of the kind," I said. "But because you've been such a good patient..."

I pulled the shredded, soaked remains of my shirt over my head and tossed it aside. More slowly, I peeled my sports bra up and then off, too. It was a hasty, incomplete striptease, but Max's lust rose as bright and golden as a sunrise at the sight. His hands twisted into the sleeping bag beneath him.

I arched my spine and thrust my bared breasts out toward Max. Rain splashed across my body. My nipples hardened at once into flushed pink peaks and I shivered. But then Max descended on me like a starving man. His lips and tongue were warm and soft in perfect counterpoint to the descending storm. I twined my fingers into Max's wet blond hair and pulled his face gently to my chest, gasping as he licked up all of the cold rainwater from my skin and left spreading heat in his wake.

My hair coiled wet and heavy along my spine. I gathered it up into a copper twist at the base of my neck so it wouldn't get in my way or obstruct Max's view. I've taken video of myself in action and it's not a sight to be missed.

With a small sigh, I pulled away from the warmth of Max's mouth. He started to draw me in again, but then leaned back against the log and stilled. I nodded my approval and slid down to kneel between Max's outstretched legs. I inhaled the scents of fresh rain on his skin, of hot testosterone and the fading sharpness of frightened adrenalin. I kissed a darkening patch of skin across the plane of Max's stomach, a bruise from his tumble down the mountainside.

I was going to tear that fucking yeti apart, but my rage didn't last long against the need growing inside me.

I closed my lips over the head of Max's cock and his jaw tightened. The heat of him in my mouth stoked the matching fire deeper within me and wetness far warmer than the rain soaked my shorts. Encircling Max's thick shaft with both hands, I began working my way up and down his length. On my knees and bowed over Max, I looked like a woman at prayer, worshiping the hard pillar of his cock. Not far from the truth.

Max was having a really difficult time sitting still. He had stretched his good arm across the log behind him, his fingers biting into the bark. He groaned in pleasure and pain.

"Yes, Lil," he said. "You feel... amazing."

I pushed my head down, swallowing every inch of Max's dick until my face was pressed into the wet denim of his jeans. I couldn't breathe, but I didn't care. He tasted too good, felt too good... I devoured Max's cock until we were both gasping on the sharp edge of orgasm.

Finally, I popped my mouth off of him with a wet slurp. Rain had collected on the plastic of the little LED lamp and cast pale, wavering light over us, like we sat at the bottom of a lake. I licked my lips.

"I guess I'm the one who got the lollipop," I said.

A gust of wind whipped the trees and sprinkled us both in pine-scented rain. Maybe I could put all this wetness to use. I lowered myself to my elbows between Max's legs and squeezed my breasts together into soft, deep cleavage around his dick. He groaned as I began sliding up and down.

"Oh fuck," Max said.

The contrast of his hot cock and the cold rain was almost too much. I squirmed against Max, kissing and sucking the flushed head of his dick into my mouth every time it thrust up from between my tits. Max's jaw was set and his eyes squeezed nearly shut. It was hard to tell if his expression was one of ecstasy or pain.

"Does it feel good?" I asked.

"Yes!" Max gasped. "Yes, Lil. So good."

"Do you want more?"

"Please, Lil! Don't stop...!"

The desperate urgency in his voice made my pussy ache with need. I wrapped my lips around his dick and swallowed Max deep once more, gagging myself on him and leaving his cock dripping wet before capturing it in my cleavage again. I stroked my breasts along him, faster and faster.

The heat inside me was growing, gushing wetter and wetter into my already soaked shorts. We were both so close... Max got there first. He said my name over and over in a low voice, like a secret meant only for me, and then the rain coming down on my skin was warm instead of cold. Max's cock throbbed against the sensitive flesh between my breasts and creamy cum splashed across them.

The power of Max's pleasure poured into me, finding and then joining my own. My orgasm echoed the steady rhythm of his and took off. It was strange to feel it thrumming through me without a cock or fingers inside me, no lips or tongue on my clit. Just Max's hardness against my heart and his cum running thick and hot over my skin.

Maybe I could have simply stayed there, reveling in the storm of sensation, but I needed Max inside me. I wanted him right down to my bones, with every part of my being. I leapt up and quite literally ripped off my shorts and panties. There was no force on Earth or beyond that was going to keep me from Max. The wet fabric tore with small sounds and I flung my remaining clothes away through the trees.

Max was still going, still cumming hard as I threw myself on top of him. He painted a ribbon of bright white along my inner thigh and then Max entered me. With one final fountain of liquid heat into me, Max finished and I began. I had been hungry and thirsty before, even scared for my life, but the feeling of Max inside me now woke a soul-deep craving that made every other need seem insignificant.

His breath became ragged as my climax squeezed his sensitive cock inside me, but Max didn't push me away or ask me to stop. I moved as slowly as I could astride him, trying to be gentle. Just like Evaine had taught me.

A pang of grief shot through me at the thought, flowing against the tidal surge of ecstasy in a way that heightened both and diminished neither. I always knew that an edge of physical pain could make the pleasure even sweeter, but this... Rain and tears ran down my face and splashed across Max's chest. He stared at me with wide, dark blue eyes.

"Lil..."

Max brought his hand up to my cheeks and traced the trail of my tears with his thumb. He pulled me down into a sweet, hot kiss. I tasted my sorrow on his lips and drew back.

"You're going to hurt yourself," I told him.

"I don't care," Max said.

"I do."

I kissed Max's fingertips and pushed his hand gently down again. He nodded and watched, forcing himself to be still as I began to ride him. It was difficult to talk while cumming, let alone move with anything like grace. But I'm an expert. Evaine had spent too long training me – I wasn't about to let her down now.

I leaned back, legs spread over Max. The rain carved curving lines through the white cum oozing all along my chest, slowly washing it away. The sight of Max's cock between my parted thighs was captivating, thrust up into the flushed, wet pink of my pussy. I swiveled my hips in tight circles, gasping and feeling him inside my body.

There was no way I could take it slow. Gentle, yes, but not slow. I needed Max too much for that. He stared as I danced in his lap. My motions were frantic, writhing to take Max's cock as deeply as I possibly could. My hair had come unwound from its coil and now flung drops of rain up into the night as I tossed my head. The hot hardness inside me was exquisite and almost agonizing in its perfection. The pleasure of Max filled me, pounded through me like a drumbeat. Like a heartbeat.

I wrapped my arms around Max's neck and clung to him while I came. He kissed me and our breath mingled in short, shuddering gasps. His lips were cold, but his breath was so warm. The rain beat down and plastered my hair across my shoulders. Flashes of lightning cast moments of brilliant illumination over us that seemed to last forever, but the boom of thunder was tiny compared to the sound of Max whispering my name into my ear.

Having Max inside me... it was like having some of his strength inside me. Not the kind of strength that let me crush stone in my bare hands, but the kind that kept Max smiling even after losing Taya and Evaine. That kept him here with me no matter the pain or danger. I held Max as tightly to me as I dared and felt his cock thrust right up into the heart of me.

"Lil, I can't stop it anymore," Max said.

His arms were around me. I don't know when it happened and couldn't find it in myself to object anymore. Max held me close, just as gently as I had, and gave me his cum. It flooded my body, my senses, my very being. I was already lost in the throes of orgasm, but Max pushed me higher. Is there something beyond climax?

Yes.

I was long past screaming. I just lay against Max and felt him inside me, trying as best I could to squeeze and milk every possible drop of pleasure from him, to return some fraction of what he was giving me.

Finally, Max let out a long breath and sagged back. He panted and withdrew his arms, cradling them to his chest with a sheepish expression.

"Are you okay?" I asked.

"Hell yes." Max smiled and blinked rain out of his eyes. "I'm not sure I have any bones left, but I feel great. How about you?"

The rain had lightened and was slowing to a stop. I touched my cheeks. My tears had stopped, too. Just like the late summer storm, they had passed. The grief wasn't gone... I would carry it for the rest of my life. But now it felt like something I *could* carry. Especially with Max always there beside me to help when it got too heavy. I gave him a long kiss.

"I'm okay," I said.

And for the first time in a month, I meant it.

Chapter
SIX

My dramatic assessment of the rain turned out to be a bit premature, so Max and I hid under a stand of pines to wait for the last showers to pass. When the storm was actually over, we ventured out from the trees again.

With Max injured, that left setting up our campsite to me. He directed me through the process and tried twice to help, but I glared each time until he sat back down. I fucked up the tent so badly that even Max couldn't figure out what the hell I had done, but then the wind started again and we retreated into the lopsided fabric dome.

With one dry sleeping bag and no fire, our camp kind of sucked and there was no way to cook dinner. So Max and I sat in the tent and fed each other marshmallows. I ate most of them, along with eight chocolate bars. Even hurt, Max kept me full to the brim with sexual energy, but I needed calories, too – a fuck-ton of calories, preferably sweet ones.

Max didn't eat as much candy, though I made certain to dose him with a handful of painkillers. He showed me a tube of a trail food called *Güp*. It was thick, gooey and white. The manufacturers might as well have named it *jizz*.

I tried a mouthful and wasn't very impressed. Actual jizz was way better. But according to the nutrition label, the stuff was more or less pure protein, vitamins and carbohydrates. Just what Max needed. I made him finish off three of the little plastic packets before letting him eat some marshmallows out of my cleavage.

After dinner, I slipped out of the tent and scouted around our lopsided little campsite. The rain hadn't started up again, but the other sleeping bag was nowhere near dry. I draped it across a couple of tree branches and sniffed the air. I didn't see or smell the yeti, but when I returned to the tent, I left the flap unzipped a few inches so I would be sure to know if the big fucker came back for seconds.

Max and I shared the remaining dry sleeping bag. He isn't exactly a small guy, so it was a pretty tight fit with both of us in there. But we needed the warmth and I didn't mind snuggling up close to Max. I made him lie on his good side and curled myself protectively around him.

We didn't sleep very much. Every sound made us both sit up and hold our breath. And each time we woke, Max's cock was poking my hip or nudging my hand. At first, it actually kind of surprised me. I can sense it when someone wants me, but I had been getting such strong and constant pings off of Max this whole trip – even while injured – that I had to measure his interest by his erection. To judge by the hard length, Max was interested. And to judge by the warm flutter in my stomach, so was I.

The night was long and restless, but not unpleasant.

In the morning, breakfast was more iodine-flavored water and some granola bars. I broke them into pieces and held each one up to Max.

"Hey, I can feed myself," he protested.

"Just because I didn't pack my stethoscope and slutty nurse costume doesn't mean that you get to start making your own medical decisions, mister."

Max laughed. "Well, I have to get up."

"No way," I said with a scowl. "You need rest to heal your stupid non-magical body. Whatever you want, tell me what it is and I'll get it for you."

"Okay, sure. Think you can go pee behind a tree for me?"

Max grinned at me and I rolled my eyes. When we were done making faces at each other, I helped Max out of the tent. The clouds seemed to have dropped their burden of rain and moved over the mountains, leaving the sky clear and blue. Still, the early morning air was cold enough to get me digging through our backpacks for a couple of Max's flannel shirts while he was off doing his business. He was struggling with the front of his jeans when he returned.

"I'm never bringing you on a job again," I told Max as I helped him with the zipper. "Unless I get some weird bounty that requires changing spark plugs or something. Non-murderous spark plugs."

"We'll see," Max said. "If you need me for anything, you know I'm not just going to sit at home."

I couldn't really argue with that. Without Max, I'd have been out of sexual energy long before we encountered the yeti. It would have torn me to pieces. Not that I liked what it did to Max any more...

I went to work breaking down camp and managed to mangle that, too. I couldn't get the tent back into its package or roll the sleeping bags up as tightly as Max had. I glared around at the camping supplies, wondering if they were magic. The evil kind of magic.

Stupid camping. Stupid yeti.

I checked Max's bandages. They had gotten wet last night in the rain, but not as badly as I expected. I'd gone a bit overboard on the medical tape, which actually served to keep the gauze beneath more or less dry. The butterfly sutures were still in place, too, despite a long evening of fucking.

When I was satisfied that nothing was going to fall out of Max, I helped him pull on a fresh shirt and used a second one to improvise a sling. It pinned his injured arm against his chest, a few inches below where the yeti had clawed him. I was actually kind of proud of the sling when I was finished. Maybe I would have made a decent Girl Scout after all. I already knew that I looked great in the uniform.

I refused to let Max carry his backpack, but we redistributed the remaining supplies so I could manage both packs more easily. But then Max unstrapped the rifle and slung it over his uninjured shoulder. I frowned and held out my hand for the gun.

"No," I told Max. "Not a chance."

"Just in case," he said.

"You can only use one arm, dummy!"

"If it's a matter of life and death," Max said with a lopsided shrug, "I'll figure it out. If it's not life or death, then I won't have to."

It was hard to tell if that was pride or practicality speaking, but I didn't really have any good arguments. And when it came down to it, I trusted Max.

I pulled some more clothes out of my backpack, selecting a pair of jeans and one of Max's flannel shirts that I tied off around my midriff. No reason I couldn't look like a mountain girl and a hot one at the same time. After I had dressed and eaten a few more marshmallows, I shouldered both backpacks and we got moving.

Max and I found our way easily enough back to the hiking trail. It was a little muddy after last night's rain, but we followed the path as it wound crookedly up the mountain. Unless the yeti had moved past us and down toward the city, I figured we would run across it eventually. Hopefully before it ate anyone else.

We hiked up through the mountains even more slowly than my first day on the trail. Max kept his pace up, but the path narrowed as we rose toward the timberline and he had only one hand to push aside branches or steady himself on the rocks. Even his right arm wasn't at full strength; the yeti's claws had cut deep into the muscles of his chest. It would be weeks or maybe months before Max was entirely healed.

I seriously considered tying a rope around Max – because of *course* he had thought to bring rope – to keep him from falling off of anything else. But that evoked all sorts of other naughty ideas and by the time I finished putting Max's back against the nearest tree and sucking another load of cum from his cock, I had forgotten all about tying my best friend up for more practical purposes.

Besides, Max was only half the reason for my decreased speed. I had no intention of letting that yeti surprise us a second time. Our last encounter with that fuzzy bastard had nearly killed Max and I would *not* risk that again.

So we scaled the mountain cautiously. I watched every shadow and scented every skirl of wind. And as the forest began to thin, I smelled something. Max saw me sniffing and unslung the rifle from his back. He held it against his hip and scanned the mountainside.

"Yeti?" he asked.

"No," I reported. "Human. The guy I smelled yesterday. He's up ahead."

I pointed along the mountain slope to a thick copse of aspen trees and purple-blossomed bushes. Max slung his rifle again and put his hand to his mouth.

"Hello?" he called.

We moved through the trees, shoving greenery out of the way. I broke several of the branches to keep them from smacking Max in the face. It was a good thing the College had chased all of the rangers out of the park for this hunt, or they would have had my ass. And not in the fun way.

Max was pushing ahead, hurrying in the direction I had indicated.

"Hey, are you alright?" he shouted.

I sniffed the air for blood or the yeti's stink. But what I smelled wasn't rotting meat, the coppery scent of blood, or even spent gunpowder. Mercury, phosphorous, fennel and myrrh. I was suddenly pretty sure I knew who owned that black Mercedes down at the base of the mountain.

"Ah, fuck," I said. "Max, stop!"

But he was already out of reach, ducking under aspen branches and waving his less-injured arm. I ran through the tangled green grass and to Max's side just as he lurched to a stop, staring. A man stood in a small clearing between the trees, pointing his wand at Max.

"Put that thing away, Doyle," I said.

"Uh... Lil?" Max asked. "What's going on?"

Doyle was a few years younger than either of us, with neat brown hair tied back from his face in a leather thong. Not the fun kind of thong. The College's most junior bounty hunter wore camouflage pants and a matching jacket covered in pockets. I smelled herbs and chemicals stored in each of them, all precisely measured and ready for whatever spells Doyle had prepared. The wizard scowled at me and kept his wand leveled at Max.

"You shouldn't be out here, Lilith," Doyle said.

"Why the hell not?" I asked. "I have just as much right to take this bounty as you do."

I flicked the tip of Doyle's wand. The polished wood zapped me like a static discharge. I pulled my hand back, shaking it. Doyle smirked briefly, then resumed glaring at Max.

"Who is this?" the wizard asked. "He's not from the College."

"He's my friend and he's none of your business," I said quickly.

Too quickly. Doyle's frown deepened.

Max smiled and waved again. "Uh... hi."

Doyle returned his attention to me. "You know that the College has launched an investigation into the demon summoned to *your* home. And now you bring a stranger – an uninitiated mortal – on your hunt? You're not building a good case for yourself, Lilith."

"A case? Wait, for what?" Max asked, his eyes going wide. "Lil, are you in some kind of trouble?"

I shook my head. "No. And I don't have to build a case for shit, Doyle. I know as much about summoning demons as you do about pleasuring women."

"Spare me your childish insults, Lilith," Doyle said, drawing himself up. "This is not your task. Not now. The yeti will be mine and you had best tend to your own increasingly suspect affairs."

I threw my hands into the air. "Oh my god! Do you guys practice that pretentious bullshit in the mirror?"

"The High Magus is watching you, Lilith," Doyle told me. He shook his wand at Max, who eyed the tip as though it were a live snake. "And will be fascinated to know what you have done here."

"Don't get me started on Vincent fucking Myrdon," I snarled. "This hunt is way over your head, Doyle. Go home!"

"How dare you!" the wizard hissed.

"Get the hell out of my way, kid. I've got a job to do and I'm not leaving this mountain without a yeti-skin rug."

Just between you and me, not really. Damn, that thing was ugly!

I stomped back through the underbrush in the direction of the path. There was plenty of daylight left. Max and I could make it to the summit by midafternoon. If the sky remained clear, there would be no rain to wash away the yeti's scent trail. Maybe I could track it instead of the other way around...

"No, Lilith," Doyle called out after me. "I'm not letting you endanger more innocent human lives!"

I didn't hear Max's footsteps behind me. When I looked over my shoulder, he still stood in front of Doyle. The wizard's wand remained leveled at his chest.

"Wait, what?" Max asked.

"I won't let you use this poor wounded fool as your bait, Lilith," Doyle announced. "I'm taking his memory of all this and getting him back to safety."

The wizard reached for one of his pockets. I smelled the cold weight of cobalt and Doyle's lips moved in the first unpronounceable syllable of the memory spell. My heart lurched to a stop and my blood seared in my veins. Max's eyes narrowed and he stepped back, hands balling into fists, but I was already there.

I was on Doyle in an instant, so fast that I doubt either of the men even saw me move. I seized Doyle's wand arm and yanked it away from Max.

"Don't you dare!" I snarled. "You have *no* idea what I would do to keep Max safe. None!"

I twisted Doyle's arm and felt the brittle wood of his wand snap in my grasp. He sank to his knees, howling in pain. Max's face went pale and I stared down at Doyle. It wasn't his wand that had broken – it was the wizard's arm. He cradled it against his chest.

"Half-breed whore!" Doyle screamed. "I always knew you would betray the College! The High Magus should have destroyed you years ago!"

To my credit, I didn't punch Doyle's stupid head off. I could have, and I really wanted to. But I just flipped Doyle off and grabbed Max's hand. I shoved an aspen branch out of our way so hard that the wrist-thick bough shattered and splinters of wood flew off into the bushes.

"Lil, wait!" Max said.

I began leading us in the direction of the trail again, but he drew back. There was no way to pull Max along without hurting him, so I stopped.

"We can't just leave him here." Max didn't have any free hands to point, so he nodded toward where Doyle sat shouting obscenities on the ground. "We're more than a day's hike from the road and everything's slippery from the rain."

"Fuck him!"

"Lil, the yeti's still out there! That thing was trouble for you with two good arms and super-strength." Max pulled away from me and began walking back toward Doyle. "He'll never make it alone."

"He was going to take your memory, Max!" I shouted.

"I know, Lil. But we have to help him. We have to get him off this mountain."

"I thought you didn't want to leave!"

"Things are different. We know who else is up here and... and now he's hurt."

"He started it! He tried to magic you!"

Max didn't say a word. He just looked at me. I kicked a rock and it went flying off into the bushes a hundred yards away.

"Okay, fine," I said with a sigh. "You're right. Doyle's not doing much magic without his wand hand and I guess we can't leave the little dickweed here to become yeti chow."

I stomped over to Doyle. The wizard had stopped shrieking long enough to crawl away from Max and was leaning with his back against an aspen tree, examining his injured arm. Doyle's attention snapped up to me and he grabbed for his fallen wand.

"Don't make me break your other arm," I told him. "Try anything and I swear I'll shove that wand right up your ass."

"What do you want now, Lilith?" Doyle asked sullenly.

I supposed he had been too busy screeching to listen. I crossed my arms over my chest. Max came to stand beside me.

"This guy you dismissed as bait talked me into helping you instead of leaving you here to become that sasquatch's bitch," I said.

Doyle scowled. "I don't want–"

"Yeah, I know you don't want my help," I finished with a growl. "And I don't really want to give it. But luckily for you, Max is a better person than either of us. So we're going to suck it up, play nice and get out of this shit together."

Chapter

SEVEN

I bent and retrieved Doyle's wand. It didn't zap me this time. I held it out to the wizard, who took the polished length of wood and tucked it into a leather holster under his arm like a gun.

"Very well," he said. "We'll leave this mountain together, since none of us are fit to hunt the yeti now."

I let that pass – barely – and helped Doyle splint his arm. Max sacrificed another shirt and I crafted a second sling. Doyle grumbled as I wrestled it into place and cast a sidelong glance at Max.

"Did she do this to you, too?" the wizard asked.

Max arched one eyebrow. "I'm just going to assume you mean the bandages and sling. Yeah, Lil's taken damned good care of me."

"Well, you're the only one getting the full naughty nurse treatment," I told him. "Doyle can take care of himself. Assuming he's left-handed."

Doyle spluttered. "Cambion slut–"

I tied the sling off behind his neck a little harder than was probably necessary. "Shut up, Doyle. You wizards always seem to conveniently forget that Merlin was a cambion, too. Without him, you would probably be studying accounting or something and wondering why you can't get laid."

Doyle began protesting again, but Max interrupted by asking if he wanted some aspirin. The wizard scoffed and went rummaging through his pockets. I watched him closely. Finally, Doyle brandished a curl of silver-gray bark.

"What's that?" Max asked.

"Willow bark," he answered.

"That's... pretty much the same thing as aspirin," said Max.

"Your aspirin hasn't been enchanted like this."

Doyle stuffed the bark into his mouth and chewed triumphantly. I uncapped the aspirin bottle and handed Max a few white tablets. He downed them with some water from his canteen and Doyle swallowed his tree bark with a grimace.

I put away the pills and shouldered our two backpacks, plus Doyle's leather rucksack. At least the young wizard looked suitably impressed at my strength. I helped both men to their feet.

"Alright, let's get you two the fuck off this mountain," I said.

I picked out the trail of broken branches and bent brush the way Max and I had come, following our own tracks back to the main path. I would make a Girl Scout yet. We found our way back to the trail and began climbing down the mountain.

A few hours later, Doyle's magic aspirin was holding up better than the commercial stuff, but the wizard just wasn't in the same physical condition as Max. Despite his youth, Doyle carried a little more weight around the middle – and I don't mean all of his ritual components. He wasn't a career hunter like Stefano.

But as the afternoon wore on, Max was beginning to flag, too. He had lost a lot of blood yesterday and wasn't exactly taking it easy. I had to stop often to help my one-armed companions past the roughest patches of trail. Max had given me plenty of sexual energy and I lamented that I wasn't quite big enough to throw one man over each of my shoulders and simply carry them down off the mountain.

The worst part of the climb wasn't far from where the yeti had tried to throw Max over the cliff. Some of the steep slope had softened in the rain and come loose, sliding out over the trail. The path was mired in mud and stones sufficiently treacherous to challenge even my footing.

After I helped Max and Doyle across the mudslide, we paused in the amber glow of the setting sun for another rest. Both of the boys were red-faced and sweating. Doyle drank the remainder of his water and wiped his arm across his forehead. Max gulped down another handful of aspirin and squinted toward the horizon.

"Lil, we're running out of light," he said.

"Yeah," I agreed. "What have you got in mind?"

"We're not too far from where we camped last night. Maybe we should stop there until morning."

I sighed. "Okay. You guys don't have so many intact limbs left that I want to risk breaking any more of them by crawling around in the dark."

"Yeah, we don't have your night vision," Max said with a nod.

And it would be nice to throw Max down – gently – and give him a proper fucking. I was willing to bet that Doyle could conjure some useful survival type stuff, too. He had been up here for a few days on his own and until I snapped his arm like a twig, the wizard seemed to have done just fine. Doyle was a dick, to be sure, but mages were never idiots and I had a lot of respect for their magic.

I shouldered our packs again and went to help Doyle stand, but froze with my hand extended. The other hunter sat against the trunk of a pine tree and scowled at me. He did that a lot.

"What is it now, Lilith?" he asked.

"Shut up!" I hissed.

I smelled something musty and disgusting – wet fur and rotten meat. A root creaked underfoot and mud squelched between claws.

I heard the deep, snorting breath of something smelling us out just as clearly as I smelled it. Tracking weak, wounded prey. I grabbed Doyle's wrist and yanked him upright hard enough to make the wizard yelp in pain.

"Max, incoming yeti!" I shouted. "Doyle, it's time to start doing our jobs!"

Rustling became loud crunching as the yeti closed in. Max swore and fumbled for his rifle. Doyle whirled on me, snatching at my sleeve with his functional hand.

"You crippled me on purpose!" he snarled. "You used me as bait, you demon bitch!"

"Get your head out of your ass and into the game, Doyle!"

I gave the sorcerer a shove and he staggered, but drew his wand awkwardly from the holster under his left arm. I struggled with the straps of three packs and managed to shake them off just as the yeti burst from the trees and out into the fading twilight. The monster was – if possible – even nastier and uglier than it had been yesterday. Mud streaked its horns and fur, but despite the rain, its claws were still black with blood. Max's blood.

And the fucker was hungry for more. The yeti didn't seem to give two shits about me and charged straight at the two injured men. To Doyle's credit, his expression remained furious but otherwise unfazed as the yeti let out a ravenous, blood-curdling howl. Max's face went pale.

I leapt into the yeti's path and it slammed right into me. The beast seemed surprised when the little human in front of it wasn't just bowled over, but not as surprised as when I jumped up and drop-kicked the motherfucker square in its ugly squashed face. The yeti was heavier than I expected, though, and the impact sent us both flying in opposite directions. Its clawed feet tore gouges into the stony mud and I bounced off across the trail.

The yeti recovered its balance faster than I did and bounded toward me again. At least I had its attention. For the moment.

Max had his rifle out and held it braced precariously against his clawed-up shoulder. He aimed and pulled the trigger. The bullet hit lower than yesterday's shots, below the monster's thick ribcage and hopefully into its more vulnerable viscera. The yeti let out a whining snarl that sounded promising, but the recoil from the gun drove Max to his knees, gasping in pain.

I moved in as the yeti spun to face Max and hammered a few rapid-fire punches into its shaggy side. My fists had a lot more mass than one of his bullets and a rib crunched under my assault. I leapt back as the yeti swung at me. It was fast enough to tear my sleeve, but not deeply into the arm beneath. I slid in behind the yeti and succeeded in breaking another rib before it could turn to face me again. I needed to soften the monster up before trying that neck-break a second time, or maybe pick it up and slam it down into some nice jagged rocks.

Unfortunately, the yeti didn't seem to have much appreciation for my plan. It slashed open my back as I was retreating, carving bloody lines across my spine that sent me sprawling into the mud. The cuts were already healing shut as I jumped up once more, but the yeti had taken advantage of the moment to lope off after the two wounded boys again. Opportunistic fucker.

Max was back on his feet and had managed to cock the rifle, firing another one-handed shot that missed the yeti entirely. He began retreating as the monster closed in, but then darted a glance down. Doyle knelt on the hiking trail, pulling paper-wrapped packages from his pockets and pouring their contents into a beaten copper bowl. With two working hands, the preparation was probably relatively quick, but Doyle kept fumbling his reagents and cursing loudly.

I threw myself at the yeti, tangling its legs with mine and dropping us both to the ground. The monster yowled and kicked at me, nearly ripping my leg off with its clawed foot. I shouted some curses of my own and rammed my knee up into the yeti's chest, just below its sternum. It snarled and head-butted me in the stomach with those huge, curving horns. I spat a mouthful of blood into the yeti's face and hammered my fist into its broad, flat nose.

Doyle finished mixing his spell and jumped up, holding the copper bowl aloft. Bright blue smoke billowed from the miniature cauldron as the wizard chanted. Before I could even try to understand what he was saying, Doyle lobbed his spell at the yeti's feet. Maybe the bowl was supposed to hit it in the head, but I couldn't blame Doyle for being a shitty shot with his off hand.

I could, however, blame him for not warning me. Fallen leaves and pine needles floated into the air as though someone had shut off the gravity. The yeti looked around, an expression of bestial confusion on its face, and then an expanding sphere of sapphire light hurled us both through the air. Leaves and mud tumbled as though caught in a hurricane.

"Lil!" Max shouted.

The yeti and I crashed through trees on the downslope side of the trail and we slammed into the ground just a few feet from the cliff where Max had come so close to death yesterday. My arms were dark with swiftly fading bruises and I was pretty sure the rest of me looked like a blueberry that had seen better days, but I charged at the yeti as it clambered back to its feet.

The yeti whirled inhumanly fast and brought its huge paws up. I seized its hands, my fingers interlocked with its long talons, and shoved. For a perfect moment, the yeti slid back through the mud and loose stone toward the cliff's edge, but then its toe claws sank into the earth and the yeti's backward slide halted. I had the high ground and barely superior strength, but that power was dwindling every time I used it and the yeti was a hell of a lot bigger than me.

I planted my heels against a tree root and pushed, but the wood cracked beneath my boots and I slipped back an inch. The yeti bit my arm, sinking dirty yellow fangs deep into my flesh. I shouted and lost another inch of ground.

"Lil!"

Max ran down the mountain toward me. His sling dangled empty around his neck and there was no sign of his rifle.

"What are you doing?" I shouted.

Max just groaned in pain as he threw his weight against the yeti. He wasn't nearly as strong as me or the monster, but he was another two hundred and fifty pounds on my side of the scales. Would it be enough?

The yeti twisted in my grip, trying to free one paw to slash at Max. I tightened my fingers on its thick, hairy hands as Max grunted like a weight lifter going for a new record and hurled himself against the yeti again. It snarled and sank sharp claws into my imprisoning hands. Blood streamed down my wrists, but I didn't let go. The yeti smashed its head into mine and I saw red stars. I still didn't let go.

"Max, get back!" I hissed.

He didn't. Max squared himself and hammered his good arm down between the yeti's legs. The monster growled and its knees softened. Just a little, but that was all I needed. I pushed and shoved with every ounce of strength. This time, the yeti moved. It slid, toppled and then fell over the cliff.

But the yeti's hooked yellow claws were still sunk deep into the flesh of my hands. The weight of the thrashing monster dragged me to my knees. I'm not ashamed to admit that I screamed. I slipped in mud and blood, kicking and writhing. The yeti's claws tore free and the monster plummeted into the darkness – but too late for me. I couldn't recover my balance.

I was falling.

And then strong arms wrapped around my waist and heaved me back up onto solid earth. Max bore me to the ground a few feet from the cliff edge, still clutching me close. His face was pale and shone with sweat. Red blossomed across his bandages and his arms shook around me.

After a long moment of trembling and panting and bleeding, I climbed to my hands and knees. The terrible slashes of the yeti's claws were already vanishing from my skin as I crawled cautiously to the edge of the cliff. I leaned out to look down below.

Sharp rocks! Yay!

Somewhere further up the slope, I heard Doyle shouting my name, sounding more suspicious than worried. I ignored him and squinted through the growing shadows. I had just enough light and sex-powered vision left to make out the yeti far, far below. There was bright red splashed across the rocks where the beast's innards had become its outards.

"Is... is it dead?" Max wheezed.

"Yeah," I said. "Yeti spaghetti."

I collapsed to the cool, damp ground beside Max once more and punched him as lightly as I could in the shoulder. It didn't matter which one anymore – they were both equally fucked up.

"That was so stupid!" I said. "Brave-stupid! Damn it, Max! We're never doing this again!"

I flopped bonelessly against Max, draping my arm across his stomach, and kissed him soundly.

Chapter
EIGHT

*T*wo days later, I pulled into the parking lot of Max's garage. I glanced around for Taya's car, but there was no sign of it. The garage doors were rolled open, so I grabbed the heavy, clinking bag from my passenger seat and walked right in. Max looked up from the engine of someone's Volvo and nodded.

"Hey, Lil."

"Hey, Max."

"So... is the College coming to wipe my memory?" he asked slowly. "Am I counting down the final moments of remembering you, Lil? If so, there are some things I need to tell you..."

"No. I convinced Doyle that I would take care of your memories with Dorian when I turned over the photos of the ex-yeti, but the College is so busy with Evaine's death and trying to find Asmodai's accomplice that I doubt anyone will notice that it didn't get done."

"But what if they do?" Max asked. "I don't want you getting in trouble because of me, Lil."

"If it comes down to that, I'm pretty sure I can get Stefano or Dorian to do me a favor. And if that doesn't work, I can always go kick down the High Magus' door. I won't let them take your memories, Max."

"Thanks, Lil."

Max moved to hug me, but then saw the grease on his hands and blushed. He turned away and went to the sink to wash them. I hoped Max wouldn't notice the dark smudge on his chin. I set my bag down on his workbench.

"How's the shoulder?" I asked.

"Sore, but working. I'm still taking it easy."

"And your chest?"

"The doctors bought the mountain lion story and told me I was damned lucky."

"They don't know the half of it," I said.

I had been the one to drive Max to the emergency room when we finally made it back down the mountain, and suggested the cover story. After all, it was the same story the College had told the yeti's other victims.

"I'm not allowed to lift anything heavier than ten pounds for at least the next few weeks," Max said. He finished washing his hands and dried them on a wad of blue paper towels. "And even then, I'll probably need some physical therapy. The yeti cut through a lot of muscle."

"I'm sorry, Max."

"It's okay, Lil. Really."

Max double-checked that his hands were clean and then gave me a hug. He hadn't noticed the grease on his chin.

"Want to see what they did?" Max asked.

I nodded. With a little help, Max managed to pull his shirt up over his head. The yeti's claw marks were jagged red lines across his chest and I inspected them closely. Max had real stitches now. The work was good and he was healing quickly, but they would still leave scars.

Actually, though... they were kind of sexy. I bit my lip. I guess chicks really do dig scars.

"What's in the bag?" Max asked.

I blinked a couple of times and then went back to the work-bench. I unzipped the bag and withdrew several shining gold bars, stacking them up on the counter. Max's eyes went wide.

"This is your share of the bounty," I told him. "Doyle wanted to go fifty-fifty since he helped. Dick. I pointed out that you helped more than he did and we finally settled on a three-way split. I love three-ways."

I grinned and Max spluttered.

"That's about thirty thousand dollars on the market today," I told him. "But hang onto it for a while. You can probably get thirty-five or forty if you wait for the right time to cash it in."

Max stared at the gold for a moment, then pushed the gleaming stack back toward me.

"I was just glad to help," he said.

I expected something like this. I pushed the gold at Max again.

"You earned it," I told him.

Max shook his head. "Look, Lil... Why don't you keep it? Put it toward the loan for the garage. It's not even a fraction of what I borrowed from you."

When he reached out to nudge the gold toward me, I placed my hand over his.

"No," I said. "I owe you a lot more than money, Max. You've been there for me when no one else was. None of the other hunters, not my father or even Evaine. She was amazing and taught me so much, but she was mysterious and unpredictable. You're the one still here with me."

Max swallowed hard and looked down at my hand on his, but he didn't argue with that. Good.

"Things are complicated right now and scary as fuck," I said, then drew a shuddering breath. "I don't understand what Asmodai needs with a cambion. With me. When the College finds his wizard buddy, I want to be there to find out. And I owe him a few good crotch punches for Reid."

Max smiled a little at that and nodded his agreement. He put his other hand on top of mine and squeezed gently.

"But no matter how shitty the rest of my life gets," I said, "I can deal with it. As long as I have my best friend right there with me."

"Always, Lil. But I don't do it for the money."

Max tightened his hands over mine and started pushing the gold bars toward me. I gave him my brightest, sweetest smile.

"I know," I said. "But if you try to give that gold back again, I'm going to shove it all right up your cute ass."

Max laughed and raised his hands in surrender. At some point during our debate, the grease on his chin had gotten smeared into a line along his cheek, like an exclamation point to his dimples.

"One condition," Max said.

"Nope," I told him. "No conditions. One way or another, you're getting the gold you earned."

Max dropped his hands again and nodded. His expression became serious. "Fine, forget conditions and rules. Just... stop staying at that hotel, Lil."

"What?"

"You're right. Things are complicated and frightening. You've lost so much and I know you're still hurting. But you don't need to be alone through this."

"Max..." I said.

"Stay here with me until you get everything else sorted out. We'll watch movies and eat junk food until I get sick and you laugh your ass off at me. Just like high school."

I drew a deep breath and looked up at Max.

"...Okay," I said.

Max blinked. "Really?"

"Yeah. I'll stay here for a while. Just until I get a new place."

Max's face lit up and he enfolded me in a hug so tight that it probably would have made his doctors frown, but I wrapped my arms around him, too. It felt good.

"When this is all done, you should think about taking an actual vacation," Max said. He didn't let go of me. "Not camping, though. Maybe a cruise or something. Get away from it all."

"Will you come with me?" I asked.

Max looked down at me, grinning. "Hmm, maybe. Two questions: are mermaids real, and are they scary?"

Dirty HANDS

Max's bed still smelled like him, but it was empty when I sat up. I smacked the pillow a few times to punish it for not being my best friend, but then I heard the distinctive clank of steel and the quiet thunder of heavy metal echoing from the garage downstairs. Max was already at work.

Staying with Max had saved me a lot in hotel bills over the last couple of weeks, but it wasn't like money was a problem. None of my bank accounts had been blown up when I lost my condo, after all. It was strange living with someone else, going to bed in someone's arms... and waking up there, too. It was all weird and new and shocking how quickly I started missing Max when he got up early.

I slid from the tangle of sheets and padded out of the bedroom. Amber morning light streamed through the windows. Waffles and bacon sat under a sheet of aluminum foil on the kitchen counter, with a note on top from Max urging me to eat up. I smiled at the note, but dropped it back onto the counter and left the food where it was.

There was something else I wanted for breakfast.

I crept down the stairs toward the garage. The old wooden steps creaked softly under my feet and I froze, listening, but there was no way Max could hear me over the sounds of Slayer and the equally metallic clank of... whatever he was working on. I like cars, but Max is the one who knows which bit is which inside of one. My expertise is a little different, though it also involves getting motors running.

So I strode past Max's office and into the garage. The old fire station's big steel doors were still rolled down until regular business hours began, but I guess Max was getting an early start. Or maybe he did this all the time – I was learning more about my best friend every day.

Max stood bent over the engine of a nice but ridiculously over-sized silver Cadillac. He pried at one of the bolts inside with a wrench that was nearly as massive and silver. Max wore a t-shirt bearing the logo of his newly opened shop and a pair of jeans that made his ass look spectacular. That part wasn't a new discovery – I knew perfectly well how great Max's ass was.

I hit the *pause* button on the stereo and Max backed out from under the Cadillac's hood. The crescent wrench remained cinched tight around one of the engine bolts. Max's hands were black with grease.

"Good morning," he said. "Did I wake you? I was trying to keep it down... Uh... Lil?"

Max straightened and stared at me. I hadn't bothered getting dressed and now stood naked in the middle of his garage. Max's deep blue eyes went wide and he grinned.

"Wow, Lil. Have I ever told you how beautiful you are?" he asked me.

I shrugged, making my bare breasts bounce, and managed not to grin back. "You've mentioned it a few times."

"Well, then maybe I should just show you," Max said. "If you're tired of being told..."

He took a step back, turning toward the sink to wash his hands, but I hooked my fingers over the waist of his jeans. Max stopped instantly, holding his grease-stained hands up away from me.

"Wait," said Max. "Lil, I need to wash my hands..."

I pulled him in closer, until my breasts rubbed against the fabric of his shirt, and stretched up onto my toes to cut Max off with a long kiss. He tasted like spearmint toothpaste. Max's words trailed off into a low groan against my lips.

His filthy hands began falling toward my shoulders, to grab me and hold me to him, but then jerked upward again. I ran my fingers along Max's chest and stomach, feeling the hard planes of muscles and the raised lines of healing scars there, then down over the front of his jeans. His groan rose in volume and dropped in pitch.

"Lil," he murmured into my mouth. "Give me just a minute to clean up and then I'll kiss every gorgeous inch of you–"

"No," I said.

My fingers reached the zipper of Max's jeans and I felt the swelling hardness there. He broke the kiss and stared down at me. I grinned at him.

"What?" Max asked. "Lil, what are you doing?"

My only answer was to grab the tab of his zipper and pull it down. That hiss of metal on metal was suddenly just as loud as his work on the Cadillac had been.

I could have waited for Max to wash up. Believe it or not, I actually *can* restrain myself a little. Max has always been fastidious about keeping his hands clean and moisturized for me, and had been doing it for long enough that he could get through the entire routine in only about three minutes. But if I didn't let Max go clean the grease off, he couldn't touch me. He would never risk getting that shit on my hair or skin.

I had Max at my mercy.

He stood there with his dirty hands held up in the air, like he had been caught doing something naughty, and stared wide-eyed as I knelt and reached into his jeans. My fingertips brushed over the cloth of his boxers and I felt the heat of his cock as though the fabric were no barrier at all. Max's jaw clenched but failed to bite back another groan. His dick throbbed in my hand and I felt a tiny spot of wetness on his boxers where the head of his cock strained against them. I rubbed my fingers over the little spot of precum and grinned up at Max.

I slipped my hand into Max's boxers and pulled out his cock. It was already longer than my hand and fully hard, making it a bit difficult to maneuver through his zipper. But no one knows their way around Max's dick like I do and it was soon jutting from his jeans toward me, flushed pink all along its length and then darker at the head.

Making sure Max was watching – which he was, raptly – I ran my thumb over the tip of his cock. He groaned again at the sensation and I brought my thumb up to my mouth and slowly sucked the warm precum from my skin. *My* hands were perfectly clean, after all. I let out a small moan at the taste and Max's raised hands clenched into fists.

"Oh god, Lil," he said. "Just let me wash my hands and I'll fuck you *so* hard, I swear…"

"Nope."

Max darted a desperate look over his shoulder, in the direction of the sink, but then I closed my soft lips around his cock and his eyes snapped back to me. His dick was smooth in my mouth, but hot and heavy, too. Max's girth forced my jaw open just a bit more than was comfortable, reminding me how huge he was. I let out a muffled little moan that made Max's hands tighten even more. His knuckles became a row of black-smudged spots of white.

I hooked my fingers through the belt loops of Max's jeans and pulled myself in, sliding his cock into my mouth and deep down my throat. I choked a bit, but I knew what I was doing. Saliva ran down the length of Max's dick not yet in my mouth and darkened the front of his jeans.

I pulled Max closer and swallowed the last thick inches of him. It wasn't easy to maneuver with so much in my mouth, but as I said,

I'm an expert. I swirled my tongue around Max's cock. The skin was silky and delicate, but the hardness beneath was like stone. Max groaned and I felt the deep note as much through his dick in my mouth as with my ears.

"Lil," he said in a low voice. "Please... I need to touch you..."

Maybe he did. But Max needed to cum, too. I felt it in the thick, hot pulse of his cock between my lips. And I needed to make him cum. My pussy ran wet with anticipation.

But not yet. I drew back, pulling my mouth off Max's cock inch by inch and leaving the flushed shaft shiny and wet. A silvery line of saliva connected his dick to my lips for a second, then spattered down to my bare chest. The tiny splash sent an electric thrill coursing through me.

I placed a gentle kiss on the end of Max's cock. He groaned. I blew a soft breath over the wet, sensitive length and his groan deepened. Goosebumps rose along Max's tensed arms. His lust glowed so hot that I wondered if it could actually burn. Even without my sex-powered super-hearing, I would have been able to hear Max's heart pounding like a drum. The muscles of his chest and shoulders were bunched so taut that they strained against his t-shirt, threatening to tear out a seam. But his black-smeared hands remained raised over his head.

"Lil, *please*...!" Max begged.

I slid my fingers across the front of his jeans and wrapped them around his slicked cock. His teeth clacked together as his jaw snapped shut against a louder sound of pleasure. I moved my hand up along his dick until I felt the larger, slightly softer weight of the head in my fingers. I twisted my hand a little, tracing a tight crescent over Max's most sensitive flesh.

With just a couple of spiraling caresses, I had Max on the edge again. I felt his pulse throbbing along the length of his cock and every stroke smeared pale precum down Max's shaft. My pussy blazed with liquid heat and wetness dripped from between my legs, leaving darkened spots across the concrete floor. I had to loosen the circle of my fingers around Max's dick, barely brushing them over his hardness, just to keep him from blowing his load. And to keep myself from pouncing on him like the cock-hungry little whore that I absolutely am.

Max's nails were biting into his palms. Thick white welled up from the head of his dick in an unending stream now, like he was cumming in slow motion. He groaned my name over and over. Begging, or maybe it was more like a prayer. Both...? Max was helpless in my hands, poised on the edge of climax and I was the one who held him there.

And the one who could release him. I tightened my fingers around Max and fed his huge, crimson-flushed cockhead into my mouth. There was only a moment to feel the searing heat of him on my tongue and then Max let out a sound that was half groan, half growl. Wetness gushed along my inner thighs from my untouched pussy. I would have felt humiliated at my own desperate show of desire if only it didn't feel so *good*.

"Lil," Max breathed. "Shit, I... I can't stop!"

Max's whole body went as rigid and hard as a statue. His cock swelled between my lips, so long and huge that I couldn't swallow any more, and then cum flooded my mouth. God, so much of it... I gulped down hot, thick cream, but still there was more. My mouth was so full of sticky semen that it ran from the corners of my lips and along my chin in bright white lines.

More... I sucked Max frantically, urgently coaxing every last drop of cum from his pulsing dick. At least half of it just streamed from my overfilled mouth, but I drank down the rest like it was the most delicious thing I had ever tasted. Because it was.

When he was done, I licked my lips and looked up at Max. He stared down at me with wide, deep blue eyes. I smirked as I swiped a finger through the cum that had dribbled down to my breasts, then raised it to my mouth and lapped at the oozing mess. Max's eyes narrowed into sapphire slits.

"You're all dirty now, Lil," he growled.

A grin spread across Max's face and he bent, wrapping his arms around my waist. His filthy hands left black streaks all over my pale skin.

"Max!" I shrieked. "Your hands! Your shoulder...!"

"It's healed up enough for this," he said.

"Healed up enough for what?"

Max threw me over his good shoulder and carried me easily toward the door out of the garage. I kicked my legs, but he just tightened his grease-smeared grip.

"What are you doing?" I cried.

"Well, since we're both dirty," Max told me, "we're taking a shower. Now."

I could have broken free easily. Even without my super powers, I'm a trained killing machine. But who would ever want to escape Max? I giggled and squirmed just enough to make it fun as he carried me upstairs.

Yes, living with Max was strange. Strange and good.

LILY QUINN BOOK #12

SPELLS OF
Binding

Chapter ONE

I sat in Max's dining room with my laptop open on the table, browsing through real estate listings... well, listlessly. There were plenty of nice houses and condominiums for sale in the city, and I had more than enough money to buy one. But for some reason, none of them seemed quite right. I kicked my chair back, resting my bare feet on the tabletop, and looked across the dining room.

"You don't have to cook for me, you know," I said.

Max smiled at me from the kitchen. He stood in front of the stove wearing a pair of boxers, a well-worn apron, and nothing else. He flipped a couple of pancakes on the griddle and shrugged his broad shoulders.

"Hey, I eat breakfast too," Max said. "I just make a little extra for you, Lil. It's no trouble."

"A *little* extra?" I repeated, nodding toward the huge tower of finished pancakes on the counter and the steaming heap of scrambled eggs beside them.

"I need more than a bowl of cereal to pull out an entire engine block. And I know you need a good breakfast to fight boogeymen, too."

Max removed the final pancakes from the stove and added them to the stack. He poured a tall glass of orange juice and then carried it all to the table. I dug into the eggs while Max sprayed whipped cream over the pancakes until the can began to splutter. We had eaten most of it off each other a few days ago. So Max topped off the pancakes with a handful of diced strawberries and pushed them across the table to me.

Maxwell Ferguson, king of best friends. Ladies and gentlemen, eat your hearts out.

I ate fast. Not that I didn't enjoy Max's cooking – I just enjoyed it quickly. I devoured twice as much as he did in the same amount of time. Max sat across from me and smirked. I've been able to outpace his appetite since we were teenagers. And Max was never a small guy, so feel free to be impressed.

Max doesn't tease me about how I eat... much. But to judge by his contemplative expression, Max was trying to come up with a really good jab. But my computer made a sudden pinging sound, interrupting Max before he could quite figure out what joke to make. I stopped with a heaping forkful of pancakes and strawberries halfway up to my mouth.

"Something wrong, Lil?" Max asked.

"Uh, not exactly," I said with a frown. I put down my fork. "Just weird. I got an email."

"If you think that's weird, maybe you've been spending too much time with the wizards."

I reached across the table and tugged on the ties that held Max's apron up around his neck. The top flopped down across the table, exposing his bare chest and the healing claw marks that a yeti sliced into him last month. Max made no move to cover himself and I smirked at him.

"No, that's not the weird part," I said. "There's no sender listed on the email."

I wiped my hands off on a napkin and clicked the notification.

There was no subject line, either. I opened the email up and read it. Then I read it again. Max watched me with obvious curiosity in his expression, but remained quiet.

"Vincent Myrdon has taken the other hunters off their current jobs," I read out slowly. "All bounties are suspended until further notice."

"What?" Max asked. "Why?"

"To... to hunt down the infernalist who created Reid."

I shoved my breakfast away and read the email a third time. Max put down his silverware and came around the table to look over my shoulder.

"You mean the wizard who works for Asmodai, that incubus who killed Evaine?" he asked. "That guy?"

"Yeah," I answered.

"But I thought the College didn't do email."

"They don't, really. But this isn't from the College," I said. "At least, not officially."

"Maybe Stefano sent it?"

A very few of the wizards – especially the younger ones, like the other monster hunters – stooped to carrying cell phones and could even use the internet when they absolutely had to. Stupid wizards don't go far, so it wasn't entirely outside the realm of possibility that a couple of them might know how to send an email. Out of character, certainly, but not impossible.

But it still didn't make any sense. Why not just call me? Why didn't the sender tell me who they were? For plausible deniability, perhaps?

Or maybe after everything I had done for them, the College *still* didn't trust me.

Of all the wizards in the city, the two most likely to slip me a little extra information were Dorian and Stefano. Dorian Vandi was a part of the inner circle of elder sorcerers and handled College bounties, including the hunters and their payment. The old mage never seemed to hold my half-demon heritage against me, but I doubted he ever used technology more recent than 1920s fare. The chances of Dorian sending an email were pretty damned remote.

That left Stefano Rossi. The other bounty hunter was the only wizard that I could actually call a friend – often friends with benefits, like sex and information.

Well, I needed one of those things right now, so I went to the bedroom to grab my phone off the nightstand and tapped Stefano's name in my contacts list. After three rings, I figured that I would just leave a voicemail, but then the line actually picked up.

"Lilith?"

I recognized Stefano's voice. He sounded surprised.

"Hey, Stefano," I said. "What's–?"

"I'm not going after that witch anymore, Lilith," he answered too quickly. "There's no information for you to squeeze out of me."

I frowned at my cell phone. Squeezing anything out of Stefano usually included a big load of his cum, too. It always drove him crazy when I beat him to his own bounty, but Stefano's *never* been able to resist me before.

"Uh…" I said. "Look, I'm more interested in the new job, the one that the College is sending everyone after now. The one on Reid's creator."

"Lilith, that's not a posted bounty. This is an internal College matter and there's no gold in catching him. How do you even know about this?"

"Don't worry about it, Stefano. I guess the witch is all mine."

I hung up and sat at the table again. I frowned at my breakfast and Max looked at me, brow furrowed.

"Sounds like Stefano didn't send that email," he said. "What about one of the other hunters? Would any of them give you the heads-up?"

"I don't think I've traded ten words with Griffith or Redmond in the entire time they've been hunting for the College. After that yeti business last month, Doyle hates me even more than usual. And I've never even seen Sabra."

"What about the other one? Clio?" Max asked.

"We've spoken a few times and I manage to refrain from making fun of her accent."

"Accent?"

"Clio's from Nebraska. Lot's of *ain't* and *y'all*. Doyle and Redmond never miss a chance to give her shit about it. Clio takes it all in stride, though."

"So do you think you should get involved, Lil?" Max asked.

"With Clio?" I spun my phone on the tabletop. "Hmm. Blonde, curvy, lots of attitude... I'd definitely go there. Just haven't had the opportunity."

"No, I mean with this hunt."

Max didn't remind me what happened the last time I forced my way into a hunt after I was specifically warned away, but he didn't have to. I remembered. Reid died. Evaine died. And for a moment, I really considered backing off. Let the College corner Reid's creator and settle it in a wizard's duel or something. But I just couldn't.

"I have to do this, Max," I told him. "If the College knows who created Reid and is helping Asmodai with... with whatever that demonic asshole's doing... then I want a piece of him. I owe Reid and Evaine that much."

Max laced his fingers together and looked across the table at me. Slowly, he nodded.

"Alright, Lil. I understand," Max said. He probably even did. "I can close up the shop today if you need me."

"What did you have in mind?"

"I'm not sure," Max admitted. "But I helped with the yeti."

"And nearly got yourself killed."

Max touched his fingertips to the healing claw marks across his chest. "I'm fine. And I'd do it all over again in a second if it would help you, Lil."

And I knew he meant it. The desire to leap over the table and pounce Max was strong. We had already fucked each other's brains out twice that morning... But I shook my head.

"I don't think you can help with this," I said. "Not yet."

"Okay. You let me know if you need me for anything, Lil."

"I will," I promised.

"Then I'll be in the garage," Max said.

He finished the last of his pancakes, deposited his plate in the sink and kissed my head before going to the bedroom to change clothes. A few minutes later, Max was downstairs, starting his day. The comforting whir and clank of tools and the double-kick beat of heavy metal echoed through his apartment.

I wolfed down the rest of my breakfast and went to get dressed, too. If I wanted to find Asmodai's infernalist buddy, I would have to play catch-up.

The other hunters were already several steps ahead of me. The High Magus had given them the job and, presumably, the information to get it done. I needed to know what they did, but Stefano was refusing to share. That left his source and hoping I had the leverage to demand some answers.

Chapter
TWO

I managed not to break any land-speed records on the freeway or even up the empty, winding road that led to the College, but I was driving fast enough that I almost crashed right into the front gate when it didn't open at my approach. I slammed on the brakes and skidded to a stop less than a foot from the thick iron bars.

What the fuck? I climbed out of my car and waved my arms at the two massive stone gargoyles perched on the posts. They didn't move, of course – they never do when I'm watching – and the gate remained stubbornly shut. I scowled at it. Somehow, I doubted this was just a random magical malfunction.

I turned my car off and left it in the middle of the driveway, then stalked to the high, ivy-covered wall that surrounded the College. Living with Max gave me constant access to his cock, which I took advantage of often and left me pretty much always full up on sexual power.

I coiled my legs beneath me, judged the distance, and leapt over the perimeter wall. I landed lightly on the other side and jogged down the driveway toward the sprawling complex of old brick mansions. The last of summer had faded and the sky overhead was streaked in silvery clouds. A misty autumn rain beaded on my old leather jacket and my shoes kicked up sprays of water from the wet grass.

The gates weren't closed to everyone, apparently. There were six vehicles parked in front of Dresden Hall and I recognized Stefano's truck among them. It was a more recent model than Max's, but in much worse shape. There were some deep claw marks in the rear fender that looked new.

Beside the bashed-up truck were Doyle's shiny black Mercedes and Sabra's big windowless van. I wasn't familiar with the other pickup truck, the motorcycle, or the gray sedan with no plates, but I could guess who they belonged to: Clio, Redmond, and Griffith.

The front doors of Dresden Hall swung open and I skidded to a stop in the driveway as the other bounty hunters stepped out. All of them – minus Sabra, of course. Stefano strode at the head of the pack, ticking something off on his fingers as he spoke. Doyle was right behind him, gesticulating with the arm I had broken last month. I suspected magical healing and scowled again. No one had offered that shit to Max when the yeti tried to carve out his heart.

I started toward the hunters. Stefano glanced up from Doyle and jerked to a halt when he saw me. The other wizards followed Stefano's gaze and fell silent.

"Lilith? What are you doing here?" he asked.

I crossed my arms. "What the fuck, guys? This infernalist is a big enough job to have you all teaming up, but you don't call me?"

"This isn't a bounty," Stefano said. "There's no gold, Lilith. I told you – this is a College matter. It's our duty to deal with it."

"And I'm not one of you, right?"

Stefano looked uncomfortable and seemed to be trying to think of something to say that would smooth this all over, but then two more figures appeared in the open doors of Dresden Hall. One of Sabra's huge homunculi was escorting an almost equally oversized human who came up short when he caught sight of me.

"Muir!" I snarled.

"Ah, shite," he said.

The big Scottish man was one of the two surviving wizards who had summoned a succubus the year before and promptly, predictably lost control of her. They tried to banish the demoness back to the Nether, but accidentally caught Ben Sung in their spell and turned him into a ghost. To cover up what they had done, Muir and Finn attempted to murder Ben a second time, along with his little brother, Rick. When I went to put an end to *that* bullshit, the two wizards managed to capture and then fuck me down in Finn's sanctum.

Okay, I didn't mind that last part so much. But Muir was supposed to be serving a life sentence in the Tower for his crimes. Unless something had changed... Had the College caught Muir doing something even worse?

I charged past Stefano before he could say another word, seized Muir by his beard and yanked his face down to mine. Sabra's homunculus reached for me, but I swatted its huge hand away so hard that one thick clay finger went clattering back through the door and across the tiled foyer.

"Was it you?" I shouted. "Did you summon Asmodai? Are you the reason Evaine's dead?"

Muir stared down at me. His eyes were wide and dark, full of a fear that I had never seen there, not even when I was beating the shit out of him in Finn's sanctum.

Good.

"Lilith, stop!" Stefano said.

He tried to pry me off Muir, but I didn't budge. Griffith grabbed my other arm and heaved, too. Neither of them could pull me away.

"If you did it," I snarled into Muir's face, "you're not going back to your cushy Tower cell–"

"He wants to help," Griffith said. "The High Magus has granted Muir a temporary release to lend us his expertise."

"Muir used to be a hunter, too," Stefano reminded me. He had stopped tugging, but his hand remained on my shoulder. "And he has... experience with demon summoning. Muir's going to help us catch–"

Griffith gave Stefano a sharp look and shook his head, setting his impressive collection of dreadlocks swinging. Stefano sighed and let go of me. He stepped away and gestured to Griffith, who did the same, though the tall hunter crossed his arms over his chest and continued to frown at me. Despite the autumn chill, Griffith's arms were bare to display dark skin thickly tattooed with curving lines of intricate sigils that suddenly reminded me of Muir's protective blue woad paint. That spell had proven frighteningly effective against my attempts to punch Muir's head off his shoulders. Griffith might not have been able to move me, but that didn't mean he would just stand idly by if I decided to kill Muir.

I looked down at Muir, who knelt on the ground with an unhappy expression on his face. Was it possible that he actually felt some remorse for the things he had done? Enough to try to make amends? I scowled at Stefano and Griffith.

"I hope you're keeping a close eye on this big bastard," I said. I released Muir's beard and took a step back. "You know he's a total dick, right?"

Stefano nodded. "He goes nowhere alone and we are controlling his access to reagents."

Muir rose slowly to his feet and didn't look me in the eye. I put my hands on my hips.

"So you're letting *this* asshole join the hunt, but not me?" I protested. "You need me! I'm the one who found Reid!"

"And killed the golem before we could question him," Clio said. The tiny blonde wore a flannel shirt against the misty autumn rain and her plaid arms were crossed, too. "You ain't a wizard and you ain't exactly got a stellar record on this."

Doyle snickered. Griffith elbowed him in the ribs.

"Ow," Doyle grumbled, rubbing his side.

I ignored them. If anyone was in charge of this shitfest, it was Stefano. He was irritatingly fuckable even now, with all that delicious olive skin, sultry dark eyes and handsome face roughened just the right amount by his close-cut beard.

"I'm the best hunter in the city," I told him in a quiet voice. "You need me. And I need this, Stefano. Let me help. We're a good team."

"Not this time, Lilith." Stefano ran his hand through the mahogany waves of his hair and his expression looked truly pained. "We have orders from the High Magus. I'm sorry. Really."

I nodded and stepped back. "Fine. Good hunting, Stefano."

"Thank you, Lilith," he said, then turned to the other wizards. "Let's move."

Sabra's homunculus took Muir by the arm again and escorted him toward her parked van. The hulking clay construct didn't even seem to notice the loss of its finger. Stefano gave me a final unhappy look, then walked away with the rest of the hunters.

Griffith fell into step beside him. "We can cover more ground if we split up."

"I'm not letting Muir operate on his own," Stefano said as they made their way toward their cars. "Let's just get what we need for the divination and see what it shows us. We can't plan properly until we have more information."

"Who the hell put *him* in charge?" Doyle grumbled under his breath to Redmond. He said it quietly, but my sex-powered hearing caught every word.

"I don't remember the last time the rest of y'all went toe-to-toe with a werewolf," Clio said. She practically had to jog to keep up with the much taller men.

"We're not hunting a werewolf," Redmond pointed out.

Clio began to argue, but then darted a glance back at me and snapped her mouth shut. I guess she knew I was listening. Without another word, the other hunters piled into their vehicles. At least they would have an annoying time getting around my i10, which was still parked in the middle of the driveway just outside the College gates.

I turned away from Dresden Hall and the departing wizards. Fuck them. I wasn't out of the hunt just yet. I stalked across the lawns and gardens toward a short, domed building cloaked in ivy – the observatory.

The big bronze doors banged open as I shoved my way through them and a dozen junior wizards looked up from their piles of star maps. An older mage raised his eyes from the telescope to watch me stride across the observatory. None of the rain outside fell into the open dome.

I ignored their shocked looks and questions as I stormed right through the observatory to the mahogany door in the back. It was shut tight. Did I really want to do this?

Yes.

I pounded on the office door and shouted. "Vincent!"

I grabbed the doorknob and twisted. It didn't turn. This had to be the first time a knob didn't do what I wanted it to... I hammered my fist against the door again.

"Vincent Myrdon!" I called out. "I need to talk to you!"

Nothing. I stepped back to give myself room and kicked the door right in the middle of the High Magus' verdigrised nameplate. I smashed into wood and metal with all of my sex-fueled strength. The sound of the impact reverberated like a cannon shot through the observatory, but the door didn't budge. My foot didn't even leave a mark.

Magic door, huh?

Fine.

I examined the marble door frame and the walls to either side. The College might have enchanted the door, but what about the stone around it? I cocked my fist back to find out.

"Just come in, Lilith," Vincent said from inside.

His voice was muffled by the door, but still hard and deep. I tried the knob again and this time, it turned easily in my hand. I pushed through the door and slammed it closed behind me.

Vincent Myrdon's office was larger than it looked from the outside, but all of that space was crowded with bookshelves and a desk so colossal that it probably took an entire oak tree to build. The leader of the College sat in a high-backed chair behind the wooden monolith and several thick tomes lay open across the top. Vincent appeared to have been in the middle of taking notes from all of them.

His silver hair was swept back and his already steep widow's peak seemed to have become even more pronounced. The streaks of auburn in his neatly trimmed goatee were fewer, too, being slowly enveloped by gray. But there was still enough left to see how vividly red it must have been when Vincent Myrdon was a younger man – the same color as my hair.

I slapped my hands down onto the High Magus' desk. His books jumped.

"Why the hell am I being left out of the biggest hunt I've ever seen?" I asked. "You've pulled every bounty hunter from the field and put them all on this. You've even let Muir out of the Tower! But *I* get shut out? Literally! The fucking gate wouldn't even open!"

"This is an internal College matter," Vincent answered in an even voice. He interlaced his fingers over one of the huge books. "You are not a member of our order, Lilith. The wizard who violated our laws will be dealt with according to those same laws."

"*I'm* the one who told you about Asmodai and about the wizard helping him. And you certainly didn't give me this bullshit runaround when I brought in Finn and Muir!"

"That was different," said Vincent.

"Fuck you." I leaned over the huge desk until my face was just a few inches away from the High Magus. "You know who made Reid, don't you? I want him."

"According to the information that you yourself gave us, that man is only a tool, an accomplice to Asmodai. I need him to answer questions about the demon lord's plans."

I hesitated at that. I knew more about Asmodai's plans than I had admitted to the College. Reid was created to be a cambion, like me – half human, half demon. In accordance with some horrifying nightmare logic, Reid was made by cutting up one of each and sewing the pieces together. I still didn't know *why* Asmodai wanted a cambion... but one of the last things Evaine had ever told me was that if the College found the answer to that question, they would kill me.

So I kept my mouth shut. Sort of.

"If you want to find out what Asmodai is up to, then why don't you just summon him yourself?" I asked.

Vincent frowned. "An intelligent man does not simply summon the Lord of Lust. A single succubus easily escaped the control of four experienced wizards last year. Even to answer my questions, I would not risk calling Asmodai into our world."

"Well, *someone* did it," I said. "Who was it? Give me a name!"

Vincent's frown deepened. "Lilith, your part in this is already suspect. When you discovered the golem, you brought him to your home. Not to us. You have not told the College what transpired between leaving the Quay Festival and the arrival of the other hunters, where the Lady of the Lake was found dead."

"You *know* what happened! Asmodai appeared in my fucking living room and Evaine fought him!"

"And what little of that encounter was captured by the scry network supports your account, Lilith. But there is more at play here."

Vincent closed the book in front of him and looked up at me with dark green eyes. I clenched my teeth and refused to say anything.

"Evaine's loss was a terrible blow to all of the Merlinic order," said the High Magus. "And your own demonic heritage only further complicates matters. It would be best if you distance yourself from this whole affair, Lilith."

"Me?" My fingers left splintered dents in the wood of the High Magus' desk and my voice dropped down into a low hiss. "You think *I* should distance myself? Like you have... *Dad*?"

Vincent Myrdon's face went absolutely white and he rose to his feet. "How–?"

"Yeah, I know the family secret. Evaine told me. So if you want to play this shit close to the vest – or robe or whatever – fine. But if you won't talk, then I will."

Vincent was silent for a long time. Finally, he heaved a soul-deep sigh and sat down again. His green eyes were tired but hard.

"Asmodai's instrument is one of our own magi," said the High Magus. "A young acolyte by the name of Zane Colton."

I knew Zane. At least, I had met him when Dorian first brought me to this office. Zane had been studying star charts in the observatory. He was the only one of the junior wizards to actually introduce himself to me.

"I know the guy," I said. "Keep going."

Vincent drew a long breath. "Zane failed to attend several important lectures and meetings during the week leading up to the golem's rampage."

"Reid," I said quietly. "His name was Reid."

"Zane was intelligent and ambitious," Vincent continued. "He had his eye on a council seat one day and we believed him capable of it. Apparently, we badly misjudged his character."

"Yeah," I agreed. "You did."

"Finn and Muir confessed to several conversations with Zane about demonic summoning rituals. He professed only an academic interest in the practice, but that's obviously no longer the case... if it ever was. Study of your condominium's remains revealed traces of Zane's magic. They were nearly undetectable through the resonance of Asmodai and Evaine's battle, but we were thorough."

Study of my condo? I briefly imagined some poor wizard having to sort through the blasted boxes of sex toys under my bed. But there were more important things right now than be either amused or annoyed at the thought of the College going through my dildo collection.

"Zane conjured a wrath demon," Vincent went on. "And destroyed a human life to create the golem... Reid. Zane summoned Asmodai through the Seal, which led to the death of the Lady of the Lake, an invaluable voice of wisdom in this world."

"Zane was reading *The Gates of Avalon* the day I met him," I said, suddenly remembering. "And it was Asmodai's shadow that came to take the book from Kalen last year."

Vincent rubbed one temple. "Yes. The shadows of sufficiently powerful demons have occasionally been able to pass out of the Nether to carry out their master's commands."

"What the fuck? I thought the Seal of Avalon stopped that kind of shit!"

"They are only shadows," Vincent said. A little defensively, I thought. "With limited power that doesn't even approach that of a true demon. The shadow which chased you was banished by the merest touch of daylight."

"Yeah, after blowing out every ward on the Marquis penthouse," I grumbled. "Why didn't you say something about these shadows before?"

"We are the heirs of Merlin. We do not advertise the weaknesses of the Seal of Avalon. But... there is good reason that many tales throughout the ages tell of terrible, faceless shadows lurking in the night."

"That's the demons still fucking with us," I said.

"Yes. And it seems their prince has some design."

"Kalen and I got away from that one at the hotel, so Asmodai didn't get *The Gates of Avalon*–"

"But gained access to the book through Zane," Vincent finished.

His jade eyes fixed on mine. "Yes, to my great shame. Though we still don't know to what end."

The High Magus wanted me to say something, to give him that answer. I didn't have it, though. I crossed my arms.

"What have you got on Zane?" I asked.

"A physical description, of course," said Vincent. "Six feet tall, one hundred seventy-eight pounds. Brown hair and brown eyes."

Dreamy eyes, I remembered. I nodded. "Anything else?"

"Zane Colton has a scar on the back of his left hand where he burned himself with saltpeter. It was his sole mistake during his final exam. But we have been unable to locate Zane using the scry network, indicating that he is somehow concealing himself from our magic."

Stefano said something about a divination just before he and the others left. I remembered the one he had done to find Dominic, the werewolf we had hunted together last year. That was powerful magic and I wondered how well Zane would be able to hide from it. But even if it worked, divination had limitations – the spell could only locate a target at noon or midnight and only displayed a picture of where they were. Maybe that would be enough to give me an edge.

"Where is Zane's sanctum?" I asked.

"115 East Sunset Avenue," Vincent answered. "But Zane is no longer there and the other hunters are conducting a thorough investigation of the premises even now. You are not a wizard, Lilith. They will understand what they find there far better than you could ever hope to."

"Watch me. I'm not giving up on this," I said. I turned toward the door, then glanced back. "Hey, you didn't send me an email this morning, did you?"

Vincent Myrdon gave me a look like I just asked if he fucked sheep in his spare time. That was a big fat *no*. I still had no idea who emailed me the tip-off. I moved in the direction of the door again.

"For whatever it's worth," Vincent said in a quiet voice I had never heard from him before. "...I'm sorry, Lilith."

I stopped with my hand on the office door.

"I didn't know of your existence you until you were eighteen years old," Vincent said. "I thought you had died along with your mother when I banished her back to the Nether. I was young and ashamed of what I had done... Ashamed that I was the kind of man a demon could love."

My fingers tightened on the doorknob. It had to be enchanted like the rest of the door, or else the brass would have been a twisted ball in my hand.

"By the time Evaine told me that you survived and that your powers had awakened, I was High Magus of the College. You were already a woman. There was nothing I could have done."

I refused to cry in front of Vincent Myrdon, but something in my chest hurt. I squeezed my eyes shut.

"Maybe if I had known earlier..." he said so softly that only my sharpened cambion hearing could catch it. "Maybe I could have been a father to you. Maybe things would have been different."

"No," I told him. "Nothing would be different."

I let myself out and closed the door quietly behind me. Vincent Myrdon was the one who tested me for demonic corruption, who watched me more closely than any other wizard in the College. My father put his work ahead of everything else in his life. That work was keeping the world safe from demons and monsters, though, and it was hard to hate him for that.

But I did, just a little.

Chapter
THREE

Okay, enough family drama! It was time to prove that I wasn't just the sexiest bounty hunter in this city.

I was the best.

The first step was to do some good old-fashioned snooping around, so I drove out to the address Vincent had given me. Zane's home was a tall townhouse up in Northbay that had a dark, neo-Victorian edifice complete with an octagonal tower ringed in windows. I supposed it was the closest thing to a Transylvanian castle that Zane Colton could afford within city limits.

I squinted through the drizzling rain at the windows, but couldn't see anything inside. The glass was pitch black, but didn't look like it had been painted or covered by garbage bags. Wizards are too refined for that kind of shit. At a guess, Zane had made some alchemical change to the glass to turn it black like that. There was no half-assing this one – I actually needed to get into Zane's house to check it out.

I circled the block a couple of times and saw no sign of Stefano's truck or any of the other hunters' vehicles. They had already come and gone. Wizards were a meticulous lot, but seven of them could probably comb through a sanctum pretty efficiently.

Was there anything left to find? I really hoped that my bravado with Vincent wasn't unfounded, that I could actually uncover something useful in Zane's sanctum.

I parked the 110 on the street and then made my way cautiously up the steep steps of Zane's house. The front door was closed, but the lock had been blasted open and was flecked with strange-smelling ash. Magical lock pick. It seemed exactly like the kind of useful spell Stefano would know. I really wished we were working together on this.

I pushed the door open and walked inside. Hardwood creaked softly under my feet. The blacked-out windows made it dark in the front room, but my sharpened vision cut through the gloom easily enough to find a light switch and flip it on.

Zane's living room was sparsely furnished. There was a leather sofa with a matching recliner and a couple of end tables. None of it was expensive, but it wasn't Ikea flat-pack, either. A fine film of dust lay over everything, though, and when I went to the kitchen, the food in Zane's refrigerator was starting to go moldy. He hadn't been back here since around the time of Reid's creation, when Vincent told me Zane disappeared from the College.

Confirming information was good, but I needed something more. The other hunters had surely taken some hair or fingernail clippings that would let them divine where to find Zane – their part and piece, as the wizards called it, like the claw Stefano used to track Dominic. Magic spells weren't an option for me. I had to find something else, something that everyone had overlooked.

I was surprised to find a laptop on Zane's dining room table. It was an older model, but I was still shocked to see a computer in a wizard's house at all. Zane was a younger mage, I supposed, and the digital world was bound to seep into the College eventually.

There were fingerprints in the dust on top. Had one of the other hunters stooped to investigating the machine? Stefano, at least, knew how to use a cell phone and probably a computer. I opened the laptop carefully, but the monitor was shattered. Frowning, I flipped it over and inspected the back. The case was cracked and the circuit boards inside were a broken jumble of green and gold. Maybe I could flash my cleavage in a computer store to get some of it fixed, but I couldn't imagine that a wizard – even a young one like Zane – would keep anything important there.

I left the laptop on the table and went to the stairs. They were covered in dust, too, but it was churned up by a half dozen different footprints. The other hunters. I followed their trail upstairs to the little cupola tower I had seen from outside and pushed the door open. I inhaled the cloying cacophony of scents of a wizard's sanctum: herbs, metal, stone, chemicals and spices. I sneezed.

The darkness wasn't absolute, but it was close. Only a few faint rays of gray daylight pushed like ghostly fingers through the blackened windows. There was no need to waste the lust Max had given me, so I searched with watering eyes until I found the light switch, then flicked it on and looked around the room.

Zane's sanctum reminded me at once of the basement where Finn and Muir had imprisoned me – and where I had kicked their asses. The walls here were lined with shelves that stretched up all the way to the high, angled ceiling. They were all filled with neatly arranged boxes, vials and jars, each labeled in precise handwriting.

The dust in here was disturbed, too. Zane's shelves had been searched, though everything had been returned to its original location. I smirked. Wizards were careful and tidy even when tossing a room.

I crouched down. Stefano and the rest had pried up the floorboards to look beneath. I checked the undersides of shelves, under all three of Zane's worktables and inside the air conditioning ducts – everywhere most people might hide their porn – but found only more fingerprints in the dust. The other hunters had scoured every inch of Zane's sanctum. There was nowhere here that they hadn't searched first.

Or was there?

I left Zane's sanctum and shut the door firmly behind me. The bounty hunters had ransacked the entire thing and if they found anything useful, then it was already gone. But there was a room that I doubted any of the wizards spent much time searching – the one where I did most of my work. *My* sanctum, if you will.

Zane's bedroom was on the second story, down a narrow hallway from his miniature tower sanctum. I pushed the door open and then stopped, blinking. I had never been in a wizard's bedroom and expected to find something spartan and functional. Well, I was mostly right...

A massive four-poster bed dominated Zane Colton's room. Like the rest of his furniture, it was functional and basic in design, with covers pulled up meticulously neat and smooth. Exactly what I expected from a wizard's bed – except for the sturdy eyebolt screwed deep into the wood of the headboard. *That* definitely wasn't part of the bed's original design. The eyebolt was shiny and new, but the metal inside the ring already showed a lot of wear. Zane may not have had it long, but he had used it hard.

Interesting.

I folded down the sheets. Whatever else Zane might have been, he was a wizard and you know what a fastidious breed they are. His sheets were absolutely clean and looked like they may even have been ironed... but my senses went far beyond human acuity. Faintly, I still smelled candle wax, blood and semen.

Zane Colton had acquired a taste for bondage. Serious stuff, too, not just fuzzy handcuffs. And given the particular wear of the eyebolt, it appeared to be both intense and recent. Was that Asmodai's influence on Zane? A sexual indoctrination at the hands of the most powerful demon in the Nether...

Fuck.

I found a few footprints in the dust. Stefano must have led the hunt through here. I managed to frown and smirk at the same time.

If Stefano had learned anything from me, it was the importance of the bedroom.

But a quick search of the nightstand and closet turned up no other bondage accoutrements. Not so much as a nipple clamp. In fact, there wasn't a whole lot in Zane's bedroom at all. There were no clear patches in the dust to indicate that Stefano had collected anything, either.

Zane must have taken it all with him when he left last month. The young wizard packed up his bondage gear, but not the contents of his sanctum? I ran my finger over the eyebolt, feeling the roughened metal. Zane must have fallen hard for the black leather to prioritize it over his magical supplies. I thought of Asmodai again and shuddered... But I'd be lying if I said it was entirely unpleasant.

None of this told me where to find Zane, though. There were a hundred bondage shops and dungeons in the city. I couldn't search them all for signs of Zane, if he had even visited any of them recently. With a sigh, I began smoothing the bed sheets back into place. If the other hunters returned to Zane's house, there was no point in tipping them off that I had been there. But something glinted at me from beneath the covers. I pulled it out.

It was a rectangle of thick black card stock, embossed with the shining gold that had caught my eye. I knew what it was before reading the gilded text. Anyone in the city would have recognized it, even if they pretended not to: an invitation to Leather and Lace. It was the biggest annual bondage ball on the west coast. Invitations were expensive and difficult to acquire. And Zane had one.

I paused beside the bed, frowning down at the black and gold invitation in my hand. Something was wrong with this whole picture. I still didn't know who sent me the email that morning. And what was Zane's invitation doing *here*? Surely the renegade infernalist had more important things to do than attend the admittedly best sex party in the state. So maybe he had discarded the invitation... by tucking it into his neatly made bed.

Yeah, right.

I put the invitation in my pocket and scoured Zane's bedroom a second and third time, finding nothing. I searched downstairs and then returned to the sanctum, but discovered no other clues as to where Zane might have gone. I stood in the middle of his sparsely furnished living room and let out a frustrated growl.

Finally, I took the Leather and Lace invitation from my pocket again and stared at it. The date embossed at the bottom was three days away. Plenty of time for me to prepare, but also plenty of time for Stefano to cast his divination and find Zane long before I could get anywhere near him.

Dead end.

I sat down heavily on Zane's couch, making dust puffed up all around me. I pulled out my cell phone, hesitated and then called Stefano again. I was surprised and relieved when he answered.

"Lilith," he said. "I'm... sorry about this morning."

"It's okay." I slumped back into the couch. "Really. I get it. Look, Stefano... I know I can't join your little hunting party. I've already spoken to the High Magus about it. But this is important to me. Like you and werewolves."

Stefano was quiet on the other end of the line. A werewolf had killed his father when he was just a kid. Stefano's mother contracted the curse, forcing him to kill her. Hunting down werewolves and lifting their demonic curse was his own personal crusade. If anyone understood my need to make Zane pay for Reid and Evaine, it was Stefano.

"Just... just tell me you're getting close," I said. I pressed my thumb and forefinger against my eyelids. "Tell me you're going to find him."

"I don't know, Lilith. We're running into problems."

I opened my eyes and sat up, frowning. "What are you talking about? What kind of problems?"

"We got what we needed, but the divination is... resisting me.

I've never seen anything like it. It may take us days to break through and even then, I'm not sure how reliable the results will be."

"Like the scry network. Zane's been hiding from that, too."

"How do you know about that?" Stefano asked. His voice fell to a whisper. So the other hunters wouldn't overhear, I guessed. "And how do you know who we're looking for?"

"I said that I talked to the High Magus."

Stefano drew a hissing breath. "And he told you? Gods, Lilith! You're really going after this, aren't you?"

"I have to. If you guys can't find Zane, I'm sure as hell going to try. You know what he did. I can't let Zane get away."

There was another moment of silence from Stefano. I heard the other bounty hunters in the background. They were arguing about the divination, all shouting suggestions and corrections over each other. I even picked out Muir's accent in the mix. Stefano sighed.

"Do what you need to, Lilith," he said. "Don't tell me what it is, though, and stay out of our way. You're right – we *do* have to catch Zane and I can't let even you stop us from doing our job."

"Yeah. Good hunting, Stefano."

"You too, Lilith."

I slipped my phone back into my pocket and stared at the invitation. It was a thin lead. Hell, it was worse than a thin lead. It was a suspicious one. But it was the only chance I had to find Zane Colton. Standing, I pocketed the invitation again.

There was something strange and doubtlessly dangerous going on. That describes pretty much my entire life and I've never let it stop me before. But if I was going to stalk Zane unnoticed through a bondage ball, I had some research to do. And some shopping.

Chapter
FOUR

*M*ax pushed me back against the bedroom wall, my spread legs hooked over his arms. His big hands cradled my ass and held me there. One of my arms twined around his neck, but Max was taking all of my weight as he hammered his cock up into me.

"What... what about your chest?" I gasped. My fingers traced the four raised lines of the yeti scars where they came up just below his shoulder. "I don't want to hurt you."

"The doctor says... I'm supposed to start exercising... the muscles again... anyway," Max said in short, low grunts.

Best workout ever. I pressed my forehead against Max's and his sweat ran down my skin. His blue eyes were open and staring right into mine. God, they were beautiful. I tasted his breath and our lips brushed with every thrust. It was a wonder that we didn't pass out from breathing only one another's panting exhales.

Hot sensation knotted and built through my body, winding around the feeling of Max inside me. It coiled tighter and tighter until it burst, sending pleasure surged through me, bright and electric and utterly consuming. I hung there shuddering in his arms as Max and my own ecstasy took me. I didn't scream or moan; I didn't want anything to drown out the sweet sounds of our bodies coming together, the wet tempo of Max's long cock thrusting into me, of our breath heaving in time.

When I could feel my limbs again, I dug my heels lightly into Max's ribs and tightened my arms around him. I had no intention of letting him do *all* the work. I slid one hand up through his damp blond hair and raked the nails of the other across the back of his neck. Max gasped and I kissed him, sliding my tongue into his open mouth. His groans were delicious.

I lifted myself almost off Max's cock and then fell once more onto the searing length of him. Again and again, riding Max and holding myself tight to him. My pink-flushed breasts rubbed against his sweat-slicked chest, and the feeling of my nipples as they trailed over the unyielding planes of Max's muscles made both of us gasp. Even pinned there against the bedroom wall, I rode him hard and fast.

Never to be outdone, Max's hands moved along the curve of my ass, dimpling the soft flesh and then spreading my pale cheeks. One long finger traced down the cleft there. My ass was slippery with the wetness gushing from my pussy. Max caressed the sensitive skin of my ass, raising goosebumps and making me shiver hotly, then circled my anus with his fingertip. Max pushed and my body accepted his touch eagerly. I moaned into our kiss as I welcomed more of him inside me.

I writhed desperately on Max's cock, feeling his finger piercing me from behind. It pressed into my ass in counterpoint to my every thrust. There was no relief from the pleasure – in and out and in again, I was penetrated and filled.

It was too much and within moments, I was at the peak once more. This time, I couldn't keep quiet. I'm pretty sure Max's eighty-seven-year-old neighbor could listen to my shrieks even without his hearing aid.

"Oh my fucking god!" I screamed. "Yes!"

Max yanked me away from the wall, turned and pressed me down into the bed without ever taking me off his dick. I fell back into the sheets and let Max drape my trembling legs over his broad shoulders. He reached out to cup my bouncing tits, adding light pinches to the swirling texture of my ecstasy. I ran my toes lightly along the side of Max's neck. He slid his hand up from one of my breasts and caught my ankle instead. Max kissed the arch of my foot and I gasped. He kissed it again, then placed a kiss on each of my toes. I squirmed and giggled.

"That tickles!" I squealed.

"Sorry," Max said. "How about this, then?"

He seized both of my ankles in one large hand and held my legs together in the air high above me. Max rose into a wide kneel and planted his other arm behind him for leverage. I clutched at the sheets and let out a sharp cry as he began hammering my pussy.

Max's thighs and rippled abs tensed every time he drove himself into me. Sweat rolled down his flushed skin and the scars across his chest stood out lividly with his exertion, but Max didn't let up one bit, not even when his jaw clenched and I heard his already racing heartbeat spike into a gallop. Max's hand tightened on my ankles and I felt his cock growing even thicker in my pussy.

"Lil, I'm close," he told me in a voice made deep and rough by pleasure.

"Don't stop," I moaned.

"I... I don't think I can."

I pressed my head back into the twisted sheets and closed my eyes, giving myself entirely over to the rich, hot sensation of Max inside me. Stretching me, filling me... A low groan rumbled up from his chest and I echoed the sound as his cock swelled.

And then Max was filling me even more. He was everywhere inside me. His cum surged into me so hard that it made me dizzy, so deep that I felt it in the pit of my stomach. Sticky, creamy white gushed from my overfilled pussy and along my ass. I screamed out

Max's name and he groaned mine until both of our voices were ragged.

Max leaned over me, panting and trembling with the effort of holding himself up. I wound my arms around his neck again and pulled him down against me, resting his head on my breasts. They make excellent pillows.

"Wow," I said. "So you like the new outfit?"

Max laughed. "I wouldn't know. Yet."

I laughed, too. My shopping bags were still downstairs in the workshop. When I came back to the garage, Max lost no time at all grabbing and kissing me, making me drop everything I was holding. I had to point out that anyone driving by might see us through the open doors, so Max had swept me into his arms and carried me upstairs. You know what happened after that.

"Hell, my outfit is so sexy it works even before I put it on," I said.

Max kissed my collarbone. "You would be sexy in a garbage bag, Lil."

"This is exactly why I couldn't take you shopping with me. We would have ended up fucking in the dressing room."

Max nodded against my chest and his sweat tickled its way across my skin.

"Yeah," he agreed. "But I missed you. And I *will* get to see what you bought, right?"

"I wouldn't want you to miss that. It's about time for me to start getting ready for the ball tonight, anyway. Help a girl get dressed?"

"Sure. Considering how often I tear your clothes off, it's only fair to help you put them on, too."

Max and I showered off together and barely managed not to make a brand new mess. While I combed out the wet red tangles of my hair, Max went back downstairs to retrieve my purchases: a tiny black leather skirt, shiny stiletto-heeled boots that came up to my thighs and brought me nearly eye-to-eye with him. And, of course, a black leather corset with steel ribbing and busks down the front.

I stood before the mirror while Max pulled on the laces of the corset. I used to have an outfit pretty much just like this, but it had gone up in flames along with the rest of my life during the battle between Evaine and Asmodai. Zane summoned the Lord of Lust to start that fight and the bastard had a lot more than my ruined wardrobe to answer for.

"Tighter," I told Max.

"Are you sure, Lil?" he asked. "This seems kind of... painful."

"Maybe a little bit, but it's not too bad. Actually, it feels kind of like armor."

I rapped my knuckles against the leather cinching my ribs and waist. The corset turned my already impressive cleavage into something positively weaponized.

"It makes me feel badass and powerful," I said.

"You *are* badass and powerful."

"Damned right."

I laughed a bit breathlessly as Max gave the corset laces another tug and then tied them off. His hands lingered on me, moving up and down the curves of my sides. The leather muted his touch, changed and transformed it into something at once more distant but also more intimate.

I looked at myself in the mirror, clothed all in black leather, and at Max standing behind me. He was still naked and his expression was awed. I reached back and raked my nails lightly along Max's bare thigh, making his breath hiss out. I was protected, but Max was utterly exposed and my every touch made him tremble.

There was heat at the small of my back, where I could just feel Max's cock rising against me. He wrapped his arms around my cinched waist and slid his hands up to my chest. His fingers tightened, but the leather hardly gave at all and Max groaned at his inability to feel the softness of my breasts.

"No!" I scolded.

Max jerked away, blinking. "Lil?"

I smiled at him in the mirror. "Just trying on the attitude. Besides, if I let you fuck me every time I looked sexy, I'd never leave the garage."

"True," Max admitted. He smiled back, but it faded quickly and he moved in close once more, pulling me around to face him. "Are you sure going to Leather and Lace is a good idea, Lil? You said the invitation shouldn't have been there at all."

"You know what this means to me, Max."

He nodded and stroked a damp copper strand of hair back out of my eyes. "Yeah, I do. And I want to make Zane pay, too. Evaine meant a lot to me, Lil, but not as much as you do."

"I *need* to put this thing to bed. Zane has to face justice – in the form of my boot up his ass – and I have to find out why he created a cambion."

Max's hands trailed down to my bare shoulders. "Evaine said that if the College finds out what Asmodai was doing, the wizards will kill you."

I glanced at my cell phone on the bedside table. Still no calls or texts from Stefano. They hadn't found Zane yet, either. I leaned into Max, resting my head against his shoulder.

"We need to understand why all of this is happening," I said. My breath raised goosebumps along Max's skin and his arms tightened around me. "What if Stefano and the others can't find Zane? We *have* to catch this guy."

"Let me help, Lil," Max whispered into my hair. "I helped with the yeti. I told you when you came to stay here: you don't have to do any of this alone."

I closed my eyes and ran my fingers down Max's chest, feeling the raised scars that ran all the way from his right shoulder to the left side of his sternum.

"Helping me nearly got you killed," I said. "Besides, aren't you sick of having me around yet?"

"Never, Lil."

I opened my eyes to look up at Max. I wanted to let him come with me. Max was smart and resourceful. He had fought twice by my side, first against a wyvern and then the yeti that had tried like fuck to gut him. I can't even tell you how scared I was each time, but it had felt good to have Max there beside me. I shook my head, though.

"You have no experience with the bondage scene," I said. "And a poorly trained sub would be too noticeable."

"You don't have much experience, either."

I stuck out my tongue. "Maybe not, but I'm a natural."

I pulled back a step and put my hands on my hips, striking an authoritative pose. Max's cock stirred again and he reached for my waist. I lifted my chin and stilled him with a single sharp, imperious glance.

"See?" I asked.

Max crossed his arms over his broad chest and smiled. "Okay, maybe you're right. I don't even know what a sub is."

"The partner in the submissive role of a bondage relationship," I told him.

"What makes you think I wouldn't be the dominant one?"

"Could you take a whip to me, Max? Really?"

"I doubt it," Max admitted. He drew a deep breath and sat down on the edge of the bed. "Okay, Lil. What's your play? You know this whole setup is suspicious as hell."

"Yeah, I know. I'll move in carefully. I don't usually go to parties early, but I want to scout out my surroundings. When I locate Zane, I'll corner him alone."

"You think you'll be able to do that?" Max asked.

"The house where the bondage ball is being held is huge. I should be able to find a quiet spot away from everyone else. Zane's magic requires a lot of material components, so I'll make sure that he's either not wearing enough clothes to carry that shit or else go for his hands first. You remember how badly Doyle fumbled his spell when I broke his arm."

Max nodded. "He nearly threw you off a cliff with his shitty aim. I almost punched him for that, broken arm or no. Do you have enough energy to take down a wizard?"

"You've kept me topped off on power for the last month. I'm *always* ready to go these days. And I took both Finn and Muir at once, who were each far older and more experienced wizards. When I'm done with Zane, he's going to have a lot worse than a few pleasant welts."

"Are you going to kill him?" Max asked.

I drew a deep breath. "I... don't know. I guess it depends on how hard he fights and what he can tell me about Asmodai."

"I don't like all of the unknowns in this plan, Lil."

"Neither do I. But we can't let Zane get away."

"He might make another golem," Max agreed quietly. "Another one like Reid."

"Or summon Asmodai. That can't happen again. If Zane's at the party tonight, he's going down."

Max kissed me. His desire enfolded me in a warm golden glow. Our kiss lingered and it was hard to extricate myself from Max's arms, but we didn't have time to go tearing my clothes off again. Not if I wanted to arrive at the bondage ball early.

I went into the bathroom and tied my hair up into a sleek red ponytail, then selected a smoky eyeshadow and deep crimson lipstick from my new makeup collection. My old one had gone up in flames along with everything else in my condo.

By the time I was done applying color to my lips and eyes, Max had pulled on a pair of jeans and a t-shirt. He stood in the door of the bathroom with the black Leather and Lace invitation and a coat draped over his arm. He held the coat out for me and then tucked the invitation into one pocket. I grabbed my cell phone, turned the ringer off and dropped it in another.

Max looked like he wanted to say something, but bit his lip and remained silent. He followed me downstairs, stopping at the door between the little lobby of his shop and the garage.

"Is there anything else you need?" Max asked. "Guns or... or some kind of weapon?"

"Where would I put them in this outfit? No, I'm good. I'm all powered up and ready to kick some ass in high heels."

"Lil..." Max took my hands in his.

I looked up at him. "Yeah?"

"I... Just be careful."

Max gave me an almost chaste kiss that wouldn't smear my lipstick and then turned away, heading for the garage.

I let myself out through the front door and made my way across the darkened parking lot, high heels clicking on the asphalt. The garage had closed an hour ago, but I heard the thunder of heavy metal and power tools from inside. In the month I had been living with Max, he never worked particularly late... But tonight, I was on a hunt, and Max was keeping himself busy.

Did he always do this? And had I really never noticed before?

I unlocked the i10 and slid into the driver's seat. Max and I both had a long night ahead.

Chapter
FIVE

*I*t wasn't that late yet, but it was autumn and the sun had already set. Tendrils of mist reached out from the bay and twined through the darkening city like some great creature intent on devouring it. The thick gray night turned downtown into a great overcrowded Stonehenge of glass and steel. Fog muted lights and sounds until they seemed worlds away.

None of that tonight. Tonight, I was going to get vengeance for Evaine and Reid.

I pulled up the music controls on my dashboard and hit *random*. Disturbed bellowed from the speakers and I raised one eyebrow. Max must have added to my music collection. I grinned and turned up the volume until the bass made my windows vibrate.

I drove north. Leather and Lace was being held in the biggest and grandest old mansion in the city: Coil House. Like I had told Max, I wanted to know my hunting grounds. So I had done just as much research about the location of the bondage ball as I did on what kind of corset to buy.

When the historic earthquake and then several fires razed most of the city back in the early twentieth century, Orson Coil was the one who lead the rebuilding efforts. He was an architect and urban planner whose ideas were far more ambitious than practical, as anyone who's ever tried to navigate downtown during rush hour could attest. But no one worked harder or poured more of their personal fortune into rebuilding than Orson Coil.

And history rewarded his efforts. Every dollar he invested into city infrastructure was repaid ten times over in lucrative building contracts, land sales and shipping agreements. With his increasing riches, Orson Coil designed and built a massive mansion for himself on the edge of the growing city.

At over sixty-five thousand square feet, Coil House remains one of the largest homes in the state's history. The sprawling forty-seven bedroom house sat in the heart of a fifty-acre private estate and contained twelve sitting rooms – whatever those were – as well as five dining rooms, three swimming pools, and two full-sized ballrooms.

Coil House's only real rival was Hearst Castle. But unlike Hearst Castle, which had become a state park back in 1954, Coil House was still owned entirely by the family who built it. Not that they lived there anymore – it was way too much house for most modern families, so they paid for its maintenance and rented the manor out at astonishing prices for movie shoots and upscale private events. Events like Leather and Lace.

Unlike Conrad's launch party the previous year, there were no spotlights set up outside Coil House to announce tonight's festivities. Instead, two men in neat black suits signaled me to a stop in front of a tall wrought iron gate. They checked my pilfered invitation and scanned a discreetly placed QR code.

"Enjoy your evening, miss," one of them said as he handed back the invitation.

He wore a pair of perfectly fitted black leather gloves that were cool against my skin when our fingers brushed. The other man opened the gate from an ivy-covered brick guardhouse. Heavy iron swung smoothly inward and then closed behind me with a low, resonate clang as I drove through.

The Coil House driveway was nearly a road in its own right, if the city council would ever approve cobblestone streets. It was wide enough for two cars to pass each other comfortably and lined in well-maintained ash trees. Small, tasteful lights illuminated acres of lawn, gardens and manicured miniature forests. It was almost a pity the Coil family didn't give up the family estate to the city; it would have made one hell of a park.

And then Coil House itself rose up before me. I had seen photographs, of course, but its sheer size and grandeur was something you just have to see in person.

Coil House was a vast gothic Victorian affair, built in an ornate style even older than what Orson Coil had plotted out for the city's rebuilding a hundred years ago. I could certainly see the appeal for Zane – his little house was a Happy Meal compared to this banquet of dark, stately beauty. Coil House had towers and minarets spaced all along its truly massive length, each finished with intricately cut gingerbread decorations. Most of the house was painted in deep browns and charcoal grays, but hints of bright gold and crimson peeked out here and there – never enough to be garish, but enough to keep the otherwise somber house lively and interesting.

Thanks to nearly a decade of monster hunting, I had some money, but places like this reminded me that to be *truly* rich was something else entirely.

Cars were parked in neat ranks all around the huge circular driveway. There had to be over a hundred of them, though not by much. I was torn between surprise to see so many and shock that there weren't more. There are always more kinky people than you realize, but I guessed this wasn't a party for just anyone who liked spankings. Leather and Lace was for the *true* bondage crowd, those who gave themselves over to the lifestyle. Like Zane, I hoped.

A woman dressed much like the two men at the gate waved me into the next available parking spot. I pulled the i10 in beside a white Tesla as the dark-suited woman guided a slick red Corvette

206 • NATALIE & ERIC SEVERINE

into place on my other side. I sat in my i10, watching a pair of hand-some young men climb out of the Corvette. They took a moment to inspect one another's matching black hair and then made their way in the direction of the front door.

I stared at my invitation. These were highly sought after and difficult to obtain even within the bondage community. That Zane had one spoke eloquently of his dedication to the fetish. But would he really show up? If I had his invitation, how would Zane get into Coil House? This wasn't exactly any old rave or college frat party that he could just crash.

At Conrad's tech launch party, I had been the crasher, invading the vampire's own home and hoping to corner him there. And I had done precisely that... after a few minor setbacks. But Coil House was a hell of a lot larger than Conrad's mansion and I wasn't even sure Zane would be here tonight. What choice did I have, though? I had no other leads.

It was time to throw the dice, as Adähr would have said. The nix was an asshole in every way imaginable, but he would have been right just about now. Besides, what was I really risking? At worst, Zane wouldn't show up tonight and I would have spent the evening at a prestigious kink party.

I could live with that.

I climbed out of the i10 and joined a handful of other guests approaching Coil House. The doors were thrown open and the expansive foyer glowed with the sparkling light of a crystal chandelier so huge that I could have taken a bath in it. The floor was finished in utterly white marble polished to a mirror sheen.

"Welcome to Leather and Lace," said a quiet voice. "May I take your coat?"

I turned to find a woman standing behind me. All I could see of her were her wide brown eyes and ruby red lips. Every inch of the rest of her body was covered in a head-to-toe black latex suit. It clung close to her every luscious curve.

"Wow," I said, then shook my head in an attempt to unstick my eyes. "Uh… Yes, thank you."

Considering how constrictive all that latex must have been, the girl in black had surprisingly little trouble helping me out of my coat. I kept my invitation, though. Unlike Conrad's party, I actually had one this time.

There were three sets of huge French doors around the foyer, each pair so wide that I could not have touched both sides of the frame at once. A tall man in an impeccable tuxedo and o-ring collar stood beside one and held out his hand. I took a deep breath and gave him my invitation.

"I'm surprised how many people are already here," I said. I was horrified to hear my voice shaking. "I thought I would be early."

The man in the collar inspected my invitation and looked up at me, taking in the boots, skirt and corset. I felt the hot golden flare of his lust, but he let none of it show on his face.

"The attendees of Leather and Lace enjoy punctuality and discipline," he said.

"But breaking the rules is half the fun, isn't it?" I asked.

This time the tuxedoed man did smile, a brilliant and wicked grin that made my breath catch. He placed my invitation along with dozens of others into a lacquered bowl, then pulled open the doors and stood to one side. He actually bowed, the motion making the polished ring of his collar dance and shine in the light.

"Welcome to Leather and Lace, mistress," he said. "And remember, we're all here to serve."

I stepped through the doors. Beyond lay one of Coil House's vast ballrooms, bigger than Max's entire garage and lined in mirrors etched with curling baroque designs in gold leaf. A dozen graceful chandeliers hung from the distant ceiling, each only slightly scaled-down versions of the one that dominated the entry foyer. The lights were dimmed – not enough to obscure anything in shadows, but enough to create a feeling of intimacy and seclusion.

Now, I'm a worldly girl and I've been around... but the bondage ball was like nothing I had ever seen before. There were people of all ages filling the ballroom, dressed in leather just like mine. But also in latex and vinyl, in lace and or painstakingly applied body paint. Proud men and women strode through the party followed closely by their subs – more than a few on leashes – while others stood alone, seeking out new acquisitions or masters. Staff moved through the ballroom, carrying trays of drinks and food, as well as small, sealed tubes of lubricant, condoms in black and gold wrappers and coils of fine white rope.

I stood in the middle of the open doors, staring. There was too much to look at, to take in at once. I smelled sex and perfume, hot candle wax and cold steel. Soft music played through hidden speakers, but it was only a melodious counterpoint to the rich, mingled sounds of conversation and moans of pleasure. I stared at a woman in a full ball gown of lace and vinyl, but then at a girl who knelt at an older gentleman's feet, his foot propped up on one of her shoulders while she polished his already shining black boots. A slender man glided by wearing nothing but a mask and bowed to a woman in silver stiletto heels so high that she walked on her toes like a ballet dancer.

"This must be your first time."

The voice belonged to a woman in a skin-tight red latex dress tied along the sides. Black lace stockings rose up her legs to garter clips that held them in place. The dress barely covered the supple curve of her ass and when she shifted her weight, I caught a glimpse of more black lace between her legs. The woman's brown hair was pulled back into a neat bun and she looked at me over the red rims of her glasses.

"I'm... sorry?" I said.

"You've never been to Leather and Lace before," the woman said. Her perfectly painted crimson lips instantly made me want to bite them. "I can always spot a newcomer. I'm Miss Rose. Would you like me to show you around?"

I glanced past the domme to a couple standing obediently behind her. One was a young man about ten years younger than his mistress, with dark hair and a dusky, chiseled body on full display. The other was a willowy strawberry-blonde woman nearly as tall as the man. Her breasts were high and small, dusted with freckles. Neither of them wore anything but a black leather collar adorned with a polished steel rose, and matching gold wedding rings.

"You already uh... seem pretty busy," I said.

"They will wait all night for me," Miss Rose answered. "If I tell them to."

Her subs stood in perfect silence, patiently awaiting their mistress' command. I returned my attention to her.

"Yeah, it's my first time," I admitted. "But I'm not exactly inexperienced."

Miss Rose gave me a smile that reminded me a little of Evaine whenever I said something dumb and she was about to correct me. God, it made me want to kiss this woman.

"Vanilla sex is sweet and a very satisfying flavor for many," she said. "But you came for something else."

Vanilla? Me? I bristled a little at that. I fucked vampires, fairies, werewolves, mummies, wizards, dryads, nixi, djinni, ghosts, half-demon golems and hunky mechanics. Hardly vanilla. But I couldn't very well explain that and besides, I needed help finding my way around if I had any hope of cornering Zane tonight.

"I'd love a tour," I said. "If you have time."

Miss Rose's smile warmed. "It would be my pleasure. Come."

She gestured and led me into the ballroom. Her paired submissives gave me room to fall in beside their mistress, then followed silently after us. The domme in red glasses walked close, keeping her voice low.

"This is the public space," Miss Rose said. "You are welcome to enjoy anything on display here."

We stopped at the edge of a small crowd gathered around a circular platform. On top, a woman was on her hands and knees, adorned in straps of white around her waist and crossing over her breasts. A man in a kilt of black leather had a fist clenched in her hair, holding the woman fast as a powerful-looking machine drove a cock-headed piston in and out of her pussy. Wetness streamed down her trembling thighs, though the ball gag buckled into her mouth muffled her screams of pleasure. The crowd clapped appreciatively.

My guide leaned in close, her red lips nearly brushing my ear. "Remember what your parents told you. Look, but do not touch. What we do here is intimate, but it is also art. Watch – that's why the practitioners are here tonight, after all – but any participation is by invitation only."

The thought of being invited up onto that stage made my breath come faster and heat stir between my legs.

"Do those kinds of invitations get extended?" I asked.

"Indeed so. This is a gathering of like minds and tastes, after all. But never presume. Consent is the first and last rule of bondage."

None of this was helping me find Zane yet, but I found myself listening attentively. I liked handcuffs and how I looked in a corset, but all of this... it was something else entirely. And I was fascinated.

We moved on through the vast ballroom. At a glance, I only estimated enough guests here to account for half of the cars outside. There was plenty of room to walk without bumping into anyone, but the huge room still felt somehow crowded. Because everything here was so intimate, I realized, exactly as Miss Rose had said. I've never been shy and even gotten naughty in public a few times, but it was always discreet, secretive. Part of the thrill was sitting through dinner across from Max and cumming my brains out while not letting anyone around us realize what was happening.

But here, it was all on display. This sex wasn't just fun, it was something to be shown off and shared in a way that made even this experienced half-succubus girl's knees knock a little.

Miss Rose moved further through the bondage ball and I followed, trailed by her pair of ever-vigilant subs. When their mistress accepted a glass of pale golden wine from a passing tray, the man wearing the rose-emblazoned collar carried it for her without even being asked.

On another dais, a hugely muscular man knotted ropes of alternating red and white around a kneeling younger man. I might have considered the second man naked if so much of his body weren't covered in rope. Strands wound back and forth across his stomach and chest, binding his arms behind him and twisting so intricately that only my sex-powered vision let me pick out the details. Complex knotwork confined even the length of his cock, but it strained impressively.

The older man took a sturdy metal hook hanging from a steel A-frame and slid it through the looping red knots between the young sub's shoulders, then pulled the bound and helpless boy to his feet. Ropes held him imprisoned as his dom invited men and women forward one at a time to examine his work. They ran curious, eager hands over the beautiful knots and the beautiful boy while he writhed in his bonds.

Miss Rose touched my shoulder lightly. I snapped my mouth shut and turned to face her.

"This way," she said.

More than a few men, women and others directed small, respectful nods in the direction of my guide. She caught me doing a double take as we passed a face I had seen on television and gave me a glance over her cherry-red glasses.

"You may see familiar faces here tonight, but try not to stare unless invited to do so," Miss Rose told me. "This lifestyle is a private one and sharing it like this is a gesture of trust."

I looked around the ballroom. I was accustomed to a lot of attention wherever I went, but no one here stared. I felt the heat of lust from a dozen places at once, but none of them leered and no one approached me. Not yet, at least. Not while I was obviously occupied with the domme in red.

"Trust and consent," I repeated.

My teacher for the night smiled and the curve of her crimson lips sent a hot shiver racing through my body. I couldn't decide if I wanted to obey her every order just to see that approving smile or disobey so Miss Rose would take me over her knee for a spanking. I glanced back at her two subs, still unspeaking but utterly attentive. Their mistress really put the *sensual* in *consensual*.

We were nearing the far end of the ballroom and I followed eagerly. Racks set up along one wall were hung with black leather straps that crisscrossed tender flesh, bound limbs together or held them apart. Onlookers stood in a ring around a man tied naked to a polished wooden X.

A woman covered with intricate tattoos held a braided whip in one colorful hand. She circled it over her head with expert skill and then the whip lashed out with a crack like a tiny gunshot. The leather left a long line of red across the man's chest and he shouted in pain, but the sound turned quickly into a groan of ecstasy. His cock stood out from his body so hard that it trembled with barely restrained pleasure.

Another woman sat chained to an unyielding metal chair with her legs parted and a bit between her teeth. Tiny clamps pinched her nipples and the delicate pink of her labia, spreading her open for all to see. A man in almost military uniform snapped on a pair of dark nitrile gloves and knelt between her thighs. He thrust two fingers into the girl and she jerked in her restraints. The man worked in and out of her pussy until the black of his gloves shone wet and gleaming.

"I've never seen anything like this," I admitted.

Miss Rose smiled and pushed her glasses up her nose. "This is only the public space. You will find many open doors in Coil House tonight. In these cases, you are welcome to treat them as any of these exhibitions and to join in if invited. But there will be closed doors, too."

"So if it's locked, they want privacy?" I asked. That must have been where everyone else was.

"For the safety of all guests, there are no locked doors at Leather and Lace."

"Safety? So accidents can happen?" I asked.

Miss Rose frowned and even that made me want to kiss her.

"Occasionally," she told me. "Certain works of fiction have popularized bondage without providing education. Uninformed newcomers have sometimes gotten in over their heads."

"What do you mean?"

"Inexperienced practitioners can make dangerous mistakes. They can injure themselves or others. Or let their trust be abused."

I hadn't for a moment forgotten why I was at the bondage ball, but Miss Rose's comment brought it all surging to the fore. It was time to get to work.

"I'm looking for something pretty hardcore," I said.

Miss Rose glanced back toward the girl chained to her chair. The man had teased her to gushing wetness and now pinched the swollen pink bud of her clitoris in a pair of forceps. Another woman handed him a hollow needle and as I watched, he lanced it through the girl's engorged clit. She screamed against the bit in her teeth and her pussy streamed as the uniformed man slid a tiny silver ring through the new piercing. My pulse skipped. It looked painful, yes, but god, the girl was squirming and squirting in the throes of absolute ecstasy.

Miss Rose turned back to me with one eyebrow raised. But if Zane had learned his tastes from the Lord of Lust, then...

"Harder," I whispered.

"Hmm. Pain can bring equal pleasure, and for those seeking extreme measures of both, there are a few rooms here tonight... But they are not generally for beginners."

"I've heard of a guy," I said slowly. "Young. About six feet tall, brown hair and sultry eyes. There's nothing he won't do."

That last part was pure guesswork, but this whole thing was a gamble. I held my breath.

Miss Rose nodded. "Ah, yes. Master Zane. He's a newcomer to our community, but has already acquired a certain reputation. Master Zane is popular with the young and impressionable."

"Is he here tonight?" I asked.

"Perhaps."

The domme brushed gentle fingers across my bare shoulders, but then squeezed it firmly. I gasped at her touch.

"Most bondage practitioners are as psychologically healthy and sound as anyone," she told me. "Sometimes more, as we have outlets for passions that many repress. But there are those who simply take pleasure in hurting others, who abuse the trust of their submissives to get what they desire."

"And Zane is one of those?" I asked.

"He is handsome and seems to have an uncommon level of skill for such a new dom... but his submissives say that Master Zane respects no boundaries or safewords during sessions. Many of them have been hurt."

Miss Rose circled me closer than the slowly swelling ballroom crowd necessitated. She trailed her hand across my back. Her fingertips remained high along my shoulders, never dipping lower to more intimate parts of my body, but I shivered and struggled to catch my breath.

"There are better teachers here than Master Zane. Whatever it is you wish to learn, I would be pleased to show you," she said, then gestured back to her two stoic submissives. "Alex? Jessica? Would you like to serve our new friend?"

The dark-haired young man and his pale, slender wife shared a glance and then looked me up and down. Alex's cock began to rise, already promising impressive length and thickness. Jessica licked her lips and a pink flush spread across her freckled chest. I felt their lust flare suddenly brilliant and golden. They held it in check all through the entire tour, but now they had their mistress' permission to speak their desire.

"Yes, Miss Rose," Alex and Jessica answered in unison.

The thought of those two serving me while the smolderingly sexy Miss Rose watched and instructed made my knees weak. My pussy throbbed with liquid heat, but I had a job to do and this was not it.

"You have no idea how much I want to accept that invitation," I said. I heard the tightness in my voice, and the reluctance. "But I have to find Zane."

The domme studied me through her glasses. "You're certain? And understand what you're seeking out?"

"Yes," I said.

Miss Rose held my gaze long enough for me to start squirming. Finally, she nodded.

"I have heard some of the others saying Master Zane is already here," she told me. "That he was the first to arrive this evening."

"Where is he, then?" I asked.

"That I do not know. He and I don't speak. But some of the submissives believe that Master Zane has something special planned for them tonight."

That sounded both promising and alarming. What the hell was Zane up to? I drew a deep breath and stared around the ballroom. Miss Rose followed my gaze.

"Master Zane spends little or no time in the public spaces," she told me. "I'm not the only one here who disapproves of his practices. Leather and Lace extends all throughout the eastern wing of Coil House tonight. He may appear here in the ballroom to acquire new subs – or else send others to do that job for him – but then will likely retreat to a more private room to carry out whatever he has planned."

"Thank you, Miss Rose," I said.

"I hope to see you again. And be careful."

"I will."

Miss Rose gave my shoulder one last squeeze and then turned away. I watched the domme and her two utterly delicious subs wind their way back across the huge ballroom. With a disappointed sigh, I returned my attention to the rest of the bondage ball.

Zane was here somewhere, and he was planning something. Did it have anything to do with the suspicious invitation left in his bed? I was beginning to wonder if it was an invitation not just to Leather and Lace, but to come and find Zane. But why? I had no idea, but I was really looking forward to beating some answers out of the renegade wizard.

Chapter
SIX

*Z*ane Colton was somewhere in Coil House, but there were dozens of men here in the ballroom alone, with more coming and going all the time. Some of them were dressed in expensive suits and ties. Many wore nothing at all. But some were covered head to toe in vinyl or latex, and others wore elaborate harlequin masks or leather ones zipped shut across eyes and mouth.

Zane could be any one of those men and I wouldn't know. He had been gone from his sanctum too long to smell like it anymore. Even if he had recently rolled in wolfsbane, I doubted that I could pick out the scent through the haze of perfume, lube, sex and sweat. For all I knew, Zane could be that guy tied to the rack twenty feet away, the one in the mask being fucked in the ass by a tall, busty woman with a huge strap-on.

Okay, probably not that one. Miss Rose had called him *Master Zane* and said he was a dom. Zane was more likely to be doing the ass fucking than taking it. But the point remained: finding one man in here wasn't going to be easy.

What did I have to work with? Well, Miss Rose had also told me that Zane would likely be somewhere more private than the ballroom and that Leather and Lace took up the whole east wing of

Coil House. That was better than having to search all of the massive mansion, but not by much. I really wished there had been room in my skin-tight leather getup for my cell phone, but if I recalled my research correctly, the east wing contained more than half of Coil House's forty-seven bedrooms. Which was why it was perfect for Leather and Lace, of course.

There were two other sets of carved mahogany doors leading out from the ballroom and I strode through the swirling, milling, fucking crowd toward one of them. Men in smooth silver masks pulled them open at my approach and I stepped through into a wide hallway with floors made of granite and marble in patterns of interlocking rings. My high heels rang off the polished stonework.

Where are you, Zane?

I moved down the hall and stopped at the open doors to one of Coil House's huge dining rooms. Well-dressed people sat in carved wooden chairs around a long table that ran down the middle of the room. The table was heavily laden, but not with food. On top of the polished table, a muscular man hammered his cock into a blonde woman's ass, his deep groans of pleasure stifled by the gag fixed over his mouth.

When he had emptied himself entirely into the panting blonde, his domme led him down from the tabletop by the leash around his neck. A man in a silk tie picked up his wineglass and at his command, the girl in the center of the table sat up into a kneel that made her legs quiver. He stroked her hair and back, whispering into her ear.

"Very good, sweetheart," he said in a low, soothing voice. "You took it all."

The pale-haired woman whimpered and gasped as her master placed the wineglass beneath her.

"Now show everyone what a good girl you are," he told her. "Squeeze all of that spunk out. Show us how big a load that boy left inside you."

The girl did as she was commanded. Her whole body trembled with the effort, but her whimper rose to a moan as bright white cum welled up from the freshly-fucked pink of her asshole. It streamed into the wineglass, nearly filling the fine crystal with cream. The blonde's master raised his glass and the gathered diners murmured their appreciation. Then he held it out to the woman still kneeling and gasping in the center of the banquet table.

"Now drink, sweetheart," he said softly. "You've earned it."

My mouth watered, but I reluctantly turned away from the dining room and moved on. Doors lined the right side of the hallway, but the other wall was made up of windows that looked out across moonlit gardens and the shimmering blue of an expansive swimming pool. A man and woman in full evening dress twined together in the water, cloth slicked against their skin like binding caresses. But the man's hair was pale and he was too short to be Zane, so I wrenched my eyes from the scene and kept searching.

There were only a few bedrooms on the first level of the east wing. All of the doors stood open and I stared through each of them, but none of the people being bound, fucked, whipped or held close – or doing those things to their subs – were Zane. By the time I reached the stairs leading up to the second story, I still didn't know what a sitting room was *supposed* to be for, but I knew at least five different ways to have naughty fun in them.

The stairs were so wide that I could have laid out comfortably across the steps. They curved around to let out on a second-story hall just as huge and grand as the one below. It was quieter up here, though, the sounds of sex softer. Not silent, not to my ears, but muted. Most of the doors along the upper hallway were closed.

But I heard something else from behind me. Footsteps.

I spun toward the noise, heart pounding, to find a pair of men about my own age standing at the top of the steps. For a moment, I stared. I recognized them: both were tall, lithe and dark-haired... but I breathed a sigh that was part disappointment, part relief.

Neither of them were Zane Colton. Actually, they looked just like each other. Brothers, if not actual twins. I *had* seen them before, though, outside Coil House as they climbed from their Corvette. They looked quite different now – both men were naked except for collars around their necks, like Alex and Jessica. But instead of gleaming roses, blank steel tags hung from the leather.

The two brothers stopped in front of me, standing side by side. Handcuffed together, in fact. They inclined their heads at the same time and smiled. One of them held a glass of wine. The other held a small silver key and I knew a handcuff key when I saw one.

"We saw you alone, ma'am," said one of the twins.

"And watching. Are you in need of good subs?" asked the other, taking over smoothly for his brother. He held out the wine.

"We're ready to serve," said the first. He offered the key.

"What makes you think I'd unlock you?" I asked with a grin, but I was still working. "Maybe next time, boys. Go find a smoking hot domme in red named Miss Rose. I bet she can help you out."

The twins looked disappointed, but they inclined their heads once more and retreated down the stairs. I watched them go with disappointment. I was at Leather and Lace to work, but so much of what I saw here was amazing. Next year, I would have to see about bringing Max. What sort of mark would I put on his collar?

Grinning, I turned back to regard the second-story hallway. A handsome older couple led a young woman into one of the open rooms by her leash and closed the door firmly behind them, but the lock didn't click. Everyone else here was playing by the rules Miss Rose had laid out.

But not Zane. Miss Rose said that "Master" Zane had a bad reputation. With a demon holding *his* leash, I wasn't surprised. So which room up here wasn't like the others...?

I stalked slowly along the hallway, all senses on alert. I heard the slap of leather against yielding flesh and the sharp moans that followed. But I didn't hear Zane's voice. Not that I recognized, at least. I had only met the man once, so I listened for anything magical, those strange syllables that go right in one ear and slide out the other before you comprehend them.

This would have been a hell of a lot easier if I could just kick down every closed door, but I figured that I could get away with that maybe twice before I pissed someone off. Angry civilians tended to complicate any hunt and resulted in a lot of memory wipes that I hoped to avoid.

I smelled musky semen and sweet flavored lube, then... blood. I closed my eyes and inhaled the scent. Blood play was a legitimate bondage fetish with a considerable following, but Miss Rose also said that several of Zane's playthings were injured on his watch. Was that what I smelled now? The demon-summoning bastard apparently had something special planned tonight, after all...

The blood scent was weak – there was no way I would have been able to track it downstairs. But now I followed it to another flight of stairs, these slightly narrower but no less ornate than those that led to the second floor. I saw the blue glow of the pool shimmering through a window. I was still in the east wing, so I climbed the steps to the third story.

The stairs let out into another wide hallway. Each of the doors stood open up on this level and I didn't hear voices from any of them. So I strode quickly along the hall, peering into the bedrooms and bathrooms, but they were all empty.

Empty of other people, at least. At the end of the hallway was not another staircase, but a pair of double doors leading into a vast bedroom. Unlit red candles sat on bookshelves and I smelled something spicy, like cardamom or cinnamon. There was a desk against one wall that rivaled Vincent Myrdon's for size, with a smooth marble top and carved ebony legs. Silver serving trays on the desk were heaped with a mix of butt plugs, dildos, strap-ons, clamps and leather binders that made my old toy boxes look almost G-rated by comparison.

But another tray held implements of another sort: pliers and knives, including one with a wavy blade like a gleaming tongue of steel fire. Those tools had been used before. Zane must have cleaned them afterward, but these blades were the source of the blood I smelled.

The room certainly invited closer inspection. But when I tried to step through the doorway, I slammed into an invisible barrier. I saw nothing in front of me, but it felt like I had just tried to walk through a brick wall. I knocked my knuckles against the hardened air. There was a ward on the bedroom door. Merlinic magic. This was *definitely* Zane's room.

Wards were serious magic. Asmodai's shadow had blasted about twenty of them to shit in the Hotel Marquis' penthouse, but I wasn't a demon lord or even a demon lord's shadow. I couldn't just tear my way through that much magic. Maybe it was like Finn's circle of binding...? Being half succubus had kept me bound, but being half human had let me break out.

Remembering how I pushed my way through Finn's spell made me shiver. That sensation of my human and demonic halves being pulled apart, snarling at each other across the ephemeral distance between them... I was in no hurry to *ever* feel that again.

But I would do it to get at Zane. In a heartbeat.

I put my hand to the hard, empty air and pushed. The warded doorway tingled against my skin and shifted subtly, like it was trying to shrug me off. I guessed that any ordinary human would simply slip away from the ward without realizing why they couldn't get into the bedroom. Handy. But I was a fucking cambion. I'm not that easy to trick.

Cambion or not, though, I pushed and shoved at Zane's spell until sweat ran down the back of my neck, but remained stubbornly out in the hallway.

I scowled at the open door. Okay, this wasn't designed to contain demons like Finn's magic circle. This was something more general.

Zane didn't want *anyone* wandering uninvited into his bedroom. I wondered if I could kick through the non-warded walls, like I had planned to do in Vincent's office, but a gaping hole in the room might have tipped Zane off.

Pressing my face against the ward, I peered around the room. The bed was huge and had a canopy of blue velvet that matched a pair of lavish armchairs nearby. But I saw no sign of Zane. There was another set of doors across the bedroom. Would he come in from there? How far did the ward extend? Could Zane pass through it? Maybe I could go down to the coat check and grab my cell phone to call Vincent or Stefano with some questions.

There were voices approaching again, but I was so focused on the bedroom that I almost didn't register them until too late. Coil House was full of people tonight, after all, and the last ones had only offered me their admittedly delectable services.

But then I heard Zane's name.

I jumped and spun to stare down the hall. It was still empty, but I picked out a half dozen female voices approaching, all speaking in hushed, awed tones.

"Did they tell you what Master Zane will do to us?"

"Are you scared of Master Zane?"

"Yes... but god, I'm so wet. Where are we going?"

They were climbing the stairs. I counted more footsteps than voices, and several pairs heavier than the rest. As silently as I could in my stiletto heels, I stepped back away from the warded door and slipped into another open bedroom just as they crested the top of the stairs. I pressed myself back behind the door, peeking out from the shadows.

There were ten of them – six girls being escorted by four men dressed from head to toe in black, including leather gimp masks zipped shut across the mouth. No wonder I hadn't heard any of them speak. Only their eyes were visible. The two in front kept their gazes fixed ahead on the room at the end of the hall. The pair in the rear surveyed the girls, the hallway and everything else. They were both big men – one of them huge enough to raise my eyebrows curiously – but none of them matched Zane's height or build.

The women were all naked. No, I corrected myself. They were *mostly* naked. Each of them wore a collar, like Alex and Jessica, complete with shiny silver tags. But these weren't decorated with a rose or even blank like the twins. Instead, each flat silver disk was inscribed with a squiggly, indecipherable mark. A rune.

I examined each of the men more closely as they marched the girls down the third-story hallway. They were harder to pick out against all that black leather, but all four wore collars with the same glyphed tag.

The group passed the doorway where I hid. The biggest gimp-suited man paused, turning his masked face my direction. Dark eyes narrowed as he squinted through the shadows, but the other guy in the back elbowed him sharply and they both moved on, following the rest down the hall.

The girls looked nervous, even scared. I smelled their adrenalin, but also their arousal. Miss Rose said that Zane's reputation impressed the younger, less experienced submissives. They huddled together in the hallway as the men motioned silently for them to wait. All four men walked right through the magically sealed door and the sigils on their collars flashed briefly with colorless light. I mentally high-fived myself. So the runes *were* keys to Zane's ward.

I needed one of those collars.

From behind the door, I couldn't see what the men were up to, but I smelled smoke and wax. Lighting the candles and preparing the room for the women, I supposed. And for Zane.

The girls milled around in the hall outside, whispering in excited, frightened voices to one another.

"Have you ever been with Master Zane?"

'No, but Bethany was."

"Isn't she in the hospital? What did Master Zane do to her?"

"Beth says she doesn't remember, exactly. But it was good. Better than good."

I wasn't sure if that was the effect of whatever Zane was actually doing in the bedroom or just a memory charm to keep his toys from spreading too many specific rumors. But either way, it was another reason to deck Zane once I got my hands on him. The wizard had a lot to answer for.

Hurriedly, I pulled off my boots, unzipped my skirt and unfastened the corset. I let out an involuntary gasp as I drew my first full breath since Max had laced it on. One of the girls looked up at the sound and I stepped further into the darkened room. I felt something cold against my back and froze.

After a moment, the whispering resumed outside and I glanced over my shoulder at what had arrested my retreat. There was a large metal rack behind me – and I don't mean a spice rack. A blindfold, leather restraints and a ball gag sat on a wooden table nearby. Zane wasn't the only one who had a fun night planned, apparently. That might prove useful...

I took a quieter deep breath and then stepped out into the hallway. I slid in beside the last girl in line, a dusky-skinned beauty with perfectly plump lips and rear. At least Zane had good taste. When I leaned in to whisper in her ear, the other woman jumped with a nervous squeak. The scent of her arousal was a sharp perfume.

"Hey," I said softly. "How long until Master Zane arrives? Do you know?"

Her dark eyes flicked over me and she swallowed hard. "I... I'm not sure. I think they said another ten or fifteen minutes."

"Have you ever done this before?" I asked.

The girl shook her head and bit her full lower lip. "Not very much and this is my first time at the ball... Master Zane sent my invitation."

Interesting. I was increasingly convinced that Zane had done much the same for me. I stared at the girl's collar – okay, maybe a bit at her luscious tits, too – and wished that Miss Rose had gotten her hands on this girl instead of Zane. Well, there was still time to set things right. I just needed to get her away from the others.

"Hey, how about some pointers?" I asked. "Five minute crash course? You wouldn't want to disappoint Master Zane, right?"

I flashed her my wickedest smile, the one I usually reserved for Max. She glanced at the other women, but I ran my finger up her arm, snapping her attention back to me. Biting those lovely lips, she gave me a small, nervous nod.

"Just five minutes?" she asked. "I... I don't want to be late. You get punished for being late."

"That's part of the fun," I said with a wink.

I took her hand and pulled her quickly into the room where I had been hiding, nudging the door quietly shut behind us.

"Let's get you less comfortable," I said.

The girl watched me with huge brown eyes, but let me push her back against the rack. I bound her wrists and ankles, spreading her arms and legs wide, then buckled the ball gag into place.

"Are you okay?" I asked. "Nothing too tight?"

She nodded, her mahogany curls bouncing. I stepped in close and she let out a soft whimper as I slid my arms around her neck. I unbuckled her collar.

"I would honestly love to stay and fuck your cute little brains out," I whispered into the girl's ear. "But I have a bad guy to catch."

I stepped back and buckled her collar around my throat. My transformation from domme to undercover bounty hunter sub was complete. The girl on the rack pulled against her restraints, but nothing at Leather and Lace was the cheap shit.

"Whnn?" she said. "Mmm-nnn!"

I barely heard her muffled voice at all. Like I said, quality gear. I moved out into the hall once more and shut the bedroom door firmly behind me. I couldn't lock it from the outside, but if the rules of Leather and Lace were respected, the closed door would be enough to keep any curious partygoers away for a while. Someone would walk in eventually – whoever had the room set up, probably – but I hoped to be long gone by then.

The other girls turned to look as I took my place in line and there were a few cautiously curious expressions. I spread my hands and shrugged.

"She just started her period," I said. "Bad timing, huh?"

The women nodded and resumed whispering nervously to each other. But we all went silent as two of the big black-clad men emerged back out into the hall. They didn't speak, but ushered us forward with leather-gloved hands. One by one, we all walked through the open double doors. The air seemed somehow taut as I stepped across the threshold, then popped like a soap bubble. I was finally inside.

The girls clustered together in the center of the bedroom. Wide eyes stared around, at the bed and the trays full of implements. The two men who had waved us inside shut the doors behind us.

And locked them.

Chapter
SEVEN

he women drew back, moving in so close that I felt soft skin and trembling limbs brush against mine. No one was talking now. The fear in the air was tangible, something almost sharp enough to cut. But there was excitement, too. Even I felt it. This wasn't the excitement of getting a step closer to Zane... No, it was something else. Something better. A shiver slid down my spine that was hot and cold at the same time.

"What are we supposed to do?" I asked.

One of the black-clad men pointed at the silver trays full of sex toys on the desk, snapped his fingers, and then pointed at the bed. The message was clear. Get started.

"What about you boys?" I asked.

The man only repeated his gesture.

Wow, Zane had these guys *really* well trained. Were they actually just going to stand there while six hot girls got busy on the bed? The other men stared at me, too. Especially the bigger pair who had taken up positions flanking the bedroom's second door. I felt their lust, but not one of them moved a muscle.

I didn't spend much time worrying about the men, though. I had better things to do.

I breathed in the taut air of growing excitement. There was a hot, heady pressure building in the locked bedroom. Heat tingled across my skin and swelled inside me. I snatched up a tangle of straps attached to a long crimson dildo and strode toward the vast, velvet-draped bed.

The girls lunged for the desk and its bounty of toys. None of them seemed to notice the last tray, the one full of blades. More magic? My demonic blood made me immune to that sort of glamour, but the other women didn't see a thing. Maybe I should have cared more, but my pussy and mouth were already watering with desire. Hurriedly, I cinched the strap-on tight around my hips until the bright red plastic cock jutted up from between my legs.

Yes. Fuck yes.

I grabbed the nearest girl, a curvy blonde with wide brown eyes and such a shy smile that she *had* to be new. The newbie hesitated a little as I pulled her into a hard kiss, but not for long before she was kissing me just as hungrily. She whimpered against my mouth and then another girl was pulling at Newbie, pressing her down into the huge bed and shoving a string of glistening black beads into her quivering ass.

I growled at having my toy taken away from me, but then heard a deliciously wet sound and looked down to find one of the other women on her hands and knees, sucking my strap-on with desperate moans. God, the sight was intoxicating. It made the deepest parts of me ache for satisfaction and demanded pleasure in a voice that would not be ignored. No wonder guys always love seeing me on my knees, devouring their dicks.

I groaned and grabbed a fistful of the girl's dark hair. God, she was tiny. Her mouth opened wide and struggled to accept the girth of my red toy cock.

"More," I told her. "Take it deeper…"

Petite let out another moan and rocked back on her hands and knees as Newbie twisted around on the bed to lick her dripping slit.

My fist tightened in Petite's hair and I yanked her forward again. I shoved my dildo down her throat, thrusting deeper and deeper.

My moans joined Petite's and I raked the nails of my free hand lightly over one breast, pinching my nipple. The sensitive flesh was already hard and flushed a deep pink. Petite's muffled voice rose and then became a squeal of utter and uninhibited pleasure. A shudder went through me at the sight of the girl with shiny-wet lips wrapped around my strap-on, her eyes squeezed shut in helpless ecstasy.

I gasped and my whole body jerked as I came. My pussy gushed and I couldn't stop myself – I forced my dildo the final inches down Petite's throat. She gagged and I imagined shooting cum into her mouth, choking her with great torrents of creamy spunk. The fantasy was so intense that it actually made me dizzy.

Petite collapsed into Newbie's arms. She had only a moment to gasp down a few breaths before another women pressed her pussy insistently against her mouth. We were all a tangle of trembling limbs, slicked fingers and shining toys. The air of the bedroom was warm and close, full of the scents of feminine lust and the music of our moans.

More. I needed more.

I grabbed another girl, one with pierced brown nipples who was fingering two of the others. Their juices ran down her skin until it gleamed. I turned her to face me and seized both of her wrists. The other women whimpered as I pulled Piercings' hands away from them and brought them to my lips. Hungrily, I sucked her dripping fingers into my mouth and licked them clean one after the other. Piercings pressed herself against me until her lips found mine and I felt her tongue sliding over them, lapping up every trace of wetness that I had missed.

The chilly hardness of her piercings brushed against my nipples and raised heat to answer the cold. My strap-on was heavy between my legs and prodded Piercings' belly, aching to be used. I tore my lips from hers and shoved her down into the knot of writhing women, then pulled her up onto her hands and knees, bent over before me. My blood burned like wildfire and my heart pounded. Sensation and desire swelled inside me.

I grabbed the dildo jutting out from my body, cool and smooth under my lust-fevered touch. Piercings moaned and lifted her ass toward me, velvety and dark and inviting. Her pussy was so slick and wet. I tightened my fingers around the strap-on and thrust it into her. Piercings gasped and pushed back urgently against me. I couldn't feel the hot tightness of her on my toy cock, but when the dildo came to rest deep inside her, it pressed the unyielding plastic back into me, hard against my clit.

I rolled my hips, staring enraptured as the red dildo emerged from the soft valley between Piercings' buttocks, shiny and wet with her juices. When I could see the narrowing tip of my strap-on, I yanked the girl back, impaling her once more. She moaned and I fucked her faster, making her voice rise until Newbie – not so shy now – pulled Piercings' face down between her legs. I slammed into Piercings hard from behind and every thrust shoved her forward into Newbie's pussy. Within seconds, both women were screaming in pleasure.

Lust raged in a golden inferno all around me. A pair of hands were pushing me down against Piercings' back and the girl with the brightly colored tattoos was there behind me, shaking vivid blue curls out of her face. I could barely move there, pressed between Tattoos and Piercings, but I would not be still. I fucked my strap-on in and out of Piercings and bit hard into her shoulder as I felt a hot, wet tongue licking from the base of my toy cock and then up. My pussy dripped against Tattoos' lips.

"Oh, god," I panted. My voice rose. "Oh, fuck...!"

Tattoos worked her way to the cleft of my ass and then pushed the tip of her tongue into my anus. I wrapped my arms around Piercings and squeezed my eyes shut in all-consuming bliss.

I curled my trembling fingers into the softness of her breasts as Tattoos licked me. When I felt the insistent hardness of a dildo against my slicked asshole, I pinched the equally unyielding metal of the rings in Piercings' nipples and tugged. A long, slender intrusion pushed into my ass. It was a much smaller toy than the one I ground desperately into Piercings' quivering pussy, but Tattoos was shoving it so deep into me that I cried out and wetness streamed from my slit. My whole body tightened like tuning a guitar string and I screamed into the smooth skin of Piercings' shoulder, while she moaned against Newbie.

Everything was a bright golden haze around me, inside me... There were stroking fingers and soft breasts and smooth, warm skin everywhere. We all moaned and came together. I didn't know who I was fucking or who was fucking me anymore. I had forgotten all about the men watching us or the house full of people downstairs. Lust burned through my body, consuming me.

"Stop."

The voice was quiet, but we all went instantly still on the bed. A man stood in the doorway, the one that we hadn't entered through. He wore a flowing pair of red silk pants, but his lean chest was bare. I drank in the sight of pale skin and thick, wavy brown hair. And those dark, dreamy eyes.

Zane Colton.

I tried to shout the name, but my mouth was full of someone's breast. All that came out was a muffled moan that was lost in the swell of half a dozen other voices.

Zane strode barefoot into the bedroom. The wizard carried a short, braided golden whip in one hand that shone in the flickering candlelight as he slapped it lightly across his open palm. There was nothing left now of the demure young acolyte I met four months ago. Had those nervous smiles and shy charms been a façade?

Or had they been real enough before Asmodai scorched them all away?

Zane inspected the bed full of women with dark eyes now more burning than dreamy. They lit on me and a predatory smile spread across Zane's face. I squirmed beneath the other girls, trying to get my feet under me, but there were still fingers and dildos inside my pussy and ass. I could only thrash weakly in the grip of the pleasure consuming me. Okay, Zane was hot and all, but not *that* hot. What the fuck was going on?

"Ah, I see you've–" Zane began, but then he stopped, staring.

The two big gimp-suited men flanking the door that Zane had just entered by were tearing off their leather masks. Long dread-locks spilled out from beneath one, a thick and impressive brown beard from the other. The slightly smaller man's face was set into a grim snarl like a lion carved from mahogany. Griffith...?

I knew the second one, too, all six and a half feet and what had to be three hundred pounds of massive Scottish wizard. Muir.

"Zane Colton!" Griffith roared. "You have betrayed the College and the legacy of Merlin!"

Muir and Griffith held up bound leather pouches, brandishing their readied battle spells. Trust a wizard to find functional pockets in a gimp suit. Zane bolted off to one side. The only weapon in his hand was the golden whip, but there was still a tray full of sharp, pointy shit on the desk.

All of the other girls were gasping and scrambling away. Tattoos yanked the dildo from my ass and I managed to roll up off of Piercings, but then someone else was kicking me in the face and I was knocked down again. Petite screamed and pulled back, falling on top of me as the orgy on the bed turned into a much less sexy tangle of terrified women. But somehow I doubted anyone downstairs could hear us.

"What are *you* doing here?" Zane cried.

As I knew all too well, Muir moved awful fast for such a big guy. He jumped between Zane and the knives, bringing the smaller wizard stumbling to a halt. Griffith held a little leather pouch aloft, chanting words that slid like oil on water, and flung it toward Zane. The loose ends of his flail rose weightless into the air as Griffith's magic congealed into physical force. Knives floated up off the desk, tangling with anal beads and a forked dildo.

Griffith spoke the final word of his spell and fine silver chains shot out, flinging themselves around Zane like a horny metal octopus. Then everything – Zane and his knives and his toys – fell back to the ground. Griffith and Muir stood over the younger wizard.

"You're coming with us, Zane," Griffith said. "High Magus Myrdon has questions about your master. And then there will be a trial, but I don't think it's going to be a very long one."

"You're not supposed... to be here..." Zane gasped as the chains tightened around him.

"Griffith?" I asked.

He and Muir turned to stare as I finally extricated myself from the whimpering knot of girls. I put my hands on my hips.

"What the fuck?" I hissed. "What are you assholes playing at? Stefano told me the divination didn't work!"

Even through the thick, honey-colored haze of lust, I was furious. But both Griffith and Muir looked more confused than proud to have stolen Zane right out from under me. Well, that and a little horny. Their gazes raked over me, along my flushed breasts and the slicked red strap-on jutting up from between my legs.

"Is Stefano around here, too?" I asked. "Just waiting to jump out and yell *boo*?"

"No," Griffith said, blinking and shaking his head like he was trying to clear it. "The divinations were... fractured. We split up to chase down all of the different visions. How the hell do you know any of this, Lilith?"

There was nothing remotely sexy about what the other hunter was saying, but something coursed through me, a wave of desire that made my knees go soft. Zane's head snapped up and Muir's eyes widened.

"Griffith–!" the big bearded wizard shouted.

Voices moaned in pleasure and I stumbled. Even Griffith and Muir seemed uncomfortably constrained in their full-body black leather. I steadied myself against one of the bedposts and glanced back at the other women. Had they begun fucking again while we were talking? But everyone in the room that wasn't an undercover bounty hunter remained huddled in the corner, where they had retreated when the magic started. Every one of the girls' faces, however, held an expression of absolute ecstasy and I suspected that the men looked the same beneath their masks.

"My master..." Zane breathed.

The candles flared with golden light and then Asmodai stood in front of the locked doors. The demon lord was dressed much like Zane, but his silk pants were black to match his long, flowing sable hair and the sharp horns arcing up from his brow. Muscles rippled smoothly under skin so golden that Asmodai appeared to have been gilded. His eyes burned like the sun.

The women behind me fell to their knees, moaning in ecstasy at the sight of Asmodai. The men knelt too, cringing back from the incubus, but sported raging boners visible even through their tight black leather suits. Heat seared through me, glowing and swelling with unbearable need.

"Asmodai!" Griffith said in a choked voice.

He sprang away with well-practiced speed, but Asmodai moved so fast that he was little more than a shining golden blur. He grabbed Griffith by the throat and lifted the hunter up into the air as effortlessly as raising a wineglass for a toast.

Muir was still clutching a sealed and stamped pouch in one large hand. I recognized that concoction – Muir had come uncomfortably close to hurling several of those fireballs right through my ribcage the last time we met. Now he bellowed the words of his incantation and flung the spell. A miniature star flared into being and streaked toward Asmodai.

But my cheer died in my throat as the demon raised one hand and caught the fireball. With a grin, Asmodai closed his long fingers around the flame. It burned for a moment and then snuffed out.

"Oh, shite," Muir gasped.

Before I could even blink, Asmodai had his other hand wrapped around Muir's neck, too, and hoisted him up alongside Griffith.

"Ah, little wizards," the incubus said in a voice so smooth and rich that the cowering women moaned in unison at the sound. "The men who carry on my treacherous son's work. Well, that is nearly over now."

"Let go of them!" I shouted.

I charged on unsteady legs and flung myself at Asmodai. I grabbed one of the demon's bare golden arms and tried to pry him off Muir. I had a split second to marvel at the irony of a universe where I was actually trying to save the big bastard, but then Asmodai swung his arm – still holding Muir – and hurled me effortlessly across the room. I smashed into one of the shelves and wood shattered under the force of my impact. Candles tumbled down around me, leaving streaks of hot wax along my skin.

With a groan, I rolled up onto my hands and knees. The pain of a few minor burns and what felt like a bruised rib should be gone already, but... no, I still ached. Something was terribly wrong. I wasn't healing. Max had fucked me just a few hours ago, to say nothing of the miniature orgy on the bed before Zane's arrival. I'd sensed the girls' lust, but no rush of sexual energy.

Asmodai. I was a cambion, but he was a full-blooded incubus and lord of the Nether. Every shred of desire, of lust in this room, belonged to him. I hadn't even felt it leaving me, like iron filings being drawn to a far more powerful magnet.

Well... fuck. I struggled to my feet. Asmodai had pulled Griffith and Muir close, long golden fingers squeezing around the wizards' throats. Muir clawed at his pockets, but his face was swiftly turning an alarming shade of red.

I yanked my strap-on. The harness should have snapped like thread, but I wasn't strong enough anymore. After precious seconds of swearing and contorting, I managed to tear the sex toy off and charged in, swinging it at Asmodai like a club. I didn't particularly intend to attack the Lord of Lust with a dildo, but I needed the damned thing *off*. It was fun to fuck with a cock and I could see why guys like it, but I don't know how they walk with one of those dangling between their legs, much less kick ass when the situation calls for it.

And kicking ass was exactly what I needed to do right now. Asmodai had killed Evaine. He was going to pay through the dick for that.

The incubus' fingers tightened around Griffith's throat and he gasped. Brilliant lines suddenly lit up all along the other hunter's body, not golden but a cold blue. His protective magical tattoos blazed through the leather of his bodysuit.

I swung my dildo at Asmodai as hard as I could. It bounced right off the demon's perfectly formed chest and the slippery plastic shaft flew out of my hand. I went in with a left hook to Asmodai's jaw, but the impact shivered agonizingly up my arm and I might as well have been tickling the demon for all my punch moved him.

Muir growled like a bear and lashed out with his huge fists and feet, but none of it was any more effective than my attack. Griffith pried desperately at Asmodai's hand and managed to gasp a single arcane word. The icy glow of his tattoos became a clear, blinding radiance. Lines of light rose up from Griffith's body, tearing his clothes away to rags, and leapt out at Asmodai like a burning hydra. They coiled around the demon prince, sprouting blade-like spines all along their lengths that drew sparks from Asmodai's skin, but didn't so much as scratch the flawless gold.

I sprinted toward the desk full of Zane's tumbled knives and my fingers closed around the hilt of the dagger with the wavy blade. But if Asmodai was shrugging off Griffith's badass magic tattoos as though they were little more than annoying puppies, what the *fuck* did I think one unenchanted knife could do? Not a damned thing... Not to Asmodai, at least.

"This is a private party," the demon said, looking between Griffith and Muir. "And you two were not invited."

Golden flames raced down Asmodai's arms and Muir screamed once as they burned over him. Griffith's tattoos wound themselves tightly against his dark skin, but their light was washed out by the glow of demonic fire.

"Lilith...!" he managed to croak.

I scrambled across the floor to where Zane lay, still bound in Griffith's chains. The wizard stared up at his master with utter adoration in his eyes and a massive tent in his red silk pants. I grabbed Zane by a handful of his thick brown hair and heaved the wizard up to his knees.

"Stop this!" I cried. I pressed the blade of Zane's own dagger against his throat. "You summoned that big golden fucker, right? Now banish him!"

Zane's grin was far too wide. It looked like it might actually split his face in half.

"Banish my master? When we're so close to breaking the Seal of Avalon?" he said. "No."

Breaking the Seal of Avalon? What the fuck was Zane talking about? I shook him furiously and shouted at Asmodai.

"Let them go! Or I'll kill the dickweed who summoned you!"

Asmodai glanced down at me. Muir was... gone. Ash sifted to the ground where he had been. Griffith's tattoos were invisible now, utterly consumed by fire. The other hunter refused to scream as he burned, but he writhed like a damned soul in Asmodai's grasp.

"Stop!" I said. "Release him or Zane is fucking dead!"

Griffith's bones glowed white-hot. I saw them blazing through his flesh. The golden flames roared and then there was just a cloud of ash. I bit back a sob and tightened my hand in Zane's hair. The young wizard wasn't even looking at me – he had eyes only for Asmodai. Zane would never stop. He would do anything for the demon lord. He had betrayed the College and created Reid. Good men and women were dead because of him.

This had to end.

Asmodai moved as fast as thought, but I didn't need to think. I had already made my decision. My knife was buried to the hilt in Zane's neck and blood ran down over his chest, leaving the wizard clad in crimson to match his red silk pants. Even as he died, Zane continued to grin like a madman.

One of the girls screamed, but still no one came running from Leather and Lace. No one knew what was happening up here.

Zane Colton was dead. But before I could be horrified or exult in what I had done, Asmodai was on me. Inhumanly strong fingers closed around my throat and I gasped in the grip of sudden pleasure that rocked me to my very core. Asmodai lifted me up, fury burning in his glorious gold eyes.

"Soon I will be drawn back into the Nether," said the Lord of Lust. "There will be no one left to summon me. The Castle and College will be forewarned and watchful now. It seems I have no more time to waste."

I moaned and grabbed at Asmodai's wrist, using it as leverage to aim a kick right where it counted. But the demon lord flung me back before my foot could connect with his balls and I slammed down hard onto the bed. Asmodai stepped over Zane, striding toward me. The wizard's body flared briefly with golden flames and then was gone.

"The rest of you..." Asmodai said, gesturing dismissively. "Go. And remember none of this."

The women let out soft whimpers of disappointment, but scrambled for the exit. One of the remaining men unlocked the door and they all bolted from the bedroom. Untouched, the doors slammed shut behind them.

"Zane's spell will hold a little while yet," Asmodai said. "Long enough for me to finish the work that I came to do."

The incubus strode with liquid grace to the bed. I scrambled back, bringing up my hands into defensive fists. They were shaking.

"Such fire," Asmodai said. He smiled radiantly down at me. "I'm glad you got my email, Lily."

I stared up at him. I couldn't look anywhere else. The shining demon prince was the only thing in the room. In the world.

"What?" I barely managed to gasp. "That... that was you?"

"Yes. And my invitation to this charming little party," Asmodai said. He trailed one golden finger over the velvet bedcovers. "But your mortal appetites are so very... vanilla."

The demon's smoothly perfect sable hair stirred in an unfelt breeze. Candlelight gleamed along the hard lines of his chest and stomach, along the curve of his sharp obsidian horns. I hated him. I wanted him. With an effort that nearly made me scream, I raised my fists again.

"Why?" I whimpered. "Why did you do this?"

"I need you, Lily. And now I have you."

"The hell you do!"

Asmodai loomed up over me, all black and gold and terrible, glorious beauty.

"Yes," said the incubus. "The hell I do."

Chapter
EIGHT

$\mathcal{A}$smodai waved one hand and the candles all around the lavish bedroom snuffed out. There was still light, a sourceless circle of pale amber radiance that illuminated the bed and nothing else beyond it.

"You have been defiant, Lily," Asmodai said. "Submit."

That word rolled through me. *Submit...* Asmodai made it sound like the best word in existence. Better than *cock* or *sex* or *fuckmyass*. I knew that was three words, but I didn't care.

No, wait... I *did* care! Whatever Asmodai wanted, I couldn't give it to him.

The incubus advanced on the bed and then stepped up into it. I tried to fight, tried to punch him right in his perfect face. But Asmodai caught both of my wrists easily and pressed me back into the velvet covers. His long golden body was heavy against mine.

"Submit," Asmodai said again.

I moaned. I should have been able to stop it, but the sound escaped my lips before I could think. No supernatural glamour has *ever* worked on me. Not fairy or vampire or even the kinds of spells that the College uses to alter memories. But this... this was something else. I didn't hate Asmodai any less for what he had done to

Evaine, to Reid, and now to Griffith and Muir. But when the demon lord slid against me, my legs parted automatically for him. Asmodai smiled down at me.

"You will enjoy this," he told me. "It is what you were meant to do, Lily, to be. Not serving the mortal wizards like a hunting hound. Another destiny awaits you."

"What... what are you talking about?" I gasped.

"A cambion created the Seal of Avalon. Only a cambion can break it."

Breaking the Seal of Avalon. Zane said that, too. That was why they made Reid, to open the Seal and release the demons that Merlin locked away centuries ago. Reid had thought Asmodai was furious with him for damaging the strange rock, but it was the other way around.

"That was the stone you made Reid touch," I said. "It was the Seal of Avalon. He wasn't a real cambion, though. The Seal cracked, but it didn't break."

The words should have been triumphant, but they came out in thin, gasping breaths. I squirmed against Asmodai. I wanted... I needed... something. *Anything* from him. A single touch, a single kiss would be enough to send me plunging over the edge into ultimate ecstasy.

"Yes," Asmodai admitted in a low voice that sent hot sensation jolting through my body. His hand tightened around my wrists.

"Then why aren't we on... on Avalon right now?" I asked with a moan. "Why not just throw me onto the Seal and... and..."

The thought of Asmodai pushing me down, bending me to his will was too much. I squeezed my eyes shut and tried not to cum.

"Merlin knew better than to craft a Seal that could be opened by force," Asmodai said. His lips brushed my ear. "You must be willing, Lily. You must touch the stone because you *want* to."

"Well, I don't want to bring back the demons. So you're pretty well fucked, aren't you?"

"No," said Asmodai. "But you will be."

He trailed one finger along my cheek, down my throat and traced the delicate arch of my collarbone. I bit my lip so hard that I tasted blood, but couldn't hold back my cry. The afterimage of Asmodai's touch was a blazing line of pleasure that burned and would not fade.

"You are so very beautiful, Lily," he said.

I moaned at Asmodai's praise. I writhed on the bed, half still trying to escape the demon pinning me there, half just trying to pose for him. Asmodai closed long fingers over my breast, brushing lightly across the oversensitive skin. I arched my back, pushing my chest into his touch, but Asmodai held me loosely and refused to give me the contact I needed.

Wetness streamed down along my spread thighs and I wound my trembling legs around Asmodai's waist. His pants were already gone – I guess an incubus doesn't have to do anything as pedestrian as get undressed. Asmodai leaned in close.

"All I have to do," he said, "is make you want what I want."

"Never... never going to happen, asshole," I said.

Well, moaned. Like a whore. *You* try resisting the Lord of Lust. Anyone who says you can't rape the willing has never had sex with an incubus.

I bit at Asmodai's lower lip with all the strength I could manage. Oh, god. He tasted like... I don't even know. Something I wanted to devour for the rest of my life. Asmodai only laughed and pressed his lips to mine. The bite became a kiss and I whimpered in helpless delight as Asmodai's tongue slid over mine.

His fingers unerringly found the peaked pink of my nipple and pinched sharply. A razor bolt of pleasure and pain lanced through my body. I felt hardness against me, hot and perfectly smooth. I rolled my hips desperately, trying to impale myself on Asmodai's cock or at least rub my pussy against his length. But the demon held himself just out of reach.

"Submit," Asmodai commanded.

His voice pierced me, that one word pouring a gallon of gasoline on the fire raging through my body.

"No...!" I gasped.

Asmodai kissed me again, hard and possessive and full of terrible, glorious power. He wasn't holding my wrists anymore. I tried to wrap my hands around the beautiful bastard's throat, but slid my arms around his neck instead and clung to him. I twined my fingers into silky black hair like starless night.

I understood now. I understood why Finn and Muir would be willing to break every College rule to summon a lust demon. Why my father had done it over and over again. I understood why Ben Sung hadn't fought when the succubus invaded his home and then his body. I *hated* Asmodai. I hated him more than anyone in any world, but I wanted him even more than that. If Stefano barged through the door right now and tried to pull the incubus off me – god help me, I'd kick his ass.

I don't know if I've *ever* felt that good, but for the first time in my life, there was no flow of sexual energy. There was lust, yes, bright and shining. Asmodai's desire burned like fucking napalm, but he gave me no power at all. The power was his. Asmodai was an incubus, a demon. He took, but he did not give.

My vision was dimming around the edges. I was still kissing Asmodai and I couldn't breathe. Just before I could pass out, he pulled his lips from mine... and I whimpered in disappointment when he did. Asmodai laughed and sat up, sliding his hands down my body. My hips rose from the sheets in a silent plea. Asmodai's touch circled my navel and then moved down between my legs, over the sensitive pink of my pussy. I wailed in pleasure and gushed wetness all along the demon's fingers.

"Do you like this, Lily?" Asmodai asked.

"N-no... Yes... Yes!" I cried.

"Do you want more?"

"Yes! Please! Fuck me!"

The words poured from my lips. I was as helpless to stop begging for Asmodai's touch as I would be to stop cumming when he gave it to me.

The Lord of Lust loomed over me. The strange, sourceless light played along his perfect muscles and the ebony arcs of his horns. There was nothing vulnerable in Asmodai's nakedness. His cock rose long, smooth and golden from his body, far more beautiful and dangerous than the sword he had wielded against Evaine. Asmodai grabbed my ankles and spread my legs wide. I whimpered.

"Beg," he commanded.

"Fuck me!" I moaned. It felt like I had spent ten years waiting for the demon, not ten minutes. "Please, please fuck me!"

With a single graceful movement, Asmodai surged into me. I cried out in mindless pleasure as he filled my body. Such rapture blazed along every inch of my nerves that it was a wonder I couldn't see them glowing through my skin like burning filaments. Every sense ignited with sweet fire at the feeling of Asmodai's cock finally inside me.

He held me there, buried to the hilt in my dripping sex. I cried out with the most whorish, most abjectly base and animal need, but Asmodai imprisoned my ankles in his unbreakable grip and would not let me move.

"Do you want to unseal the Nether, Lily?" he asked in a voice completely smooth and unperturbed as I writhed in his grasp. "Do you want to stand beside me as I tear down the world my son took from me?"

"I... I'm cumming!"

I squeezed my eyes shut, drowning myself in the sensation of Asmodai inside me. It seemed to have replaced everything hard within my body, as though his cock were the only thing holding me up.

"Wrong answer," Asmodai said.

The demon's too-strong fingers tightened around my ankles and spun me easily onto my hands and knees in the sheets. I whimpered as Asmodai withdrew his cock from my pussy, then screamed out as he plunged the steely-hard thickness up my ass.

"Fuuuuck!" I cried as the huge head pierced and then slammed deep into me. "Oh fuck. Oh fuck!"

Asmodai seized my long red hair in one fist, holding as though onto a leash and pounded himself mercilessly into my asshole. The muscular tightness had no choice but to yield to Asmodai's brutal, intoxicating invasion. I lifted my hips, offering myself up to the onslaught.

I was disgusted with myself for wanting to please Asmodai, for wanting him to watch his thick golden shaft penetrating my ass again and again. Asmodai's lust surged and poured through me like a drug. He moved faster and I squealed in utter ecstasy. Hot wetness gushed from my empty pussy and made Asmodai's corded thighs gleam like those of a shining statue. His cock drove into me relentlessly and I couldn't breathe. There was no room for anything but pleasure inside me. Pleasure and Asmodai's dick and...

"I... I need your cum," I gasped.

The incubus pulled back on my hair, yanking me upright against his chest. He bit at the side of my neck hard enough to make me shudder in sweet pain.

"Do you want it?" Asmodai's breath was a soft caress over my bruised flesh. "You want my load deep up your ass?"

"Yes!" I screamed. "Oh god, yes! Fill my asshole with cum!"

Asmodai didn't groan or relent at all in fucking me. His cock simply swelled at will, stretching me almost unbearably, and liquid heat surged into my ass. One huge, throbbing pulse and then another and another, more and more. So much cum flooded my body that my eyes rolled back and my limbs twitched beyond my control. Every muscle, every nerve, every part of my entire being was consumed by impossible pleasure.

I was riding the incubus. I had no idea when we moved or how much time had passed. My consciousness felt loose and slippery inside my head. Everything was a swirl of black and gold and insatiable need.

I sat astride Asmodai and speared my pussy onto his dick as fast and hard as I could. Wetness glistened across his rippled stomach and I was already cumming. Had I ever stopped? Every time I slammed down onto Asmodai's perfect cock, it forced a hot stream of his spunk from my overfilled ass. My skin was slicked with semen and it never seemed to end. How much had he pumped up into me?

Asmodai lay back in the blue velvet pillows with an arm behind his head, black hair fanned out around him. He caught one of my breasts in his hand, squeezing painfully as I rode him. I loved it.

"You are a credit to your people, Lily," Asmodai told me. "You fuck like a true-blooded succubus."

I moaned. His words wounded and flattered at the same time. I willed myself to stop, to pull myself off of the demon lord and run, but I swiveled my hips and reveled in the feeling of hardness impaling wet softness. Cum oozed from my ass and I moaned again.

"I have dreamed of what I will do when the mortal world is mine once more," Asmodai said. "Of the concubines I will take in their millions. But you, Lily... I will keep you for my own. You will be my consort."

I moaned at the thought. This could be my life: being Asmodai's little fuck toy, his whore and his slut. Yes... God, I wanted that, to feel like this forever...

"No," I whispered. My voice was ragged, wild and raw from so much screaming.

Asmodai's eyes blazed and his fingernails left angry red marks across my breast. His cock seared inside me and then sensation exploded through me. My body didn't seem big enough to contain the pleasure. My pussy certainly wasn't... Asmodai's cum filled me in seconds, then gushed out and ran in rivers down my thighs.

I faded again, gasping for breath and my heart pounding so hard that my whole being thrummed with the drumbeat. When I could open my eyes once more, I was sprawled across the bed. Hot semen welled up from my pussy and ass, running along my skin in thick drops that made me shudder with helpless ecstasy.

Asmodai loomed over me like a conqueror, the fingers of one hand wrapped around my throat and holding me pinned against the bed. With the other, the demon stroked his long cock. I writhed weakly in the twisted sheets, trying to entice the incubus into shoving that gorgeous prick back inside me. My pussy, my ass, my mouth... I didn't care which hole, as long as Asmodai fucked me. I never wanted to do anything else ever again.

"Still you resist me," Asmodai said. "And I'm impressed. But you're half human. That part of you is weak, Lily. All humans are. There's another part of you, though. A beautiful part that knows her lord and master."

Asmodai's cock throbbed in his hand and cum laced through the air. This was the first time I had actually seen it. The lust demon's cum wasn't white, but a precious gold just a few shades paler than his burnished flesh. It splashed in gleaming ribbons across my breasts and stomach. I gasped at the sensation of it, the tingling heat like liquid lightning.

"All I have to do is wake that part up."

The Lord of Lust snapped his fingers and the bright cum began to move across my skin. It gushed from my ass and pussy in hot rivers, turning my gasp into a rising cry of pleasure. Molten gold writhed and pulsed as it slithered from my body, fucking me in reverse until I was crying out, and then slid the wrong direction from between my trembling legs. Gilded cum swirled with the load Asmodai had just unleashed across my belly and streamed up over my chest.

For a moment, my breasts and neck were painted brilliantly gold, and then I was opening my mouth as Asmodai's cum poured itself down my throat, choking out my delirious screams. It burned inside me, Asmodai's essence and... and something else. Something that rose to answer the call of her prince.

"Your human nature will always fight me," Asmodai said. "But soon that will be burned away. You'll come to me, Lilith. Willingly. Obediently."

He stood. I gulped desperately, but couldn't speak. Asmodai smiled, shockingly white against gold and black.

"Then we will break the Seal of Avalon," he told me. "Together."

I didn't know if Asmodai faded away, if Zane's spell had finally lapsed and pulled him back into the Nether, or if it was just my own vision failing. But everything went dark.

Chapter
NINE

When I opened my eyes, I was in my bedroom again, back in my old condo. But everything looked fine now. Maybe I had gotten the place fixed up, but I didn't remember doing that. Wasn't I staying with Max ...?

Something wasn't right here. I blinked at the bedroom windows. My view should have been of the bright glass of downtown and distant red spires of the bridge. But I saw only misty gray darkness outside, as though my condominium floated in some otherworldly void.

What the hell? Was this the Nether?

The question brought me up short. Asmodai, I remembered. The trap he had laid for me at Leather and Lace. The incubus dangled Zane out like bait and I had bitten. And now... what, exactly? What had Asmodai done to me?

I had to figure out what the fuck was going on. Starting with where I was. I went to the window for a better look. Or tried to, but I couldn't move.

I might have been surrounded by something that looked like my bedroom, but I wasn't in my bed. I stood, dangling from the ceiling in silver chains that reminded me of the ones Griffith had used to capture Zane. They bound my wrists together over my head and then stretched up toward a ceiling so distant that perspective concealed it in darkness.

The chains rattled as I yanked against them, but didn't break. I still had no sexual energy. If that even mattered here. No way was this place real. Some kind of vision or dream, maybe? I felt strange, weaker in a way that had nothing to do with my lack of supernatural strength. Something inside me ached with a cold, hollow pain. Something was missing.

But Asmodai's overpowering presence was gone, too, and I could think more clearly now. Time to think of a way out of this, then. I swore a few times under my breath and then began scanning the weird dream-bedroom for anything useful.

I stared in shock at the mirror suddenly standing in front of me. No, not a mirror. I was looking at myself... almost. I recognized my own long legs, round tits and wicked smirk. But the woman before me had bright golden eyes and her hair was pitch black. A pair of slender ebony horns rose from her brow.

The other me put her hands on her hips. Her nails were a shiny obsidian color and looked terribly sharp. She wasn't chained up or even dressed like me. I had been stripped naked, but she still wore the leather corset and boots I'd bought for the bondage ball.

"What the fuck?" I asked.

But the words came out as a muffled grunt. I was gagged.

"Don't you recognize me?" the black-haired woman asked in my own voice.

I shook my head.

"I'm your better half," she said. "Your stronger half, the part you inherited from your mother. The only part of you that's going to matter soon. I am Lilith."

I started violently. I *knew* the strange feeling inside me. I had experienced it before in Finn's sanctum, when I forced myself through his circle of binding. For just a moment, the ward pulled me apart into two women – one human, one succubus. Now that demon half was standing right in front of me, while the human part was bound in chains.

Oh, shit.

Lilith stroked my cheek lightly and I shuddered. Her touch was electric. Fuck, did it *get* more masturbatory than this? My nipples rose at once to hard little buds and heat pulsed between my legs. I squeezed my thighs together, but that only made it worse. Lilith ran her hand lightly along my neck and over the curve of my breast. I bit down on the gag. Lilith knew exactly how I/she liked to be touched and I writhed in my chains.

"Don't struggle," Lilith purred. "You can't fight yourself, Lily. Just give yourself to me."

Was that what I sounded like? Damn, I was hot. I moaned into my gag.

Lilith reached toward my pussy with slender, pale golden fingers, but I kept my legs squeezed together – which was admittedly kind of a first. Lilith drew back with a frown that made me long to bite that pouting lower lip.

"Why are you fighting me, Lily?" the succubus asked. "Give me control. You'll like it."

I shook my head. *Go to hell, bitch.*

"You *will* give me control," Lilith purred. "And you *will* like it. I can show you."

The succubus snapped her fingers and chains rattled. But I had not moved...

Lilith stepped aside, revealing someone behind her. He was too large for her lithe body to have possibly concealed, but nothing in this place worked the way it was supposed to.

It was Max. He was naked, too, with arms chained overhead like mine. The pose held him up, drawing the muscles of his chest and stomach taut. His blond hair was tousled and he blinked slowly.

"Lil...?" Max asked in a fuzzy voice.

Lilith walked a slow circle around him, hips swaying seductively with every step. I tried to call out to Max, but only a soft groan escaped past the gag in my mouth.

"Maxwell Ferguson," Lilith said. Her fire-eyed gaze roamed all over his hard body and then back to me. "Your favorite toy."

She stopped before Max and wrapped her slender golden fingers around his dick.

"Lil...?" Max said again, staring between me and the succubus. "Wait, two of you? Wow. Best dream ever."

His cock grew in Lilith's hand, swiftly too long to fit in her grasp. I would have licked my lips hungrily, but the damned gag was in my way. Max just smiled dreamily and groaned.

"Toys are made to be played with," Lilith said.

She ran her hand along Max's dick, down to the thick base and then curled her fingers around his balls. The demoness squeezed them. Hard.

"Aagh!" Max cried.

The delicate skin between Lilith's fingers swiftly turned a terrible scarlet color. Max thrashed in his chains.

"Let... go..." he grunted.

"No. You're mine, Max. I'll do whatever I please with you. And you'll love it."

Lilith raked her sharp, gleaming black nails down Max's chest, leaving four parallel lines of blood that mimicked the scars left by the yeti. Max wasn't gagged and his gasp of pain echoed through my ethereal bedroom.

Stop! I tried to cry, but the gag stifled my shout.

Lilith seemed to understand me just fine, though. She smiled and raised her fingers up to her red lips, licking Max's blood from them. He stared in horror, but his long cock twitched.

"Stop?" Lilith laughed. "Why? What else is a mortal man for but to use? To dominate?"

"Lil, what's going on?" Max asked. "Are... are you okay?"

It wasn't exactly clear which of us he was speaking to. Lilith backhanded Max hard enough to set him swaying in his chains. A line of blood ran from the corner of his mouth. I cried out again and strained toward Max, but the silver chains held me fast.

"Am I not beautiful?" Lilith asked. She placed one hand against Max's chest. "Don't you want me to touch you?"

"...Yes?" he answered hopefully.

"Good boy," Lilith purred.

She stroked Max's bruised jaw and then trailed her hand down his bleeding chest. He grunted in pain and Lilith kissed him, turning Max's agonized groan into one of pleasure. She drank in both sounds.

"Tell me that you want me," Lilith murmured.

Her fingers left crimson lines as they slid down Max's stomach to circle his dick again. He panted hard, chest heaving as he tried desperately to push himself into Lilith's touch, but he didn't have the leverage. Sweat ran from his tangled blond hair.

"I want you, Lil," Max answered, shaking his head. "You know that. I've always wanted you."

"Say *I want you, Lilith*," she demanded.

"I... what?"

Lilith's hand moved along Max's cock, up to the crown and back again. Pale precum beaded at the tip and then dribbled across her fingers. Damn, she had him on the edge already. I yanked harder against the chains that bound my wrists.

"Tell me that you want *me*," Lilith said. "Not her."

Max blinked and struggled to focus. Did he know this was real? Did *I* know if this was real? Max looked at Lilith, then back at me.

"What? I want her, too. I mean you. You're both Lil," Max said slowly. "Aren't you?"

Lilith's hand stilled on his cock and she curled her sharp nails into his vulnerable flesh. Max's jaw clenched and I heard his teeth grind together.

This might not be real, but it was definitely dangerous. My succubus half was trying to take over, and she would hurt Max to do it. Bitch.

"We're *not* the same," Lilith hissed. "She is human. Weak. I am a demon!"

She raised one long, leather-clad leg and hooked it dexterously around Max's waist, still seizing his cock. I struggled against my bonds, but couldn't get any closer as Lilith sank herself onto Max. She was no longer wearing the skirt I had bought for the bondage ball and I watched Max's dick vanish into her pussy, inch by inch. I heard the slick sound of him penetrating Lilith and smelled the fragrant tang of her in the air. It was terrible and it was beautiful.

The succubus pressed herself against Max. She tossed her head and hair like spilled ink cascaded down her back. One sharp black horn slashed along Max's tightened jaw and blood welled up, dripping across his skin. Tears streamed from my eyes, but wetness streamed from my pussy, too.

"You want me, not her," Lilith told Max. "I am stronger. Better! Say it!"

Her position wasn't an easy one, but that didn't seem to matter. Lilith rose and fell onto Max's cock with unearthly grace, almost dancing as she writhed sensually on him. I watched myself taking Max and burned with fury and desire.

Lilith let out a wild cry and bit at Max's chest as she came. He squeezed his eyes shut in mingled pleasure and pain. Lilith looked back at me with Max's blood on her lips like a vampire. I was going to fucking kill her. Or just fuck her...

"I... I'm going to cum," Max panted.

Lilith pulled herself up and off his long dick. It was shining and wet and flushed deeply with desire. But the demoness lashed out, striking Max across the jaw hard enough to rock him back on his heels, then grabbed his cock to yank him forward again. Lilith sank to her knees on the bedroom floor.

"You belong to me," she said. "Not her!"

Lilith swallowed Max's dick in a single gulp, taking it all the way down her throat without the slightest sign of gagging. She worked her mouth up and down Max, but her lips were still blood red... Nightmare visions of the succubus using her teeth replaced my hot flush with cold chills.

"Oh god... please let me cum," Max groaned.

Lilith spat his dick out, still dripping wet. She licked her lips and stood, then brushed one fingertip along Max's achingly hard length.

"Tell me you want me," Lilith demanded again.

"I want you, Lil! More than anything!"

"I am Lilith!"

"Lil, why are you–?"

My demonic half closed her fingers around Max's cock and her razor-edged black nails bit into sensitive flesh. Blood ran and he shouted in pain.

"Max!" I screamed.

The gag was gone from my mouth. My voice rang out through the ghostly echo of my bedroom. Lilith released Max and spun to face me. Her golden eyes were wide, but narrowed to blazing slits.

"Are you finally tired of just watching, Lily?" she asked.

"Get away from him!" I snarled.

The demon's crimson lips turned up in a delicious smile. She sauntered toward me, hips swaying and high heels clicking out a sharp staccato against the floor. Lilith inspected her fingernails as she drew near. They were still tipped in red.

"Submit to me," Lilith demanded in a low, sultry voice. "To Lord Asmodai. Open the Seal for him and you can have anything you desire."

"No," I said.

"You will serve the Lord of Lust. You'll be his willing slave, but humanity will be yours."

"No!"

Lilith smiled and I clamped my teeth down on my own lip against a scream as Lilith seized one of my breasts. Her nails sliced into my skin.

"Lil!" Max shouted.

She bit my nipple and I twisted in my chains. It hurt, but it felt so good that my nerves burned with the pleasure. Lilith's tongue lashed my soft flesh like a cracking whip and hot blood ran down my skin.

"Please," I said through clenched teeth. *Please stop* or *please let me cum*, I didn't know.

"Submit," Lilith commanded.

"I... can't..." I panted.

It was heaven; it was hell. My head spun. Lilith's nails raked my ass and thighs, carving equal parts agony and ecstasy into my flesh. I screamed.

"Lil!" Max pulled at his chains, muscles knotting and straining, but he couldn't move. "Stop hurting her! Please, whatever you want, I'll do it! Please, just let me help her... Let me touch her..."

Max stared at me, horror and desire warring across his face. He yanked so hard against his bonds that the metal cut into his wrists, but his cock was still long and thick. Lilith took her mouth from my breast and kissed me. I tasted the copper tang of my own blood. Our blood.

"See how he begs?" Lilith asked. "This could be all men before you. Break the Seal of Avalon and Lord Asmodai will lead our people into the mortal realm once more."

I shook my head weakly. "No..."

"Those dommes you saw tonight were nothing, pathetic shadows of *our* power. We will enslave the world and you will be a true mistress of men. I am a part of you, Lily. I know what you want."

I hung shaking in my chains. How long could I fight Lilith for control? How long until she did something worse to Max? Until *I* was the one hurting him and enjoying it? Lilith was right... She was a demon and she was a part of me.

This was all in my head. This was all me, all *my* fault. Lilith caressed my cheek and I felt something else warm there. Not my blood or sweat, but my tears. The succubus grinned triumphantly.

"Leave her alone!" Max said. "Lil! Lil, it's going to be okay. Look at me, not her. Look at me!"

I blinked through tears and looked past Lilith to Max. His entire body was taut and shone with sweat as he fought against his chains. But this was my nightmare and he couldn't move one inch.

Lilith seized my chin between her thumb and forefinger. Bright red beads of my blood stood out on the black leather of her corset like rubies. My body screamed with agony and ecstasy.

"You are mine," said Lilith. "You are me."

"Lil, no!" Max shouted. "Don't listen to her!"

"I can't do this anymore," I whispered.

"Yes, you can," Max said. "You're strong, Lil. You've fought monsters your whole life and you're not about to let one win now."

"But you *are* the monster," Lilith told me.

She was right. But so was Max.

And so was I. This was my nightmare, my own internal struggle for control.

Mine.

My chains were suddenly gone and I stood beside Max. He still hung in his restraints, staring with wide blue eyes. Lilith was bound naked in my place, wrists lashed up over her head in the chains that had held me. She writhed like... well, like a furious little hellspawn, long black hair and pale golden limbs thrashing.

Now I was the one wearing black leather. There wasn't a mark on my skin.

"Lil, are you okay?" Max asked.

"Yeah," I said. "How about you?"

"Uh..."

I smiled at Max and brushed his bleeding chest with one hand. The wounds vanished. Gently, I touched Max's face and chest and still-hard cock – everywhere Lilith had touched him. Everywhere she'd hurt him. The blood and cuts disappeared as if they had never been there.

"Can you get me out of these?" Max asked, rattling his chains.

I hesitated. This wasn't over yet. As long as the succubus half of me wanted to obey Asmodai and fought against the rest of me, I would be just like Reid: a tormented monster.

"Max," I said. "Do you trust me?"

"Always, Lil."

I gave Max a long kiss and then stepped back from him. I held out my hand and hoped that I really had as much control over this weird vision as I seemed to. My fingers closed around the handle of a leather riding crop. Yay for dream logic!

I snapped the crop up against Max's cheek. He didn't flinch.

"Do you want me?" I asked Max.

"Of course I do," he answered.

"He wants *me*," Lilith hissed like a wildcat. "He desires the demon in you. Who would want an ordinary woman after they have fucked a succubus?"

I kept the riding crop against Max's cheek. "Do you want me?"

"Yes," he said.

"Do you want her?"

I used the crop to turn Max's face toward Lilith. The succubus had gone still in her chains. Her black hair was a wild cloud around her shoulders and she panted, making her breasts heave.

Max hesitated. "I... uh..."

I pulled back the crop and brought it down on Max's ass. It left a pink stripe across his skin. Max gasped and his cock twitched. I put the crop against his cheek again.

"Do you want her, Max?" I asked. "Tell me the truth."

His eyes flickered between mine and Lilith's bright golden ones.

"Yes," Max breathed.

"You see!" Lilith cried. "Give me control and you will have him! You will have any man or woman you desire!"

"I already have Max," I said. "And as for other guys and girls... Do you even know what I do for a living?"

Lilith's beautiful lips turned down into a pouting frown. Max stared at her and at me, his hands clenched into fists. They shook in their chains, making the silver links chime. I cracked the riding crop against my open palm. Both Max and Lilith snapped their attention back to me.

"You called the mortal dommes mere shadows of you," I said, pointing my riding crop at the succubus. "But do you even know what *they* do?"

"They subjugate their slaves," Lilith snarled.

"No. What they do is about trust, about taking ownership and control of someone else's pleasure. What the demons do is just abuse. All Asmodai wants to do is hurt people, Lilith."

The succubus' eyes narrowed. "So now you'll hurt me?"

"No," I said, shaking my head. "Max?"

"Yes, Lil?" he answered.

"What do you want to do to her?"

"Kiss her," Max said at once.

"Where?"

"Her... her hip."

I looked at Lilith. Her skin was smooth and unmarked by any of the wounds she had inflicted on me, as fine as pale golden silk. I held the riding crop to Max's lips. His eyebrows shot up and I slapped his cheek with it.

"Kiss," I said.

I pressed the leather to Max's lips and he kissed it. I advanced on Lilith and the wild demoness tried to draw back, but the chains bound her just as securely as they had me. I cracked the riding crop across the delicate curve of Lilith's hip. She bit her lip.

"Now where do you want to kiss her?" I asked Max.

"Her belly," he answered breathlessly.

Max kissed the crop when I offered it again and I delivered his caress with another sharp smack of leather. The crop left a bright mark on Lilith's smooth stomach, as though I could see Max's kiss on her skin.

"Where?" I asked Max.

"Her breast."

Smack!

"Her neck."

Smack!

"Her ass!"

Smack!

Now it was Lilith's turn to writhe in the silver dream-chains. She twisted and shied away from my riding crop, but the leather came down wherever I aimed it. Lilith whimpered and then moaned with each blow. Pink marked her pale flesh like a dozen roses.

Max leaned forward to kiss the riding crop again and I pulled it back. He frowned and I slapped it across his hard, sweat-slicked chest.

"Remember who's in control here," I said.

"Yes, Lil."

"*I'm* in control," Lilith said. "Asmodai awakened *me*."

"Where?" I asked Max.

"Her... her lips," he answered.

I let Max kiss the flat end of the crop once more. His eyes fell shut and his mouth lingered there, as if he could taste Lilith on the leather. His cock hadn't flagged one bit and remained utterly hard, as flushed as the rosy red my crop left on Lilith's skin.

I walked slowly across the room to the succubus and held the crop up in front of her. She regarded it with a hungry, greedy expression on her lovely face, but I withdrew it and Lilith hissed at me. I waved one finger at her, but offered the riding crop again.

Lilith looked at me skeptically, then back to the black crop. She whimpered softly, but I didn't touch it to her lips. I let Lilith close the final distance and press her mouth against where Max's had been. She kissed the crop hungrily and bit the leather between her teeth to stifle a sharp moan.

My demonic half was one hot little bitch. Watching her made my pussy drip and left shining streaks of wetness down the dark leather of my boots. Max's dick was as hard as I had ever seen it and twitched with every reluctant sound of Lilith's pleasure.

I pulled the riding crop away from the demon's mouth. She fought against the chains to keep her lips on it.

"What do you want?" I asked.

"I want you to be me," Lilith said.

I slapped the crop across her ass. She let out a high, keening wail as I striped her golden skin.

"What do you want?" I asked again.

"I want to serve Asmodai!"

I flicked the crop sharply across her breasts, raising another pink line. Lilith whimpered.

"But... but you could have the power of a true succubus," she pleaded. "Let me be you!"

I tapped the leather riding crop lightly against Lilith's cheek and leaned in close, my lips nearly touching hers.

"What do you really want?" I asked.

Lilith bit her lip. The succubus' long legs trembled so hard that they couldn't hold her weight any longer. Only the chains held her up now. I ran the crop along Lilith's inner thigh. She gasped and when I pulled it away, it shone wetly. Lilith stared, open-mouthed and panting, as I offered the shining crop to Max. He smiled at Lilith and then licked the taste of her from the leather.

"I want..." Lilith said.

"What do you want?" I asked.

"I want to cum. No... I..."

I slid the riding crop down Max's chest and stomach to his cock. He let out a low groan as I trailed it over the sensitive crown. Max left a pale streak of precum across the leather. I held it out to Lilith and she licked the crop clean, then whimpered when it was gone.

"I want him to cum," Lilith whispered.

Drawing a deep breath, I cracked my crop against her chains. They vanished. Suddenly unsupported, Lilith fell to her knees in front of me.

"Max, do you want her?" I asked.

"But... isn't she a demon?"

"Yeah, she's a demon. A succubus. But she's also me." I put the crop against the back of Max's neck and pushed until he looked down at Lilith. "Do you want her, Max?"

"Yes, Lil. I always want you. Every part of you."

The riding crop was gone from my hand and I grabbed Max's cock. He gasped and threw back his head. His thick length was like iron hot out of the forge. Lilith drew herself up into a kneel, gold eyes staring raptly at Max as I stroked him.

"Make him cum," she begged.

"Help me," I told her.

Lilith put both of her hands over mine. Her fingers circled his flushed crown, but carefully. The succubus' nails didn't cut and Max gasped at our touch.

"Oh god, Lil," he groaned. "Lilith...!"

Max's whole body went taut as a drumhead and then trembled at our touch. Long streams of cum – pure, bright white instead of demonic gold – shot from his dick and painted pale streaks through Lilith's midnight hair. It beaded like pearls along her black horns and splashed in glistening ribbons across her face. Her burning eyes were wide, her mouth open in an expression of wonder as Max gave her his huge load of creamy spunk.

Finally, I released Max's dripping cock and he staggered. His chains were gone, too. We were done with chains.

Max rubbed his shoulders as though expecting pain, but then gave me a surprised look and shrugged. More dream logic.

I knelt next to Lilith. The black-haired succubus whirled and grabbed me by the throat. Max started forward, but I held up one hand. My domme skills must have been getting pretty good because he actually stopped. Lilith's razor-edged obsidian nails bit into my skin, but not hard enough to draw blood. I put my hand over hers.

"I need control," she said in a breaking voice. "I have to become you...!"

"You already are," I told her. "You're a part of me, Lilith. And I want you back."

I kissed her. Lilith went rigid against me, but then the succubus closed her eyes and returned my kiss.

Chapter
TEN

The soft creak of an opening door woke me. I sat up on the bed and blinked slowly through the bright morning sunlight at a woman standing in the doorway. She wore an apron stuffed with rubber gloves and cleaning supplies. Hurriedly, she turned away and scampered from the bedroom.

I was still at Coil House, sitting in the tangled bedding where Asmodai had left me last night. The sheets were clean, or at least not stained gold with magical demon spunk. The ashes that used to be Griffith, Muir and Zane were gone, too, though I still smelled smoke faintly in the air. I stared at the carpet where their remains had been. Fucking Asmodai...

I unbuckled the stolen collar from around my neck. The little metal charm hanging from it was blank now. I guess Zane's ward had lapsed, and so had the magical key to get through it. I dropped my collar into the rumpled sheets and stood.

My clothes were still in the next room, folded neatly on a table beside the bed. The woman whose collar I had taken was gone, as well as the rack where I had secured her. I searched around the bedroom, but didn't smell any trace of blood or ashes.

I breathed out a long sigh of relief. Whoever found the girl, it didn't seem to have been Asmodai.

My long hair was a wild red mess and I couldn't tie my corset very well on my own, but soon I was dressed again. It felt good to be armored in leather once more. I zipped up my thigh-high boots and stepped back out into the hallway.

The cleaning crew was gathered at the top of the stairs. They whispered to each other as I passed, but didn't otherwise look particularly scandalized. I supposed that the bondage aficionados who ran Leather and Lace contracted companies that knew how to deal with lube and cumstains. One accidental leftover from the bondage party wasn't going to ruffle their feathers very much.

I waved to the cleaners as I made my way down the curving staircase. My coat hung from an otherwise empty rack in the foyer. I dug my phone out of the pocket and found several texts from Max.

> - *Late night. Everything okay?*
> - *Think you'll be home for breakfast?*
> - *Fell asleep in the shop & had the weirdest/hottest dream about you...*

I headed out of Coil House and across the circular driveway in the direction of my car. It gleamed sleek and silver in the bright morning sunlight. A chilly autumn wind stirred through the trees of Coil House's vast grounds and tugged at my tangled copper hair. I tapped out a message back to Max as I walked.

Long night, I texted. *Need a big breakfast. I'll tell you the whole thing while I stuff my face.*

When I hit *send*, my cell phone vibrated again, still on silent. But it wasn't another text and it wasn't Max. I stared at the name on the screen. Stefano was calling me. He needed to know what happened last night. But what could I tell him? Evaine was right... If the wizards learned Asmodai wanted me to break the Seal of Avalon, the wizards would do *anything* to remove me as a threat.

I didn't like keeping secrets, but Evaine had told me to keep this one. And it was safe enough now, wasn't it? Zane was dead and Asmodai himself said that the College and Castle would be watching too closely for anyone else to risk summoning him back to Earth. Maybe the wizards could put some putty on that crack in the Seal of Avalon.

Asmodai's attempt to enslave me to my own demonic nature had failed, too. The incubus needed me to touch the Seal willingly, or it wouldn't open. As long as I never did that, Asmodai was pretty well fucked. I grinned. Any day that started with Asmodai not getting what he wanted was a good one.

My phone had stopped vibrating. I unlocked the i10 and slid inside, then pulled up Vincent Myrdon's number. I would catch Stefano up later. I tossed my phone into the passenger seat beside me as the car's Bluetooth picked up the call. The College deserved to know what had happened to Griffith and Muir, what I had done to Zane, and I would tell them what I could.

While the call rang through to my father's office, I drove away from Coil House and down the long cobbled driveway toward the city. It was time to go home to breakfast and Max. Maybe breakfast on Max.

LILY QUINN BOOK #13

Sealed

WITH A KISS

Chapter
ONE

Max held me close, his strong arms wrapped around my waist. His body pressed against mine and the bed sheets were a tangle of white all around us, like ocean foam on a crashing wave. Max surrounded me, filled me, and the feeling of him was overwhelming. I pushed my face into the pillow to muffle my cry as the pleasure surged up from deep within me.

When I ran out of air, I breathed in the scent of Max from the bed. Of *us*. I lay on my side in the bed with Max curled around me, inside me. I felt the swift, powerful beating of his heart like a metronome in high tempo against my back. I gasped and grabbed at the sheets, twisting the already hopeless mess into knots around my fingers.

"Don't stop," I told him. "Just... just like this. Please don't stop. Don't ever stop, Max."

"Never, Lil," he said into my ear.

Max trailed warm lips down the side of my neck and kissed the back of my shoulder. His cock slid smoothly in and out of my pussy, keeping up the steady, unhurried pace. I fought the urge to move faster, to seize Max's hips and pull him in, or push him down and ride him hard. Letting myself lie back against Max took every ounce of self-control I had managed to learn over the last year.

Max's cock filled me, hot and thick and so good that I had to stifle another loud scream. Something was building inside me that I couldn't name. I've had a *lot* of sex in my life, so it's not often that anything in bed gives me pause. But this warm, full sensation was not confined to my pussy. It was in my chest, too, behind my ribs and making my heart feel too big for my body. Every beat made pleasure pulse through me.

And with every tight thrum of ecstasy, Max was right there beside me. Inside me. It made me remember our first time together, when my powers awakened. And just like that night nine years ago, something between us was waiting for me to close the circuit, to cross some final distance...

With every thrust of Max's dick inside me, every kiss along my spine, white-hot pleasure built and pushed me higher than I'd ever gone before. His cock fit me perfectly, stretching the tightness of my pussy just short of pain. Max matched my rhythm as though we danced together. He swept me into a swirl of sensation, a storm that pulled me up and up and would not let go. The ecstasy was almost agonizing in its sweetness.

You really should try it. But not with Max. He's mine.

Max slid one big hand along my hip and up to my chest, gently tracing his fingers over my breast and raising goosebumps across my skin in his wake. I moaned and snatched his wrist. He let me pull his hand up to my mouth and I bit the end of one finger. Max's cock turned to molten steel inside me as I circled his fingertip with my tongue.

"Lil," he whispered.

Max repeated my name like it was a prayer. He buried his face in my red hair and inhaled deeply. Even after giving me a dozen orgasms or more, Max was still trying to hold off his own climax. But I was too close now and so was he.

I arched my back and finally grabbed Max's hip, pulling him as deep into me as I could. His cock throbbed inside me like another heartbeat and then pumped thick heat into my pussy, feeding my orgasm like throwing gasoline on a fire. Fuck, like throwing *dynamite* on a fire.

"Max!" I screamed. I swear the windows rattled. "Fuck! Yes!"

He held me tight against his chest as we came together. That sensation of *more* was just a breath away now. Hurricane-force pleasure swept through me, sending my thoughts spinning and soaring. I writhed in Max's arms, drowning in the feeling of him. I never wanted to feel anything else ever again.

After a short, sweet eternity, Max withdrew slowly from inside me. Cum spilled from between my legs and into the tangled sheets. I whimpered a little and Max pulled me in close again, his cock nestled in the cleft of my ass. He kissed me gently behind the ear.

"That was... intense," Max said in a voice still ragged around the edges.

"Yeah," I agreed. I wriggled back against Max, content just to feel him holding me. "It was, wasn't it?"

"Are you okay, Lil?" he asked. "You seemed kind of distracted for a bit there."

I blinked my eyes open again. Max had noticed? Of course he noticed. I tried to smile and frown at the same time, but managed neither. Luckily, Max was still spooning me and couldn't see my face at all.

"Me?" I told him. "I'm always fine. I'm Lily Quinn, half-succubus monster hunter extraordinaire."

Max laughed and kissed the back of my neck, then continued on down between my shoulder blades. I shivered pleasantly and nearly punched Max when he stopped. He sat up with a groan.

"Shit, it's almost noon," Max said. "I better get out to the junkyard now if I want to find those parts for the Daewoo. Unless you need me to stay?"

I sat up next to Max and yawned. When I stretched, my spine popped.

"No, go get your car parts," I said with a sigh. "As much as I like your boy parts. You've never let a customer down before and you're not about to start now. Besides, I've got some stuff to do, too."

"New bounty?"

"Shopping, actually," I said.

"Well, at least you're all charged up."

"Yeah... If anyone else goes for the last jar of fabric softener, they're fucked."

"It comes in jugs, Lil," said Max.

"Whatever. There's a joke in there somewhere about my jugs, but I can't quite find it."

Max stood up and leaned over the bed to give me a kiss. "If you can't manage to hunt down one joke about your breasts, then it's a good thing there are monsters out there to catch."

"Hey, fuck you! I'm hilarious."

I grabbed Max before he could get away and put a kiss on each of his dimples. He kissed me back, pressing me down into the bed. I squirmed a little beneath him, but didn't push him off of me.

"Lil, I..." Max began.

His voice shook and my heart suddenly jumped in my chest, hammering against my ribcage like a prisoner demanding release. But Max only sighed and gave me another dimpled smile.

"I've really liked having you here," he said. "I'm so sorry for everything that happened with Asmodai and Evaine, but... but the last month has been absolutely amazing. Thank you for being here with me, Lil."

"Thanks, Max. I couldn't have gotten through this shit without you."

Max and I lay together in the twisted sheets, just staring into each other's eyes. Finally, he let out a low growl and stood.

"Right," Max said in an explosive exhale. "Clothes now or I'm never leaving this bedroom."

I lingered in bed as he went into the bathroom to clean off, then over to the closet to pick out some clothes. When he bent to retrieve a pair of boots, I whistled and Max blushed. He returned to the bedroom to dress and I watched him zip up his jeans with a predatory smile. When Max saw my expression, he offered a second time to stay home, but I waved him off.

"My own things to do, remember?" I said.

"Okay." Max kissed my hair. "See you later tonight, Lil."

I hoped that he would get back before dinner or we were having pizza again. Not that I have anything against pizza, but Max's cooking was far better than anything I could order online.

Finally, I climbed up out of bed and gave Max one last goodbye kiss. He retreated from the bedroom and I heard the door close downstairs, so I went into the bathroom to mop up the slick mess still running from between my legs. There was cum everywhere, dripping warm and white from inside me.

When I was finished cleaning, I wadded up the towel to throw into the laundry basket. But then I grabbed the edge and pulled. The terrycloth stretched and a single thread snapped.

That was it. I sighed.

Two weeks ago, I lost my powers. Shit, huh? I could still hunt monsters for the College without super strength, speed and senses. Hey, give me *some* credit – I'm a genuine badass all on my own. But cambions are half lust demon. We don't just lose our powers, not unless we can't get laid. And that clearly wasn't my problem. Something else was going on. Something big.

I had my theories, but luckily, there was a test to be sure.

Chapter
TWO

*B*y the time I finished what I needed to do, the fading sunlight had turned the streaked clouds into long pink and magenta streamers stretching out from the glittering silver sea. Shopping didn't take all day, but nerving myself up did.

Now my jeans lay tangled in the bathroom door, leaving me wearing just my t-shirt and panties. And because the floor was cold in October, my admittedly tattered old bunny slippers. One of the eyes was missing from the left slipper and the ears on the right hung at angles you would never see on a healthy rabbit. The slippers had been reduced to an ashy, sodden mess after the destruction of my condo, but I wasn't about to throw them away.

I stood in front of the bathroom sink, staring at myself in the mirror. I didn't *look* any different. I didn't even feel very different, really. But something had changed and I didn't even realize it was happening.

Shit.

I hadn't told Max yet, not about the loss of my powers or about the test. Maybe it sounds stupid, but I wanted to be sure before I said anything. Well, now I was sure... But Max was still out trying to salvage a new transmission and compression valves for the little black Daewoo downstairs in his garage. The Korean manufacturer had shut down years ago, so finding replacement parts was kind of a pain in the ass. But Max's client adored her car and he was going to make her day when he got it fixed up.

I turned my head this way and that, inspecting my eyes in the mirror. The light still reflected off the golden threads in my hazel irises, that same demonic gleam that's been there since I turned eighteen – since my cambion powers appeared.

Sometimes I almost expected to hear that succubus half of me speak in her own voice again. But aside from that hot/weird vision thing Asmodai forced on me last month, there was no one else in my head. Lilith wasn't a separate person anymore and the only time I spoke to her was when I talked to myself.

Too bad. I could have used some advice right about now.

I sighed and shook my head. Bright red hair swirled along my back... and then kept flowing around my shoulders as though I stood underwater. Max's toothbrush floated up and bumped gently into the white plastic test stick. They tumbled together in slow motion through the air.

Magic.

Shit!

I hurled myself to the floor as the mirror exploded into silver glass shards and flames whooshed over my head. Burning plaster and scorched red brick rained down around me. I smelled brimstone and witchwood on the hot air. Some fucker just threw a fireball at me!

There was a crash from somewhere else in the apartment and I jumped to my feet. I leapt over the broken mirror and ran out into the living room, sliding in my slippers. Heavy footsteps pounded across the floor and I squinted. The lights were still off in the rest of the apartment and without my sex-powered super-senses, I had only the fading sunset to see by. But it was enough to catch the glint of metal as two figures charged toward me.

My home invaders were a pair of homunculi, thick man-shapes that only stood about waist-high, both plated in steel. That meant Sabra was here somewhere, directing her creations. What the fuck?

The homunculi reached for me, large hands outstretched. They looked tough and heavy, but the little clay bastards were also slow. I bolted around the first one and kicked. Without my supernatural strength, I couldn't just smash it to pieces, but I put all my weight against the homunculus and pushed hard. It rocked forward and toppled, limbs thrashing like an overturned toy. The living statue clattered noisily against the hardwood as it struggled to right itself.

I kicked the coffee table up onto two legs and shoved it at the second homunculus. Sabra's golems were slow in the head, too, and this one seized the table in steel-shod hands. By the time the homunculus figured out that it wasn't holding a pissed-off, half-dressed cambion, I had already grabbed the stock of the shotgun taped beneath the table. After Asmodai's appearance in my old condo, Max had agreed that a little more proactive home security might be a good idea.

The homunculus dropped Max's coffee table and I fired point-blank into its armored chest. Twisted metal and damp red clay sprayed across the living room rug. My handjob skills paid off as I quickly pumped the shotgun and hammered two more slugs into Sabra's golem. Its stumpy limbs thrashed weakly.

The first homunculus had managed to get up onto its hands and knees. I sprinted across the room and put the last two shots into its blobby head. Both of the clay and steel bodies finally lay still, but there were more footsteps on the stairs.

I tossed the empty shotgun aside and then yanked my couch gun from between the cushions. What, you don't have a couch gun? Sure, sometimes the nine-millimeter poked me in the ass when Max and I were playing video games, but tonight made it all worthwhile.

"Drop it, Lilith!" shouted a familiar voice.

SEALED WITH A KISS • 279

I whirled to face Doyle. The young bounty hunter wore black fatigues still so crisp and new that even in the wan light, I could clearly see the sharp creases. Or maybe he ironed them. I wouldn't put it past Doyle. He leveled an engraved rowan wand at me.

So Sabra wasn't the only one on the job. Had that been Doyle's fireball in the bathroom or were *all* of the hunters converging on me? The last time that happened was to hunt down Zane Colton, one of the College's own corrupted wizards. If they were after me now, this was bad. Really bad.

Doyle and I stood at the top of the stairs, holding each other at gun/wand-point. Spells take a lot of material components, chanting and gesticulating, while my gun only required a single finger. But even if Doyle was an asshole – and he was – he was a wizard of the College. One of the good guys. Dismantling the homunculi was one thing… I didn't understand the magic very well, but Stefano told me once that Sabra's golems only carried some rudimentary reflection of her mind. Breaking them was pretty much like breaking a mirror. But shooting Doyle was something else entirely.

"What the fuck?" I asked. "Fireballs? Homunculi? I know we fuck with each other sometimes, but not like this. What the hell is going on?"

"The High Magus has called a hunt on you, Lilith."

There was no fear or even glee in Doyle's voice, though neither one would have been a surprise. Doyle never liked me, but all I heard now was cold resolve. I wasn't going to talk Doyle out of this.

"What are you doing working with Sabra?" I asked. "I thought Zane had to be a damned special case to get you to pull your head out of your ass!"

Doyle didn't rise to the bait. He shook his head and kept his wand pointed at me. "You're too dangerous, Lilith. The Castle and the College want you dead."

My head spun and my blood turned to ice. The wizards were going to kill me, just as Evaine had warned. I had to get out of here.

"Don't–!" Doyle shouted.

I shot him in the shoulder. Doyle shouted and fell, bleeding across the hardwood. His eyes flicked up between my legs as I kicked the wand out of his hand and I felt the golden flicker of his lust. Good to know that I still had that half-succubus sense, at least. But Doyle scowled at me and I supposed lust and disdain weren't mutually exclusive.

"Give it up," Doyle said, groaning with each word. "You're too dangerous, Lilith, and you can't stop us all!"

A voice echoed up from the garage downstairs. I couldn't understand the words, but I recognized the midwestern twang – Clio. She was here, too. The High Magus had called a hunt on me and every hunter in the city must have answered.

That shouldn't have hurt, but somehow, it still did. There would be time for pain later, though. Right now, I had to survive.

I grabbed Doyle's wand off the floor and ran into the bedroom just as gale-force winds began whipping through the apartment. Back in the living room, Doyle shouted and I heard a lamp crash to the floor. I kicked the screen from the open window and hurled Doyle's wand out into the darkening evening. It would take him a while to find it again and by then, I hoped to be long gone.

I scooped my keys and cell phone off the nightstand and stared out the window as Clio's storm shrieked in my ears. Shit, that jump was going to be a lot harder without my powers, but I didn't have a lot of other options. I switched the safety on my gun – no point in escaping the bounty hunters only to shoot myself by accident in the process.

Doyle staggered into the bedroom, shouting something that I couldn't hear over Clio's howling wind, and I dove out the window. The fall probably should have snapped both my legs, but Evaine taught me better than that. I tucked into a roll that dispersed the force of my landing, then skidded to a grass-stained stop on hands and knees on a narrow strip of side yard lawn.

I sat up, panting and swearing. One of my slippers had flown off during my fall and I scrambled toward it, but an arrow thunked into the wooden fence that ran beside Max's garage, only a few inches from my face. Delicately etched runes glowed with pale blue fire all along the shaft. I jumped back, reflexively throwing my hands up as Redmond's enchanted arrow exploded with light. It shone so bright that I could clearly see the silhouette of my bones through the flesh.

I whirled away, blinking back stinging tears. I could *just* make out the figure crouched on the garage roof, barely visible against the night sky in his black clothes. For a die-hard Tolkien buff, Redmond sure got his Gandalf mixed up with his Legolas.

"Oh, come on!" I shouted. "Not you, too!"

I badly wanted to flip Redmond off, but my hands were full of keys, gun and cell phone. The other hunter fitted another arrow against his bowstring, chanting in a low voice. The arrow began to glow, scarlet this time instead of blue. I didn't know what spell Redmond had carved into that shot, but I sure as fuck didn't want to stick around to find out.

I threw myself flat against the brick wall of the building, out of Redmond's line of sight, and made an awkward crab-crawl dash around toward the front of Max's garage to the parking lot. There was my i10, just a few yards away...

Sabra's big black van roared into the parking lot, tires screaming across the pavement. Without my magical sex vision, all I could make out through the dark glass were indistinct shadows.

"Fuck!" I cried.

I brought up the pistol I had grabbed from the couch, thumbed off the safety and fired at the van. Even now, I didn't really want to shoot Sabra, so I aimed at the passenger side, figuring I would put a few bullets into the seat there or maybe a homunculus riding shotgun.

My first shot barely chipped the glass. Sabra must have made some alchemical transformation and I could only pray that the van wasn't entirely bulletproof. The second and third shots slammed into the van and milky spiderwebs raced out across the glass. My fourth finally hammered a tiny hole through Sabra's windshield. It wasn't much, but it must have been enough to make the hidden sorceress flinch because her oversized van veered off course and spun a screeching half-circle in the middle of Max's parking lot.

I pulled the trigger again, but missed entirely and the bullet dug a furrow into the asphalt. My next shot, though, punched into one of Sabra's tires. It didn't blow out, but even over the screaming of her brakes, I heard swearing and clanking from inside the van. The whole thing overbalanced and toppled onto its side with a thunderous crash. I really hoped Sabra had her seatbelt on.

Redmond sprinted along the length of the roof and I saw the glowing red of his arrow. Ember light illuminated the hunter's eyes, narrowed as he lined up his shot. I bolted around Sabra's van, but Redmond's perch was high enough that the fallen vehicle provided no cover at all.

The back doors of the van had burst open when it overturned, spilling homunculi of all sizes and builds. Several of the smaller golems were crushed beneath the car, but one of the bigger constructs wedged steel-plated fingers under the bumper and struggled to pull it upright again. The hulking homunculus saw me coming and dropped the van, moving in for the kill. I guess catching me was its pre-programmed first priority.

Redmond took his shot. I ducked the homunculus' fist and his glowing crimson arrow thunked into the golem's lumpy shoulder. The arrow didn't hurt it much, but then the fireball spell exploded and flung clay in every direction. I shouted and hopped in a circle as my remaining bunny slipper caught fire.

"Shit! Sorry, Sabra!" Redmond called from the roof.

Max's front door burst open and Clio came stalking through, blonde hair billowing in gale-force winds. I kicked off my burning slipper and kept running. Redmond had pulled another arrow –

this one a bright, poisonous-looking green – and fired, but Clio's magically-brewed storm knocked his shot right out of the air.

"Dang it, Redmond!" Clio shouted.

I hit the unlock key on the i10's fob, yanked the door open and dove inside. I punched the start button and threw my car into reverse. Sabra's van still lay on its side like a beached metal whale and I clipped my rear bumper against hers, setting the dark bulk spinning. A pair of homunculi grabbed for my i10 and I jammed the shifter down into *drive*. My tires screeched on the pavement, but they caught before Sabra's golems did and I lurched forward.

One of Redmond's arrows slammed into my back windshield. It didn't have the mass to break through, but the spell exploded on contact and shattered the window, peppering me with embers and broken glass. Swearing, I stomped on the accelerator and burned twin tracks of black across Max's parking lot as I raced away.

Chapter
THREE

I drove through the darkening night without destination, knowing only that I had to get away. After I put a few miles between me and the garage, I managed to make myself slow down a little. Racing around the city in panties and one of Max's t-shirts might have been ideal for charming cops out of speeding tickets, but the police weren't my biggest problem right now.

Did the College know my powers were gone? Probably not... Doyle and the rest were geared up for a serious fight. There was no way the College would have dispatched all four of them to deal with a single unmagical human woman. The only reason the High Magus hadn't sent more was because Asmodai had killed Griffith. And Stefano...

I frowned and shook broken glass out of my hair. Had Stefano been there at the garage and I was just lucky enough to avoid him? I doubted it. When the College hunters tracked down Zane Colton, Stefano had them a hell of a lot better coordinated than this. The other hunters weren't used to working together and they were dis-organized.

That was probably what saved my life tonight. If Stefano had been there, I'd be dead.

Rush hour was over, but I stayed off the freeways. They felt too open and exposed, *especially* after rush hour. It would take only a single magical nudge from a College hunter to send my little silver car smashing into a concrete divider or over the edge of any of the bridges criss-crossing the bay. So I stuck to surface streets, eventually winding my way south down the Parkway. The curving oceanfront road was dark and quiet.

I considered calling Stefano to ask what was going on, but figured that I already knew the story: the College had realized I was the key to the Seal of Avalon. I was a cambion, just like Merlin, and the first one born since he created the Seal to keep the demons locked up in the Nether. All I had to do was willingly touch the Seal of Avalon and it would break, freeing the demons to start the Dark Ages all over again.

I briefly wondered if my current powerless state had changed any of that. I didn't have any of my other sex-fueled half-succubus abilities. No superhuman strength or speed or healing... Maybe I couldn't open the Seal anymore. But no, I had felt Doyle's lust back at the garage. I was still a cambion, only without any of the perks.

How the hell did the College know about me and the Seal? The only others who knew were Reid and Zane, but both of them were dead. Evaine had kept the secret my whole life and *I* sure as fuck hadn't told anyone. Well, anyone beside Max.

Wait, Max...!

I jabbed the phone button on my steering wheel.

"Call Max," I said. My voice shook.

The phone rang through the i10's speakers. And rang. The readout on my speedometer rose with every ring that Max didn't pick up. Maybe his hands were just covered in grease and he was trying to get them cleaned off...

"Hi, this is Max Ferguson. I can't come to the phone right now," said his voicemail. "So leave a message and I'll get back to you as soon as I can."

"Max, it's Lily! Don't go home!" I shouted. The wind whistled through the shattered remains of my window. "The hunters came after me there and it's not safe!"

I needed to see Max, to make sure he was okay and plan our next move. But it was entirely possible, even probable, that the College was tracking me through the scry network even now. Were they listening in on me?

"Go to... to the place where we were first together," I told Max's voicemail. "Before all of this began. I'll meet you there. Be careful."

I hung up and stared through the shadowed curves of the Parkway. Alright, I knew where I was going, but how long could I stay there before the wizards converged on me again? I had to hope that Max got my message soon.

The Quay vanished behind me and I drove down into Southport. No one pulled me over, though. The police had all but given up on this part of the city back when I was in high school, and any cops who might have pulled the short straw to patrol Southport were probably busy answering calls for toilet-papered houses and smashed jack-o-lanterns.

Southport was a warren of old warehouses and piers left over from when the city was a center of shipping, instead of tech start-ups and rent gouging. Every street corner was spray-painted with graffiti and half the streetlamps were dark. I wasn't afraid of Southport, though. I had grown up and survived here since before I had either tits or superhuman powers.

No, I was afraid of who might be following me into Southport. I watched my rear-view mirror obsessively and studied every pair of headlights so intently that I nearly missed my turn. I swore and jerked the steering wheel almost too late, turning and screeching down a narrow side street.

The pavement was ancient and cratered with potholes like a shitty knock-off version of the moon. Crumbling and gang-tagged buildings swiftly gave way to sandy earth dotted with a few scrubby coastal willows. Faded signs directed me toward the ocean with unconvincing green paint promises of a vista point and telephone access.

The road dipped and then climbed sharply, finally letting out in a tiny gravel parking lot. The bulbs of the streetlights had been shattered and the line of pay phones were long gone. Someone had yanked the phones out of their plexiglass boxes years before I ever set foot on the old overlook.

The view had changed a bit since high school... A few more of the decrepit warehouses sagged like drunks now or had collapsed entirely, and a little more of the northern hills were eaten up by condominiums, but the steep slope of the overlook still dropped away to offer its old view of the shimmering silver bay waters.

The nostalgia washed over me so hard that it brought tears to my eyes. This was where Max and I were first together, tangled in the bed of his truck and fumbling through our virginity the way all teenagers do. This was where I had discovered my powers, even if I didn't understand what they meant at the time. Max had run away from me that night, but he came back and promised never to leave again, no matter how fucked-up and scary things got. And Max had kept that promise ever since.

But where was he now?

There was no sign of Max's truck. The isolation of the overlook was no competition for what I guessed had to be a hundred Halloween parties, so there were no teenagers parked here tonight, cars rocking on their shocks as they went at it inside. My only company was a primer-gray racer with flat tires that sat crookedly against the guardrail. The windshield wipers bristled with parking tickets and a yellow tow warning curled in the driver's side window.

The vehicle seemed abandoned and the wizards didn't usually engage in that level of deception, but I was taking no chances tonight. I parked next to the other car and looked in through the dusty windows, but it was empty.

Slowly, I let out the breath I had been holding and turned off my engine. I smelled salty, bitter seawater outside, and hot pavement cooling in the night. The late autumn wind whipped in through the broken rear windshield and blew my hair into my face. Were Doyle and Sabra and the rest still at the garage? If Max showed up there, I doubted that they would hurt him. But they certainly didn't give a shit about his shop and would erase a lot of Max's memories before dumping him back into the world with no idea who I was.

That was *not* going to happen. I tried calling Max a second time, but after four more rings, his voicemail picked up again. Growling in frustration, I tightened my fingers around my phone and half wished that I could just crush the damned thing into a twisted ball of glass and metal. Instead, I dropped it onto the passenger seat and pressed my hands against my stomach, trying to soothe the butterflies there. I winced. Those were some bitchy butterflies... And I was in for months of this crap.

I watched the night for headlights. As soon as Max got here, I was going to jump him for the world's most ferocious quickie. I was a professional sex beast, after all. I could get his pants off and cock into me within ten seconds. Twenty if I was being ladylike. And once I showed Max just how worried I had been about him, we could figure out what to do next. Run for a safe house, maybe?

I really needed to get a safe house. Every badass in the movies had one. *Movies...* I suddenly remembered the night before. Max had cooked dinner and we watched a movie. I only made fun of him a little for getting teary-eyed when the boy and the girl finally kissed at the end, then took Max to bed and had sex all night long.

Thank god we slept in this morning, giving Max his late start on collecting the Daewoo parts. What if he had been home when the other hunters attacked? I couldn't imagine Max just standing aside while Sabra's homunculi tried to rip me apart. Max was good at a hell of lot of things and had helped me a few times in my hunts, but that wasn't the same as fighting a group of trained wizards, even disorganized ones.

After what happened back at the garage, I was pretty sure Clio and the rest were *getting* organized. I checked the time on my phone again, then stared out through the night. A thick silver fog was rising from the bay below and crept up the headlands toward me like a great, prowling gray dragon. The stars were concealed behind thickening clouds. Hiding, just like me.

Still no Max. Alright, maybe I would have to skip even a quick fuck. As soon as Max arrived, we had to get moving. Probably in his truck. Even if I pried off the license plates, every hunter in the city would still recognize my little silver i10 on sight.

With some more muttered swearing, I climbed out of the car. I found a duffel bag in the trunk and dug up a pair of black cargo pants and a long-sleeved shirt from inside, the kind I wear on the job. At least on jobs where the dress code isn't *slutty*.

I go through a lot of clothes in my profession and had long ago learned to pack spares. No shoes in this bag, though. I pulled on the pants and threw the shirt back. The night was growing quickly cold, but I was still too amped on adrenalin and worry to feel it much. I buttoned and zipped up the pants, then shut the i10's trunk. I hadn't been on a hunt in a while, I realized. There was Zane last month, but that wasn't even a real job. More like me walking into Asmodai's trap and then beating him at his own game because I'm awesome.

The last bounty I'd actually gotten paid for was... the yeti? The job where I snapped Doyle's arm like a stick and Max was nearly thrown off a mountain. The memory of that last part still made my gut clench. But come to think of it, I had stopped looking for new houses, too. I was happy living with Max and had no desire to leave.

Holy shit... Was Max my boyfriend?

My cell phone rang. Gravel bit into my bare feet as I ran around the car and yanked open the door. I grabbed my phone from the passenger seat.

"Max? Where are you?" I asked. "Are you okay?"

"Lilith."

It wasn't Max. I pulled my phone away from my ear and looked down at the screen. Vincent Myrdon's name glowed there in bright white letters. The High Magus of the College. I lifted the phone again.

"Hi, Dad," I said.

"You need to come to the College, Lilith." Vincent's voice was heavy and solemn.

"Why? So you can kill me yourself?" I snarled into the phone.

"I'm sorry, Lilith. It has to be done. You're dangerous. We all knew this day might come. You were warned when Evaine brought you to us."

"I'm your daughter!"

"We would be forced to pass this sentence on any cambion. You don't understand the threat you pose to this entire world, Lilith! You have the power to open the Seal of Avalon—"

"I know that," I snapped. "How the hell do you?"

"We've been studying Zane's notes, the passages he copied from the *Gates of Avalon* and his... schematics for Reid's creation. Both were magically encoded, but Finn knew Zane well enough to help us decrypt them."

Finn, fucking me even from prison. I wanted to wrap my hands around his neck and squeeze until something popped. At my current power level, that would probably just be my knuckles. Well, I could still bounce Finn's skull off the wall of his Tower cell a few times.

The sound of raised voices derailed my fantasies. I whirled, staring around the overlook, but I was still alone. The shouting was coming through my phone from wherever Vincent was, but it was muffled and without my heightened hearing, I couldn't make out the words.

"What's that?" I asked.

"Stefano Rossi," Vincent answered. "He is... debating the necessity of my orders with Dorian."

So that's where Stefano was when the other hunters invaded Max's garage, arguing for my life while my own father commanded my death. I wanted to punch something.

"How did you find out about your link to the Seal of Avalon, Lilith?" Vincent asked. "Why didn't you tell us at once?"

"Evaine told me," I said. "And she warned me the College – that *you* – would hunt me down because of it. So of course I didn't tell you!"

"The Lady... was involved?"

"Yeah. That's why Evaine was chasing Reid, to get to him before your hunters did. She died trying to protect me! From Asmodai and from you!"

"None regret the loss of the Lady of the Lake more than the Merlinic order–"

"Oh, fuck you!"

"–but Evaine fought since before the founding of the Castle to protect this world and others from the demons who would tear them apart," Vincent went on in a voice like stone. "You understand the danger that you pose, Lilith. You've faced Asmodai. And you must know what he and his kind would do to the Earth. No one life is worth that risk. Even that of my own daughter."

Not that family was exactly a big priority for Vincent Myrdon, but I was pretty sure that the High Magus would have taken a ritual dagger to any one of his own wizards if they were as dangerous to humanity as I was. The College and their leader were dead serious about their job.

"But Asmodai can't *force* me to open the Seal of Avalon," I protested. "I have to be willing when I touch the stone or it doesn't work. Right?"

"Yes," Vincent admitted slowly. "That's our understanding, as well. But Lilith, the risk is too great. Asmodai is an ancient being of unimaginable power, immortal patience and infinite guile. Even the djinni dared not face the demons openly. As long as any cambion lives, we are all in danger."

"Maybe you should have thought about that before summoning a succubus and knocking her up with one!"

"Yes, perhaps I should have," Vincent agreed softly. "But Merlin banished Asmodai – his own father – to protect humanity. How can I refuse the same sacrifice to keep our world from becoming play-things to demons of lust and violence, of greed and fear?"

I remembered Reid down on his knees in the empty street, begging me to put a bullet in his skull before that could happen. Evaine tried to save me from the demons and the College, but now she was dead. Asmodai killed her to get to me.

"You're such an asshole," I said. My voice cracked. "It's not your sacrifice, Dad. It's *mine*. You're asking me to die!"

"To protect the world, Lilith... yes."

The world. The whole world and maybe others. I squeezed my eyes shut.

"Okay," I whispered.

"...What?"

"You're right," I told Vincent. "Asmodai needs me to break the Seal of Avalon. He'll spend the rest of my life plotting ways to make that happen. We can't give him the chance to succeed."

There was stunned silence on the other end of the phone line. I opened my eyes again and looked out across the foggy bay. The sea and sky were indistinct silvery smears through my tears.

"I'll turn myself in," I said. "Tonight, at the College. Just give me until midnight to take care of a few things. But no more hunters. No scry network and no spells."

"Lilith..."

"Promise me. Please, Dad."

"Very well," said Vincent. God, he sounded tired. "You have your freedom until midnight, Lilith. After that–"

"I'm pregnant," I blurted.

"Pregnant?"

"Yeah. And sex doesn't give me powers anymore."

"But there's only one reason that sex would no longer fuel your succubus heritage," Vincent said. "And why you could conceive a child. Lilith, that means–"

"I know what it means," I interrupted. "My mother fell for you and when she did, sex couldn't feed or power her anymore, either. If I were a full-blooded succubus, I would do your job for you and just die, too!"

I could practically hear the High Magus flinching at that.

"Lilith... Your mother was a demon. To know that a creature like her had such feelings for me almost destroyed me. I could never return them..."

"Yeah," I sighed. My heart was a pounding knot of pain in my chest. "I know. And none of this changes what needs to happen."

"Maybe it won't come down to... that." Now it was the High Magus' voice that was unsteady. "Perhaps we can hide you away somewhere that Asmodai can never reach. The Tower may be an option."

"Yeah, sure. Life in prison."

Vincent may have been reluctant to execute a pregnant woman, but it was too late to start backpedaling now and we both knew it. Even if Vincent somehow convinced the rest of the Merlinic council to spare me, the Castle would never buy it and I had the feeling that the College's big brother got the final say. Sooner or later, the wizards were going to kill me. And I was frighteningly okay with that. It was better than a world full of demons.

"I'll see you at midnight, Dad," I said.

I hung up.

Chapter
FOUR

"Max, it's me. It's okay to go home. I'll be there," I told his voicemail. My voice dropped to a whisper. "Please be there, Max. I need to talk to you."

I drove back into midtown, but parked a few blocks away from the garage and approached carefully through the fog. It was only about eight o'clock and there should have been at least a few trick-or-treaters roaming the street, but I saw only a couple of other people on the road. The College, of course. They had cleared everyone out. There's a good reason that most of the world doesn't know magic is real.

Mister Martinez, Max's ancient neighbor was outside, shuffling alongside his equally ancient and arthritic dog. He waved as I passed, but didn't seem to notice my bare feet or the garage's shattered windows. I wasn't sure if that was a result of the College's magic or just Mister Martinez's cataracts, but I waved back and hurried across the parking lot before the old man could pull me into yet another conversation about his dog's pooping habits.

Sabra's van was gone, although there were still gouges in the asphalt where it had fallen, and the ragged hole pounded into the ground by one of my bullets. Other than the tarp-covered silhouette of my Alfa Romeo, the parking lot was empty. I circled Max's garage slowly, scanning the deep shadows, but didn't see any sign of the other bounty hunters.

The front door into the lobby was open, the lock scorched black by one of their spells. I checked the door frame for weird runes – I wouldn't put it past Doyle or Redmond to set a trap for me, some kind of binding spell or magical bomb – but I didn't see or smell anything. I stepped inside.

"Max?" I called out.

The garage and office were empty, and so was the apartment upstairs. Sabra's homunculi were gone, too, though the broken lamp lay in smashed pieces across the hardwood floor. I ignored the mess for now – I only had until midnight and there were a lot more important things to do with my freedom than clean house.

I searched every room, calling Max's name... like he might be hiding somewhere, waiting to jump out and surprise me. God, I would have punched Max for that. And then kissed him.

I even checked the bed. The sheets were still rumpled and they smelled like sex. They smelled like Max, like us. It was amazing how quickly I'd grown used to falling asleep with someone else in the bed beside me. How nice it was to wake up with someone.

No, not with *someone*.

With Max.

I ran a hand over his pillow. Max should have been back hours ago. The salvage yards and auto shops were all closed by now. I tried Max's phone again, but still nothing. Was his battery dead?

Max was supposed to be here. There were things I needed to tell him and a text message just wasn't good enough. The least I could do was write Max a real note. Not that a letter was good enough, either, but it was better than an email. I had almost four hours until midnight... Surely Max would come home by then. In the meantime, I could at least get my thoughts written down.

Just in case.

I searched for some paper. The office downstairs was a mess of forms and invoices kicked up by Clio's magical windstorm, but I didn't want to leave my final words on the back of a work order. Surely Max kept a notepad or something around the garage... Why the fuck was everything digital these days? I suddenly felt a little bad for all the times I teased the wizards for being so old fashioned.

I grabbed a pen from Max's desk and then went back upstairs. I hadn't turned on any of the lamps, but the curtains were all open and the windows filled the living room with pools of multicolored city light. Floorboards creaked under my feet as I walked.

Other than worrying about Max running late, I was weirdly calm. I was going to die. Probably tonight. Even if Vincent actually tried to spare my life, I knew the Castle wouldn't go for it. I was too dangerous. I could break the Seal of Avalon. The wizards have been protecting the Earth against that kind of threat for over a thousand years and they weren't about to start gambling the world's safety just for me.

Me or my baby.

Hell, maybe that even made it worse in their book. Any child of mine would be a quarter succubus. Did that count as a cambion? Would my son or daughter be able to open the Seal of Avalon, too? The College and Castle would never risk that. And I couldn't blame them. One woman and one unborn child... That wasn't such a high price to keep the world safe. Most people would have paid it. I guess I was about to.

There were a few cookbooks in the kitchen and an ancient binder from Max's high school home economics class, but all of the pages were filled with his neat handwriting. No blank paper.

I moved through our shadowed, silent apartment back to the bedroom, but found nothing useful in my nightstand – even I can't write a letter with sex toys. So I circled the bed and tried Max's side. I fished around the drawer of his nightstand for paper or a notebook, maybe a diary.

My fingers closed on something small and square inside, with rounded corners. I felt velvet and slowly drew the object out. My hands shook as I held up the little box. It was dusty, showing stark black prints where I had touched the velvet. It had been in that drawer for a long time, but there were other spots in the dust where it had been touched before. The fingerprints there were bigger than mine, though. They were Max's.

I almost dropped the box twice before I managed to fumble it open and stare at the contents, nestled in a clean bed of white satin and safe from dust. The engagement ring shone with the soft, warm glint of gold and a small diamond – the best Max could afford on a mechanic's pay – glittered at the top like a tiny, perfect star.

My head spun and my heart raced. A handful of girlfriends had passed through Max's life, but few of them deserved this. Taya, maybe? But no, there was too much dust on the box. This ring was older than that. Max and Taya started dating just last April. And then Max left her. Because of me. For me.

I was the only woman who had been in Max's life that long.

This ring... it was for me.

I don't know when I sat down, but I was on the edge of the bed, cradling the little black velvet box in shaking hands. Max was there beside me through everything, every job I took and every guy I fucked to do them. And the whole time, Max had this ring hidden away beside his bed.

How long had he felt that way about me? Five years? Longer? Since high school? I looked at Max's fingerprints on the box. How many times had he sat here just like this, staring at the ring he bought for me? Max never said anything. Even as kids, when Max and I played house, I was playing. He wasn't.

And I never noticed.

I snapped the little velvet box shut and tucked it into my pocket. I wiped my eyes and checked the clock on Max's nightstand. There were hours left until midnight, but if he wasn't back home by then, fuck my deal. Fuck the letter. I would call Vincent and renegotiate. I wasn't going *anywhere* until I saw Max one last time.

There was no warning before the flames roared up around me. I threw myself across the bed and down into a crouch on the other side, but there was no detonation. It wasn't another fireball.

Cautiously, I stood and peered over the bed. There was a little fire extinguisher in the kitchen, but the flames hadn't spread. They burned in a perfect circle of leaping gold on the floor, but inside the ring was... something else.

It was like looking through a window or screen. I stared through the bedroom floor at a strand of empty beach that I didn't recognize. My view was from high above, showing waves as black as ink washing up across pale sand. The beach was narrow and gave way swiftly to the tall green spires of trees whose species I couldn't quite identify. I saw mountains in the distance, too, sharp silhouettes against the star-studded night sky. But the ground below was dark – there was no sign of buildings or cars or civilization of any kind. Not so much as a single streetlamp. The only light was the cold glow of the stars. Where was this?

I barely had time to wonder before the scene inside the ring of fire was moving. It raced away from the beach and down through the forest, soaring smoothly along a wooded valley between two of the steep azure mountains. The trees parted to reveal a clearing and circle of towering stones in the center. They jutted up from the grassy earth, gray and mossy and ancient. Stonehenge was on Salisbury Plain, not a mile through some uninhabited forest beside the sea, but this place looked an awful lot like it.

In the center of the ring crouched a smooth-cut altar of plain white rock. Max lay on top, his eyes closed.

"Max!" I cried.

I reached through the fire toward him, but my fingers only smashed into the bedroom floor. Without my sex-power cambion strength, I couldn't even crack the hardwood. The ring of flames flared, singeing my hand and I snatched it back with a hiss. Okay, this was just a projection of some kind, not a portal. I could look, but not touch. Fuck!

I leaned over the edge of the bed, heart pounding, and studied the image. Max's eyes remained shut, but his chest rose and fell slowly, evenly. He was alive. But where the hell was he? Was any of this even real? Max was wearing the same jeans and t-shirt that he had put on that morning. The shoes were right, too – a pair of well-worn but well cared for black leather work boots. If that wasn't really Max that I was staring at, it was the best damned illusion I had ever seen.

"Max!" I shouted. "Max, can you hear me?"

He stirred on the altar and his blue eyes fluttered open. But Max wasn't looking at me. Three women had stepped into the ring of up-thrust stones, strutting naked and graceful through the mist toward Max. They had long, dark hair and slender black horns arcing up from their brows. Their flawless skin was a fine, pale gold color that I knew all too well.

Succubae.

"Stop! Don't touch him!" I cried.

I had no idea if they could hear me, but I could hear them. The succubae spread out to encircle Max, their bright eyes flashing in the silver starlight. With musical sighs so sensual that they made me shiver, they ran slim golden hands over him. The demons' lips curved up into deliciously kissable smiles as they felt out the hard lines of Max's body.

His eyes moved slowly across the scene around him, glassy and glazed. Was he drugged or charmed or something...? Max was only human. He didn't have my immunity to supernatural glamours. He just smiled dazedly at the three succubae as their fingers tightened on him and sharp, shiny obsidian fingernails sliced through his clothes, cutting and tearing them easily away. Within seconds, Max lay naked on the stone altar.

The picture in the ring of flames moved in close, giving me an all too perfect view of one of the demon women pressing her perfectly red lips to Max's. His deep groan echoed through the bedroom. Max brought his hands up, but he didn't push her away. I doubted that he could. Max slid his fingers into the succubus' midnight hair and helplessly pulled her deeper into the kiss.

I grabbed the edge of the bed as the scene widened again. Whoever was directing this vision had a promising career in porn – the cinematography was amazing. My hands curled into useless fists in the bed sheets.

The other succubae trailed kisses along Max's skin, one working her way down over the scars slanting across his chest while the last moved up his thigh. Max groaned again, the sound muffled but deepening. I watched his body tighten at the demons' touch. His cock began to flush and swell, making the horned women let out a chorus of sensual moans. The one kissing her way along Max's tensed stomach looked up right at me through the gold flames.

"Get off of him, you succubitches!" I snarled.

The demon whore winked at me, then grabbed Max's dick and guided the growing length into her mouth. His hips rose off the smooth stone as her full lips moved up and down his cock, making it slick and wet. One of the other succubae hissed like a cat and descended on Max, too. She bit his inner thigh hard enough to leave a swiftly darkening bruise, then attacked his balls with her long pink tongue.

The first succubus finally pulled back. Even as he panted for breath, Max reached out for the golden-skinned demoness with desperate need. She ignored his wordless plea and stepped lightly up onto the altar. The silver starlight seemed to cling to her lithe body, making her look like some gilded statue to feminine sensuality. She stood straddling Max's broad shoulders and he stared up at her with those wide, wondering eyes.

"No," I whispered. "Max!"

"Yes..." he groaned helplessly.

The succubus knelt over Max and he clutched the curve of her hips, pulling her pussy down to his waiting mouth. I watched his jaw work as Max eagerly, hungrily licked her. And to judge by the demoness' moans, he tongued her pussy with all his usual skill and enthusiasm. Within seconds, shining wetness ran from the demon's flushed golden slit and down Max's chin. The succubus rocked her hips against his mouth and her fingernails drew red lines across his chest where she held herself steady.

I squirmed on Max's bed. My pussy was growing swiftly slick and hot at the sight of the three succubae crawling all over him. What could I do? Look away? It wouldn't stop what was happening to Max and I had to know what was going on. Where was he? Why were they doing this to him? And how...?

The other two demonesses were still fighting over Max's cock, both of them licking and sucking every long, flushed inch. They alternately moaned in pleasure and hissed at one another when their tongues met. Two mouths and four hands stroked Max. There was no way he could hold out against them. Already, pale precum ran along the dark crown of his dick and the succubae lapped it up, racing each other for every drop.

My fists tightened nearly hard enough to tear through the bedsheets even without my cambion strength. The gesture was one of powerless rage, but also served to keep me from ripping open my pants and jamming my hand down there. I *hated* the succubae for what they were doing to Max, but I was getting so damned wet watching it happen.

Max strained, but the demons were far stronger, and they were merciless. His fingers curled into the soft golden thighs of the succubus kneeling astride his face, but she wouldn't even let him up for breath. Not that it seemed to slow Max down one bit as he devoured her. He was always a dedicated and selfless lover, but now the succubae would take everything Max had to offer and more.

His entire body went rigid and I recognized that long, deep groan, the one that sounded like it welled up right from the bottom of Max's soul. The pair of demonesses sucking his cock looked at me through the flames as cum began to fountain from Max. It hung bright and white in the air for a moment, then splashed down across their upturned faces. They didn't even take their lips off of Max's dick as his load painted them in beads of ivory that shone like drops of moonlight on their gold skin and black hair.

One of the succubae licked her way to Max's flared head and the ring of flames showed me a single long jet of semen shooting into her mouth before she sealed ruby-red lips around his cock. Her cheeks bulged as she drank up another spurt, but then the other lust demoness was grabbing Max, snatching at his still-pulsing dick and feeding it into her own mouth. The first succubus whimpered as her toy was taken away, Max's load running down over her chin.

I squeezed my legs together. I could taste Max's cum as though I were there. I smelled him in the sheets and wrapped them around my hands. Furious tears ran down my cheeks.

"Why are you doing this?" I cried. "Leave him alone!"

The vision drew back to show me the succubus who had been riding Max's face now prowling down along his hard body. He was gasping breathlessly even as he licked his lips and begged for more. The succubus gave a feline hiss and the other two pulled their mouths from his cock with loud wet sounds. Cum ran down their faces as they closed slender golden fingers around the base of Max's dick. They held him there while the first succubus mounted Max. Her lips pursed into a perfect O of pleasure as she took his entire length in one smooth thrust.

"No," Max said in a strained voice. "I can't... It's too much..."

The demoness on top of him didn't care. She leaned forward, balancing herself against Max's thighs and displaying the rosy gold of her spread pussy. One of the others darted in, licking frantically at the juices dripping along Max's cock. When her sister demon plunged herself down, impaling herself on Max again, the succubus growled and lapped at her asshole with her wet pink tongue. They alternated between hissing venomously at one another and then moaning like whores.

Max groaned and gasped, thrusting himself up into the welcoming, addictive heat clasping his cock. He reached out blindly, desperately. His hands shook, but came down on the third she-demon's hip. Max pulled her closer to the head of the altar, his eyes wide and dark, until he could bury his face in the silky gold of her breasts. He kissed savagely at the soft swells and then descended on her peaked nipples like a starving man.

Or more like a man throwing himself into the sea to drown.

I bit the sheet clenched in my hands. A single succubus could bring men to their knees, make them fuck so hard and so long that their hearts burst. What would three of them do to Max? But god, how my pussy ached as I watched him with them. I wanted so badly to shove my fingers between my trembling legs. But I refused to give these Nether bitches the satisfaction.

Although it looked like they were getting plenty of satisfaction. The three succubae were all equally lovely, ethereal, and a little difficult to differentiate. I couldn't tell if the second demon whore had replaced the first, but now one of them straddled Max with his dick impaled to the hilt in the tight pink hole of her ass. She rode him hard, shrieking as she speared her anus on his thick cock. The succubus arched her spine in a graceful contortion that I could never have managed, craning her head back to kiss the one at the top of the altar. The third succubus was between her spread thighs, devouring her streaming pussy and Max's length every time it emerged from the other demoness' stretched, quivering asshole.

All three succubae erupted into a chorus of musical moans and Max let out a rough cry. His body tensed and his hips rose up off the stone altar. He thrashed, but the black and gold demons pushed him back down. Held him prisoner.

"Oh... oh god!" Max gasped.

The sound was full of pleasure, but there was a strained note of something like pain, too. Succubae were demons, and to demons, humans were just animals, livestock. Playthings.

Max came again. Hard. His cock swelled in the demon girl's ass and then gushed such a huge load into her that it spurted free in creamy drops all over the face of the succubus licking between her legs. Max pumped her full of cum until it ran in gooey rivers down her shining thighs. He collapsed back onto the stone, panting and streaming sweat.

And then the succubae began again.

"Stop this!" I screamed into the fire. "You're killing him! Stop, please!"

The flames roared. I still heard Max's breath laboring as the view suddenly swung around, away from the altar. Asmodai smiled up at me through the fire. His bright eyes shone like gold wedding rings.

"You bastard!" I snarled. "How did you get Max? What the fuck are you doing to him? Let him go!"

The Lord of Lust's voice was as smooth and lovely as ever, like if chocolate were a sound. Max's groans rose to answer that voice and I had to fight not to echo him. The bright circle of flames rippled with each word.

"Lily. I await you on Avalon. Come to me. Alone."

"Fuck you, asshole!" I shouted.

"Come to me," said Asmodai. "Come for him."

The fire went out.

Chapter
FIVE

I jumped up off the bed. Asmodai had Max! I wasn't sure exactly why the big golden fucker was on Avalon or how he had gotten Max, but I could guess the second part. The last time Asmodai wanted something he wasn't supposed to have, he sent a shadow to the Hotel Marquis to retrieve it. If Asmodai's shadow could chase me through the College's strongest wards, snatching one human mechanic was a piece of cake.

But Max was tough and he was strong. He had faced a yeti and survived. And he kept up with me in bed for years. Those succubae had their work cut out for them... In the end, though, the demons *would* kill Max. I couldn't just leave him in Asmodai's hands. There was no way I was going to let those bitches fuck Max to death.

That was *my* job.

I paced back and forth across the bedroom. It was obvious what Asmodai wanted – he was using Max as bait to lure me out to Avalon so I would open the Seal for him. Even if I were willing to do that, I'd seen too many movies and knew Asmodai too well to think for a second that he would let Max go.

This wasn't a hostage exchange. This was a trap... but I *had* to get Max back.

Could I call the College? It was the wizards' job to protect all of humanity against scary supernatural shit... Max was only one man, though, and not even a very important one. Not to them. If Vincent Myrdon was willing to kill his daughter and unborn grandchild to deny Asmodai, I doubted that Max's life even registered on his radar. I had no intention of *ever* giving Asmodai what he wanted and was willing to let the College kill me just to fuck the smooth golden bastard over forever, but I was the only one who would care about saving Max.

Okay, what were my other options? Stefano had argued with the College about killing me. Did his friendship extend to helping me rescue Max? Maybe, but Stefano was one mage. Merlin was the only wizard who had ever managed to defeat Asmodai alone. Even if Stefano agreed to help me, it wouldn't be enough.

Who else could I call? Who owed me favors or... a wish?

A wish!

I grabbed the cell phone out of my pocket so fast that it jumped from between my fingers. I swore and snatched the stupid device out of the air before it could crash to the floor. I had played diplomat to Madu Tau about six months ago. And by that, of course, I mean we had a lot of hot sex in his ridiculously opulent penthouse fifty stories above Cairo. As a reward for my performance in bed, the powerful air djinn had given me a single wish. But I didn't actually have Madu Tau's phone number.

I ran into the living room and switched on the lights, but then turned a slow circle, scowling. Madu Tau had given me a business card, but that went up in flames along with just about everything I owned when Asmodai and Evaine's battle destroyed my condo. I screwed my eyes shut and willed my heart to stop hammering so hard. I could barely hear anything else.

What had Madu Tau told me about the wish, about how to cash it in? I thought I remembered, but I still felt a little silly when I opened my eyes again and spoke to the empty air.

"Uh, Madu Tau? I'm ready to make my wish," I said.

My heart slammed twice against my ribs and then there was a swirl of scented smoke. When it cleared, Madu Tau stood in the middle of Max's living room. The air djinn looked exactly as I remembered: over seven imposing feet of powerful muscle and dark midnight skin. He wore an exquisitely tailored white suit and his gleaming black beard was immaculate. Madu Tau gave me a radiant smile.

"Ah, the gorgeous Lily Quinn," he said.

Madu Tau took one of my hands and closed his fingers over mine. They were so long and large that my entire hand vanished in the djinn's grasp. He gave a gentle squeeze and looked around the apartment, at the shattered lamp, the broken coffee table and the craters in the living room floor where the homunculi had fallen. Madu Tau's smile faltered slightly and he released my hand.

"I had hoped to fulfill a pleasant whim," he said in his deep basso rumble. "What do you need from me? Are you in danger?"

"I... I'm ready to make my wish."

"Very well. What do you desire?" Madu Tau asked.

"There's a man on Avalon," I said. My voice shook so hard that I could barely speak. "They took him. His name is Maxwell Ferguson. Big, blond, sweet. I wish for my Max back. Please!"

One of Madu Tau's dark eyebrows shot up, but he smiled and sketched a small bow. "As you wish, my lovely one."

He vanished in another puff of scented smoke. I bit my lip and tried not to pace. My fingers and toes felt like they were made of ice. I pressed my hands against my stomach. Max would be back here and safe soon. Then I could tell him all the things I needed to...

Madu Tau reappeared in the living room. Alone.

"Where's Max?" I demanded.

The djinn was frowning deeply. "I... was unable to retrieve the mortal."

"What? Why not?" I cried. "Did you see him?"

"I did, yes. The boy is there. But powerful enchantments have been raised on Avalon. There are demons on the island, too, that guard him – wrath demons and succubae. And I saw Asmodai himself. I am powerful, Lily, but even I dare not challenge the Lord of Lust."

"So you can't get to Max?" I asked. "Shit!"

"Avalon is closer to the Nether than any other place in this realm," Madu Tau said. He shook his head. "But the demons were banished centuries ago. What is going on, Lily? Why is Asmodai on the mystic isle?"

"I'm not sure," I answered, shaking my head. "I thought he was stuck in the Nether, too. But he's on Avalon and he's got Max!"

"Strange winds are stirring," said Madu Tau.

I couldn't help it now. I paced back and forth across the living room. I kicked a broken shard of the lamp out of my way. Both of Madu Tau's eyebrows rose this time. He reached out as I passed and placed one large hand on my shoulder, halting my stalking progress through the apartment. I turned to look up at Madu Tau and his hand slid down to the curve of my lower back. Effortlessly, the djinn pulled me close.

"I would be pleased to grant some *other* wish," Madu Tau said. "Perhaps you even desire to earn another...?"

His presence was warm and protective, but I took his wrist and pried his hand off my ass. Luckily, Madu Tau let me. Even with all of my powers, I'm not sure I could have forced a djinn to do anything. Without my sex-fueled strength, I was a kitten.

"Sorry," I said. "Pass. I have to get Max out of there."

"I am obligated by honor to fulfill your desire," Madu Tau told me. "There must be something I can do for you."

I chewed my lip for a moment. "What did you say about enchantments on Avalon?"

"There is a powerful ward of demonic making around the glen where your mortal is being held. I am unable to pass."

"I know a guy," I said. "If anyone can get through Asmodai's wards, it's him."

"Who is this man?" Madu Tau asked with another frown.

"An Unseelie thief named Kalen Silverwind. Kalen's so good at what he does that Asmodai hired him last year."

The air djinn's frown deepened. "Thieves and Unseelie are neither to be trusted. Especially one who's been in the employ of your enemy."

"I need him. I arrested Kalen for the College and they've been keeping him locked up ever since. Can you spring him for me?"

Madu Tau considered. I held my breath.

"I am bound to grant your wish, if I am able," he told me. "But the djinni have made agreements with the Merlinic order. If I grant this wish, Lily, then the repercussions of violating those rules must fall upon you."

"Fine," I said. The College and the Castle already wanted me dead. What else could they possibly do to me? And getting Max back was worth any price.

"This is your wish, Lily?" Madu Tau asked. "For Kalen Silverwind's freedom and his aid?"

"Yes," I answered at once.

"Where is Kalen being held?"

"The Tower," I answered. "It's a weird micro-realm–"

"I know it," said Madu Tau. He smiled brilliantly at me. "In fact, there are a pair of sphinxes serving as guards there with whom I am familiar."

With another swirl of blue-gray smoke, Madu Tau vanished. He was gone longer this time. Long enough for me to resume pacing.

I paused at the door of the bedroom and pulled the little velvet box from my pocket. I flipped it open and stared at the ring inside. The sparkle of the tiny diamond made rainbows dance across my vision as tears filled my eyes. I closed the box and stuffed it back into my pocket.

I was going to save Max, no matter what. I even had the beginnings of a plan, but I would need help. A lot of help.

Madu Tau was gone for an eternity that according to my cell phone, lasted just over six minutes. When he reappeared, the djinn held Kalen Silverwind by one slender arm.

He still wore the uninspired linen clothes that the wizards had given him, but nothing else about the fairy could be called plain. Kalen's rakishly tousled hair was vivid indigo and every inch of his skin was a lickable butterscotch color, right up to the tapered points of his ears. A pair of long dragonfly wings extended from between the thief's shoulders, shining with every color I could think of, plus a few new ones.

"What the...?" Kalen asked. His bright violet eyes lit on me and widened. "Lily? What am I doing here? How did you get me out of the Tower?"

"I need your help," I said.

Kalen rubbed his wrists. The iron manacles the College had used to keep the fairy from performing his magic were gone. He glanced up at Madu Tau, who released his arm and stepped back.

"I'm really quite grateful to you and your mysterious friend for the prison break," Kalen said with a grin. "Truly. But I'm afraid I have to go."

He snapped his fingers, but nothing happened. Kalen frowned and snapped again, then glared suspiciously at me. I spread my hands. I certainly didn't have an off switch for his magic.

"I told you the Unseelie have no honor," Madu Tau said. "I suspected he might try to abandon you at the first opportunity. You wished for Kalen Silverwind's help, Lily, and you shall have it."

"So... Kalen *has* to help me?" I asked.

The air djinn nodded. "Yes. Kalen may use any and all of his magic to aid you, but not to leave your side. Not until your task is completed."

"Thank you," I said.

I stood up on the tips of my toes and still had to put my arms around Madu Tau's neck to pull him down for a kiss. He grinned hugely, but I bypassed his lips and planted the kiss on his cheek. Madu Tau sighed.

"This mortal must be a man of great value," he said.

"You have no idea," I answered. "Won't you stick around? I could really use a djinn tonight."

Madu Tau shook his head. "No. I granted your wish, my dear, but after what I have seen on Avalon, I fear that I have concerns of my own that I must see to."

"But I have to stay?" Kalen grumbled. "Wow, thanks."

The air djinn ignored him and took my hand delicately, kissing it. "I wish you good fortune tonight, my lovely one. For your sake and the sake of us all."

With that, Madu Tau vanished one final time, leaving behind only a few wisps of smoke and the sweet smell of incense. Kalen flipped off the spot where Madu Tau had been standing and then turned toward me with a smirk.

"Now that he's gone, let's talk about how I can help. I seem to recall that my help last time involved a lot less clothing..."

Kalen winked and raised one hand, his thumb and forefinger pressed together. I wasn't sure if the restraints Madu Tau had placed on Kalen's magic would keep him from snapping off my clothes like when we first met. I felt Kalen's lust and smacked his hand.

"Stop that!" I told him. "We have work to do."

"Well, I was *trying* to get to work," Kalen said with a theatrical sigh. "Maybe you better tell me what's going on, Lily. How the hell did you get a djinn wish? And why did you use it to get me out of the Tower if not to fuck me until neither of us can walk straight?"

"Asmodai stole my boyfriend. He's holding Max prisoner on Avalon and thinks he can use that to make me open Merlin's Seal for him."

Kalen jerked back as though I'd slapped him.

"Asmodai? Avalon?" he gasped. "Boyfriend?"

I crossed my arms. "Asmodai has put demons and wards around Max. You're going to help me get past them to steal Max back and get him home safe."

"If you know about Asmodai's involvement, then you know that he's the one who made me steal *The Gates of Avalon*," Kalen said. He grabbed my shoulder with a shaking hand. "You remember what happened when just his shadow came after us, Lily! What makes you think I would be crazy enough to get near Asmodai again, let alone cross him?"

"You have to help me, Kalen. Madu Tau's magic won't let you go until we get Max back. But we're going to need some more help."

"Help?" Kalen protested. "Lily, there's nothing in your world or mine that can fight the Lord of Lust! By the Queen, are you mad?"

"The jury's still out."

"You have no idea the danger of what you're suggesting, Lily."

"And it's even worse than I'm telling you," I said.

Chapter
SIX

Kalen spent the next twenty minutes trying to talk me out of my insane idea. He made a lot of good points, too, but I was stubborn and desperate. And maybe it could actually work. It had to... I was the only one who could save Max from Asmodai.

I needed to make some phone calls, so I shoved Kalen into the bathroom and told him to enjoy a shower while he could get one. The fairy tried to pull me in with him, but I shut the door in his face. When I heard water running on the other side, I fished the cell phone out of my pocket and started dialing. Mostly, I had to leave messages and cross my fingers.

Once that was done, I went into the bedroom for a change of clothes. My barefoot-and-fatigues look wasn't going to cut it for assaulting Avalon. I walked into Max's closet, running my hands over the clothes on his side.

The shirts branded for his new garage all hung together in a neat, clean row. But Max's collection of ancient metal band t-shirts still smelled like him even after being washed a hundred times. I pressed my face into the fabric and fought back tears. I *would* get Max back, no matter the cost.

The other side of the closet was all my stuff – Max had insisted on making room when I moved in. I pulled on a pair of jeans and tucked the engagement ring box into my pocket, then chose one of Max's old AC/DC t-shirts and some sturdy athletic shoes. I went to the mirror and made sure I collected all of my hair as I tied it up into a ponytail. But when I finished, I found myself still staring at my reflection.

I slid my hands down my body, smoothing the t-shirt against my belly. Did it show? I almost imagined I could feel a second soft heartbeat under my fingertips. That was impossible... It was far too early. My powers only disappeared two weeks ago. That was the earliest I could have gotten pregnant. It was too soon to show, but I gave myself a rueful little smile in the mirror.

"You idiot," I told my reflection. "You should have told Max right away. But you wanted to be sure. You wanted it to be perfect, didn't you? Because he deserves it. And now we're out of time."

The shower was still going when I emerged from the bedroom. I went into the living room again and briefly reconsidered cleaning up the shattered lamp, but the doorbell rang. Already?

I ran down the stairs, taking them two at a time. The garage's *OPEN* sign was dark in the window and the door sat ajar, the lock burnt to cinders by the hunters' attack... God, was that really only a few hours ago? But Edward Ashton stood out front, ringing the bell despite the unlocked and broken front door. I waved him inside.

"Ash," I said. "You're here! I wasn't even sure you would get my voicemail."

The half-dryad man stepped into the lobby and looked around, pushing his glasses back up his broad nose.

"I don't usually take phone calls," Ash said. "But as luck would have it, I was in the city to inspect one of my factories."

That made sense. Ash was dressed in professional brown slacks a shade darker than his wood-colored skin and a button-down shirt instead of the jeans and flannel he had worn at our last meeting.

The paper manufacturer lived high in the mountains outside the city, in the forest of his dryad mother and aunts. If Ash had been at home, he probably wouldn't have cell reception. Ash was the first call I had made, but I didn't expect to see him until nearly midnight, if at all.

"What can I do for you, Lily?" Ash asked as I led him up into Max's apartment. His shockingly green eyes took in the damage as we crested the stairs and he whistled. "I'm happy to do what I can. But perhaps we should discuss it at my house, if this place isn't secure. If nothing else, it would make for a more... intimate setting."

The half-dryad's smile was warm and inviting. I felt the swiftly kindling spark of his lust.

"Not you, too," I groaned. "Listen, I need a favor and I'll pay for it, but in gold. Nothing else."

Ash shrugged and smiled again. "Ah, I see. Well, I'm certainly happy to at least consider your proposal."

Kalen finally came sauntering back out into the living room, toweling off his dark purple-blue hair. He was shirtless, wearing only a pair of skin-tight black leather pants that certainly hadn't come from Max's closet. Kalen's iridescent wings fluttered, shaking off water in a fine mist. Ash eyed the half-naked fairy with a contemplative expression.

"Good to see you again, Mister Silverwind," Ash said. "It's been some time."

Kalen finished drying his hair and dropped his damp towel to the floor. He held out one long-fingered hand and a silvery silk shirt appeared in it. I wasn't sure if Kalen was conjuring clothes out of thin air or just from some remote fairyland closet, but it seemed like a useful trick either way.

"Ashton," Kalen answered as he shrugged into his new shirt. "What are you doing here? Did Lily's djinn steal you, too?"

"That's right," I said. "You two already know each other. Kalen stole the dryad's ring for you, didn't he?"

Ash actually winced a little at that. "*Stole* is... such a harsh word. I prefer *acquired*."

Kalen laughed and the Seelie man blushed darkly. I was just about to tell the two fairies to play nice when the doorbell rang again and I hurried back downstairs. A young Korean man leaned in through the open door, peering around the front desk. A handsome smile lit up his face as I descended the stairs, but the air in the garage felt as cold as ice and goosebumps rose all along my arms.

"Lily!" he said. "Thanks for calling."

"Ben?" I asked.

"Yeah. My brother loaned me his body to meet with you," Ben said. He ran one hand through his short black hair. "I think Rick might be hoping for another... uh... encounter with you. I'd be lying if I said I didn't have my own hopes. In my incorporeal state, physical sensations are so rare."

"Sorry," I said. I put my arms around Ben and pulled him into a hug, shivering a little in the ethereal cold of the ghost's presence. "But I didn't invite you here for sex. I need your help."

Ben nodded. "Anything you need, Lily. We're all yours."

I led him upstairs and made awkward dual introductions for the unhomed spirit and his brother's body. Kalen didn't seem to care, but Ash was instantly fascinated. He removed his glasses and polished them on the sleeve of his shirt before replacing them to lean close and examine Ben.

"A ghost? Truly?" Ash asked. His leaf-green eyes positively sparkled. "Most haunting entities come from the spirit world, incarnations of pain or loss that attach themselves to scenes of trauma and play out the events there. But you seem to be something else."

"I was human," Ben said. "Just a normal guy until some wizards caught me in their banishment spell. They were trying to send a succubus back to the Nether. My soul couldn't go there, but the magic had already ripped it out of my body."

"And so here you remain," said Ash.

"Yeah."

I looked up at the clock. It was past nine. Only a few more hours until I was supposed to turn myself over to the College. How long would Vincent wait before deciding I was too late and have me brought in by force? Long enough for me to pull off my insane plan, I hoped.

"How much longer do we need to wait?" Kalen asked.

"I'm not sure," I admitted. "We're still waiting on two more and honestly, I have no idea if they will show."

"Then if I'm going to die tonight," Kalen said, "I'd rather not do it on an empty stomach. Is there anything to eat around here?"

Still deep in conversation, Ash and Ben began searching the refrigerator and pulling out leftovers. It hurt to see them in Max's kitchen, cooking Max's food. The smell of last night's chicken parmesan being reheated was so painful that I had to excuse myself to the bedroom for a few minutes so that I could cry without anyone watching.

Everyone had almost finished eating – I couldn't bring myself to join them – when I heard the rumble of a truck in the parking lot outside. I jumped to my feet and ran down the stairs. By the time I reached the bottom, the broken front door was open again.

Stefano Rossi stood in the ruined lobby, looking around at the damage with dark eyes narrowed. They widened when he saw me bounding down the steps, but he hung back as another man appeared in the door. The newcomer was about ten years younger than Stefano, lanky and deeply tanned with sun-bleached blond hair. Dominic grinned up at me.

"Hey, Lily," he said.

"Hi, Dominic," I answered. "How're you feeling?"

"Not like a werewolf anymore, if that's what you're asking. Cool garage you've got here. Maybe I should bring my car in."

"Are you hungry?" I asked, pointing back upstairs.

"I could eat," Dominic answered, nodding enthusiastically.

"There's some food if you want to have a bite before we get started."

"Thanks! Hey, I got whisked off to this other totally weird place and never really got to thank you properly for helping Stefano catch me. You saved a lot more than my life, you know."

"You're welcome," I said. If the impatience showed in my voice, Dominic didn't seem to notice.

"The College guys are great," he went on. "They've been letting me work as... a sort of assistant, I guess. No magic, but I file books in the library and measure out weird shit for them. That kind of thing. It beats the hell out of serving coffee."

"Mmm-hm," I said.

Dominic flashed me a dazzling smile and slung one long arm around my waist. He leaned down to whisper into my ear.

"I'm a little fuzzy on how we met, actually. The wizards say they can't wipe my memory, but the werewolf curse still did a number on my brain. Did we hook up? Or was that just a *really* great dream on my part? Either way, we should absolutely do it again."

I sighed and pulled away. "Yes, I fucked you. But we really don't have time for that right now. Why don't you go get some dinner?"

"Okay, cool," Dominic said. He sounded a little wounded, but headed up the stairs in the direction of food.

When Dominic was gone, Stefano finally stepped forward. I threw my arms around the other hunter and hugged him. Stefano hesitated for a moment, then returned my embrace and squeezed me tight. He smelled like herbs and metal.

"About damned time," I said in a choked voice. "I wasn't sure you were going to show."

"Neither was I," Stefano admitted.

"I heard you fought when Vincent put the bounty out on me."

"I told the High Magus that you deserved better than to be hunted like a monster, that you should have the chance to turn yourself in peacefully."

I released Stefano and slugged him in the shoulder. Without my cambion superpowers, he didn't even flinch.

"You dick!" I said. "I thought you were telling the College not to kill me!"

"Lilith, you can open the Seal of Avalon." Stefano didn't sound happy about it. "You know that can't be allowed."

"You don't kill werewolves."

"You're more dangerous than a werewolf. And now you're asking me for a meeting, to bring Dominic and to keep it all secret from the College."

"Did you tell them?"

Stefano stared at me with jaw clenched and an almost painful intensity in his dark eyes. He was a wizard and it was his duty to kill me. But Stefano sighed.

"No," he said. "And the High Magus is keeping everyone off the scry network until midnight, just as you asked. The College has no idea I'm here."

I hugged Stefano again.

"You never could say *no* to me," I said. "Thanks, Stefano."

"I'll help you if I'm able... But I can't let you hurt anyone or put the world in danger."

"Yeah, I know."

I took Stefano upstairs. At some point, one of the guys – my money was on Ash – had cleaned up the broken lamp and righted the cracked coffee table. Dominic had seated himself at the dining room, heaping leftover chicken and pasta onto his plate. I cleared my throat.

"Ash, Kalen, Ben in Rick's body," I said, gesturing to each man in turn. "This is Dominic. He was a werewolf."

"All better now," Dominic added cheerfully. "Caught and cured thanks to Lily and Stefano."

"What's *he* doing here?" Stefano asked, stabbing an accusatory finger toward Kalen. "He's supposed to be in the Tower."

Kalen sat back in his chair, long dragonfly wings rippling lazily. "I'm sorry, I don't think we've actually met. But to judge by the spell-stink, you must be one of Myrdon's hunting hounds."

"He repeatedly refused to warn us about Asmodai's involvement in the *Gates of Avalon* theft!" Stefano snarled. His hands clenched into fists.

"Hey, are those wings real?" Dominic asked, leaning over the table to squint at Kalen.

"More real than your hair color, blondie," the fairy answered with a smirk.

Dominic flushed and Stefano's face was becoming dangerously dark. Ash stood and placed a hand on the hunter's shoulder, but Stefano still seemed about ready to throw a punch. Or at least clap Kalen in irons and drag him back to the Tower.

"Okay, that's enough dick measuring," I said in a loud voice. "Look, I need your help. All of you."

The five men shared quick, guilty glances at one another and then all looked at me. I snapped my fingers until their eyes moved above my shoulders. Stefano let out a long breath and nodded.

"Alright, Lilith," he said. "What's going on? What do you need?"

"Asmodai's kidnapped my boyfriend. And we're going to rescue him."

Kalen already knew the plan, but he still seemed every bit as horrified as everyone else. Even Ben and Dominic stared, open-mouthed. Stefano looked like I had just kicked him in the balls. Twice.

"Lilith, if Asmodai has taken a hostage," he said slowly, "then you know that he's done it to force you into opening the Seal of Avalon. And you know that can't happen."

"Yeah, I know," I told Stefano. "And I have a plan. Asmodai's taken Max to Avalon–"

Both Dominic and Ben raised their hands.

"Questions already?" I sighed. "What is it, Dominic?"

"What's Avalon?" he asked.

"Avalon is a magical island," I answered. "I... don't know exactly where, because it's not really on Earth. At least, not *entirely* on Earth. I was born there and it's where Merlin constructed the Seal of Avalon, but that's about all I know."

"Avalon exists in all realms and all times," Ash said, making an expansive gesture with both hands and then bringing them back together, one on top of the other. "It serves as a sort of lynchpin between the worlds and keeps them connected. That includes the Nether and the fae realm, as well as a number of other planes. That's why Merlin placed the Seal there."

"Okay, cool," said Dominic.

"What was your question, Ben?" I asked.

The ghost pointed to Dominic. "He already asked, but I have another. If Avalon isn't really on Earth, how are we getting there?"

Kalen leaned forward. No one was eating now.

"Avalon chooses who comes and goes from its shores," the fairy answered. "If you're supposed to be on Avalon, then you'll arrive. If you're not, then none of this planning will matter."

"Well, Asmodai told me to come there," I said. "He seems to think that I can make it to Avalon just fine. It sounds strange to say, but let's hope Asmodai is right."

Kalen let out a musical little hiss of discomfort. Stefano and Ash shared an unsettled look and even Dominic was now regarding his dinner plate with a slightly sick expression. I drew a deep breath and pressed on.

"Getting to Avalon is only the first part of my plan and not even close to the hardest part. There's a djinn named Madu Tau who promised me a wish, but when I wished for Max back, he couldn't do it. He said Max is being protected. So once we get to the island, our next barrier is a demonic ward."

"If Asmodai wants you to come to him, then why would there be any barriers at all?" Ash asked, frowning.

"To keep everyone else out," Stefano answered. "Asmodai must realize that the College and Castle won't just sit idly by while he attempts to break the Seal of Avalon. Asmodai doesn't want any interference."

I nodded in agreement. "I intend to bring friends tonight and Asmodai won't like that."

"That's where I come in," Kalen said. "Apparently. I'm supposed to take down the ward, or at least open up a hole in the defenses."

"Preferably without alerting Asmodai," I added.

Stefano frowned deeply for a moment, then looked over at Kalen and sighed.

"You stole *The Gates of Avalon* from the High Magus' own library without tripping a single ward or alarm," the hunter admitted. "You may actually be able to slip unnoticed through Asmodai's protections."

Kalen raised one indigo eyebrow. "Um... thanks for that ringing endorsement."

Dominic snorted with laughter and Stefano rolled his eyes. Ash winced a little. He was only half fairy and Seelie, but I wondered if he felt some responsibility for how Kalen acted. I tapped the table-top and pointed to Dominic.

"Don't relax just yet," I told him. "You're up next."

"Me? Sweet. What's my job?" Dominic asked.

"Asmodai brought some other demons with him," I said. "Madu Tau saw them when he tried to get Max for me. There are at least three succubae and several wrath demons."

"Wrath demons?" Ben asked.

"Big red guys with wicked horns and claws," I said. "They're scary as fuck. I fought just half of one a couple months ago and he kicked my ass."

"But the demons shouldn't be able to manifest on any plane of existence without being summoned there. Not even on Avalon," Ash objected.

"We believe that the Seal has been damaged somehow," said Stefano. "It's... leaking."

I nodded. "That was Reid. He cracked the stone."

"A golem created by Asmodai," Stefano explained to the others. "He was half human and half demon."

"Like me," I said. "Reid wasn't a true cambion and he couldn't open the Seal, but he was close enough to damage it."

"That must be how Asmodai and the other demons managed to manifest on the island at all," Ash said grimly. "But we're lucky, at least a little. Even the Lord of Lust wouldn't be able to force many demons through a single crack in the Seal."

"Avalon is the only place of overlap between the Nether and Earth. So with the Seal still in place, the demons can't leave the island," Stefano finished.

"But they're still enough to cause us some real problems," I said. "Which is why we need a werewolf."

Everyone turned to look at Dominic, who raised his hands defensively. "Whoa, hey! I got cured, remember?"

"I know. But Stefano still has your claw, right?"

Stefano nodded slowly. The werewolf claw he had pulled out of me after we fought Dominic the first time was a dangerous but invaluable bit of magical equipment.

"We could curse you again," I said.

"Lilith, have you lost your mind?" Stefano asked. "You want to turn Dominic into a savage monster? A werewolf is just as likely to tear your boyfriend apart as to rescue him!"

Dominic had gone pale and pressed himself back into his seat. I gave him what I hoped was a reassuring smile and pointed again. This time, everyone looked at Ben.

"I'm not asking you to make Dominic into a monster," I told Stefano. "I'm asking you to give *him* a powerful new body."

Ben frowned.

"Me?" he asked.

"Yes, you," I said. "Next to the demons, werewolves are the deadliest creatures in the world. That's the whole point of the curse, right? To change some poor human into a mindless murder machine. But Ben can possess Dominic and control his transformed body."

Ben's frown became thoughtful. Slowly, the dead man nodded.

"In theory, yeah," he said. "My mind in his body. It could work."

"Holy shit..." Dominic breathed.

Stefano's hands were still clenched into fists so tight that his knuckles had turned white. "Lilith, no! You can't ask Dominic to do this! You know what werewolves are like, that this isn't just about changing his body. That curse turns its victim into a monster, corrupting his very soul!"

"It's the only plan I've got, Stefano! And the curse can be lifted. You've done it before," I said. I turned to face Dominic, though. "But you don't have to agree to this. Stefano isn't wrong about how brutal it is. I'm sure I could find someone else."

"No... wait," Dominic said in a shaking voice. "I didn't say I wouldn't do it."

"What?" Stefano asked.

Dominic looked up at the wizard with earnest eyes. "Working for the College is the first thing I've done with my life that ever really mattered. You and Lily saved me. I want to help her."

Stefano grabbed Dominic and heaved the younger man up out of the chair by his arm. Dominic shouted and kicked out, flailing in Stefano's grip and making plates and food jump across the top of the table.

"No," Stefano snarled at Dominic. "I'm not letting you do this!"

"Stop!" I cried.

Stefano paused, though he was still holding Dominic by the arm. I put my hand on Stefano's wrist and he slowly released Dominic, who sagged down into his chair again. Ash took a step closer, but I waved him back.

"Stefano, I know what I'm asking you to do is hard," I said quietly.

"You want me to create a werewolf," he said in a ragged voice.

"Yeah," I agreed. "And I'm sorry. But I need you. No one else can do this."

Stefano met my gaze with raw pain naked in his eyes. I felt sick. Hunting werewolves and fighting their magical disease was Stefano's crusade, his whole life. And I was asking him to knowingly infect someone with that curse. I would have felt less guilty asking him to cut out his own heart.

I slid my hand up Stefano's arm and felt the muscles so tight there that they trembled. But he nodded.

"Alright, Lilith," he said. "For you."

I pulled Stefano close and leaned in, pressing my lips lightly to his. I didn't deepen the kiss, but the other hunter's eyes fell shut for a moment. I released Stefano and he stepped away.

"Thank you," I said.

"Just get Dominic out of there alive and back to the College to be cured," Stefano said.

"I'll do my best," I promised him. "But let's see if we can stack the deck in our favor. Ash?"

The half-dryad had politely averted his gaze during the conversation with Stefano, but now he looked at me again. "Yes?"

"One werewolf isn't going to be enough. Not against wrath demons. But you collect all sorts of weird and arcane stuff, right? Please tell me you have something useful. A holy sword, a magic ring or crown... something like that?"

Ash took off his glasses and polished them on his shirt, then put them back on. He nodded at me.

"Actually, I know just the thing. A piece of wood from a Roman cross. Not the one on which Jesus Christ died, of course, but the crucifix of a man who hung beside the human savior. When driven into the earth, it will consecrate the immediate area."

"And that's... good?" I asked. I looked helplessly at Stefano.

"Yes," the wizard answered with a nod. "On ground consecrated by any sufficient infusion of faith, demons will be ill and weakened. For a while, at least."

"And you have one of those, Ash?" I asked.

"I do, yes."

"But it's not made by dryads," I objected.

"I'm eclectic, and hardly exclusive to the lore and artifacts of my family," Ash said. He directed a warm smile and wink at Dominic. "I enjoy all things wood, if you take my meaning."

"Uh, no?" Dominic said.

Kalen smirked. "And they say *I'm* insatiable."

"How long?" I asked. Kalen laughed even as I scowled at him. "I mean, how long will the consecration last? And how large an area will it affect?"

Ash and Stefano engaged in a short technical debate about the size of the crucifix spar, the type of wood and state of preservation. I didn't understand a single word of it, but the two finally seemed to reach some kind of agreement.

"It should consecrate an area about one hundred twenty-three yards in diameter," Stefano announced. "How long it affects the demons will depend entirely upon their individual strength."

"I don't know that it will do very much to Asmodai," Ash said, shaking his head. "But the succubae and wrath demons should be substantially hampered."

I nodded and put my hands on my hips. "Right. Ash, I'm going to need to borrow that stake. I'll pay you whatever you want for it, up to and including every penny I've got."

Ash polished his glasses. There was no way they needed to be cleaned again; it must have been a thoughtful habit, not a cleanly one.

"The Roman cross spar is yours if you'll do something for me," Ash said. "Bring back a seed or acorn from one of Avalon's trees."

"Deal," I agreed, then held up my hand and ticked off points on my fingers. "So here's the plan. We re-infect Dominic with lycanthropy. Ben possesses him so he fights for us and doesn't rampage. We go to Avalon – if the island will let us – where Kalen will get Ben-slash-Dominic past the wards. Once we're in position, we use the cross stake thing. Ash, how do we do that?"

"Simply drive it into the earth," he answered.

"Alright," I said. "We put the stake into the ground and then charge in. Ben, you don't have to fight to win. Just keep the demons busy long enough for me to grab Max and get him to Kalen."

"But then what?" Ben asked. "Even with a werewolf fighting on consecrated ground, Asmodai still sounds like a problem."

"I'll deal with Asmodai," I said.

"You?" Stefano asked. "Lilith, how? What if Asmodai forces you to open the Seal of Avalon?"

"He can't," I reminded him. "Asmodai can't just throw me at it."

"You have to touch the Seal willingly," said Ash, nodding. "Or else it won't open."

"Exactly. I'm going to keep my middle fingers pointed firmly at the big golden fucker the whole time. Don't worry, I've managed to tell Asmodai to go back to hell before."

Even Kalen looked impressed at that. I smiled and nodded to the fairy.

"Kalen, you grab an acorn or something, but make it quick. As soon as Max is free, I want you to get him, Ben and Dominic off of Avalon as fast as you can. My wish to Madu Tau will be fulfilled, so you should be able to just teleport away."

"What about you, Lilith?" Stefano asked. "If you plan to fight Asmodai, you're going to need every ounce of power you can get. You need sex."

Dominic raised one hand and pointed vigorously to himself with the other. Kalen grinned and so did Ash. Even the oppressive chill of Ben's deathly presence warmed a little. Stefano's expression was intense and hungry as he regarded me. With the bounty that the College had put on my head, I was fruit more forbidden than ever and Stefano clearly wanted a taste so badly that he could... well, taste it.

"No!" I shouted. "No one is fucking me! Stop asking!"

All of the men gathered around the dinner table looked deeply disappointed. Kalen was the one to voice the obvious question.

"Why not?" he asked.

"Two reasons," I said, then let out a sigh. "Guys, I don't have my powers. They're gone."

Kalen cocked his head at me. "I'm not usually one to repeat myself. But... why not?"

"I have..." I hesitated and then tried again. "Look, something happened. Sex doesn't give me a succubus' strength or speed anymore. It wouldn't matter if I threw you all in a big pile on the bed and dove into the middle. I can feel your lust – thank you for that, boys, though you can turn down the volume now – but I can't do anything with it."

Stefano was staring at me with suspicion in his dark eyes. He was a wizard – if he didn't already know what was happening to me, he was certainly beginning to suspect. There weren't many things that could rob a cambion of her power. I gave Stefano a grim smile.

"And there's the second reason," I said. "The College is right about me. I'm too dangerous to be allowed to live."

"But you said if you're unwilling, the demons can't use you," Ben objected.

"Asmodai is immortal," I said. "He's smart and he's stubborn. After he tried to turn my own succubus half against me, I thought he was all out of plays."

"He wasn't," Kalen hissed in a low voice. "The Lord of Lust is *never* out of plays."

"You're right," I agreed. "Asmodai took Max. Asmodai will keep hurting and manipulating people trying to make me open the Seal.

He may even find a way to make it work. And I can never let that happen."

"So... what?" Dominic asked. "What does that mean?"

I drew a deep breath. "It means that for all of you, this is a rescue mission. But for me, it's a suicide mission."

Everyone started talking at the same time, shouting questions and objections. I banged my fist down on the table.

"Shut up and listen!" I said. "Asmodai needs me alive. That's the only reason I'll be able to get close to Max. But once I get Max away, Asmodai's going to figure out pretty damned quick that I'm not a useful tool anymore. By then, I want you all gone. And take the holy stake thing with you, too. We need to be damned sure those wrath demons can do their job."

"Their job," Dominic repeated. "You mean..."

"You can't actually expect us to let you die, Lily," Ben said.

"Yes, I do. Don't you dare come back for me," I told him.

"Lilith, we could do it at the College," Stefano said. "We could... take care of you... so it won't hurt."

"You can say *kill me*, Stefano. But do you want to be the one to execute me? Or Dorian or my... or the High Magus?"

"I..." Stefano began.

But he didn't seem to know how to finish the sentence. Stefano didn't want to kill me. He would want to even less if he knew I was pregnant. I didn't want to stick anyone else at the College with that shitty job, either.

"And you guys are stodgy and slow as fuck," I said in a shaking voice. "How long will it take to fill out the parchments to execute me? That's more time for Asmodai to come up with a new plan. No. I die tonight. But save Max first or I swear I'll haunt every last one of you!"

No one laughed. All five men looked at the floor and none of them said anything this time. Kalen's wings rustled in the silence. Finally, Stefano spoke again.

"I can give you until midnight, Lilith," he said. "Like the High Magus agreed. But after that, I have to tell the College what you're doing. There are demons on Avalon and you're going willingly to them… even if you don't plan to survive the encounter."

"I know," I told him. "How long will it take to get the claw? It's in your sanctuary, right?"

Stefano nodded. "I can get there and back inside an hour. But I need to leave now."

"Thanks."

The bounty hunter hesitated for a second, then hurried down the stairs in the direction of his truck. I turned back to the others.

"Ash? The Roman cross thingy we need is at your house, right?"

"Yes," said the half-dryad man, adjusting his glasses again. "But I'm afraid that trip takes considerably longer than an hour."

"We don't have that kind of time. Kalen, can you teleport Ash home and then bring the stake?" I asked.

"Your djinn shackled me with his magic," Kalen answered. "No teleporting, remember?"

"You have to help me get Max back. This is helping me to do that, right?"

The fairy combed fingers through his damp indigo hair. "If this doesn't work, you can blame your djinn."

"Sure," I said. "Consider this a dry run for teleporting everyone off Avalon."

"Can you bring my car?" Ash asked. "I'd rather not have to retrieve it later."

Kalen rolled his eyes. "Fine. I'll bring your car, too. Let's go."

He took Ash's hand. The half-dryad had just a moment to grin and wink at Kalen before they vanished from Max's living room. I hoped Kalen would hurry – there were only three hours left until Stefano had to report me to the College. By then, we had to be gone.

Chapter
SEVEN

*T*wo hours later, I stood with Kalen and Dominic in front of the darkened south gate of the Palace Marina. Well, Kalen and Ben possessing Dominic's body.

"Be careful," Rick said.

"I'm already dead," Ben assured him. "I'll be fine."

Rick pulled him into a tight hug. I supposed it was the first time the two had been able to do that since Ben died. When the brothers released one another, Stefano stepped forward.

"Are you ready for this?" he asked.

Ben nodded. There had been a short argument about using Dominic at all – Rick was hesitant to be separated from his brother and offered up his own body for the werewolf curse. Ben refused to let Rick risk himself, of course. The ghost had a protective streak wide enough to drive along. Dominic had argued with Rick, too, pointing out that his "bitchin' body" had been through the curse and its removal before. In the end, Rick was outvoted.

"I'm ready," Ben said. "Do it."

Stefano wore a pair of thick leather gloves and held a small, sturdy-looking ebony box. A silver lock sealed it shut and I saw no sign of a keyhole, but Stefano murmured a few arcane words and it clicked open. He withdrew Dominic's claw from inside. It was as long as one of my fingers and ended in a wickedly sharp point. Stefano handed the box to Rick and then took Ben's wrist.

"Forgive me," Stefano whispered.

He pressed the claw into Ben's forearm. It didn't take much. The point of the claw pierced Ben's borrowed skin and a single bright red drop of blood welled up. Stefano jumped back and we all held our breath.

Ben sagged to one knee, gasping, and began to change. His body swelled and grew, tearing through Dominic's jeans and t-shirt. Huge furry paws ripped through his shoes and long claws dug furrows into the concrete. The werewolf straightened into a gray-furred, nine-foot-tall living monument to violence. The beast turned its elongated lupine head toward me and stared with burning yellow-gold eyes. Slowly, he raised one massive paw and curled it into a fist with the thumb sticking up. I released the breath I had been holding.

"Holy shit. It worked," I said, then looked at Stefano. "But why did he transform already? I thought werewolves didn't change until some demonic passion made it happen."

"A ghost's existence is fueled by a great deal of pain and rage. And probably plenty of lust with you around. Benjamin Sung has access to the passions that drive werewolves, but because the body is not his own, he has voluntary control over the transformation," Stefano said, then hesitated. "...I think. This has never been done before."

"Ben?" Rick asked in an unsteady voice. "Are you okay?"

"Yeah," the werewolf answered in a bone-jolting growl.

In nearly a decade of monster hunting, I had never heard a werewolf speak. And to judge by how Stefano's eyes flew wide, it seemed to be a first for him, too. I put my hand on Rick's shoulder. He looked up at me.

"Time to go," I said.

Rick nodded. Stefano sealed Dominic's original claw back into the ebony box and secured it in a locking toolbox across the bed of his truck, then climbed up behind the wheel. Rick went around to the passenger side.

"Good hunting, Lilith," Stefano said in a heavy voice, like he didn't think he was ever going to see me again.

Well, that was the plan.

"It's been fun, Stefano," I told him with a smile. "Good hunting."

He twisted a key in the truck's ignition and the engine rumbled. If Rick had any parting words, I couldn't hear them as Stefano drove off through the dark fog.

When they were gone, I turned to Ben and Kalen. The fairy's blue-purple hair was still in disarray. According to Kalen, a brisk wind had whipped up as soon as he teleported to Ash's house. Apparently, Madu Tau's little reminder had chased Kalen the entire time until he returned to me.

The misty night air was quiet now, but Kalen still looked uncomfortable. He held a long, seven-inch splinter of wood in one hand, tossed it quickly to his other hand and then back again. It was ancient and colorless and utterly unimpressive to look at. I really hoped that Kalen had actually gotten the right piece of wood from Ash and not picked up some random detritus from the forest floor. But Madu Tau probably wouldn't let Kalen get away with that shit.

And to guess by the low, dull ache in my head when I stood too close, the aged gray stake was the real thing.

"Want me to carry it?" I asked.

Kalen stopped fidgeting with the piece of wood and stuck it into the pocket of his conjured leather jacket. He shook his head. "It's not pleasant, but it's better than cold iron. And it's our best demon-fighting weapon, so I'd like to keep it close."

"It'll be a lot less pleasant for the demons," I said, rubbing my temple. I spoke with authority.

"I just hope this thing doesn't break when I try to stick it in the ground. I don't trust dryads. They're great in bed and all, but Seelie girls are always trying to screw me over."

"Imagine that," I said in a flat voice, then nodded to the marina. "So... you're the one who asked to meet up here, Kalen. How do we get to Avalon? Swim?"

Ben stretched his long, shaggy new arms and shrugged. A werewolf could probably swim for days, but we didn't have days. Kalen clicked his tongue at me.

"I'm a thief, Lily," he said. "Pick a boat."

The marina gate was locked, but Kalen just tapped a few apparently random numbers on the keypad and the stainless steel mesh door creaked open. He gestured with a little flourish. Ben ducked through the gate and I followed.

Palace Marina was silent and dark. It was one of the smaller marinas on the bay, tucked away at the bottom of the Quay and quiet at this hour. The fog had begun to settle again by now, leaving the piers and boats all beaded in sparkling dew. But there was still enough evening mist to conceal us from any other late-night marina visitors.

I picked the fastest-looking speedboat and Kalen had it hotwired in ten seconds flat. I climbed down into the boat, then held on as Ben leapt in beside me. The boat rocked violently under the additional six hundred pounds of weight and Kalen grabbed onto the canopy until it stilled again.

"Sorry," Ben growled. He flashed long, sharp teeth in a rueful lupine grin. "New body."

"You'd better get familiar with it real quick," Kalen told him. "We're going to need you in peak condition soon."

Ben nodded his furry head. I checked the time on my cell phone as the fairy pushed up on the speedboat's throttle. Almost eleven thirty. Half an hour until midnight.

"How long will it take to get to Avalon?" I asked.

Kalen watched the dark water as we slid out into the bay. He shrugged, making his wings shimmer.

"No idea," he said. "That's up to Avalon."

"Then where are we going, exactly?" I asked.

"We're following the moonlight."

I looked up into the sky. The clouds were thick and I could see only a few stars glittering between them. No moon. But I trusted Kalen... You know, sort of.

My cell phone rang in my hand and I glanced down from the sky. Vincent's number flashed on the screen. I hit *ignore* and then tossed my phone out into the bay. I wasn't in the mood for any more father-daughter bonding.

Ben and Kalen watched me with wary gold and violet eyes. I offered them a small smile, then returned my attention to the sky and water. The bay was flat and black, like we moved out across a vast obsidian mirror. Fog blurred the city behind us and even the lights of the bridges ahead were just fuzzy, indistinct points of radiance. Kalen guided us under and then past the great red pillars of the big bridge, out into the open ocean.

This was worse than foolish. I knew that. The College and my father were willing to execute me and my unborn child to keep the world safe from Asmodai. Two lives for the safety of the world. Was adding a third really such a terrible price to pay?

Yes. A world without Max wasn't one worth saving.

I felt as weak as a soap bubble, but as strong as a mountain at the same time. I was going to get Max back, damn it. I didn't care if I died when it was done, but I sure as hell wasn't going to check out without seeing him one more time.

"I'm coming, Max," I said. "Just hold on a little longer. We'll get you out of there."

Ben and Kalen glanced at each other, but they didn't say anything. I guess girls on suicide missions are entitled to act a little weird.

The city and even the bridges vanished swiftly into the distance. Dark gray fog closed in around us and only the growl of the boat's engine and slap of water against the sides told me we were moving at all. The clouds above us had cleared, though, and the stars shone so bright and close that they almost eclipsed the pale golden glow of the full moon.

Full moon? But there was no moon tonight...

Something dark emerged from the fog ahead. Ben pointed with a long clawed finger.

"Is that a boat?" he rumbled.

"No," said Kalen. "We've arrived."

"Avalon? Already?" I asked.

Kalen nodded. "Someone must really want you here."

The shape in the mist resolved itself into a tall, craggy island. A narrow band of sandy beach ran around the edge, but quickly gave way to dense, hilly forest. Trees thrust up from the fog like an army of great green swords and a slender stream wound its way out of the woods to spread silvery fingers of water across the beach in a miniature delta.

Even Kalen was quiet and somber as he steered the boat toward Avalon. I touched his arm and the fairy jumped. His high cheeks darkened.

"Thanks for doing this," I said. "I know how afraid you are of Asmodai."

"Not as afraid as you are." Kalen gave me a smirk. "Besides, I'm impressed. This heist is almost Unseelie."

When we got close, Ben leapt down into the water and heaved our boat up onto the sand with one hand. Kalen turned off the engine and flew gracefully down to the beach. I waved off Ben's offered paw and stood at the prow, looking out across Avalon. The full harvest moon etched everything in silver and gold.

This was a one-way trip. I only needed two things to finish the job tonight.

I checked my right pocket for my gun. The nine-millimeter wasn't very powerful, but it didn't have to be. It was just for insurance, after all, in case something went wrong and I couldn't count on Asmodai or his demons to kill me. I had to be ready to do it myself.

From my other pocket, I pulled out the little velvet box and removed Max's ring. It was small and heavy in my palm. I tossed the box away into the water, where it fell with a splash. Slowly, I slipped the slender gold band onto the ring finger of my left hand. It fit perfectly. I wasn't sure if Max had borrowed one of my rings to get it sized or he just knew me that well. The tiny diamond caught the pale moonlight and burned like a star plucked down from the sky.

Something inside me rose to answer that fire, something bright and clear and blinding. Something like recognition.

A soft noise echoed out across the water and I tensed at the prow of the boat. It sounded like a voice, but it didn't belong to Ben or Kalen. No, this voice was higher and more musical. Feminine. It sounded like... Evaine? I grabbed the edge of the boat and strained to hear more, but the voice was gone. If it had even been there in the first place.

From the shore, Kalen and Ben gave me quizzical looks. I shook my head. Maybe I was starting to go crazy. At this point, it certainly wouldn't surprise me.

I jumped down from the boat, kicking up a spray of wet sand. Cold water swirled around my ankles as I stalked up onto the beach toward the fairy and the werewolf.

"Come on," I said. "Let's get Max back."

Chapter
EIGHT

*B*en and Kalen followed me across the beach and up into the forested hills of Avalon. The slope was grassy and a lot steeper than it appeared from shore. Kalen spent more time flying than walking and Ben dug his long claws into the ground for traction, leaving me alone to struggle with the climb.

Evaine told me that I was born here on Avalon. She had taken me away to the human world when I was only a baby, so I didn't recognize anything.

It wasn't hard to find our way, though. There were no roads or even trails on Avalon, but I quickly discovered that with just a little concentration, I could feel Asmodai's presence on the island. My half-demon soul was drawn to its prince, though not in the horrible way that tore me apart before. Asmodai had awakened my succubus side once and she tried to take over, but that human-versus-demon shit was over. I was one person and every part of me wanted Max back. If only for a moment.

"This way," I said, pointing to another deceptively steep hill.

Ben and Kalen nodded, keeping pace effortlessly as I panted my way up the slope. The night air was cold and clear. It was strange not to taste every breath. I might have been born on Avalon, but I was raised in the city. Every lungful of air there had been shared first by thousands of people and cars. Avalon felt ancient but empty, like we were the first and only people ever to visit the isle.

But we weren't alone on Avalon, and at the top of the hill stood the reminder of that. A sharp line of golden light flared beneath my feet, playing over my body. The air tensed around me as though waiting for something as I passed through Asmodai's ward. But when I looked back, Ben hit the light and bounced off. He growled and slashed his claws against the ward. The golden glow flashed again, but seemed otherwise unimpressed by the werewolf's angry display.

"Stop that," Kalen told Ben. His voice was slightly muffled by the magic barrier between us. "You're going to need those claws later."

"Can you get through?" I asked.

Kalen didn't answer. His iridescent dragonfly wings hummed and he flew a few yards into the air, examining the ward. I was just about to ask if we could hurry it up when Kalen began singing a series of small, intricate notes. Light flashed along the ward, sparks of color like miniature fireworks, and then Kalen landed once more. He gestured to Ben.

"Go on," Kalen said.

The possessed werewolf gave him a skeptical look, but stepped forward. The line of golden light flared, but Ben passed unchallenged through Asmodai's ward. Kalen sauntered through the barrier after him.

"Did you disarm it?" I asked.

"What? And tip off the demons that something's wrong?" the fairy scoffed. "You offend me, Lily."

"Then what did you do?" Ben asked.

"Well, that ward was obviously designed with an exception for Lily," Kalen said. "Asmodai wants you here, remember? There's a guest list and I simply added us to it."

I frowned. "What about Max? You have to be able to get him out of here."

"Relax. He's already on the list. Asmodai had to get him here somehow, after all."

I grabbed Kalen into an impulsive hug. I knew the fairy didn't have much choice in helping me, but I was no less thankful. Without him, I really would have been fucked. Kalen grinned and pulled me in close, his lips seeking mine. I put my hand against his chest and shoved him back.

"Easy there," I said. "I'm not *that* grateful."

"Can't blame me for trying," Kalen answered with a sinuous shrug. "After all, we're all probably about to die."

Ben had hunkered down at the crest of the hill and I knelt beside him, looking down the slope. The trees parted just ahead and the grassy starlight-silvered ground leveled out into a narrow valley that I recognized all too well. A circle of huge, weathered gray rocks rose up from the earth around a large block of white stone and the shapes writhing on top. I couldn't make out the details from this distance, but I caught flashes of blond hair and golden skin: Max and the succubae.

Kalen gave a low whistle. I punched him in the arm.

"Stop that! They're killing him," I hissed.

The fairy rubbed his shoulder and scowled. "While it certainly seems like your boyfriend is having the time of his short mortal life, that's not what I'm looking at."

He pointed and Ben growled deep in his throat. The succubae weren't the only demons down in the glen. Seven massive, blood-colored shapes stood between us and the circle of standing stones. Between us and Max.

Reid's demonic half, Orbias, must have been the runt of the litter. These wrath demons were all bigger and redder, like Satan fucked a monster truck and had a brood of huge, angry babies. They were twice the size of Dominic's werewolf form and rippled with muscles. Long black horns spread from the demons' temples that were wide enough to kick a field goal through.

"Holy shit," I whispered.

"Which one of them is Asmodai?" Ben rumbled.

I squinted. "I... don't see him, but I don't have my super senses right now."

"I can't see Asmodai, either," said Kalen. Even with seven wrath demons in our way, the fairy still sounded relieved.

"Where is he?" Ben asked.

"I'm not sure," I said. "Close, though. I can still feel him. But if Asmodai's stepped out for a pee break, let's not waste the opportunity. Kalen, can you teleport us in there to grab Max?"

The fairy thief raised his hands, interlaced his fingers and then pulled them apart. A tracery of silver light glowed in the air between them that made absolutely no sense to me, but Kalen shook his head.

"There's another ward between us and your boy," he reported. "I'll need to get closer before I can start making modifications."

Ben pointed to the outside of the narrow mountain valley. "We can circle through the trees there before we have to charge out into the open."

I nodded and we crept along the forest's edge, keeping a few trees between us and the glade full of demons below. Ben dropped to all fours and was soon padding silently through the shadows. Kalen flew beside him, just a couple of feet up off the ground. He snapped his fingers once and the soft buzz of his wings abruptly stopped, like switching off a vibrator.

That left me feeling like the clumsy one as I darted between trees. I've been a hunter for nine years and can be pretty quiet when I put my mind to it, but not nearly as silent as a prowling werewolf or a fairy thief. Damn, I missed my powers.

Not that they made me any quieter, but once we got close, my plan was to run straight into the middle of that heap of succubae.

They might not have been as strong as wrath demons, but three of them were plenty powerful enough to make getting Max out of there difficult.

We were jumping across a narrow, stony stream when I heard the voice again, the same one that called to me from the ocean. The one that sounded like Evaine.

I held up one hand, signaling Ben and Kalen to a halt, and I looked around the forest. The stream led up the slope, away from the valley, and appeared to be trickling out from the mouth of a small, dark cave tucked into the hillside. Was that where the voice was coming from? I concentrated, but it was just too soft to make out any words.

"Do you hear that?" I whispered.

Kalen gave me an almost pitying look. "You mean the sound of three succubae getting off with your boyfriend?"

"What?" I spun away from the cave and stared down into the shallow valley. "God, I wish I could tear those bitches apart...!"

I knelt behind a tree that looked a bit like an alder but wasn't. I stared down the hill at the circle of stones and the white altar in the center. I could see Max down there, the trio of succubae crawling all over him. And there were still seven wrath demons in my way, too. Even if I had all of my old powers, those weren't good odds.

Time to improve them.

I nodded to Kalen and he alighted silently on the dew-dampened grass beside me. Ben stalked along behind us to the edge of the forest. We were just a hundred yards from the closest demon now. The huge crimson-skinned creature sniffed the air with a broad, flat nose. He growled something in a voice even deeper than Ben's and in a language I didn't know. It didn't sound friendly.

"Now!" I hissed at Kalen.

He yanked the fragment of Roman cross from his pocket and stabbed it down. The wood didn't break. It sank like a knife into the earth and I felt the consecration ripple outward – it felt like being kicked in the stomach and I only barely managed not to throw up all over Kalen.

But the full-blooded demons were having an even stronger reaction. The wrath demons doubled over with groans that sounded like an avalanche, all clutching at their stomachs. The closest one fell to his knees and vomited up something that looked like crude oil into the moonlit grass. Another towering red demon staggered and sagged against the standing stones.

The succubae were inside the area Stefano and Ash had agreed upon, too. The demonesses threw themselves back, screaming and grabbing their slender black horns. Their outlines blurred and shimmered like mirages.

"Ben, it's show time!" I called out.

The werewolf didn't seem to be affected by the consecration. I wasn't sure if it was because he was only cursed and not actually a demon or if it had something to do with Ben's possession, but I cheered aloud when he gave me a lupine grin and loped out from the trees.

His long-legged stride ate up the distance quickly and then he was pouncing on the nearest wrath demon. The reeling monster whipped around to face Ben, but too late. My favorite werewolf descended on him, bearing the demon to the ground. Ben slashed huge claws through the huge red chest and blood sprayed, burning black scars into the grass. The wrath demon managed to get his horned head up and gouge a ragged line into Ben's jaw as the werewolf darted in, teeth bared.

Ben tore out the demon's throat. He raised his bloody, smoking gray muzzle and howled. The sound of it was loud and savage and triumphant. The remaining wrath demons were still clutching their heads or stomachs, but they turned toward the howl and answered with their own bellowing challenges.

"Get me in there!" I shouted to Kalen.

"Lily, the ward!" he protested.

"You work on breaking through it," I told him. "But I should already be on the guest list, right? I'm getting Max!"

Kalen nodded and held out his hand. I took it and the fairy snapped the fingers of his other hand. Swirling colors closed in around me as Kalen's magic took hold and then we appeared just outside the circle of ancient standing stones. The fairy's hand was still wrapped around mine when I bolted forward, toward the altar. Golden light played harmlessly over me, but Kalen smashed into the sudden wall of radiance like it was made of bricks. He drew back from the ward with a sibilant hiss.

Behind Kalen, the wrath demons were closing into an uneven circle around Ben. He pounced on one of them, tearing out a huge red thigh muscle. The demon snarled and slashed hooked black claws across Ben's snout. The werewolf let out a snarl of his own, but the gashes along his face were already healing shut. Ben kicked the demon away and it struggled to rise again on its injured leg.

"Kalen!" I shouted.

Two of Asmodai's oversized red guards had noticed the fairy. They lunged toward Kalen and he launched himself into the air, dragonfly wings beating frantically. One of the wrath demons reached up with a long, hugely muscled arm and sank his hooked ebony claws into Kalen's boot. The fairy shouted and flicked his fingers. Vines and tree roots erupted from the earth like furious green serpents. They wrapped themselves around the two demons and pulled them down to the ground.

"Learned that from a dryad," Kalen panted. "Guess they *are* pretty useful sometimes."

I laughed. The sound was wild and edged in madness even to my own ears. The wrath demons yanked against the imprisoning plants, making wood snap and leaves fly. Kalen raised outstretched fingers and more vines rose up from the island.

"Go get... your boyfriend..." he grunted as the demons shattered another tree root as thick as my arm.

I sprinted across the wet grass and between the upthrust gray stones. They were larger than they had appeared from a distance, towering over me like petrified sequoias. Moss and lichen covered the rock in looping whorls that made me dizzy to look at.

The circle was bigger than it had seemed, too. But in the middle stood the altar of smooth white stone. The three beautiful, black-haired succubae writhed in the grass around it, moaning now in pain instead of pleasure. Max lay alone on top of the altar, naked and panting. His blond hair was dark with sweat and plastered to his forehead, but he was *right there*. My heart leapt.

"Hold on, Max!" I shouted.

Yes! I make the best plans!

I jumped over one of the reeling, retching succubae. She made a weak grab for my ankle, but I kicked her hand away and ran to the altar. Max's blue eyes fluttered open and he stared up at me.

"Max, I'm here," I cried. "And I'm going to get you out."

I reached desperately for Max... but my hands passed right through him. I felt hard stone instead of warm flesh against my skin and Max wavered like moonlight on water. Then he vanished.

There was no altar. My hands lay flat on top of a smaller waist-high stone that thrust up from the grassy earth. A narrow crack ran down the middle of the rock. The one Reid had put there.

I was touching the Seal of Avalon.

"Get us out," Asmodai said. "Yes, that sounds about right."

The Lord of Lust laughed. He stood at the edge of the ancient stone ring, dressed in black and his golden fingers closed on the real Max's shoulder.

I jerked my hand back, but it was too late. Cracks raced down the ancient stone and a fiery, hellish light seared from inside. Lines of furious red flame shot out all around me, tracing deep fissures and unreadable runes across the ground. They blazed and the Seal of Avalon exploded into pieces.

Shit.

Chapter
NINE

*A*smodai had played me. Again. I grabbed the gun from my pocket, but what good would that do? I'd already broken the Seal of Avalon. Killing myself wouldn't close it now.

The circle of standing stones smoldered with crimson light, as though breaking the Seal had turned them somehow molten, but the night had gone colder than ice as the Nether opened. A shivering pulse of furious, frozen scarlet rippled out from the ring and impacted against a clear, clean white brilliance. The consecration of the Roman cross... But the hellish fire blazed and the light died. My ears were full of a terrible, thunderous chorus, like a million monsters roaring in triumph – all of the demons of the Nether preparing to return to Earth.

The wrath demons on Avalon stood up, grinning viciously as dark red blood stopped running from their wounds. One of them caught Ben mid-pounce with a backhand that sent the six-hundred-pound werewolf flying through the air like a stuffed animal. The demons that Kalen had snared were suddenly covered in flames, swiftly incinerating the roots and vines that bound them. The huge monsters shrugged off the ashes and laughed with terrible, deep booming sounds.

Max and the altar might have been an illusion to make me willingly touch the Seal, but the succubae were all too real. The three demonic women leapt to their feet and prowled toward me. I let out a single sob, but that was all the self-pity I could afford. Max was right there, standing beside Asmodai. The real Max. *My* Max. Asmodai regarded me with bright golden eyes. His smile was one of complete and utter victory.

"Max!" I screamed.

He sagged forward in Asmodai's grasp, naked and glassy-eyed. What the hell had they done to Max? My heart clenched agonizingly inside me.

Somewhere outside the ring of glowering blood-colored stones, Ben howled, but the sound cut off with a pained whine. I heard Kalen swearing in a dozen languages as something creaked and crashed. I dropped my gun into the grass – it wasn't going to help me against demons – and held up my hands in surrender.

"Okay, Asmodai! You got what you wanted," I cried.

Asmodai laughed. "Of course I did. I am the Lord of Lust. Everything you have ever desired, Lily – revenge, pleasure, salvation – has only served me."

"Let Max go!"

Now the demon lord's golden eyes were almost curious, but the fire in them was no less cold. "You really came here for the mortal man. Pathetic. That's why you are weak, Lily. Why all humans are."

"But Merlin was your son!" I shouted in desperation. "His mother was human. You must have loved her!"

"Love," Asmodai snarled. He made it sound like a curse. "Love is a weakness, a disease. Love has made you powerless and now it will bring your whole world to its knees. Starting with you, Lily."

He gestured to the succubae. I ran at Max, but the demons were already leaping at me. They were going to tear me apart. Asmodai didn't need me anymore. I'd done everything he wanted. Max's eyes were still so faraway and glazed. He didn't even see me charging

348 • NATALIE & ERIC SEVERINE

toward him. But what else could I do? I had already condemned the entire world. The least I could do now was die trying to get to Max, to use my final breath and tell him how I felt...

One of the succubae was right there in front of me, grabbing for me with razor-sharp black nails. I punched the demoness in her perfectly smooth golden stomach. It was a pointless, stupid attempt to drive her back, to get me a little closer to Max before I died.

My fist went right through the succubus. Was she just another illusion? But no, the demoness reeled as brilliant silver light consumed her body. She vanished with a scream, leaving behind only a few bright sparks that quickly faded into the moonlight. The other two succubae drew back, their eyes wide. I held up my hand in wonderment. Max's engagement ring glinted on my finger.

What the hell? I didn't have my powers anymore and even when I did, they were never like this...!

"What are you doing?" Asmodai shouted. "Kill the cambion!"

The remaining succubae lunged at me again. One of them managed to grab a handful of my hair and bent me backward. She raked her blade-edge nails across my throat, but they just scraped harmlessly over my skin, drawing a spray of glowing silver sparks.

I seized the succubus' wrist and twisted, easily forcing her down to her knees. She was a full-blooded demon with all the terrible might of the Nether bleeding through the open Seal of Avalon. Was that what was strengthening me now? But I was only half demon and even that half had lost its power... Right?

The succubus kneeling down at my feet screamed. The other one lashed out with a high kick that came at me so fast her leg was little more than a blur of pale gold. But I was faster. I grabbed her ankle, yanked and the demoness fell on her ass. Both succubae writhed and shrieked in my grasp.

Hey, they just spent all night having their way with my boyfriend. I was allowed a little jealous rage. Light flashed and with a final pair of wails, the succubae were gone.

I charged through the falling swirl of silver embers at Asmodai. The incubus threw Max to the ground and raised his hand. Flames rose from between Asmodai's fingers, outlining the burning shape of his sword, but I hit him first. My fist connected with Asmodai's face and the demon lord went flying. He smashed into one of the blazing crimson stones and cracks raced out across the glowing rock. There was blood on Asmodai's golden skin.

I fell to my knees beside Max. He slumped naked where Asmodai had dropped him, eyes closed.

"Max!" I cried. "Max, are you okay?"

He only groaned quietly in answer.

Cold scarlet light streamed up from where the Seal had been and the cracks in the earth yawned open like raw red wounds. I wasn't even certain if Kalen was still alive or if there would be a world left beyond Avalon for much longer. But I pulled Max into my arms.

"Max? Hey, can you hear me?" I asked. My voice cracked. "Max, there... there are some things I need to tell you..."

"No!" Asmodai said.

He stood, brushing away shards of shattered stone. Asmodai was far more powerful than his succubae and the bruises were fading swiftly from his gilded flesh. I jumped up and threw myself between Asmodai and Max. Avalon shuddered beneath us.

"I don't know where you found the strength to harm me," Asmodai growled. "But you will pay for that insolence! And I know just how to break you."

The demon's beautiful voice rang like a struck bell.

"Max!" he commanded.

Max jerked to his feet and his eyes snapped open, fixing on Asmodai. I've always been immune or at least resistant to supernatural powers, but Max was only human. The demon prince pointed to me.

"Take her," he said. "Ravage her. Ruin her!"

Max whirled on me. Asmodai's rage smoldered in his dark blue eyes and Max seized my arm. His fingers dug hard into me and tears sprang into my eyes.

"Max?" I gasped. "What are you doing?"

His fist curled into my shirt and the cloth tore easily in his strong hands. The icy red flames of the broken Seal burned without heat all around us and the terrible cold seeping out from the Nether raked across my skin. Max tossed aside the remains of my shirt and advanced on me.

"No, Max!" I shouted. "Stop!"

Max ignored me. His naked, muscular body bunched like that of a hunting cat about to pounce. And his cock... god, Max was as hard as I had ever seen him, flushed darkly and jutting out toward me like a bared weapon. Max grabbed my bra and yanked it away with a snarl of ripping fabric. The Lord of Lust loomed over us.

"Ah, Lily," Asmodai said. "I am going to break you in so many ways. But first, I'm going to break your heart. And then Max's, when he realizes what he's done to you."

"Max, please! Listen to me," I cried. I pushed Max back as gently as I could. "This isn't you! Asmodai is—"

Max lunged at me with a wordless snarl. He grabbed my hair with one large hand and shoved me down to my knees. There was no way to fight Max, not without hurting him. I didn't understand why I had the power that I did right now, but I wouldn't use it to hurt Max.

His hand closed into a fist in my hair and Max yanked me forward. I only had time for a single desperate gasp of air before Max shoved his dick down my throat. I choked instantly and tears sprang into my eyes. I'm an experienced little cocksucker, but Asmodai was making Max attack me. Making him rape me.

"Ah, but you were so enthusiastic this morning," Asmodai said. "Yes, Lily, I was watching you together. Watching and waiting to take him from you."

My throat convulsed around the invading length of Max's dick, but under Asmodai's twisted influence, he just groaned, a sound of pleasure that I knew all too well. Max fucked my face hard and fast, his smooth cock sliding over my tongue. My jaw ached from being forced so wide and saliva ran down from my lips, leaving shining streaks across my breasts that reflected the burning light of the shattered Seal.

I couldn't breathe and my vision was going gray around the edges from lack of air. Only Max's fist wound tight into my hair and his cock rammed down my throat kept me upright. But what I felt wasn't pain. Wet heat surged between my legs as I brought my hands up against Max's thighs. His groans rose in volume and I couldn't help myself... I moaned in answer.

"Or perhaps you *do* like it?" Asmodai taunted.

I tried to push Max away, but he was holding me too tightly and his cock kept plunging into my mouth, over and over. There was no way to stop this without hurting him. And Asmodai... the demon was right. I *did* like it. Fuck, my pussy was dripping.

Asmodai made a slashing gesture with one hand. At his command, my remaining clothes ripped themselves to shreds and fell to the grass. Max yanked his cock out of my mouth and threw me down. He was on me in a heartbeat, grabbing and pinning me against the earth. Asmodai had left my panties just so Max could violently tear the lace away. He stared down at me with eyes so dilated that the blue was swallowed entirely by black. I turned my head so I wouldn't have to watch as Max held up the dripping wet remains of my panties while Asmodai grinned.

"Lily, once I thought you worthy of your demonic blood," the incubus said. "But now I see how weak you are. You can't stop even one mortal man."

"No... Max," I gasped.

He was panting for breath, too, nearly growling as I squeezed my legs together. Max pushed one knee between my slicked thighs and I whimpered with the effort of trying to keep him out. The urge to spread my legs for him was unbelievable. Max's unyielding cock burned where it slid against my skin. An electric thrill ran through me, like I had been struck by lightning, and my back arched. My breasts thrust up toward Max, my nipples almost painfully hard. Was it Asmodai's presence making me feel like this? I remembered the helpless, slavish lust that the demon had forced into me once before.

No, this was different. I wasn't the victim Asmodai said I was. I just... wanted Max. Even now, even as entire worlds stood on the brink of destruction and Asmodai turned Max's body against me.

But not Max's heart. Never his heart.

I wrapped my arms around Max and pulled him close. Max hurled himself against me and grabbed a fistful of my hair, forcing my head back. He bit the side of my neck hard enough to draw blood from any other woman, but I was stronger than that.

"Asmodai's wrong," I whispered into his ear. "Love doesn't make us weak. It makes us strong. You can't hurt me, Max."

My legs parted and Max let out a bestial snarl. His hips thrust forward and Max hammered himself into me. The invasion of my pussy was violent, but it was somehow perfect, too. Like Max was meant to be there inside me. Like the first night we were together, when we discovered what I was. Max fit me as exactly as his ring on my finger.

I coiled my legs around Max's waist to pull him in, to accept him. The sensation of fullness made me gasp and pleasure burned out through my body. Max filled places inside me that I had never known were empty. I wound my fingers into his hair and brought his face down to mine.

"I love you," I whispered against his lips.

I kissed him. Max resisted, trying to tear away from me. He managed to struggle upright into a sitting position, but I was right there with him.

"You're not running away again," I told him. "You promised me. And now I'm promising you, Max. I'm here with you. Always."

I kept my arms around Max and my lips pressed to his. He grabbed my shoulders, straining to push me away and snapped at my tongue with his teeth, but then... Oh god, Max's lips finally parted under mine and he returned my kiss. Nothing in the history of all the worlds has ever tasted as good as Max's kiss.

"No!" Asmodai snarled. "Make her hurt, Max! She ruined your life. Everything terrible that has ever happened to you was because of *her!*"

Max's eyes fell shut and his hands slid down along my back, settling on my hips with easy familiarity. I curled my legs around his waist and Max moved inside me, lifting me and thrusting instinctively in the dance we both knew so well. I kissed Max like a woman drowning and his breath was the only thing that could save me. And maybe it was...

"No! Release her!" Asmodai shouted.

The demon's roar shook the broken earth beneath us, but it still sounded so far away. Unimportant.

I moaned against Max's lips and Avalon shuddered again. He filled my body and senses so utterly that nothing else existed. Max pulled me down onto his cock with pure hungry desire now, not violence. His hands moved over me as though exploring me for the first time. He did more than find the sensitive places inside me – Max created new ones that belonged to him alone and came alive only at his skillful touch.

I drew back and Max's eyes opened. Even in the flickering red light, they were so blue.

"Lil?" Max asked.

My heart leapt at the sound of my name on his lips and the ecstasy of it coursed through my entire body. I cupped his face in my trembling hands.

"I love you, Max," I said.

His eyes went wide and his pulse raced faster than I'd ever felt it before. Max's hands tightened helplessly around my waist and his cock blazed gloriously inside me like a pillar of flame.

"You love...?" Max gasped. "Lil, I love you. I love you!"

Asmodai's shadow fell over us. The demon lord railed in fury, but I couldn't look away from Max. I knew his face better than my own, but I was seeing it for the first time. Max's dimpled grin and wide blue eyes were so full of love and desire, all of it for me. I felt the fire within him, burning out Asmodai's poisonous control. It wasn't the golden flame of lust, but something so much brighter and purer. Max loved me. He was inside me and filling me and the feeling of it was almost too much for words.

Except three.

"I love you," I said again.

The pleasure soared beyond sense and sensation. Max kissed me and his cock throbbed inside me. He held nothing back now. Max poured his cum and his love into me, white-hot and searing through my body. I could feel it along my skin, taste it in my mouth, hear and smell and see it all. Max filled me to bursting with all I could take and more.

Max and I burned together, and I'm not just being metaphorical: that silver-white light I used to fight the succubae blazed off both of us now. Asmodai's shadow was blown back behind him, thrown into stark relief by our radiance. The glow rippled and flowed like light shining through water, clean and bright. Asmodai threw his hands up over his face.

"What are you doing?" the demon cried. "You're a cambion! Love should make you powerless!"

I stood and pulled Max to his feet. My fingers remained entwined with his. Icy razor wind whipped our hair and raked our skin, but the fire that burned between us pushed back the cold. Max stared around at the cracked and broken earth beneath us, but he strode beside me as I advanced slowly on Asmodai.

"Powerless? Is that what happened to you?" I asked. "You fell in love with a mortal woman. She couldn't love you, though, just like Vincent couldn't love my mother. But Max loves me."

"Stop this!" Asmodai shouted.

I didn't stop. I walked through the center of the ring of glowing red stones, toward Asmodai.

"Sex doesn't give me power anymore," I told him. "But love does, and it's so much stronger."

Asmodai snarled in pure demonic fury and lashed out. Not at me, but at Max, trying to take away the source of my power. Or perhaps to strike down the love he had never known. Asmodai's black-nailed hand slashed lines of darkness through our light, but Max didn't flinch.

I thrust my hand into the center of Asmodai's chest and closed it around his heart. He screamed. I felt the cold emptiness inside Asmodai, his hatred for the woman who had spurned his love; his hatred for Merlin, the son who bound him away for a thousand years. The demon's soul was a bottomless abyss of hate.

But I had more love... I poured our light into Asmodai. His scream rose and radiance blazed through him. Asmodai's gleaming golden body burned white-hot and then he was gone, leaving only an afterimage that shone for a moment before that faded, too.

The hellish glow wavered and wild roars boomed across Avalon. The rage demons... They dropped Ben's furry body and charged toward us.

"Lil?" Max asked.

"Stand with me," I said.

Max's fingers tightened around mine. "Always."

We stood our ground as the towering demons closed. I waved my hand and the light surrounding us flashed in a line that arced out across the glen. It sliced through the wrath demons like an impossibly sharp silver blade and they toppled like felled trees, burning swiftly away to nothingness.

My new powers were awesome. I grinned, but Avalon convulsed and would have thrown me to the ground if Max hadn't been there to hold me up.

"Right, I better do something about the Seal," I said.

Max and I walked together into the center of the stone circle. Avalon pitched and split violently beneath us, but Max held me steady. I knelt and thrust my hand into the broken earth, just like I had with Asmodai, and pushed the Nether back. The red cracks groaned, shifted and grated thunderously closed around my hand. I clenched my fingers into a fist and lifted it out of the ground. Stone rose under my hand, smooth and gray and whole – a new Seal of Avalon.

The crimson light and otherworldly cold were gone. Moonlight shone through the little valley again and even the blinding silver fire around us finally died away.

"Well, that takes care of that," I said. "We're pretty amazing."

Max swept me up into his arms and I kissed him.

Chapter
TEN

Max and I hurried out of the circle toward Ben. The werewolf pulled himself up to his feet and pressed huge gray paws to his stomach, looking surprised to find it intact. Kalen sauntered through the trampled grass in our direction. His grin was as cocky as ever, but his leather coat hung in shreds and one wing dangled uselessly against his back.

"So, that didn't go at all according to plan," he said. "And this must be Max..."

Ben sniffed the air and opened his fang-filled maw to say something, but then figures were pouring out from the trees – wizards. Dozens of them in street clothes and robes, with wands and staves and herbs clutched in their hands. Asmodai's wards must have collapsed. I couldn't imagine Kalen letting the sorcerers in.

I recognized Redmond and Clio and the other bounty hunters. Dorian Vandi was there, too. The balding little mage looked shockingly fierce in old-fashioned black robes and leveling a wand of polished ebony at Ben. Stefano ran out ahead of the other wizards, throwing himself in front of the werewolf.

"No!" he shouted.

Stefano was dressed for battle, but his rugged face was pale. He looked shocked to see any of us still alive.

I couldn't blame him.

The ring of wizards tightened and Ben raised his huge paws in surrender. His demon-wolf form warped and shrank down into Dominic's naked human body. He was streaked in gore, but other than the tiny new scar where Stefano had pricked his wrist with the claw, seemed unharmed.

"Where's Kalen?" Stefano asked.

I guess my super senses were back in full force because even through the shouting, I clearly heard the soft snap of fingers. There was a burst of multicolored sparkles behind one of the standing stones – Kalen making his exit. My wish to Madu Tau was fulfilled and Kalen was free again. He had certainly earned it.

Remy Saville shoved his way through the circle of mages. The French hunter wore a broadsword on his belt and his hand glowed blue with painted runes. The College had even called in big brother tonight. Were the Castle wizards here to stop me or the demons? Either way, I had to admire their bravery.

Remy pointed to Ben. "Release the boy."

Ben looked down at me and then nodded. Dominic suddenly sagged forward, sweaty and panting. Stefano caught Dominic and lowered him to the grass. With my new senses, I saw the indistinct shape of Ben standing over them. Dominic shivered violently and Stefano pulled a blanket out from his coat, wrapping it around the younger man. Dominic opened his eyes.

"Did we win?" he wheezed.

Vincent Myrdon pushed Remy aside and stalked toward me. Wind whipped the High Magus' flowing robes and he gripped a tall wooden staff. Vincent glanced at Stefano, then turned his furious gaze on me. Max coughed and tried to cover his cock, but a single hand was not enough and I wasn't ready to give up the one I was holding just yet. I stared Vincent down and didn't even try to conceal my nakedness. Let them look.

"Lilith Quinn," Vincent said in a loud, clear voice. "You have invoked a djinn's wish in sovereign College territory, unlawfully removed a prisoner from the Tower and conspired in the creation of a werewolf!"

I nodded. Yeah, that all sounded about right. And pretty badass.

"You *knew* the danger that you pose to all of existence, yet you ran," the High Magus said. "Against all wisdom, you came to Avalon and to Asmodai."

Vincent raised his hand and lightning flashed between his outstretched fingers. Max pulled me closer, but he didn't run. Neither did I.

"You know the sentence, Lilith," Vincent told me in a breaking voice. "And I'm sorry."

I held up my hand toward the High Magus as the bright, jagged line of electricity lanced out toward me. Radiance flared around my body and Vincent's lightning splashed harmlessly against it. Vincent drew a hasty step back, and some of the other wizards took more than one.

"Ease up on the wands, everyone!" I called out. "Asmodai's gone. The Seal of Avalon is safe and stronger than ever. No more shadows. No more summonings. You're going to find a lot of empty spell circles and disappointed infernalists now."

A murmur rippled through the wizards. But Vincent didn't back down. Couldn't, maybe.

"You're still dangerous, Lilith," he said. "You're a cambion and you have powers now that we've never seen before."

I turned my glowing hand over, folding in all but my middle finger. Max raised one eyebrow at me, but he was grinning.

"You always seem to forget that Merlin was a cambion, too. You need us," I said. I smirked at Vincent. "Besides, do you really want to fight me?"

My father looked right past the luminous hand flipping him off and held my gaze for a lingering moment. Vincent's hair and beard seemed to have gone entirely gray and I didn't think that was just a result of the silver moonlight. Eventually, the High Magus nodded.

"Stand down!" Vincent called out.

Slowly, the other wizards lowered their wands and handfuls of sulfur and iridescent crystals. Dorian trotted forward, looking decidedly less impressive as he shrugged out of his robe and reached up to throw it around my bare shoulders. Beneath, the old sorcerer wore an actual tweed suit, complete with leather patches on the elbows. I finally let go of Max's hand long enough to give Dorian a huge hug. He got some breasts mushed in his face and I didn't care if his boss was right there to see.

Stefano came forward, holding out his worn and battle-scarred trench coat. Max took it hesitantly and then pulled it on. He was a little taller than Stefano, but at least his cock wasn't swinging in the breeze anymore. Avalon was no longer icy cold, but the evening air was brisk.

"Thanks," Max said.

Stefano regarded Max for a moment, then finally nodded and returned to Dominic, probably to prepare a teleportation spell. The surfer was still cursed, after all, and had to be cured again. Stefano would make sure it got done. I turned back to my father and made my expression hard. There was one last problem to deal with.

"You're not wiping Max's memories," I said bluntly. "Asmodai took Max from me and I kicked his ass. I'll do it all over again if I have to!"

Vincent blinked a few times. And then to my utter shock, the High Magus laughed. I blinked. I didn't think he even knew *how* to laugh. Max and I exchanged a confused look.

"Lilith, if I intended to remove Maxwell's memories, I would have done so years ago," Vincent said. "But he's proved willing and capable of keeping your secrets, and ours."

SEALED WITH A KISS · 361

"You... you knew about me?" Max asked.

"Evaine told me. She always suspected the two of you shared a special bond. I couldn't be there for my daughter, but I could at least prevent the College from taking away the man who was. And when Lilith said that she was pregnant, I knew that Evaine had been right."

Dorian's bushy white eyebrows shot up. "Daughter?"

"Pregnant?" Max asked.

I pressed his hand under my borrowed robes and to my bare belly. "You're going to be a dad."

"A baby? Us?" Max said, his voice cracking. "But Lil, I thought cambions couldn't get pregnant."

"They can when they're in love," I told him.

Max jumped up, pumping his fist in the air, then dropped to his knees and put a kiss on my navel. I laughed and hugged Max against me. We were both crying.

"Vincent?" Dorian asked softly.

The High Magus sighed and nodded. "Yes, I know. And as soon as this matter is resolved, I will resign my position. Peacefully, on the condition that my decision concerning Maxwell Ferguson's memories is maintained."

"I'm sure that can be arranged," Dorian said.

He and Vincent shook hands and Dorian stepped back. Vincent watched the other wizard go without much regret. My father had worked hard and given up a lot to become High Magus, but after the events of the last year, he seemed more than ready to retire.

Vincent cleared his throat meaningfully and Max climbed to his feet again, but he didn't look at all sorry. He was grinning like an idiot and my cheeks hurt from smiling back.

"Convincing Avalon to allow us here at all required considerable magic," Vincent announced. "And we should not abuse our welcome. Remy, take as many as you need and conduct a sweep of the island. Make sure that no demons escaped."

I could have told him the island was clean. The Seal was whole again and through it, I felt every demonic presence on Earth – more of them than the wizards probably wanted to believe. There were still vampires and werewolves, too, but the demons were locked away once more in the Nether. If it made the mages feel better to check, though...

"Hey, there's something I want to check out, too," I said.

Vincent glanced back, but Dorian and Remy were organizing the wizards as they spread out to search Avalon. He hefted his staff and followed at a distance as I began walking across the grass. Max kept up easily beside me, even as he stared around the island. I guessed that he was a little too busy and demon-charmed to see much of it earlier.

We reached the edge of the forest and I paused beneath a tree to dig around in the leaves until I found an acorn. Who knew if Kalen had picked one up like I asked, or if he would deliver it to Ash now that he was free of Madu Tau's power? The acorn had a silvery sheen to it that might have just been the moonlight, but I doubted it. I handed the seed over to Max, who examined it for a moment and then dropped it into a pocket of Stefano's coat.

"I'll explain later. It's going to be a long story," I said.

Max smiled. "I want to hear everything. When there's time."

We wound our way through the trees. Max wasn't the only one who had a busy night and I was having a bit of trouble retracing my steps. Max put his arm around me as we walked. The warmth of him beside me felt good.

"I missed you, Max," I said with a sigh. "So fucking much. What happened? How did Asmodai get you?"

Max ran his free hand through tangled blond hair and thought for a moment. "I was... on my way back to the garage, I think, but someone jumped right out in front of the truck. The sun had just set and I couldn't see much of anything."

"Only a shadow?" I guessed.

"Yeah. I was too close and I clipped the guy. When I pulled over and went to check on him, though, he... *it* grabbed me. The rest is pretty fuzzy. That must have been Asmodai. He brought me here so... so you would come for me."

Max stopped walking. I stopped, too, and looked up as he gently brushed a strand of red hair back out of my face. Vincent waited in silence a few yards away.

"Lil, why did you come for me?" Max asked. "It was dangerous. For the whole world, apparently."

"Because I love you, dummy," I said.

Max's eyes fell shut for a second and he smiled. "God, I never thought I would hear that from you, Lil. I've loved you since... forever. Since I was a kid. Since before I knew what I was feeling."

"I know."

Max opened his eyes again and we resumed walking. Leaves and grass crunched quietly beneath our bare feet and the midnight dew was cold against my skin. I really missed my bunny slippers. Max kept his arm around me.

"You know that was okay, right?" he said. "I never expected you to return my feelings, Lil. You were my best friend and that was enough for me. I was really happy."

"I know," I told him again. "But you're happier now, aren't you? Even after everything that's happened?"

Max grinned down at me, dimples cranked up to full. "Yeah, Lil. I wouldn't trade a moment of it. Not the yeti or the demons or anything. I love you."

"I love you, too."

I leaned against Max's shoulder as we walked together through the forest. Finally, I heard the soft hiss of water and we followed it to the little stream that I had seen before, then back up the slope. Max pointed to the cave.

"Is that it?" he asked me. "Is that what you wanted to take a look at?"

I nodded and cocked my head, listening. There... I could just make out the sound of a voice from deep inside. Even with my new love-powered super senses, though, the words were lost.

"Do you hear that?" I asked.

Max nodded. "That voice? Yeah. But I can't tell what it's saying."

Vincent caught up to us and stared at the cave entrance. It was nothing impressive, just a rough circular hole into the hillside with tree roots wrapped around the edges. The stream that flowed out from the darkness was shallow and ran along a bed of jumbled stones. But Vincent's expression was awed.

"I... haven't been here since I first became High Magus," he said.

"What is this place?" I asked.

Vincent gave me a hard, suspicious look. But with a visible effort, he relaxed and gestured toward the cave. "I suppose the two of you have earned the right to be here. Come and meet him."

"Him?" Max asked.

I shrugged. This part was new to me, but I wasn't frightened. Not with Max there beside me.

Vincent led us down into the earth. Max had to duck through the opening, but the ceiling beyond stretched quickly up and away. Vincent produced a pinch of fine black powder from one sleeve and with a word, it kindled into a tongue of flame between his fingers. It was just a spark, really, but the flickering light spread out across the cavern as though Vincent held an entire bonfire in his hand.

The cave was huge. It wound far deeper into the hill than I would have thought possible without collapse, but nothing on Avalon worked the way it was supposed to. The rocky floor was swept clean and the little stream we had followed ran from a ring-shaped pool in the center. The pond was still and the surface covered by a thick layer of pale mist. A single line of stones thrust up from the foggy water, creating a narrow walkway that led out to an island in the middle.

"This way," Vincent said.

He escorted us to the edge of the subterranean lake and then across the rocks to the island. The ground here was as smooth and even as the rest of the cavern but for a simple white marble bier rising from the center. It looked just like the one Asmodai showed me in his devastating illusion and I grabbed Max's hand as we approached.

A man lay on top of this stone altar, too, but he wasn't naked. He wore armor and I recognized the style; the main hall of the College was filled with suits exactly like this. It even had the same surcoat emblazoned with two dragons locked in combat – one red, one white. The man had dark hair and a closely cropped beard shot through with silver. I guessed he was somewhere in his forties and carried his age well in his wide, firm jaw and powerful build. A plain steel band circled his head. It didn't look much like one, but I knew a crown when I saw it.

Vincent bowed his head deeply, respectfully. "Behold Arthur Pendragon, king of the Britons."

"No way," Max breathed.

I whistled.

"Here he sleeps away the centuries," Vincent said. "It is written in *The Gates of Avalon* that he will rise again in Earth's darkest hour to defend us all."

Max looked back toward the cave's entrance. "I'm not so sure about your legend. We really could have used him tonight."

"Or," Vincent said, "that was not our darkest hour."

Well, *that* gave me the willies. Arthur's gauntleted hands were folded across the hilt of a simple, battle-scarred sword. I recognized the blade, though I had only seen it once. Excalibur. I guess the sword had returned to its master when Evaine was done borrowing it. Oh, Evaine...

The fog across the pond eddied and rose into the ghostly shape of a woman in a long white dress. Curling hair of swirling mist cascaded down her back.

"Evaine!" I cried.

I ran to the water's edge with Max following close on my heels. Evaine's silhouette reached out and trailed spectral fingers down my face. I felt a cold tingle at her touch, but nothing more. Hot tears ran down my cheeks.

"Lily," she said. Her voice was soft and echoed across some impossible distance. "If you can hear me now, then you've returned to Avalon, the island of your birth."

"I'm here, Evaine," I told her in a choked sob. It was so good to hear her voice again. "I'm listening."

"The circle is complete. If you do not already, then you will soon carry Max's child." The ethereal image of the Lady of the Lake smiled. "If I know him at all, Max stands beside you even now. Lily, you have proven that a cambion can love and be loved in return. Not even Merlin possessed such power. The world has never seen anything like you."

Max kissed my wet cheek. "Damned right."

"Your daughter will be raised in love," Evaine's echo said. "And her love will determine the fate of all the worlds. Great things are coming, Lily. Great and terrible things. But love each other and the light will never die."

Evaine's misty silver image rippled and began to fade. I reached for her as she turned away.

"Wait!" I cried.

The woman on the dark water actually paused and looked back at me.

"I love you," I told her. It was easier this time.

"And I love you, Lily."

And then Evaine was gone. All that remained was a sheen of mist on the water's surface. I wiped my eyes and stood, turning to face Vincent.

"Thanks for showing us this... Dad," I said, trying it on without bitterness this time.

Vincent's expression was already shocked and awed, but he only barely managed to keep his jaw from dropping at that. He took a deep breath and drew himself up.

"You are... welcome, Lilith," Vincent said. He drew himself up and let out a long breath. "Important things have occurred today. The Lady's final words must be recorded and studied."

He turned away and hurried out toward the cave's exit. Max and I had to trot to remain in the light of his spell. From there, it was a short walk back to the beach. A shorter walk than it had been on the way in, but I was beyond being fazed by Avalon's weirdness anymore. The wizards had reconvened and were now filing into four old-fashioned wooden boats lined up neatly on the island's sandy shore. They must have finished searching for demons and come up empty.

Told you.

Vincent rushed off toward the rest of the mages. I didn't think he was done with us just yet, but that could wait until later. Discreetly, I pointed Max in the direction of the speedboat Kalen had stolen. I felt like we should return it.

"You can drive that, right?" I asked.

Max nodded and climbed in. I grabbed the prow and shoved the boat effortlessly out into the water. When it was a dozen yards from the shore, I jumped, arcing up through the air, and landed gently in the back. It was almost like flying. Even at my most sex-charged, I had never felt so light.

My new powers were amazing, but still mysterious. How far did they go? What else could I do?

Max revved the engine and steered the boat away from Avalon. He had buttoned Stefano's coat shut, covering everything but his bare feet and muscular calves. I pointed my finger at him and thought *really* hard about his clothes vanishing. Both Kalen and Asmodai had been able to do it... My finger glowed, but nothing happened.

Max raised an eyebrow and I shrugged.

"Only testing my powers," I told him. "I guess I still have *some* limits."

Oh well. I would just have to tear Max's clothes off the old fashioned way. He was still staring at my hand, though, at the diamond ring shining there on my finger, bright and simple and perfect.

"Lil, that... that's my ring!" Max said. "You found it? And you're wearing it! Does that mean...?"

"Yes," I answered. "If you still want to marry me. That box was pretty damned dusty."

Max shouted and released the wheel. Our boat fishtailed wildly through the dark water, but Max was already grabbing me. He picked me up and whirled me in a circle.

"Yes! Yes, I want to marry you," he shouted. "Lil, I love you!"

I was never going to get tired of that. Max kissed me again and again before finally setting me down and then wrestling the speedboat back onto course. Fog had closed in around us, concealing the island once more. I told Max to head southeast and hoped that Avalon would take us home.

"So what's next?" he asked.

"You mean after we get married?" I said. Max did another little happy dance at that and I grinned. "Well, your shop is uh... going to need some repairs and a new room for the baby, but they should have that done by the time we get back from our honeymoon."

"What about you?" Max asked. "Back to bounty hunting? There are still monsters out there, right?"

"No demons, but plenty of other shit," I agreed, nodding. "You're going to be in bed all day keeping me charged up."

"I thought you didn't need that anymore."

I stuck out my tongue. "Fine. I'll come up with plenty of other excuses to fuck your brains out."

"We don't need excuses for that," Max said.

"Just keep loving me and I can take on anything," I told him. "And keep our little girl safe until she grows up to save the world."

Max laughed. "Any monsters under her bed are in for some serious trouble."

He kept one hand on the wheel this time, but Max pulled me close again. I kissed him and didn't stop for a long time.

EPILOGUE

Arthur. It is time.

The voice was soft but insistent. Every part of me felt heavy, dusty, and I ached to sink deeper into endless dreams. It had grown difficult to tell my body apart from the stone on which I slept. But I was summoned, and bound to answer the call.

Awake, Arthur Pendragon. You are needed.

With an effort that made me groan aloud, I forced my eyes open and looked around. I still lay on the stone bier that had been my bed for... How long had I slept? To judge by the ache in my neck and the fullness in my bladder, a long time indeed.

The hollow hill seemed much as I remembered it, though, large and empty and silent. The only light was the glow of the moon filtering in from outside. It reflected off the circular pool surrounding me and shimmered through the cave.

My armor clanked as I sat up and hefted Excalibur's familiar weight. There was a new notch in the worn blade, one that had not been there when Merlin brought me here to sleep so long ago. I frowned and shook my hand out of its gauntlet to run the thumb along Excalibur's bright steel edge. It was still sharp enough to draw blood.

The dim light gleaming off my sword shifted. There was someone else in the cave.

A woman stood on the shore of the lake, watching me. How had she gotten so close? Wind that smelled of earth and water tugged at her long, pale hair. Her golden eyes flashed in the darkness.

Demon! I leapt off the stone bier, putting it between us. I raised Excalibur and the steel came alive in my hand.

The woman wore a white dress that flowed around her legs like ocean foam. She looked young, with pale skin and a coppery tint to her blonde hair when it caught the light. Her bright eyes shone the gold of something priceless and precious. She was beautiful, but beauty had tricked me before.

"You will find me no easy prey, demoness," I said. "What are you doing here?"

The words came out in a rough growl. How long since I had last spoken? The young woman walked closer, slowly circling the tiny island toward me.

"Welcome back to the world, Arthur," she said.

I started. Hers was the voice that had roused me from Merlin's magical sleep, but it was not a voice I knew.

"Who are you?" I asked.

"In time, the wizards will call me the Lady of the Lake. Keeper of Avalon."

I stared. This golden-eyed woman was *not* Evaine, but she was here on the isle and she had woken me. I felt the power of her presence, too, and saw the same ageless and immortal beauty that had been Evaine's. But there was something... else. Cautiously, I lowered Excalibur. The new Lady of the Lake gave me a smile that would have been gentle were it not for the wicked curve of her lips.

"My name is Eva Quinn," she said. "And it's time to take up your sword, Arthur Pendragon. I need your help with something."

I still didn't know who this woman was, but I had the feeling she was going to get me into a lot of trouble.

A LILY QUINN EPILOGUE

Magic MAX

Magic
MAX

"Well, that's going to complicate things," I said. "But thanks. Really. I owe you."

I finished my phone call and hung up as Max emerged from Eva's room with a colorful children's book tucked under his arm. My husband is over six imposing feet of blond hair, muscles and typically a few grease stains from working in his garage downstairs. Right now, though, he was just grinning like a big goofy kid.

"Success," Max announced. "She's finally asleep."

I jumped up off the couch and bounded across the living room to put a lingering kiss on that victorious smile. Max circled his arms around my waist and pulled me tight against his hard body. He was still holding the kids' book and one corner pressed into my back, but that was actually kind of sexy. Fatherhood was a damned good look on Max.

"Eva loves the sound of your voice," I told him. "She gets that from me."

"We like your voice, too," Max said.

"Thanks, though I think Eva prefers *The Wheels on the Bus* to your favorite song."

"Yeah? What song is that?" Max asked.

"*Oh fuck, I'm cumming!*" I said. "And I'm usually screaming it."

Max smiled again and showed off his dimples. "Well, I *do* like loud music."

"Good," I said. "Because I need to sweet-talk you."

I took Max's hands and pulled him back to the couch. He dropped his storybook on the coffee table and then let me push him down into the cushions. Not that he had much choice – I've always been a lot stronger than Max. But it's his fault, really. Our love gives me super-powers.

Most of the lamps were still turned off, but city lights streamed through the window and filled our living room with a mosaic of glowing colors. I dropped into Max's lap, straddling his waist, and wound my arms around his neck. Max settled his hands on my hips and silver moonlight glittered along the curve of our wedding rings.

Max smiled up at me. "Alright, Lil. What's going on?"

"I need you to go to The Junk Yard," I said.

"What do you need at a junkyard?" Max asked. "Am I out of parts for the garage or something?"

"Nope. Not *a* junkyard. *The* Junk Yard. It's a strip club. A male strip club."

One of Max's eyebrows shot upward. "Okay, then. I get why you would visit a club like that, Lil, but why do you want *me* to go?"

"It's for a job," I said. "A bounty that the College just posted."

"At a strip club?"

"A lot of the guys from The Junk Yard are calling in sick. Some of them have even been admitted to the hospital for exhaustion and it's not from dancing."

"What, then?" Max asked.

"The College thinks it's the work of a jakhai."

"I've read about them a few times," Max said. "Aren't they from southeast Asia?"

"India, mostly. And that's geomancer territory when it comes to monster hunting, so the College doesn't know much about jakhai.

But lucky for them, I met a very nice young geomancer when I was in Cairo on the quicksilver job."

"Is that who you were just talking to on the phone?" Max asked.

I nodded. "Jun says that the College is probably right about there being a jakhai prowling around The Junk Yard. The symptoms all match, and so do the victims. Jakhai magically steal youth and vitality from men – especially beautiful ones – to feed their own fucked-up brand of immortality."

"So that's what she's doing to the guys at the Junk Yard? Stealing their life?"

"Leaving them sick and exhausted," I said, then drew a deep breath. "Not for much longer, though. I'm going to take care of the bitch. But I need your help to do it."

Max cocked his head at me. "I thought you didn't like me getting involved in your bounty-hunting, Lil."

That's my job. I'm a monster hunter for the College, a secret society of Merlinic wizards. Max had his garage downstairs and it was doing great, but I'm the one who bought the building. I get paid a small fortune for each bounty I hunt down, and I love what I do... But it *is* dangerous.

I'm half demon – a cambion, as the wizards call me. Sex used to be what fueled me with the strength to be tossed through a brick wall by a vampire and then get up again to return the favor. Now Max's love for me and mine for him gives me more power than I've ever dreamed of.

It was awesome.

But Max was still only human. And he was right – I really didn't like getting him involved. Have I ever told you about the time Max tried to fight off a wyvern with nothing but a tire iron and a road flare? While he was naked? Or the time he nearly got thrown over a cliff trying to help me hunt down a yeti? Or how he was taken by Asmodai, the most powerful demon prince of the Nether, and held hostage on Avalon?

I got him back, though, and Asmodai is dead. I cut him in half with love-powered lasers.

No one hurts my Max and gets away with it.

Max brushed his fingers along my cheek and up through my long red hair. I placed my hand over his, leaning into the warmth of his touch.

"I'm not involving you in the hunting part," I told Max. "I would *never* put you in danger. I just need help with reconnaissance. I can get into The Junk Yard easy enough – all I have to do is pay the cover charge and walk inside. But there are places I can't go in there and things I can't do."

"That's what you need me for?" Max asked.

"Yeah. Pretty much all of The Junk Yard employees are male. I can't get backstage or behind the bar without someone noticing. That's why I need you to get a job with security, so you can go where I can't and talk to the boys."

"Talk to them? I can't imagine you having the slightest trouble getting a bunch of hot men to chat with you, Lil."

"But they'll be working," I said. "Trying to sell me lap dances and smiling for a nice tip."

Max laughed. "Oh yeah, I bet they want to do *something* with their tips."

"Maybe, but only you get to. You're not jealous, are you?"

"Not a chance. You're the best monster hunter in the world, Lil. You keep us all safe from the shit that goes bump in the night. And I love you for it."

"I love you, too," I said. "You know that, right?"

Max kissed me. He took my waist in his big hands and pulled me tight against his chest. Max's cock was growing swiftly long and hard in his lap beneath me. It was delicious and distracting...

I pulled myself from the circle of Max's arms just long enough to kick my pants off and shove soaked panties down my legs. Max smiled up at me and opened his mouth to say something, but I was already back in his lap and he drew me in close again. Through cambion senses I've never been able to explain, I felt Max's love and his lust for me, burning like a star.

And I felt the heat of his cock against my pussy, even through his jeans. I kissed Max again and didn't stop until I could no longer stand not feeling his skin against mine. I yanked Max's shirt up over his head and raked my nails lightly down his flushing chest. Four raised scars ran from his right shoulder and across his pectorals, claw marks left by the yeti bastard that tried to fling him off a mountaintop. I've always thought the scars looked damned sexy on Max, but don't tell him that... I never wanted him to get more of them.

"Capture or kill?" Max asked as I came in for another kiss.

"Hmm...?"

"The jakhai," Max said. He ran strong fingers along my spine and down to cup my bare ass, tracing fire over my skin and making me shudder with pleasure. "Are we capturing or killing it?"

"Oh, yeah. The job," I said. "Kill. Jakhai are pretty fucking evil. Sorry, I got distracted."

"I would tell you that I'm sorry," Max murmured against my lips. "But I'm not."

My pulse pounded through me in a hot red drumbeat of need. I reached between our bodies and pulled down the zipper of Max's jeans. He bit back a groan as I slid my hand into his pants and closed my fingers around the growing length of his dick. If that jakhai wanted strength and vitality, Max would have been one hell of a meal.

But I had no intention of using my husband as bait.

"Why don't you call Stefano?" Max asked in a tight voice as I pulled his cock free. "If you're nervous about sending me into that club, I mean. You two work well together."

"We do," I agreed. "But Stefano's down in Louisiana on another job."

"Werewolf?"

I nodded. It was always werewolves with Stefano. My friend had spent his whole life on a one-man crusade to wipe out lycanthropy and I wondered if he would ever stop long enough to actually find some joy.

Like I had. I stroked the smooth, hard length of Max's cock and groaned at the heat of it against my skin. Max shot a glance back in the direction of Eva's bedroom door, but I winked at him. Since the birth of our daughter, I had become a master of silent sex. Like a sex ninja.

Well, sort of.

"So... uh... what's the plan?" Max asked me.

For hunting down the jakhai. Right. I had gotten distracted again. That's what happens when Max is being sexy. Which was all the time, so I figured that I should do something about that. I lifted my hips and grabbed Max's cock, guiding him up into my pussy. There, no longer distracted. I think better with his dick inside me, anyway.

Max gripped my waist and pulled me down on top of him. Hard heat spread and then filled me, forcing a soft moan from my lips. Max's head fell back onto the cushions of the couch, eyes wide as I took every inch. He was the first man I ever fucked – though certainly not the only one – but whenever we're together, Max stares at me in absolute wonder. Like it's the first time all over again. But so do I... It took me far too long to realize how much I loved him and that knowledge hits me like a lightning bolt every single time.

I laid my hands flat against Max's chest to steady myself and began riding him slowly, feeling the hard planes of muscles underneath my fingers. I rocked his dick smoothly in and out of me. Every movement made me gasp.

"The plan..." I said breathlessly. "Right. Well, jakhai only reveal their true forms when they attack. Until then, they just look like human women."

"Have any of the sick performers from The Junk Yard reported seeing a monster?" Max panted. "Or given a description of the last woman they danced for?"

"No. Jun says that jakhai take a lot more than physical strength from their targets. It's a spiritual draining, too, and most victims never remember what happened to them."

"That must make them pretty hard to track," Max grunted.

"It does. So I need you to keep your eyes and ears open for tired strippers with weird gaps in their memories. Tips they don't recall getting and that sort of thing."

"Where will you be?" Max asked. He slid his hands down to my hips and ran his thumbs over my stomach as he pumped his cock up into me.

"At a table, enjoying the show," I moaned. "Maybe at the tip bar, like a good paying customer. Don't worry, I'll be... close."

I gasped the last word as the pleasure built inside me. I arched my spine and gripped the back of the couch so hard that the frame creaked under my fingers.

"When I locate the jakhai, I'll make my move," I said in short, panting bursts. "I can corner her somewhere away from everyone else and take her out."

Max nodded and slid his hands back down along the curve of my ass. He didn't stop there, though, and traced his fingers over my pussy where I was spread wide on his thick cock. Max's touch was strong but gentle, moving in soft counterpoint to the hard thrust of his dick and guiding me expertly up into ecstasy.

"Oh fuck, I'm cumming!" I screamed.

Or tried to, but Max was *fast*.

He clapped one hand over my mouth and I screamed the words into it as I writhed on the end of his cock. Max held me tightly, muffling my slutty moans while I clung to his shoulders. I closed my eyes and surrendered myself to Max, trusting him to give me what I needed without waking Eva.

Max stood up suddenly from the couch – still holding me in his arms – and threw me face-down into the cushions. I grabbed a throw pillow and bit into it as Max mounted me from behind. He sank his long cock into me, inch by inch, until I was gasping and squirming. Max put his hand on the back of my neck, curling his fingers up into my coppery hair.

"You okay down there, Lil?" he asked.

I nodded and Max pressed my face into the pillow.

"Good," he said. "Because I'm not done with you."

Between the pair of us, I usually claimed the title of domme. I have the outfit and the training and everything. Since becoming a father, though, Max has learned that a loving but firm hand is sometimes required. He's mastered a clear, strong voice that always brings Eva to a halt before she can pry the cover off an electrical socket or crawl over the top of the stairs. When Max uses that voice on me, I just melt.

Max held me down and drove his cock relentlessly into my gushing pussy. Spots of light flashed in front of my eyes like stars and I screamed into the pillow. I thrashed in the grip of ecstasy, but Max pinned me there and pounded pleasure through me until it burned along my whole body. Every long stroke of his dick made wetness stream from between my legs and drip down my trembling thighs.

I felt Max's dick swell inside me, his already impressive girth stretching my pussy almost more than I could take. Max slammed himself deep into me and came. Molten sensation flooded through my body and sent me spiraling over the edge. I bit the pillow until the cover tore and white stuffing billowed up from inside to match the fountain of cream Max poured into me. I couldn't think, I couldn't do anything but scream in absolute and utter abandon as Max filled me.

Finally, we sat up, panting and sticky. Max and I looked across the living room toward Eva's door, holding breathlessly still in the *did-we-wake-the-baby-?* pause. But a few moments passed with no sound from our daughter's bedroom. Yes, go sex ninjas!

Max stood and grabbed his cock, stashing it away in his jeans once more. His chest shone with sweat and I laid back on the couch to enjoy the view until Max offered me his hand. I took it and let him help me upright. White spunk ran down between my legs.

I smirked at Max and he flushed. Not long after I got pregnant, he agreed to a vasectomy. Good thing... Eva had been a wonderful, life-changing surprise, but I wasn't in a hurry to do it all again and Max would have knocked me up with triplets to judge by the size of the load he left inside me.

"So... will you help me find the jakhai?" I asked. "Did I successfully sweet-talk you?"

Max smoothed down my shirt and put his arms around me. He gave me a dimpled smile.

"You don't need to ask," he said. "And you didn't need to talk me into anything. I've always got your back, Lil."

I stood up onto my toes and kissed Max until neither of us could breathe anymore. Then I grabbed his hands and towed him toward our bedroom, which I had spent a small fortune soundproofing and where I promised that Max would *definitely* have my back.

———

"I need you, Lily. And now I have you."

"The hell you do!"

"Yes," I said. "The hell I do."

Or to be more accurate, Asmodai had said. Now the part of the demonic Lord of Lust was being played by a plastic tyrannosaurus rex, which I waggled menacingly at a stuffed bunny standing in for yours truly. Eva giggled and grabbed the toy dinosaur from my hand, then stuck it in her mouth. She chewed on Asmodai's head.

"Good girl," I said.

Eva had her father's pale blonde hair, but there was a distinct red tint when the sun caught it just right. Her otherwise nondescript baby blue eyes were developing a ring of bright demonic gold around the pupils, too, that made me wonder if Eva was going to inherit any of my abilities.

I heard the door open downstairs and so did Eva. She dropped the dinosaur and waved her chubby little arms in the air.

"Da, da, da!" Eva burbled. It wasn't quite a real word, but she was getting close.

"That's right," I said. "Daddy's home."

Max climbed the steps and grinned when he saw us playing on the floor. His blond hair was damp, and dimpled cheeks a little flushed. I smelled sweat and wondered if Max had been nervous about his interview at The Junk Yard. I was pretty damned sure he didn't need to be. With a body like his, Max could have gotten a job as the bouncer in Valhalla, tossing Norse gods out on their ears when they got too rowdy.

"How are my favorite girls?" he asked.

He sat down at the top of the stairs and picked up one of Eva's toys, a model Ducati motorcycle. He rolled it toward Eva, making growling engine noises.

"We're great," I said. "Did you get the job?"

"Well... uh... yeah," Max answered. He drove the motorcycle up Eva's leg. "My first shift is tonight, actually."

"Good. That jakhai is damned near killing strippers. The sooner we can put the bitch down, the better."

I clapped one hand over my mouth and glanced down at Eva, suddenly worried that her first word was going to be something a lot less socially acceptable than *daddy*. But my daughter was fully absorbed by chasing Max's toy motorcycle with her t-rex, making squeaky little engine noises of her own.

"Can we get your parents to baby-sit this evening?" I asked. "Or maybe I should call my dad."

"Your father is one of the world's preeminent wizards," Max said. "I'm not sure he appreciates being asked to baby-sit."

"Actually, I think Vincent likes being a grandpa. And you know he believes Eva is some kind of chosen one prophetic child or something. I'm certain we can drop her off for a few hours tonight. My dad can watch Eva, you can start your new job and I can bust a man-eating monster."

Max laughed, but quickly sobered and his cheeks went pink again. "That sounds good, Lil. But... uh... about the job..."

"Pendragon," said Eva.

Max and I blinked. We stared at Eva, up at each other, and then back down at our daughter. She clutched the motorcycle in one tiny hand, the plastic tyrannosaurus rex in the other and began banging them enthusiastically together. Eva laughed.

"Did she just say...?" Max asked.

"Pendragon," I said. "Like King Arthur Pendragon."

"To be honest, I was kind of hoping her first word would be *daddy*," Max admitted.

"Me too," I agreed. I wasn't jealous – Max was the best dad in the history of dads.

"We saw Arthur asleep on Avalon," he said. "Do you think this means something?"

I smirked. "Yeah. That this is what we get for letting wizards baby-sit our daughter. Eva's going to be learning spells as soon as she can string together a sentence."

"Oh boy," Max said. "How do you baby-proof a house against magic?"

———

I carried Eva across the manicured gardens of the College to my father's house. Vincent Myrdon was no longer the High Magus, but he was still an important wizard and lived in one of the oldest, largest sanctums on the grounds. His tower was built from deep red bricks, dark and imposing and cloaked in thick ivy. The windows glowed with warm amber light, though, and I sniffed the air as I approached. There was something cooking inside that didn't smell like a spell.

Vincent met me at the iron-banded door, dressed in sweeping black robes like an archaic judge. His hair and beard had finished going steely gray, but he took Eva from my arms with the closest thing to a smile his stern old face seemed capable of.

Something had softened since Vincent admitted to fathering me and resigned his position. Making a half-demon baby was absolutely forbidden by the College and Vincent's indiscretion had very nearly released the demons from the Nether to plunge the world into a second Dark Age. But in the end, I had done a lot more good than harm and the College didn't seem very interested in punishing their one-time High Magus.

"She's growing quickly," Vincent commented, cradling Eva in his arms.

"That's Max's cooking," I said. "Dinner may get run through a blender, but it's still delicious."

Vincent glanced back over his shoulder at something inside the tower that I couldn't see. "Has Eva eaten her supper already, then?"

"Yeah, but she's pretty much always hungry. If you feel like risking your walls, go for it."

"My... walls?" Vincent asked.

"Eva's an enthusiastic eater."

He still looked confused, so I waved my hands and pantomimed flinging imaginary food. Eva squealed at my demonstration and my father frowned down at her.

"I see," said Vincent. "I shall proceed with caution."

I couldn't help smiling at him. Vincent was so bad at all of this, but he was trying. That had to be worth something. I lingered in the door, wondering what to say to my father. Being Vincent's daughter was as new to me as being Eva's mother.

"She said her first word today," I told him at last.

"What was it?"

"Pendragon."

Vincent's eyes went wide and he stared in shock at the baby in his arms. Eva giggled and grabbed his beard. Vincent winced.

"That is astonishing," he said, the words distorted as Eva yanked on his face. "Did she say anything else?"

"No. She just pooped her diaper and Max changed her," I answered, then wrinkled my nose. "Speaking of which…"

My half-demon senses were a hundred times more acute than any human, which served as an invaluable early warning system when it came to dirty diapers. I backed quickly away, waving to my baby girl and leaving her in the capable hands of the world's most powerful wizard.

Hey, Vincent missed out on raising me. So really I was the one doing him a favor by letting him experience these treasured moments with his granddaughter.

I walked back out in the direction of Dresden Hall, making my way through another one of the College's vast and perfectly arranged herb gardens. Dorian Vandi stood beside a patch of red flowers and lectured to a pair of robed apprentice mages who were scribbling furiously in their notebooks. The two student wizards looked up as I passed and gave me deep nods of respect that were nearly bows. Their desire was far less restrained, but they were young and it wasn't their fault I could sense lust.

Dorian waved and a wide smile creased his face. I wished that I could stop to chat with Dorian and was sure the old wizard wanted to know how Max and Eva were doing, but I was in a hurry tonight. The sun was already setting and I needed to get out to The Junk Yard before the club filled up too much. I didn't think the jakhai would show until she had a bit of a crowd to blend into, but I had to be in place before that. So I settled for waving to Dorian and reminding myself that I would be back soon to collect the bounty on one dead stripper-sucking monster.

A silvery veil of fog was rising from the bay by the time I climbed back into my new Model X – complete with baby car seat – and pulled up The Junk Yard's address on my phone. I drove away from the College, through the massive black iron gates and past a pair of watchful stone gargoyles. The GPS guided me out of the hills and toward the freeway downtown.

I checked the time. With any luck, Max was already at The Junk Yard, bonding with strippers and starting his first shift. And I was already nervous. The love that Max and I shared gave me some pretty fucking amazing powers – we didn't even know the full extent of them yet – but what if Max got hurt? Would any of my abilities be able to help him?

If only jakhai came from the Nether. One of the powers we *did* know about was my nose for anything demonic. I could sense hell-hounds, vampires and werewolves from across the world. If the jakhai were a demon, I wouldn't need Max's help to find her.

The sun finished setting and a thick layer of gray clouds covered the moon and stars. But the city glowed with its own lights in every color. I drove through green and red, blinking yellow and incandescent white until I spotted the neon orange letters scrawled against a background of corrugated metal: The Junk Yard.

I parked at the far end of the lot, climbed out and locked the Model X. I glanced at my phone for messages from either Max or Vincent, but the notifications screen was empty. So I pocketed my phone and made my way across the parking lot to the club's front door. I waited through the short line and paid my cover charge to a man in an unbuttoned blue work shirt. He winked at me as I headed through onto the main floor.

The Junk Yard lived up to its name. Chain-link fences separated out the sections, and the walls inside were festooned with car parts.

I chose a table near the back covered in bumper stickers – *If you think this car is dirty, try a night with the driver.* My chair was a black leather bucket seat that had been reclaimed from a sports car at some point and welded onto a new steel base. In a pinch, I probably could have used the thing to beat a minotaur to death.

And then there were the men. A bartender with massive pecs and brightly colored tattoos all along his thick arms stood behind a counter finished in more corrugated aluminum. He was only half wearing a pair of coveralls unzipped to the waist, with the sleeves tied around his hips. He poured gin into a metal shaker, clapped the lid on top and tossed the whole thing tumbling up through the air. He caught it with a flourish and emptied the martini out into a glass, then garnished it with a skewered olive. A short woman with luscious curls cheered and tucked an impressive tip into the waist of the bartender's coveralls before taking her drink.

Half of the lights were dimmed through the club and the rest strobed in time with the pounding music. Up on the main stage, a young man with black hair and a red g-string held one of the shining brass poles in a chokehold between his thighs. He leaned out from the pole, every svelte muscle tensed on well-oiled display, and spun a slow circle for the audience. A dozen women at the padded edge of the tip bar clapped and I joined in their applause. I knew from experience that shit takes a lot of strength – and the stripper up there didn't have my supernatural advantages.

My view of the stage wasn't good from the back of the room, but it was the customers I was there to watch, not the dancers. Any of these women might be a monster in disguise. There were several middle-aged ladies working off their menopause one dollar at a time at the tip bar. Or maybe the jakhai was masquerading as one of the already drunk professional types blowing off steam after a long day at the office. Or one of the younger girls trying to nerve herself up to get close to the stage and hoping to take home a genuine stripper tonight.

And then a group of women in tiaras and a bachelorette party buzz swooped in to add to my suspect pool.

Any of them could be my mark.

On stage, the dark-haired stripper dismounted his pole with an acrobatic backflip. Everyone cheered and he rewarded us with a few sinuous pelvic thrusts that elicited another round of applause. He moved around the edge of the stage, sweeping up dollar bills and smiling at the women before finally trotting back behind a drop cloth curtain.

The stage lights dimmed and I looked around The Junk Yard. Where was Max? According to the big chrome clock over the bar, his shift had definitely started. But I didn't see my husband at any of the doors. Was there already something going on backstage? I checked my phone again, but there were still no calls or texts from Max. He would have let me know if he found anything, right?

The music faded out and the DJ leaned over her microphone.

"And now The Junk Yard brings you our newest performer," she announced. "I've seen his audition and I guarantee he'll get your motors running, ladies. Please welcome to the stage... Maximus!"

What? That sounded a lot like...

The DJ slammed the music back up, blasting Tool through the strip club, and the curtains flew open to reveal Max.

My Max.

His blue eyes darted nervously over the crowd as Max walked out across the stage toward us. He wore mechanic's coveralls with a few familiar grease-stains and the *Max's Garage* patch in red and white on his chest. Lights pulsed across the club and women were already jumping up from their tables, practically running for seats in front. If it weren't for my supernatural speed, I would have been tossing some lady out of my seat at the suddenly packed tip bar.

I sat right next to the stage and stared up at Max. He raked one hand through his hair and gulped visibly. I tried to look furious, but it wasn't anger that made my hands shake. Max met my eyes and grabbed the front of his coveralls. He twisted his fist into the fabric, pulled and ripped the entire thing off his body. All around me, the women cheered.

Holy shit. I knew tear-away clothes and that was no Velcro. Since when had Max been able to rip off a full work suit with one hand?

I wasn't sure, but damn it was *hot*. Max strode to the edge of the stage in nothing more than a black g-string and stopped there. He was trembling, but my husband was still watching me and his expression was hard, determined. He raised his hands and laced his fingers behind his head, just the way I always told him showed off the muscles of his arms and chest. Max's yeti-scars rippled across his pecs as he made them jump in time with the music. It took every ounce of self-restraint I've ever learned not to leap up onto the stage and grab him.

The audience screamed for more. Max gulped and his eyes flickered around the entire club, over everyone staring at him. But then they fixed on me again and Max smiled. I caught just a flash of his dimples, a deep breath and then he was stepping back into the center of the stage.

Max reached up and seized one of the poles in both hands. Lights played across his broad chest and tensed stomach. Max's hands tightened on the pole and then he lifted himself off the stage. Without even breaking a sweat, Max pulled his legs up over his head, toes pointed toward the ceiling. He held that pose for a heartbeat, the hard muscles of his back on perfect display, and then hooked a knee around the pole.

Max let go and suspended himself by one leg. He spun and stretched out toward the second stripper pole, but even as tall and long as Max was, he couldn't reach. So he planted his foot against the first pole and jumped, twisting through the air. He caught himself on the other pole with one hand and swung all the way around it like the hottest gymnast I've ever fucking seen.

Other women were half out of their seats, hurling dollar bills onto the stage and shouting at Max. I grabbed a hundred out of my wallet and slapped it down. The money was quickly piling up on stage and I wondered if I should retire from bounty hunting. Sure, I was pretty much a professional superhero and the College paid me ridiculous amounts of alchemically transmuted gold for it, but damned if Max didn't look *amazing* up on that stage. But this wasn't the job he was supposed to get hired for!

Max raised his legs outward until he held his body perpendicular to the pole like a human flag. I was tempted to stand and salute as he spun for us. Max circled twice and then hooked one leg around the pole again, released his hands and slid slowly down the brass without their assistance.

The women howled as he came to a rest at the bottom and crawled obediently across the stage toward us. At the edge, Max pushed himself to his knees, legs parted, and planted one hand on the ground behind him. He locked eyes with me and Max's g-string struggled to contain him. I could clearly make out the length of his dick silhouetted inside the black satin. Max thrust his hips and a collective moan went up from the audience. I couldn't stop a short cry, either, helplessly imagining myself there on top of Max and accepting that long, hard thrust of his cock.

Max's eyes went wide and his cheeks darkened, like he knew exactly what I was thinking. Or like he had thought it first. Max sat up and leaned down over the edge of the stage toward me. His body eclipsed the club lights and seemed almost to glow against them. The need to kiss Max, to throw him down and fuck him right there for everyone to see was nearly irresistible, but he pulled himself away with a growl that I heard even over the thump and pound of music.

Max had a job to do and he danced the way he did everything else in his life – wholeheartedly and with dedication. He strode a circuit of the stage and then leapt back onto one of the poles to the sound of cheers. It takes a lot of excited voices to drown out cranked up heavy metal, but that was exactly what Max got.

He knotted his knees around the pole and then arched his back to grab it below. Max released his legs and tensed his well-muscled arms, falling heels-over-head in slow motion until he landed on the stage once more. The end of his song was utterly lost in the storm of wild applause.

Even the DJ let out a whoop that thundered throughout The Junk Yard.

"I hope you enjoyed Maximus as much as I did, ladies," she said into the microphone. "I'd say he was a hit. Wouldn't you?"

Max flushed brightly at the shouts and whistles as he gathered up loose bills and the shreds of his torn coveralls. He backed toward the curtain and waved sheepishly at me before disappearing backstage. I forced myself to start breathing again.

———

I sat at my table in the back again and drummed my fingers against the lacquered-over bumper stickers. A few other guys came and went from the stage, jiggling their junk and giving the club its name. But none of them earned as much applause as Max, I noted with pleasure and dismay.

The crowd was getting pretty thick as the evening went on and I struggled to watch all of the women scattered across the darkened strip club. This was exactly why I needed extra eyes tonight. But nothing so far had gone according to plan. Finally, the DJ came on the microphone again.

"Get ready," she said. "In just a moment, our performers will be prowling The Junk Yard for your pleasure. Buy a lap dance and check out your favorite parts!"

The door that led backstage swung open and a mouth-watering line of hot men filed through, all barely clad in their tiny g-strings.

Max was the third to emerge and a crowd of women was on their feet in a heartbeat, all surging toward him. I got to Max first, though I admit that it may have required a bit of shoving. I promise, no one got hurt.

Not yet, at least.

"Lap dance," I ordered. "Right now."

"Sure, Lil," Max said.

I towed him across the main floor to another set of doors, these ones outlined in glowing neon hotrod flames and yellow placards warning that it might get hot inside. There was a smaller stage in the lounge, and cushioned alcoves lining the remaining walls. Each one had a heavy velvet curtain that wasn't exactly in keeping with the rest of The Junk Yard aesthetic, but I supposed was perfect for maintaining privacy.

I stalked to an alcove in the back and Max followed me inside, pulling the curtain shut behind us. I dropped into the padded seat and yanked him down on top of me to straddle my waist. I strained upward and kissed Max hard, furiously.

"What the hell were you doing on that stage?" I asked.

"Uh... dancing?" Max answered. "Did I do okay?"

"You were amazing," I told him. "But how do you even know how to pole dance?"

"I watched some YouTube videos this afternoon. And we have the pole I put up for you in the bedroom... I didn't choose that stupid name, though. The whole *Maximus* thing was Saffi's idea."

"Who?"

"She's the DJ tonight."

"And how the fuck did you rip off those coveralls?" I asked.

"I'm... not really sure," Max admitted in a quiet voice. "But you do it all the time. I have to order new pairs every month."

"I'm a love-powered half demon that can shoot death beams from my fingertips. You're *human*, Max. Which is exactly the point! You were supposed to get a job with security."

I smacked one hand down across Max's bare ass and my husband reached out to steady himself against the padded sides of the private alcove. But not because I had knocked him off-balance with all my supernatural strength, as far as I could tell. Max's breath came faster and his cock stirred where it was pressed along my stomach.

"They weren't hiring security," Max said. He moved his hips in a slow circle, grinding the growing bulge of his dick against me. "No one here knows that they have a monster problem, so they weren't looking for more protection. But The Junk Yard is down almost half their performers, so..."

"So they hired you to dance," I finished with a growl. "Why didn't you tell me?"

Max's eyes fell shut as he slid his cock against my belly. It was growing longer and thicker with every movement. I felt the heat of him through my clothes and my heart sped.

"I meant to tell you, Lil," Max said. "I promise. But then Eva said her first word and I forgot all about it."

"You should have turned down the job."

Max opened his eyes again and looked down at me. He let go of the booth walls and trailed his fingers down along the delicate arches of my collarbones. Goosebumps rose across my skin where Max touched me and I gasped.

"You need help finding the jakhai, Lil," he said. "I've always got your back. Whatever you need."

"And you think I need you to be a stripper?" I asked. The question came out in a gasp as Max moved slowly against me.

"Tonight? Yeah, you do."

Fuck... I yanked Max's black g-string down to reveal the full hardness of his dick. He groaned when I stroked my fingers over the flushed length. Max hadn't broken a sweat dancing up on stage, but now perspiration beaded along his hairline.

"I don't want you to get hurt," I said.

"I don't want anyone *else* to get hurt," Max panted. "And that is exactly what's happening as long as that jakhai is hunting here. If putting on a g-string and getting up on that stage will help you stop her..."

"You're not a piece of meat, Max."

His cock throbbed in my hand. Sweat ran down over Max's tensed muscles and drew glistening lines across his skin.

"I kind of felt like one up there," Max admitted. "Everyone was staring at me and shouting for more. It felt... good."

"Every woman in that room wanted you. They all want to be right here, stroking your cock."

Max groaned and thrust his dick urgently into my touch. Pale precum dripped from the huge, flushed head and across the back of my hand.

"What about you, Lil?" he asked in a low, rough voice. "What do you want?"

I turned beneath Max and pulled my knees onto the seat. I leaned against the padded back of the booth, pushing my ass out toward him. Max shoved my skirt up around my hips and yanked my thong down.

"I want you to fuck me," I answered.

"Yes, Lil," Max growled.

He grabbed my waist and slammed himself forward, his cock spearing deep into me. The sensation of penetration was enough to make me cry out, and this time Max didn't quiet me. Thank god for the loud music pounding off the main floor, or the entire club would have heard us.

I braced myself against the back of the booth as Max hammered his dick into my pussy. Pleasure coiled through me and knotted deep in my belly. I reached around and grabbed one of Max's wrists, then desperately bit two of his fingers to muffle my cries as the orgasm surged through my body. Max gripped my hip tightly with his other hand and fucked his fingers in and out of my mouth.

When the tide of ecstasy ebbed just a little and left me panting there on the end of Max's cock, his hand withdrew. I gulped down a breath and struggled to speak.

"I don't like this, Max," I gasped. I pushed myself back onto him. "I mean, I like *this*. But I didn't want you to be bait. And as soon as you stepped out on that stage, that's exactly what you turned yourself into."

Max ran one dripping wet finger down the cleft of my ass. I moaned as he moved his fingertip in tight circles over my anus. Max pressed himself against me from behind.

"I'm not helpless, Lil," he said into my ear. "You're here and I know you would never let anything happen to me. I trust you."

Max always believed in me, even when I didn't believe in myself. I could do anything as long as I had Max there beside me. Maybe he felt that same strength when I was near...? The idea was warm, intoxicating.

I moaned louder and lifted my ass up toward Max in a silent plea. He pushed in time with the hard, rhythmic pounding of his cock, his finger spreading my asshole and then popping inside me. It was too fucking much and in a single smooth thrust, Max shoved me right over into another orgasm. I gasped at the sensation of fullness in front and back.

I don't know how long Max kept me reeling wildly between the pleasure in my pussy and in my ass, but it was getting to be way too long for a lap dance. Max didn't seem at all worried or ashamed, though. He shoved a second finger up my ass, curling both of them inside me, and hammered his cock deep into my pussy.

Max's flawless rhythm began to falter as pleasure took over. He was close. God, his dick was as hot as molten steel inside me. But if I walked out of here with cum oozing down my thighs, someone was sure to notice. Max would lose his job at The Junk Yard. If he was truly determined to bait the jakhai and help me catch her... I couldn't fuck that up.

I looked over my shoulder and licked my lips. Max nodded once and pulled himself out of my pussy. His bared cock dripped as I quickly slid to the floor and turned to face him. I fed his slicked shaft into my mouth and Max reached down to sink his fingers into my hair, cradling the back of my head.

I swallowed as much of Max's length as I could and wrapped my fingers around the tightening weight of his balls. It was like holding live coals in my hand. Max gave a low growl and his cock pulsed between my lips. Cum gushed into my mouth and then down my throat in a creamy torrent. I drank it as fast as I could, but there was so much... Hot drops of cream leaked from the corners of my mouth and along my chin.

Finally, I released Max's dick, licking my lips again. I wiped my chin with the back of my hand and lapped at the streak of sticky white semen, then pushed sex-tangled hair out of my face to look up at Max.

"All clear?" I asked. "I don't want to get you fired for improper conduct with your customers."

Max nodded at me. "You're clean."

"Maybe my face is," I said with a snort. "But my mind is always filthy."

"Hell yeah," Max agreed and gave me a wide, dimpled smile. He tugged his black g-string back into place and raked his fingers through his sweaty blond hair. "So... does this mean we're changing the plan, Lil?"

"Only if you haven't already heard something helpful from one of the other dancers," I said.

"Not really," Max admitted. "There are a few regulars, but none of the guys here tonight know them very well."

"Makes sense. The strippers who have actually come face-to-face with the jakhai are the ones who are at home sick."

"Or at the hospital," Max finished. "And can't remember anything."

He helped me back to my feet in the close confines. I replaced my underwear and smoothed down my skirt. After a final kiss, I stepped out of the alcove.

"Then I guess you better get back out there," I told Max. "There's a whole line of women waiting for your attention and with any luck, one of them is a monster."

———

I followed Max back out of the lounge and toward the main floor. He paused in the door, wreathed by the neon flames, took a deep breath and steeled himself. There was a small crowd waiting for Max and they surged forward. He ran his hand through his hair and rubbed his chin, not-very-subtly flashing the gold of his wedding ring, but that didn't deter a single one of his admirers. Of course, we weren't really trying to chase off the determined ones... like a jakhai looking for her next meal.

I ordered a soda from the big tattooed bartender and withdrew to my table in the back. The Junk Yard was filling quickly and the DJ had cranked up her music to drown out the loud buzz of conversation. There had to be two hundred women in the club now, plus another fifty or so men. Finding a lone jakhai in all this was getting increasingly difficult.

Or would have been if I wasn't dangling a delicious piece of blond bait. Max was right – this *was* a better way to locate the jakhai. I've pulled the bait-and-beat trick a few times, luring my mark close and then taking them down. And Stefano is the fucking brass-balled master of that exact technique for hunting werewolves.

And now Max... I was torn between gut-wrenching terror and a pride in my husband so fierce that it threatened to make my heart leap out onto the table and do a dance all of its own. Most of us trained for years to hunt monsters. Max was just doing it because it was *right*.

Not that he was doing it alone. Max didn't have to do anything alone ever again. Not if I could help it.

I must have been a nervous drinker. When I glanced down again, my soda was already empty. It was a damned good thing my magical metabolism was resistant to shit like drugs and caffeine, or else I would have been jittery enough to start juggling my chair about now. I wasn't sure if my jakhai knew there were monster hunters in the city, but there was no reason to tip her off that she might not be the only supernatural bitch at The Junk Yard tonight.

I went back to the bar. I was seriously tempted to get something stronger than cola, but I *am* capable of getting drunk when there's enough alcohol involved and I didn't want to risk losing a nano-second off my reaction times. So I ordered two more sodas and turned to watch the strip club while the bartender poured my new drinks.

The boy with the black hair was back on stage, climbing his way sinuously up one pole to show off his lean and well-oiled muscles. A dozen other strippers prowled across the floor, trailing seductive touches along patron's shoulders or even dropping down to sit in a shocked-looking businesswoman's lap. They hadn't sold any dances yet, but the night was still young.

Max emerged from the lounge again, blushing and following an extremely pleased middle-age woman. She tucked another twenty-dollar bill into his hand and stood up on her toes to kiss his flaming cheeks. She practically skipped back to her table, accepting giggles and high-fives from the rest of her party.

Max saw me across the floor and grinned sheepishly, but then a woman with a cascade of dark hair almost down to her knees charged out of the crowd toward him. Her pretty face was all business and within seconds, she was sweeping Max away into the lounge for her lap dance.

The bartender returned with my two sodas and I paid, making sure to leave a generous tip on the counter. Max was picking up a ridiculous amount of cash tonight and the least we could do was return some of it to The Junk Yard staff. The inked-up bartender grinned at me and promised to mix up something special if I ever got tired of soda. I thanked him and carried the glasses back in the direction of my table.

I was halfway across The Junk Yard when I felt... something. Shock and fear. I dropped my drinks and whirled, staring. A table of sorority girls shrieked and jumped away from the sudden splash of soda.

"Hey, are you okay?" one of them shouted over the music.

No. I wasn't. I was terrified. But why?

Something sharp slashed along the side of my neck. I gasped and pressed my hand to my throat, but I didn't feel anything there. No cut, no blood. What the fuck...?

The bartender was rushing toward me, snatching a towel from somewhere beneath the counter as he moved. A couple of the sorority sisters jumped up and reached for me.

"Shit, is she about to pass out?"

"Grab her!"

I felt hot blood running down my skin and tasted acidic terror in my mouth. But... there was nothing on my fingers. Because I wasn't the one who was bleeding, I realized. I wasn't the one who was scared.

Max was.

I ran. I ran faster than I ever have before. The bartender blinked in slow motion as I suddenly vanished from his sight and the wind of my passage tugged at the closest girl's hair. I *had* to get to Max... By the time I slammed through the lounge doors, my feet were no longer even touching the floor. I streaked through the air a few inches up off the ground.

Yeah, I can fucking fly now.

Max was next to the smaller stage inside the lounge. It was still empty, but the woman with the knee-length hair stood behind him.

I could only make out half of her face through the thick fall of her black hair, but what I could see was stunningly beautiful – Indian features, dark skin and darker eyes.

The jakhai. She was nearly a foot shorter than Max and had to reach up to grab his neck, but her sharp fingernails had already sliced a ribbon of blood from his throat. The jakhai yanked Max back and bright red dripped down his bare chest.

"Let go of my husband, bitch," I said.

"If you move, I'll kill him," she hissed.

Shit, stalemate. I was sure I could burn the jakhai down with my crazy love powers even from across the room. It would take less than a second... but I didn't know how fast jakhai were. Could I get a shot off before she slashed those razor fingernails through Max's throat? I couldn't risk it.

"He's strong," said the jakhai. "Strong enough to resist me and strong enough to sustain me for years."

So she hadn't drained anything from Max yet. Which explained why she still looked human. Max must have realized something was wrong not long after the jakhai brought him here and then he tried to fight back. That's when I felt Max's fear and her grabbing him.

I stood my ground in the lounge doorway and the jakhai watched me from behind Max.

"Get out of my way," she hissed. "I'm leaving with this man. You won't see me again. Or him."

"You're shit at hostage-taking," I told the jakhai, but my voice shook. "You're supposed to promise me you'll release him if I let you go. Now what's my incentive to do what you tell me?"

"I sense your bond with this man," said the monster. "I've never encountered anything like it. You won't risk hurting him. But I will."

"It's alright, Lil," Max told me. "I... I think I can do this."

"What the hell are you talking about?" I cried. "Do what? Max!"

There was a blur of blond hair and black satin g-string. Max grabbed the jakhai's wrist in one hand and rammed his other elbow back into her chest. She screeched and squirmed in his grip like the world's most pissed-off cat, but Max yanked the jakhai up over his shoulder and slammed her down onto the floor hard enough to leave cracks in the concrete.

Max jumped back as the jakhai slithered to her feet again. Her really gross feet... The monster's mouth-wateringly beautiful disguise had melted away in an instant, revealing her true form. She was as withered and knobbed as an ancient tree, covered in sagging gray-green skin. Her hair remained long and black, but so was her tongue. It whipped and snapped like a snake.

The jakhai lunged toward Max. She *was* fast, but I was faster. I brought up one hand and silver-white light lanced out from my fingertips, severing her lashing tongue. She shrilled and recoiled, but I was already in front of the jakhai before she could turn on me.

I flattened my hand like a blade and sliced it through her midsection. Two pieces of what used to be a monster hit the ground and collapsed in on themselves, flesh shrinking against the skeleton. And then even the bones crumbled into dust.

"Max! Are you okay?" I cried.

He stood a few yards away, panting. He touched the cut on the side of his neck, inspected the smear of blood on his fingers and then nodded.

"Yeah," Max said. "Yeah, Lil. I'm alright. I've taken worse hits at the garage."

I ran to my husband and threw my arms around him. I laid my head against his chest to hear his heart pounding loud and strong in my ear. Max held me tight, breathing hard into my hair.

"Thanks for saving my ass," he said. "How did you know what was happening in here?"

"I felt it." I leaned into Max. I didn't care about the sweat or blood. "When you were afraid and when that bitch cut you, like it was all happening to me. It almost took me too long to figure out what was going on."

"That's... weird," said Max.

"So was you throwing that jakhai around," I told him. "She was a lot faster than a human. Not as fast as me, but still! And what she said about your strength..."

I squinted up at Max. He had torn the coveralls off on stage, and done that whole impressive routine on the poles without breaking a sweat. The night before, Max held me down on the couch when I was threatening to wake Eva. Sure, I still could have chucked him across the living room if I really needed to... but maybe not quite as easily as I thought.

"What're you thinking, Lil?" Max asked.

"Falling in love gave me a ton of powers," I said slowly. "And I'm starting to think that it gave you some, too."

I loved Max. But he had to love me in return, or the circuit wasn't complete. That was where my powers came from. Our love had to go both ways... and perhaps the magic did, too. Max's blue eyes widened and he stared down at me.

"Holy shit, Lil," he said. "Are you serious?"

"We need to talk to my dad to be sure and the wizards will want to do some tests on you, but... yes."

Max kissed me until we were both breathless, then finally released me with a grin.

"So... does this mean that I get to help you hunt monsters?" he asked.

I blinked. "What?"

"Look, I'm not talking about shutting down the garage, Lil. But you know I always wanted to help. Anything I could do, anything you needed. And now I can do more."

I stared at Max, but then I nodded. Neither of us ever had to face anything alone again. No matter what, Max and I had each other's backs. Always.

"If you really want to help me hunt, then we better get started," I told him. "I doubt anyone out there heard us over the music, but someone's going to come back here eventually. We need to get you and the jakhai cleaned up."

"I'm on it, Lil," Max said. "I think I saw a broom and some garbage bags backstage."

"And then you have to get back up on the main stage."

"Uh... why?" Max asked. "Is that part of our getaway strategy?"

"No," I said. "I just want to see you dance again."

Max laughed and he kissed me. "I'm going to love working together, Lil."

"Yeah," I agreed. "So am I."

For more stories by
Natalie and Eric Severine,
visit us at **LLStories.com**

www.ingramcontent.com/pod-product-compliance
Lightning Source LLC
Chambersburg PA
CBHW050110120726
47904CB00004B/1290